Upon These Azure Shores

Upon These Azure Shores
On the Water's Edge Tahoe Trilogy

Kathy Boyd Fellure

BOOK JACKET PRESS

Book Jacket Press – P. O. Box 1209, Ione, CA 95640
www.bookjacketpress.com

Scripture quotations marked KJV are taken from the Holy Bible,
King James Version, Cambridge, 1769.
All author quotes are Public Domain.

Editor: Daniele Johnson Araujo
Interior sketch art © Donna Plant
Cover design © Kim Van Meter
Typographer ©Aaron Cameron
Cameroncreative.co
Author bio picture © Hidden Hills Photography

Print ISBN 978-1-7347031-0-8
Library of Congress Control Number: 2020907275

EBook ISBN 978-1-7347031-1-5

Dedication

In memory of my grandparents Charles and Floyce Boyd
who taught me the language of the lake.
&
Lynn Cordone ~ my lifelong friend who is true Tahoe Blue.

Part One
Time
Selma

Chapter One
Vikingsholm, Lake Tahoe, California ~ Late Spring of 1931

"The resplendent era on the lake is changing. I watch for the reach of Black Friday to touch these waters, but as yet we are separate unto ourselves here upon these azure shores." ~ Lora Josephine Knight, June 28 of 1930, as spoken to a friend.

Astrid hung precariously over the edge of the boat lowering her arm into the lapping, frothy waves. She longed to shed the burden of her cumbersome clothing, dive into the crystal clear lake, and swim leisurely backstrokes from the shore and out of the bay back to the deep cerulean waters. The steamboat ride from the north to the west shore had crossed over shallow teal and turquoise water, then sailed beyond the deeper sapphire hues before docking on the shoreline at Vikingsholm. Astrid was mesmerized by the changing shades of blue.

The almost thirteen-year-old gathered her gabardine traveling skirt inches above mid-calf and wandered from the ferry landing party at the edge of the pier. She slipped away amid the bustle of distracted disembarking adults caught up in commotion as porters unloaded their trunks, plunked stacks of luggage and numerous hat boxes on the creaky planks. The steam whistle continued blowing shrill greetings, puffing white clouds skyward drawing attention from her departure.

Captivated by the forest of towering cedars, firs, and pines, she inhaled the enticing vanilla-scented bark and lost herself in the forest's majesty. With each step, her button-up boots secured solid footing on the needled carpet. The mighty rush and rumble of a waterfall echoed through lofty branches and stirred her imagination. She quickened her pace.

Massive granite boulders jutted out of the earth with an alluring untamed beauty. Astrid removed a glove and stroked her bare palm over the grainy rock; her soft pink flesh prickled by the bumpy surface. Running her hand over the stones was not enough. Leaning against an indent in the slab, Astrid set free the abundance of her chestnut hair from clips underneath her cloche hat, then tucked the cap under her arm, and shook her head.

Astrid's name carried on the breeze from a distance. Someone had been sent to fetch her. Ignoring the call, she savored the moment soaking in the rays of sunshine filtering warmth and light through the canopy of treetops. She would find this place again. She memorized the alignment of tree trunks in the small grove, and the staggering outcrop of moss-covered rocks, mapping a route in her mind as she retraced her steps toward the castle at Vikingsholm.

***

"Astrid! Answer me now." Her father's authoritative voice grew closer.

2

She hastened to meet him before he stumbled upon her newfound secret refuge.

"Father?" She answered out of breath, her cheeks flushed from exertion. Her hem hung up and tore on a low-lying tree limb. She stepped back to release the fabric as it tugged and ripped again. *Mother will be furious. But dear Tessa will mend it for me this very day.* Astrid was quick to hide the damage to her expensive ensemble in a fold of her skirt. She recalled with clarity the transformation of her father's usually pleasant disposition when billing slips continued arriving in the post for her and her mother's holiday trousseaus.

"It is dangerous for you to stray from the companionship of Mrs. Knight's guest party. You are to remain beside your mother or myself for the entirety of the fortnight." His stern scowl, eyebrows arched and creased forehead, contradicted the nervous manner in which he rubbed the tips of his raven black moustache between his thumb and finger.

"Yes, Father." She looped her arm under his and strode close beside him in meek compliance, thankful her spoiled garment went unnoticed. Her hat tumbled to the ground.

He fanned the loose curls on her shoulders. "There are coyote, fox, and bear throughout these woods, though you may not see them." He scooped her hat up, brushed the dirt off, and held it out to her. "You do not yet know the perils of the real world."

Astrid put her hair up while slipping her glove on and placed her hat at a daring angle. She interlocked both her arms about his again and clasped her hands together. "Thank you, Father. You do take care to protect me." She matched his gait and listened intently as he spoke, his bowler bobbing on top his head and his frockcoat flapping open in the breeze.

"Astrid, it is a great privilege to be invited to this mountain retreat. Construction was completed a mere two years ago." He gave her a corrective glance, "We'll be among the first to marvel at the Scandinavian architecture and art, and some reproductions of actual museum pieces." He looked ahead as they walked. She stole glances backward until the grove faded from her sight.

"Father, are you sneaking in a history lesson? You most always wait to do so until supper." A warm smile radiated across her face accentuating her petite nose.

Her attentiveness pleased him. William Hughes continued expounding on the various species of evergreens in the forest: sugar pine, Jeffrey, and cedars. The soles of their shoes crunched on cone and pine debris as he pointed out the differences in the shape and size of the prickly and smoother pinecones. All facts that Astrid found both interesting and curious.

"Many indigenous trees at Lake Tahoe sprouted after a volcanic eruption of tremendous magnitude." He picked up a long, slender cone without pointy edges, then placed it in her brown gloved palms. He brushed back rogue strands of black wavy hair that swept across his brow.

Astrid accepted the woody treasure. "May I please keep it?"

Her father continued without answering. "The conifers, proper botanical name, strobilus, are both male, producing pollen, and female, producing seeds."

"It is different here from at home on Lake Michigan with the white birch trees." Astrid breathed in a gulp of air.

"Yes, it is." William halted. "Well, then here we are, back at the compound."

Before Astrid the massive stone castle, trimmed in by Tahoe fir and pine, spread out into east and west wings. A turret rounded out the far end of the home. The mighty fortress appeared to rise from the earth like an ageless guardian from another time, another place, and bespoke a commanding presence. She inched back to take in the full view. The distant granite mountain peaks ringed around the lake and beyond dwarfing the hidden castle.

Astrid stood spellbound, gazing at the intricately carved, wooden dragons' head roof at the courtyard buildings on the east side. "I have no words." The young girl uttered in hushed reverence.

"All the leaded, stained glass pastel windows were imported from Sweden," her father explained. She stood still, eyes riveted upward, her mouth agape. "The castle replicates Scandinavian wooden churches and homes in Norway along with stone castles in Sweden dating back to the eleventh century. The dragons reflect old Scandinavian superstitions from the first introduction of Christianity. They were carved onto churches to provide added protection against all evils, mirroring the heathen temples in those days."

"Why would the Christians use the same dragon trim the heathen built for pagan purposes?" She questioned, her boot heels weighing deep into the soft soil.

"Because at first they weren't certain their new beliefs would be enough." William answered. "End of lesson for now. It's time to refresh yourself and dress appropriately for tea. The ladies are boating over to Fanette Island while the gentlemen relax with their cigars before supper."

"Why must I take tea? Do the women never join the men for a goblet of wine or to smoke a pipe?" The serious tone in Astrid's voice startled him.

"On occasion the gentlemen take tea with the ladies." Her father said and smoothed out the wrinkles in his tan pleated trousers. "Mrs. Knight does not serve illegal alcohol on these grounds." He reprimanded her with a frown. "Let us go to the house and I will formally introduce you to our hostess who awaits your safe return, as does your mother." He winked. "She sent me out on this mission in the wild timberland to find you."

"Is she irritated with me for roaming?" She rose to her tiptoes to ask him, eye to eye.

"Your mother is not pleased though she will be much relieved to find you are well." The corners of his mouth upturned as he said, "try to conform to the rules while on holiday." A glimmer of humor shone in his sea-green eyes. "Or they will feed you to a bear."

Astrid laughed and relaxed down on her heels. She pulled her sable-trimmed bolero jacket tight as they stepped into the shade. "Will I need an evening wrap?"

"Most certainly. The days here are warm but the evenings turn brisk. It will be a new experience to celebrate your birthday." He led the way along the path to the ornate front door clasped by three extensive wrought iron hinges and bordered by clear leaded glass windows. Crisp air and a heady whiff of pine infused the impressive compound that was seamless with the forest.

A floor clock painted Swedish style greeted both father and daughter in the hallway entrance. "May I introduce, Selma?" William Hughes smiled and bowed to the wooden maiden.

"She is precisely my height." Astrid marveled, standing beside the life-size clock.

Selma stood, one hand on a hip with her back against a wood wall panel and her lacquer painted black shoes stationary on the stone floor. A ruffle of strawberry blond hair cropped above her round clock face and the rest was tucked beneath a bright orange scarf. The perfect Scandinavian hostess had one hand in her apron pocket and appeared ready at any moment to bend her knee, curtsy, and offer you fresh flower petals from the castle gardens.

"I see you have met my official greeter." A woman's gentle voice surprised the young girl.

"Yes, ma'am." Astrid's cheeks blushed warm as she turned to acknowledge her hostess.

"Mrs. Knight, my daughter, Astrid." Hughes said as he stepped forward.

"I do apologize for my tardy arrival." Astrid said politely. She studied the gray-haired older woman whose wire-rimmed spectacles settled slightly awry on her slender nose. Her casual attire was quite unexpected right down to scuffed black leather shoes and woolen socks that slouched unevenly at the hemline of her plain brown skirt.

"Dear girl, if anyone understands the desire to explore these woods, it is me." She leaned in and gave her guest a hearty hug. "I do hope you will boat over to the island to take tea with me. We depart within the hour." Mrs. Knight spoke in a welcoming, genuine tone. The sparkle of a kindred spirit twinkled in her knowing eyes. "The climb up the rocky hill to the teahouse is a bit of an adventure, but well worth the conversation and company."

"Thank you for the invitation. I will dress appropriately and be waiting on the beach precisely at the quarter hour." Astrid promised.

"Perhaps we can walk down together?" Mrs. Knight suggested.

"That will be most pleasant." Astrid nodded in agreement and straighten her stance.

"I look forward to chatting with your daughter this evening, William." Lora said, then disappeared down the hall and up the winding staircase.

"She is lovely, Father. Much like I imagined her to be from her letters these past years." Astrid whispered and kissed his forehead.

"Make haste to prepare yourself for the evening and I will make peace with your mother. Go now." He urged her toward her room. "I'll send Tessa to help with any needs."

William Hughes' ears tuned in to the echoing clip-clip of Astrid's boot heels against the stone floor that became a softer tap-tap when she reached the hall rug. Soon a door opened and closed. He expelled a deep sigh and pulled a cigar from his vest pocket. A cigar aficionado, he traveled with a cedar-lined humidor that housed his Cuban specials. He ran the rolled and crushed tobacco leaves under his nose and mustache, inhaling with anticipation. "Politics, religion, and Prohibition. Tonight promises to be a stimulating debate among Democrat, Republican, and one proclaimed socialist." William licked the length of the cigar, the bitter tobacco nipped at the tip of his tongue before he slipped it back in his pocket and headed into the library. "There will be no five cent, cellophane wrapped domestic White Owl's to chew on tonight." He settled contentedly in a leather armchair, opened a newspaper and tried to concentrate on reading while pondering the day's events. Yet his thoughts wandered.

Vikingsholm seemed a magical kingdom on these distant shores isolated from the rumors brewing in Europe breeding fears of the possibility of another Great War. Could this mountain haven offer a needed respite from the residual of the rampant decadence the Roaring Twenties caused in American cities? The great United States now strived to repeal the Prohibition Act of the previous decade, to be untethered from the profiteer bootleggers. Would there ever be any relief from the constant rhetoric dividing fellow countrymen? Either financial recovery would soon rebound for all classes, or this terrible depression would cause devastation for years to come. William hung onto hope while he struggled with a mixture of guilt and gratitude that his family had thus far escaped the ravages of financial ruin.

Chapter Two
Early summer of 1940

"We could not hide from nor be protected from the onslaught of the war. Father does not understand our country's reluctance to take a stand with the European nations already suffering losses. I heard his fellow flyers' rants through the walls of our study. Soon all lives will be much altered. I know Mother does not agree. But I do. I wish I could go with them." ~ Astrid journal entry, June 10 of 1940

Rose Hughes cast a last glance on the pristine waters from the steamer as it circled Fanette Island leaving the warm sunlight, to enter the shade of a cooler early dusk before paddling out of the bay. The emerald shoreline widened into the massive blue lake. It was as difficult to leave Vikingsholm this summer as it had been her first visit, nine years before.

Astrid called up to her from the lower level. Rose descended the upper deck stairs, her steps heavy and her thoughts unsettled. Their holiday had been interrupted by a telegram delivered by messenger who boated in late the previous evening while Lora Josephine Knight reclined with her guests and sipped brandy in the rattan chaise lounge chairs along the beach. In the shadow of candlelit poles lining the beach, Rose read the concern on her husband's face as he folded, then slipped the telegram into the breast pocket of his jacket. He resumed the preceding political discussion, though she noted his attention now diverted away from the men, toward her and their daughter.

Two perfect fortnights of swimming, hiking, and croquet matches came to an immediate halt. Rose relished their annual family adventures at Lake Tahoe. While here, she'd hoped Astrid would forget her foolish intentions to volunteer at the hospitals in London. She had grown so fond of the Tahoe locals. Over the years they'd been drawn in by her daughter's compassionate heart and cultured intellect which she lavished upon the poor children on the south shore. These days she spent little time primping while on vacation, she simply wove her lustrous henna mane into a thick braid. Astrid read to any child who joined her in the forest clearing to hear fanciful fairytales and continuing chapters of novels borrowed from Mrs. Knight's extensive library.

A motor car outing around the picturesque lake planned for the next day had been cancelled. Instead, her husband sped out at dawn on a mahogany Garwood racing boat with local Alton McDuff. Lora Knight had awakened early to pack a lunch hamper for their journey. She joined Rose and Astrid to see William off at the pier where precious few words were spoken. Rose now wished she had said more to her husband. Perhaps if she'd clearly stated how much she was against him flying with the Royal Air Force in England, he might have listened.

As she watched her daughter's hazel eyes rest in pensive contemplation on the choppy waves, Rose questioned how much information her daughter needed to know.

"How long will father be gone?" Astrid held her cape closed with the hood down.

"Until his mission in Washington D.C. is completed." Rose sat beside her daughter on the damp wooden bench and clutched the edges of her shawl tight, her long blonde curls cascading down her back. She blinked and closed her grey eyes against threatening tears.

America will soon declare war. She'd overheard snippets of discourse drifting from their study on the rising tobacco smoke of the pilots gathered together before their family headed out west. Many American pilots want to fly with the Royal Air Force, to help defend England even if the United States didn't officially declare war before a great battle to save Britain waged. Most of the senior Hughes family still lived in Norfolk, East Anglia, in London, and the fishing villages of Cornwall. The younger generation had immigrated to America and become U. S. citizens. Still, the matriarchs remained rooted in Great Britain.

Rose knew her husband. William would volunteer to fly with the RAF. She took her daughter's hand, pressed it between her palms and held snug. Astrid was so young, so innocent, and led a protected life in the small east coast town she was determined to leave for the intrigue of the beckoning world.

Astrid's sun-bleached tresses blew like wheat grass in the wind. Her slender body felt slight beside Rose's full figure. Together the women formed an unwavering breaker facing the increasing white capped swells slapping hard against the steamer, rocking the bow.

"Perhaps your father will be allowed to come home before he deploys." Rose whispered her heart's desire into Astrid's chilled ear.

Astrid managed to offer a weak smile for her mothers' sake. She kept her inner thoughts to herself rather than risk another confrontational explosion like the last time she'd shared the deep longing of her soul. Biting her lower lip, Astrid leaned forward and set her eyes straight ahead.

Rose watched the castle disappear behind the ancient forest winding around the outer edges of the last stretch of Emerald Bay. The captain steered his vessel toward rugged Rubicon Bay under faded crimson layers of the setting sun. The lake appeared to be swallowed whole as the dark of night spread its enfolding cloak.

Chapter Three
Another Drought Year ~ September 1 of 2017

"I am feeling older and less useful these days. My daughters live farther away, and I'm no longer needed to help with grandchildren that spent considerable time in my home or at my bookstore. Turning sixty is for the birds, not Nana's sweet birdie friends, but rakish ravens of disquiet." ~ Emily journal entry, August 9 of 2017

The heavily wooded mile hike straight down to Vikingsholm was more taxing than Emily and Jack had anticipated in the unseasonably humid Indian summer heat. Wasps that usually came and went in the month of August buzzed along the path, irksome and persistent.

"The low water level from this seven year drought is a breeding ground for these pests." Jack bent on one knee to tie his dangling boot laces. "Another dry winter is expected." He shifted the weight of his backpack and adjusted his shoulder straps as he stood.

"Oh, I'm feeling it." Emily batted at the insects, worked in a couple of squats, and stretched her legs. "It's going to be harder

14

hiking the mile back." She gazed up the trail and took note that no one was making their way down behind them.

"The natural beauty of these mountains is changing." Jack moved beside her.

Emily arched her back, pointed to the stone fortress and said. "The State of California has preserved this so far, or what would have happened to these unique grounds?" She glanced at the thatched roofs usually sprouting a vibrant profusion of either spring or summer wildflowers; now barren, the sod hardened and cracked from the lack of water. Emily added. "The sprinkler system must be turned off."

"The surrounding woods are quenched and it's definitely taking a toll." Jack lamented running his fingers through a nearby branch of brittle brown pine needles that rained down to his feet. "Every green thing is shriveling up."

"The Tahoe of our youth is disappearing and becoming a tinder box for the next fire to devour." Emily's voice drifted to a far off place. Turning to Jack, she tapped his shoulder and tried to flash an encouraging smile. "Bet your girlfriend Selma is still faithfully going tick-tock, tick-tock inside. You know she's waiting with that flirtatious Swedish clock face, standing with one hand on her hip wondering why it's been so long since your last visit."

"Are you jealous?" Jack grinned and led the way into the compound and through the heavy wooden doors past a straggling group of tourists strolling the grounds waiting for the docent. The temperature was unusually high outside, so he motioned for the people to follow them inside where fans blasted on the highest setting.

"Not quite the usual end of summer crowd," Emily commented, her hand cupping her mouth.

"Not at all." Jack answered. "This is the last place I expected business to be lacking." He pointed toward the grand piano in the living room. "Please say yes when they ask for a volunteer to play this time."

"That's for the tourists."

"It's for anyone they ask."

"I'll think about it." Emily walked over past the roped-off area and placed her fingertips on the black and white keys but resisted the temptation to play a few notes. A, *Please Do Not Play the Piano*, sign was posted in clear view.

"Are you going to say yes this time?" Rachel asked. "Maybe Beethoven's *Für Elise*?" She pinned on her docent name tag and stroked her frizzy auburn hair off to one side and behind an ear.

"I'm sure someone in the tour will be thrilled to play."

"Not a very big crowd today." Jack mentioned.

"Mostly foreigners from across the pond. That means we'll sell lots of souvenir books. Locals don't buy the books. They don't need to; they know the stories by heart." Rachel dusted the top of Selma's head with a red bandana from her jean pocket.

Emily's eyebrows peaked.

"We've had to cut back on the housekeeping." Rachel spoke in a muted tone. "Everything is strictly volunteer now. I try to come in an hour early to feather dust, but my babysitter showed up late this morning."

"What's going on?" Jack questioned and walked over to his wife.

Rachel motioned for the couple to join her on the other side of the roped-off area. "The State of California doesn't have any money for parks. We've been filling in for almost a year now. I was actually going to ask you two if you'd be willing to volunteer to help with the grounds or with housekeeping." She flashed a big smile with bright white perfect teeth and waved to a couple drawing closer armed with brochures and cameras.

Jack and Emily looked at each other and nodded. "Of course, anything to help. We'll adjust our schedules for whenever you need us." Emily promised.

Jack's voice dropped below a whisper. "Selma seems to be losing time." He glanced at his watch. "She's nineteen minutes late."

"I know. No funds to fix her." Rachel hedged. "Has to be done for free."

"We have a friend in Reno. He's a clock maker. He can get Selma back in sync," Jack offered. "I helped his mother when the flu epidemic hit last winter." Jack straightened when he caught sight of a family with little ones checking their watches, hands raised in the air and fingers on the eleven o'clock hour.

The group started the mile hike up the path an hour before dusk. The sun bore down as the temperature hit a record 100 degrees. Pockets of shade from the imposing pines offered momentary respite. Jack noticed an elderly woman with a cane. He hadn't seen her at the castle. She stumbled on stones and wobbled in her hiking boots on the uneven dirt while trying to make it to one of the strategically placed benches for rest stops. Jack leapt forward and anchored one of his arms under hers. She reached out, bracing herself for a fall. Her knobby cane rolled down the path, but she grabbed Jack and held on.

"Oh, thank you." She bumped into an immense granite boulder near a cluster of Indian Paint Brush flowers emerging half-in and half-out of the sunlight.

"I think I might have taken on a little too much today with this heat." She plopped on the flat surface of the rock and her legs dangled limp as she tried to catch her breath. The trunk of her body swayed to the right, knocking her straw hat on the ground exposing snowy white hair pinned up in a loose bun.

The woman's face flushed a bright pink and her arm and hand were hot against Jack's cool skin. He instinctively checked her pulse. "Ma'am, I'm a doctor. I think you are experiencing heat stress. What is your name?" He knelt beside her and checked her pulse.

"I'm tired, so tired." She leaned forward and slumped on Jack's shoulder.

"Are you nauseous? Your pulse is too rapid and it's not slowing down."

"Canteen in my satchel." She reached for the bag that rested near her feet.

"Only tiny sips." Jack opened the worn pack, slipped out the tin canteen, and unscrewed the cap. He poured a few drops across his forearm. "Water's too hot. Em?"

"Ahead of you, honey." She opened her backpack and pulled out a bottle of water. "It's completely thawed out. Nice and cool, not too cold."

"What is your name?" Jack persisted as he patted some of the cool water on the woman's wrists, then tipped the bottle for her to sip from. "My name is Jack." He focused in on her eyes again trying to engage her for information. She had dressed properly for the hike and had worn a hat for protection from the sun. Her rumpled white shirt was tucked into her loose-fitting jeans. Jack figured her to be a local; a very aged woman with lots of grit. He noted the lack of any perspiration and dampness on her matted down hair.

"Better." She said after a few more sips. "Better now. But it will be a while before I can make it up the rest of the way." The admission seemed to embarrass her. "I must look a mess." She struggled to brush back the straying tresses of hair from her sagging bun. Her wrinkled, crepey skin rippled with rivers and outlets of bulging purple and blue veins.

"I didn't see you at the castle, during the tour." Jack shifted from his right knee to his left. "Were you there?"

"No. I hike down and head into the forest, eat my picnic lunch, then walk the grounds." She offered a timid smile. "I prefer not to mingle about with the tourists." Her eyes scanned the direction her cane had rolled down the hill and under a tree. Emily went to get it.

Jack helped the woman to stand. She leaned on him, still shaky. "Why don't my wife and I take it slow and walk beside you? Or we can call for help from the castle. They can meet us

down at the lower road and give you a ride up to the parking lot."
He paused and asked. "Did you drive here?"

"If you escort me to that bench over where I was heading,
I'll be fine after a rest. I can make it back to the top." She swallowed a few more sips of water. "Can you hand me my bonnet,
please? It helps to block out the sun." She released Jack's hand
and tried to steady herself. Emily placed her walking stick under
her palm. "Thank you for coming to my assistance." Her hazel
eyes settled upon Jack's. "My name, is Astrid."

Chapter Four
Snippets of Memory

"My Nana used to say that people and things aren't always who or what they might seem. She possessed what I thought was a southern wisdom that I lack. Then I realized it was actually spiritual discernment." ~ Emily journal entry, September 7 of 2017

"What did you think of the old woman we met at Vikingsholm last week?" Emily said and pulled into the driveway. The deep-groove tread of the new tires on the truck spit gravel sideways until she stopped inches in front of the tallest pine on the edge of the property.

"She's old." Jack shrugged his shoulders and said. "And in pretty good shape for someone in her nineties."

"She's ninety?" Emily released her belt buckle and opened the door.

"I asked her when we got to the top of the path. She's ninety-seven. I was concerned there wasn't anyone waiting for her at home." Jack's seatbelt snapped back against the inside vinyl panel of the truck. "I was right, she said she lives alone." He locked his door and rounded the vehicle to her side and held it open while they gathered supplies, then nudged it shut.

"Where?"

"Tahoe City now, but she used to live on the south shore."

"All her life?"

"Why the inquisition?" Jack turned the key in front door until it clicked open. They filed in one after the other carrying cardboard boxes overflowing with medical supplies.

"I saw her yesterday, when I was shopping at the Safeway." Emily lowered her boxes on the sofa. "We can sort through these after dinner tonight." She shifted diabetic syringes to the center of one and buffered them with fluffy cotton ball bags and twelve-pack pouches of antibiotic ointment.

"Did she speak to you?" Jack placed his stack of four boxes beside hers. He followed Emily into the cozy kitchen where sunlight flooded in and illuminated a tidy, sunny room painted buttercup yellow and bordered with a hand-stenciled floral print. He went to work and promptly started sifting through towering stacks of color-coded medical files set in neat rows on the table. A post-it note was attached to the top files denoting dates back to the 1980's.

"Not at first. I only noticed her because she was watching me. You know—how you can feel someone's eyes boring a hole through you. It completely unnerved me, so I hurried over to let her know that I saw her, and I said hello." She began loading files, one stack at a time into empty boxes stored under the oval oak tabletop.

"Did she remember you?"

"Yeah she did, but—well, she wasn't friendly at all."

"Maybe she already forgot meeting us. She's almost one hundred years old." Jack said and crammed the last records for all his remaining patients into the biggest cardboard box. He heaved a heavy sigh. "Hardly seems possible this is all that is left of my thirty-one year medical career." He stood with his head hung low casting an elongated shadow over the files.

Emily ran her hand over his and rested it there for a few seconds. "This is hard for you, cleaning out your office and bringing everything home." She spoke in a supportive tone.

"It's so final." He lifted a box and carried it into the new makeshift office in the former bedroom now converted into a temporary storage room.

"And, no, that wasn't the problem." Emily called out to him while organizing the piles by year of admission to the practice. Some of the files dated back to when Doc and Annie ran the practice next door. "A short, wiry middle-aged man was with her and she didn't introduce me. He kept turning nervously until he walked out of the store without saying a word."

"She might just be a private person." Jack returned for another load.

"I saw him hand her an envelope before she stuffed it in that same satchel she had that day on the trail."

Jack shrugged. "What's so strange about that?" He headed back with a box tucked under each arm, his muscled biceps bugling from the strain, pulling his shirt sleeves taut.

"When I got closer, I saw a lot of money in it. Not tens and twenties, but hundred-dollar bills." A frown marred Emily's face.

23

"Maybe he's helping her out through these hard times. She probably needs a little financial assistance. Don't think she has a job this far past retirement age." Jack picked up a hefty carton spilling over with extra folders on top.

"Why hide the money?" Emily mentally scrutinized the possibilities while helping Jack with the last load. Walking a step behind him, she bent forward from the unexpected weight of the paperwork.

"You said she put it in her pack." He topped off the pile of boxes sitting next to a tall four-drawer filing cabinet in a corner of the room. Light filtered in from a nearby open window and the eyelet lace curtain rippled in a mid-afternoon alpine breeze. The coolness of the air offered momentary relief and Emily lingered in the direct flow of the stream after unloading the heavy burden on top of the cabinet.

"She did, and then she left without any groceries. She didn't purchase a thing." Emily scrunched her face up striving to retrieve a thought from the back storage section of her brain.

"So, you're saying Astrid's crime is not buying groceries? Maybe it was money to help her pay the mortgage." Jack employed his puppy dog pout face. "Let's move past the idiosyncrasies of a very senior citizen. I'm hungry."

"I'm serious. It was weird, secretive. And there was something else off, different, I can't quite pinpoint what."

"We may never run into her again. I'm grateful we happened along when she needed medical help. She could have gone from heat stress to heat stroke that day. You know the elderly can't handle it when the temps soar at this elevated altitude." Jack brushed his fingers through Emily's honey hair and gave his wife the look—his eyes locked onto hers in a penetrating stare. No more playful pout, he meant business.

Emily let it go, but during the course of the evening she remembered exactly what the something was. Astrid's eyes were hazel that day at Vikingsholm. Today, they were blue.

Chapter Five
A Beloved Young Woman

"This season of drought is singing the majesty of the Sierra Nevada Forest from the stateliest pines on down to saplings, and seedlings just sprouting. Most recent fires have been contained in the subalpine zone, but the species at the higher elevations are beginning to decline." ~ Tahoe Daily Tribune, September 17 of 2017

"I've done some more checking on our mystery woman, Astrid." Emily announced as Jack fired up the propane grill on the back deck. A cool breeze blew in through the lumbering pine boughs spreading across the wooden-planked west corner where their Adirondack loungers and ottomans waited for them. Emily fanned herself anyway. She knew the welcomed relief was not going to last into the evening like it usually does. She tossed their farmer's market organic salad in a wooden bowl on the picnic table completing the dinner setting, then headed for her chair.

"Really." Jack replied and placed two lean filet mignon steaks on the grate. The meat juices immediately hissed a low sizzle. "Why?"

"Well, I guess because I keep running into her in town." Emily stretched her short legs until her feet rested on the sage green painted ottoman. She flipped her zories off and they hit the deck below. She wiggled her toes and flicked a mosquito off her thigh where the cuff of her shorts lay against her tan skin. "I met someone at Vikingsholm who knew of a young woman who used to travel from Michigan with her parents to visit Lora Knight in the 1930's."

"Do you think that young woman was Astrid?" Jack poked a fork into the steaks, shaking his special garlic and onion seasoning mix lightly over as he turned them. He winked at his wife.

"Yes, I mean I think so. Can't be sure unless I ask her." She didn't wink back. "This person was well-known for almost a decade. She came for four weeks every summer, then quite abruptly she and her family never returned." She shifted sideways waving away a little cyclone of mosquitos flitting in the rays of sunlight. "Don't you find it odd that the family's regular visits ended without any explanation?"

"Remember Lora died in 1945 a little over a month after World War II ended. The war changed a lot of lives. Maybe that had something to do with it." Jack turned off the propane and brought the meat to the table. "Not so mysterious."

"I think it is. No contact at all with anyone, no letters, no phone calls, no photographs?" Emily wandered over barefoot and sat beside her husband. "What happened in that gap of time?"

"Ask her." Jack suggested, took her hand, and prayed a blessing over their meal. "The woman we met is well-acclimated to the mountains. She hikes daily and walks everywhere. I understand she doesn't drive a car, and she probably shouldn't at her age."

"I saw her riding a bicycle yesterday. It was a 1950's no-speeder with a worn wicker basket attached to the handlebars. She rode easily and slowed down to stop without any trouble. You might expect an elderly woman to teeter a bit. When I first saw her, she seemed to be a younger woman." Em dished out the greens and handed Jack a tray with clinking bottles of balsamic vinegar and olive oil. "I wonder why she faltered so that day at Vikingsholm."

Jack stopped for a moment pondering Emily's observations. "Well, I want to be like her when I'm that old." He mused before slicing his knife through the browned and crusty seasoned top of his filet. He cut all the way through the tender meat until a steady stream of blood flowed from the dark red center. Jack smiled his stamp of approval after the first bite then looked to his wife for validation.

"Melt-in-your-mouth perfection." She mumbled while savoring a chunk of the meat.

"The barter for meat with Sanchez was a great deal for both of us. This is the last of it."

"That entire side of beef in the deep freezer is gone?" Emily appeared surprised.

"Em, you donated a good half of it to the Riker Fire Fundraiser." Jack reminded her. "You give it away as fast as it comes in."

"Helping Hector's brother with his cattle was the right thing to do." She ran her hand on back of Jack's neck twirling his wavy hair of short lose locks into a thick tangle around her fingers.

"He still had a healthy herd, not like a lot of the remaining ranchers whose steers are starving. Our tire blew for a reason that day near Carson City." Jack polished off his meal and leaned back into his chair. "I struggle with the hard times everyone around us is experiencing—loss of jobs, homes, and forced retirements. I can relate to that last one. And I like that you share." He drew her to his chest, planted a kiss on her forehead. The warmth of his breath fell upon the back of her neck and on the cusp of her ear, firing an electric current throughout her body.

Emily relaxed in his hold, safe and secure. She was home in his arms. They still had a cabin and a paid off one at that, even though the exorbitant new taxes were quickly draining their dwindling resources.

"Why so curious about this particular old woman?" Jack mulled over his words as he considered Emily's remaining brain trauma complications that still cause unforeseen struggles.

"Because in the depth of my soul, I know something is off even though I can't figure out what. I've run into her five times in the weeks since she first crossed our paths. I wasn't thinking about her at all until she kept popping up everywhere I went—the Safeway, the post office, the bank, the thrift store, and today the foreclosure at the Miller's home on the east shore." Another wave of the breeze caught the wind chime and played a soft tune of tinkling notes.

29

"What was she doing there?" Jack stacked their plates, helped her clear the table and carry everything inside. He stood holding the door open while balancing the dishes.

"I have no idea. She ignored me this time too and hurried off again. I was delivering a meal for the children. Six little ones under ten. What are they going to do?" She sighed a heavy lament and halted. "Those children gobbled down that full pan of lasagna and ate the entire loaf of cheese bread. Their parents just ate the salad and drank coffee. They asked me to stay." Emily's voice cracked. "More hardship brought on by financial loss."

"Be glad we could help. They were patients for twelve years, since they first married, just teenagers, not even twenty." Jack leaned against the counter. "One day at a time." He whispered in her ear. "That's the best any of us can do."

Emily nestled into Jack's welcoming embrace and tried to nudge Astrid out of her mind. Her noticeable lack of any compassion for the Miller family, and her unexpected presence at their residence left more questions than answers.

Chapter Six

A Reluctant Leader on the Lakes Shores

"The years have taught me to choose my words with great care and to speak at the precise moment what I have to say will incur the impact I desire. Too much time is wasted on foolish banter and reckless abandon that will accomplish the exact opposite. I do not intend to spend the end of my life backtracking, but rather to leap from the present into the future." ~ Astrid at a Camp Richardson Tahoe gathering. September 30 of 2017

Astrid unpinned her silvery-tipped white locks and let them uncurl into a slow tumble to her waist. The vanity mirror in front of her was tilted with a slight downward slant so she could gaze at her aged features at a more flattering angle. Her fingers followed the wrinkles that creased deep across her forehead and left rows etching each decade of nearly a century. A frown crowned her brow as she reached for the natural boar bristle brush and began her nightly ritual of thirty repeated strokes until her hair lay flat, shiny, and smooth. She returned the brush to its proper place on the table, still staring into the looking glass.

A vast array of jarred creams and bottled oils cluttered around the vintage brush and comb set. Astrid unscrewed an opaque oval jar and slathered the clotted, white creamy mixture on her cheeks, forehead and neck. In long upward movements she blended the moisturizer up her crepey neck, and in a circular motion on her dry cheeks and forehead. Within minutes the cream absorbed until not a trace remained visible. She then uncorked an ornately beaded bottle and dotted her fingertips with pearl-size droplets of amber oil and gently massaged it onto her eyelids and the bagging skin below her eyes; leaving a glistening sheen with a more supple appearance.

Clasping her trembling hands together on the vanity, she tried to still the hand tremors involuntarily interrupting her nightly routine. "Not again." She murmured.

After several moments of waiting, her hands steadied enough that she could continue. With a quick jerk, she pulled open the drawer beneath the table and retrieved a small double-compartmented plastic container and a two ounce squeeze bottle. She wiped her palms dry on a folded paper towel and gazed up into the mirror while she popped the cap open to one side of the small circular case. In one swift swipe, Astrid removed a hazel contact and placed it in the bowl, and then repeated the procedure on her left eye. Without a flinch she squirted a few drops of cleansing solution into both miniature bowls, then snapped the lids shut.

The old woman raised her head and beheld the image before her through clouded blue eyes that once radiated a striking sapphire iris. Tears pooled, hugging the inner corners until her eyelashes lowered and brushed against the liquid but did not soak it up. Her shaky hand touched the beveled glass and wiped away the watery beads from the old woman. "Nothing to cry about now. Be strong. Be courageous." She urged.

Applying a thick serum to the top of her hands she completed the sequence of her nightly habit by rubbing them together, careful not to waste any of the expensive salve on her palms. Her shoulders sagging, she gathered her pale pink cotton nightgown up to her chin. Heaving a deep sigh, she let the exasperation of the days disappointing events flow out as she distanced herself from what should have happened but didn't. She closed all the ointments yet lingered in her chair as if she still had some task to finish; some ceremonial rite to complete, some additional technique to enhance and preserve her appearance. After a few more seconds, she flicked off the light, then retreated downstairs to the family room.

Astride tried to make sense of the failed speaking engagement under the huge revival tent at Camp Richardson. The turnout was five times larger than she had hoped for, because the organizers had come through on their end. She was the one who didn't. Her shameless promotion intended to draw in the less fortunate that were in foreclosure, who had already walked away from their homes, and were now living in their vehicles—had all backfired.

The people wanted to voice their anger and frustration. They wanted to be heard, they had zero interest in listening to a weak old woman who appeared to have nothing to offer. Legitimate rants of injustice took over and the stifling heat made the meeting unbearable. Too many locals stuffed too close together under a muggy pitched circus canvas soon spun in a totally different direction.

She lost control of the crowd.

"I should have held it out in the open air, under the early evening shade of the tall pines and sheltering cedars." Astrid shook her head and rocked harder in the oak spindle-back chair, its curved bands bearing heavy on the Persian rug in the middle of the family room.

"We'll get it right next time." A mousey man, short in stature, with thin black hair plastered to his head mumbled from across the room.

"People will remember how I failed tonight."

"People will forget, they always do." He pulled a pack of cigarettes and a matchbook from his Hawaiian shirt pocket. "Wait a couple of weeks. Let the temperature drop ten, maybe even twenty degrees if we get lucky." He struck the match against his boot heel until it lit, sucked in a deep draw, then exhaled a stream of smoke out the open sliding door. "They'll come again." The palm trees on his shirt seemed to sway each time he took another drag.

"I don't know."

"I do. It's human nature. I've seen it everywhere I've been." His dark beady eyes narrowed, and a malevolent grin crept icily across his face.

"A lot of the people left early."

"Yeah, it's those very namby-pamby do-gooders you got to watch out for. They were all saying how they are going to trust the Lord to provide for them. People are praying. Geeze." He stepped outside and squashed the burning embers of his cigarette into forest floor.

"Please make certain that butt is out." Astrid rose, her petite frame lost in the billowing full-length nightie flapping in the incoming breeze.

Detert stamped out the butt a second time. "Don't dwell on it." He kicked up some dirt and pine needles to cover his trash, then turned to face her. "We still took in a small bundle of cash. Next time, we can triple that amount." He pulled out another cigarette and offered one to the old woman.

"I don't smoke." She rebuffed him.

"Maybe you should." He pursed his lips. "Relax. We're just getting started."

Chapter Seven
Time Passages

I learned from watching my Nana live because it lined up with what she said. She was more of a listener than a talker. It took me decades to discover the power of silence and the wisdom of restraining my tongue, fine tuning my ears, and observing the movement surrounding me, or noticing what is missing that should be present. ~ Emily journal entry, October 1 of 2017

The deeper Emily dug for information the more frustrated she became. No one knew this Astrid's last name. It was beginning to seem she possessed a unique star quality like Cher, Prince, or Sting. How ridiculous.

  Fred at the hardware store told her that he only knew who she was because she came in frequently to purchase rather odd amounts of kerosene, wicks, and old-fashioned glass oil lamps. One day her snowy hair would be pinned up in a tight bun smack on top of her head, and the next time it would be flowing like a river down her back. Sometimes she wandered in alone and sometimes a slick weasel accompanied her, practically attached to her hip. She always paid in cash. No checks, credit, or debit cards.

And so, it was at the Safeway market, the post office, and the local bakery.

Kerry at the bank said basically the same thing.

"But you have to know her last name to take a deposit or transact a withdrawal." Emily persisted in a low whisper as she deposited the first check for her new editing services.

"I can't give out that kind of information about one of our customers to another. I could lose my job." Kerry shook her head of thick blonde curls. "But I will say," her eyes met Emily's, "there is an air of confidence, almost an arrogance about her." Kerry handed Emily a receipt.

"That, I already know." Emily huffed a cloud of defeat, took the paper and turned to leave. "Next thing you'll tell me is that she goes by the name of Smith or Jones."

"Actually," Kerry leaned in and took her time before speaking. "You may have something there."

"Astrid Jones? You've got to be kidding."

"Hmmm…"

"Astrid Smith?"

"Isn't Smith such a common name?" Kerry replied just as her boss walked behind her. She straightened up, and smiled, "thank you, Mrs. Conner. Please say hello to Jack from Gil and me." Then she motioned the next customer to come forward.

"Yes. Unusually common." Emily muttered with an intense sense of satisfaction as she exited through the double glass doors.

***

Jack had reassembled his office in the back bedroom. Nana's old room. Whenever Emily entered it, she overlooked the gleaming rows of metal filing cabinet and the bookshelves lined with medical journals. She still saw her grandmother's mountain high, queen-size poster bed covered in handmade quilts. Emily radiated a sly grin.

"What?" Jack glanced up and asked, a stethoscope hooked around his neck and he was all decked out in his snazzy green surgery scrubs. "What are you up to now?"

"I picked up the molly bolts at the hardware store," Emily shook a small brown paper bag. "You can hang your body charts and art to add the finishing touch." She scooped up his prize Madeline Bohanon canvas and pointed to the wall across from his desk. "That way you can look at art while you're working."

"I love her watercolors." Jack eagerly accepted both the bag of bolts, and the painting of the lake lapping at the shoreline—teal, aqua, and sapphire washing over the canvas edges. "The water has a texture to it, not just the fabric beneath the colors, but a liquid fiber."

"She was an amazing artist." Emily left Jack with his hands full and slipped out before he could question her further. While he puttered, she fully intended to fire up the computer and google all the Astrid Smiths in the Tahoe/Reno region. Then what, she asked herself? Track them down while running all the errands to get Jack's practice started up again? And ask them what? Astrid hadn't committed a crime or anything. She simply had aroused Emily's distrust. Was a slumbering beast lurking below her outer surface, Tahoe Tessie-esque?

"Have you thought it all the way through yet?" Jack emerged from the kitchen doorway after hammering and mounting most of the art.

"Enough to leave it be for a while."

"Good."

Jack turned and flash kissed Emily. Then he kissed her again, a slow tender sweep across her lips that weakened her knees and sent a tingling sensation down the back of her neck to her spine. Their bodies pressed closer.

"I just want you to know that I still have it in me." He breathed the words in her ear and nibbled on her earlobe before pulling himself back to his work.

Emily leaned onto a dining room chair to steady herself. "Oh, I know you do, Dr. Conner." Her thoughts muddled into a hazy maze. In the background she heard Jack whistling clearly in her left ear. Although her right ear, the one he had spoken into, was still non-functioning in a very pleasant sort of way.

"You clever, clever man." She watched Jack hoist up a framed medical poster of the human body depicting all the muscles with tag names listed in strategic places. "Good try."

Emily sat facing the computer screen, stuck. She decided she would do it her own way and stacked eight phone books on the dining room table to begin her search. After paper clipping together the Smith section in each book, she poured herself a hot cup of coffee from the warming carafe. She grabbed a few highlighters from the junk drawer. "There can't be too many Astrids to weed through."

As it turned out an hour later, there wasn't a single Astrid listed in any of the phone books.

"You should have just gone online." Jack gloated. A chuckle escaped that he muffled under his breath as soon as she glared up at him.

Her cheeks burned red hot. The wasted time and failure added to her annoyance. Em rubbed her hand over her shoulder and neck, then rolled her head back and forth until a repeated popping sound signaled the realignment of her bones and the ability to get back to her previous plans. "When is your first patient arriving?" Emily picked up a stack of charts and clipboards.

"When Brock can break from his job. Most likely during his lunch hour." Jack took the paperwork from her and went into his office to prepare the necessary lab slips and test vials for the blood work. "I'm pretty sure he has cancer. He's only thirty-nine." He sighed.

"What can you do for him if the insurance company won't authorize the needed tests?"

"I can get a diagnosis. We'll have to take the system head-on."

"Brock is young enough. They may allow more testing and treatment, right?"

"There are no absolutes anymore with this new national health plan." Jack threw his hands up in disgust then tightened his grip on the lab slips. "Brock may have a better chance if it's in the earlier stages." Jack knew full well he would apply for every authorization possible and only a paltry few would make it through, if any.

Emily watched a familiar shadow fall across her husband's face. It shaded the twinkle of blue that used to dance in his eyes and had aged him beyond his years; stripping the vitality from his handsome features. She respected his refusal to accept defeat as so many of the other local physicians had; closing their offices, one by one. Jack couldn't afford to renew his rental in Tahoe City, but he worked around the system and discovered their cabin was still zoned like Doc's for a home office. He paid all the extra taxes and expensive permits to get the green light. They both knew it was a matter of time before the county would shut them down based on some obscure code violation or a new excessive processing fee for an additional tax.

"I left some files in my truck." He gave her a peck on the cheek and was careful not to let the screen door slam behind him.

Brock walked in the kitchen soon after Jack left. He needed to stoop to get his six feet eight inch lanky frame under the door jam. He held the screen open for his wife Asia, a young woman of petite frame and an overly abundant belly bursting with child. Her hands cradled her cumbersome load as she stepped over the threshold. Jack followed behind them.

"We were due yesterday." Asia announced. "Don't worry, not even a twinge let alone a contraction yet." She shifted awkwardly; her feet packed snuggly in tiny ballet flats. A puffy swelling rounded her ankles and puffed out at the top of the slippers where the elastic bands cut in reddened lines. "Nothing fits me, nothing." She tugged at a tight faded Giants t-shirt that left little room to spare.

"She's been wearing all my shirts." Brock offered the information with a hint of pride to which his mortified wife shuddered.

"It's okay, Honey. The doctor understands." Brock tried to reassure her.

"It's just part of being pregnant." Emily wrapped an arm around Asia and guided her to a recliner in the living room. "You elevate your legs for a good twenty minutes while the fellas discuss all the medical and insurance technicalities."

"But I wanted to go in with Brock, that's why I came."

"You'll have plenty of time to talk with the doc." Emily inserted a roll pillow behind Asia's lower back and a round one under her knees, then slowly cranked the lever to raise the footrest. When it popped into place, she gingerly guided a therapedic foam pillow into position as a head rest and support for Asia's upper back.

"Well, I…" Asia adjusted and sort of melded into the chair. "Oh, this is just wonderful. No throbbing, no pressure on my spine." She closed her eyes. "Okay, I'll wait here."

"I'll let you know when it's time to join them." Emily sat beside her and picked up a magazine. Jack needed to give Brock time to absorb the wide scope of possibilities that cancer might have on both his family and his job. He never brought up the big "C" word unless he was ninety-nine percent certain that was the diagnosis for his patient. All Mr. and Mrs. Benton should have to contend with today was the imminent birth of their first child, not cancer.

Asia appeared to be dozing off when her eyelids opened wide as if forcing herself out of an ensuing, relaxing slumber. "Does Dr. Conner think my husband may have cancer?"

"What?" Emily was caught off guard.

"Cancer. Can it be cancer?" She was now fully alert and cast her stare upon Emily.

"Why do you think that?" Emily stumbled for words knowing she could not share Jack's pre-diagnosis without violating doctor patient confidentially.

"My father died of lung cancer. He was a three-pack-a-day smoker. I swore I'd never marry a smoker. But you don't pick who you fall in love with." Asia's voice drifted along with her glance out the picture window to the huge expanse of the lake on the other side of the glass.

"Have you and Brock discussed this?" Emily stalled.

"Yes. He quit. Went from two packs a day, to one, to half. Then just a couple of cigarettes, to one, and then to none." She looked to Emily, eyes tear-filled and red-rimmed. All the sweetness of her countenance dissipated. "He hasn't smoked for three years." Her tone lightened a bit. "But I know the signs. The hacking cough, the shortness of breath and wheezing. Brock is losing his appetite and he's down about ten pounds." She wiped away a tear. "And he's so tired all the time. He just collapses into bed after work."

"Will he be honest and tell Jack all these symptoms?" It slipped out. Emily's heart ached for the young couple. She lost herself for a moment and didn't have time to regroup.

43

"Yes, but only because he's scared he won't be around for the baby. It's a boy." Asia smiled a beautiful, hopeful smile.

"Do you have a name picked out?"

"We were going to call him Jake, but I want to name him after his father, Brockway Benjamin Jr." She laughed. "We'll just call him Benny. My husband never liked his full name."

At that point, Emily drew Asia into a long discussion about family names, nicknames, and little boy troubles that grown men later brag about in various degrees of exaggeration or full-blown fantasy.

Asia laughed with gusto. "Yeah, Brock has some..." She halted in mid-sentence, glanced over in the direction of the office door and checked the time on her watch. "They've been in there for an hour. That can't be good."

"I'm sure they'll send for you soon."

"My dad died at forty-nine. I was nineteen. Sometimes it's hard being an only child."

"I am so sorry." Emily hesitated. "My mother died right after I married. My father followed her a year later."

"Was it cancer?"

"Yes."

"Then you know."

"I do." Emily struggled to hold herself back when the door finally opened.

Brock came over to get his wife. He helped her out of the recliner which was more of a feat than either of them had antici-pated. He walked and she waddled. Neither of them said a word. Jack was waiting. He closed the door after they sat down at his office desk. Before long, a string of sobs flowed out and filled the house with a grieving Emily hadn't remembered for decades. Fear of the unknown, of the known, and of loss. How quickly the memory returns to steal, Emily thought. But she had learned how to tame the beast with prayer. She asked God for hope and praised Him for mercy. And if the long road of cancer was still to be ahead of them, she prayed for grace.

Jack came out first, Asia followed, and Brock emerged red-eyed, fostering a mild smile. Husband and wife held hands; his long pale fingers interwoven with her slender tan fingers. Jack waved a stack of paperwork like a victory banner.

"We battled on the phone with the insurance company, but I got the approval for the lung biopsy. Can you fax this right away, Em?"

"I'll do it now." Emily reached for the forms he fanned over to her.

"Emily," Asia joined her in the kitchen, "thank you for listening. I so needed someone to just listen to me."

Em turned to answer her. Trickles of water dribbled down Asia's legs. The edges of her shorts turned a deeper shade of denim when a gush of water flowed into a growing lake around her ballet shoes, overflowing the grout lines on the tile floor.

Brock's mouth dropped open.

Emily rushed to grab a couple of towels from the laundry room, then handed two to Asia to put between her legs. "It will be a damp ride to the hospital." She dropped the rest on the floor.

"I am so sorry about the water." Asia sidled over to the door. "It's everywhere." She continued to drip while trying to balance the towels between her legs with each soggy step.

"It's baby-birthing time." Jack grabbed his leather bag.

Brock didn't move.

Chapter Eight
Benny's Birth

The unexpected events in life arrive like uninvited visitors. This is not necessarily a bad thing. For the list makers and organizers, it is unsettling to lose control over the course set into motion. Attitude dictates the outcome. Either you learn to roll with it, or you scramble to regain any semblance of direction to chart a new direction. ~ Emily journal entry, October 3 of 2017

Asia didn't get any farther than the deck. A steady flow of blood intermingled with the amniotic fluid and turned the clear puddles wherever she walked, into crimson-stained seas. Brock carried her back into the house while Jack dialed 911. Labor pains hit hard and fast. Shock overtook Asia's panicked face when a second contraction surprised her.

"Ohhh…no!" She moaned, burying her face deep onto her husband's chest, her arms wrapped tight around his slumping shoulders.

Even as first time parents, the young couple instinctively knew this was not normal.

"Not good." Jack murmured to Emily. "They asked for the proof of health insurance." He aided Brock as he tried to help his wife get up on the examining table in the office. "Em, can you help her get into a gown?" Jack grabbed a stack from under the table.

"Isn't the ambulance on the way?" Brock's voice rattled in and out of pitch.

"It may not get here for a while so let's prepare for the baby." Jack answered so matter-of-factly that his air of confidence seemed to momentarily calm the Benton couple. He and Emily washed their hands and scrubbed their forearms at the kitchen sink.

"I feel pressure." Asia tugged on her husband's shirt with a firm enough grip to drag him inches from her lips. "And it hurts!" Her voice deepened into a deep guttural tone that made Brock's eyes widen. He attempted to step back but Asia clutched his t-shirt and wouldn't let go.

"Emily, I need to cut her shorts off and check out the bleeding." Jack motioned his wife to move to the opposite side of the table and handed her surgical gloves to put on after he snapped on a pair himself. "Brock, dial 911 again. Brock!" Jack pulled Brock away from his bewildered wife, snipped down the shorts seam line, then handed Emily the scissors to shear off the other side. She glanced at her watch. "Three minutes between contractions, Jack."

Emily slid the fabric out from under Asia, cut her panties off the same way and covered her with a gown that opened in the front. "Wash up and put some gloves on after you call, Brock. You may be helping deliver your own son." Emily urged him to hurry. Brock rushed to the sink, turned the water on full blast. It sprayed in every direction as he soaped up while turning backward to keep watch over Asia.

"The baby is crowning. That was fast." Jack sopped up blood with sterile towels Emily handed him. "Do you have a family history of short labors?" he asked Asia.

"Yes. Most women in my family deliver in one to three hours." She shifted to reposition herself and winced in pain, her nose crinkled, and eyelids closed to mere slits as Jack's hands mapped the baby's location on her abdomen, "Sunny-side up." He mouthed to Emily.

"What can I do?" Brock stood at a distance.

The sight and smell of blood permeated the room, something most first time fathers think they can handle but many find that is not the case once they are in the midst of natural childbirth. This was anything but natural. Something was wrong. The bleeding had increased with the past two contractions, which were mere minutes apart.

"Trade places with Emily and give her the phone." Jack stated.

Brock froze, eyes wide as his face paled.

"Quick now, give Em the cell." Jack leveled his tone and met Brock's glazed-over stare until he responded and relinquished his cell as Emily pried it from his deadlock grip.

"Em, tell the operator, we have an emergency. There is a rupture somewhere."

Jack calmly told Brock and Asia, "We want them to get here right away. Do you both understand?"

"Is the baby okay?" Asia sniffled. "I need to push." She squeezed her husband's hand.

Jack grabbed a bulb syringe. A small face appeared. Dark hair coated in a white vernix and blood mixture slid onto Jack's green-gloved hand. He immediately squeezed the bulb into one nostril at a time, and then he made a clean sweep of the mouth. Tiny muddy blue eyes opened and blinked at Jack.

The baby made no sound, not a whimper or a cry, nor a gasp for air. Nothing.

Chapter Nine
Saying Good-bye

"Life is precious. Every breath is measured, every hair on the head is numbered, and every tear is bottled. If I did not believe this to be absolute truth, I could not bear the sorrows that befall those with hearts full of love for the ones that leave no matter how we long for them to stay." ~ Emily journal entry, October 7 of 2017

The shrill sound of the ambulance sirens reverberated down the street. But it was too late.

Brock stood vigilant over his wife, fighting off the woozy nausea that buckled his knees. Jack delivered Benny's shoulders—first the right, then the left. A river of blood gushed as a tiny person was pushed out into the world, arms stretched wide, legs kicking. The faint cries of life sounded more like the weak mews of a newborn kitten.

Asia lifted her head to see her son. Jack laid the baby on her chest facing his mother and called Emily over to hold him for her. Asia reached to touch his fingers and toes, then collapsed, her body convulsing on the table.

The baby was red and blue, not tan, white, or pink.

Benny's cries grew louder.

Jack scrambled to stop the bleeding. He could only guess what was causing it. Most likely a ruptured main uterine artery. Asia needed to be in an operating room, stat. Mother and child were still attached by the umbilical cord. It pulsated between them, a bluish-grey tangle, knotted and twisted.

Brock knelt near his wife's head, sobbing, stroking her face, telling her how much he loved her, how beautiful their son was.

Asia's brown eyes rolled back, and her lids opened and shut, her body jerked in sharp, quick movements, arms flailing, hands and fingers clawed inward. Only a few animal-like moans escaped her gaping mouth.

Brock drew back.

Benny's cries grew stronger, louder.

Emily realized at some point Jack had donned one of the gowns and put a paper mask over his mouth. She couldn't remember this happening. She and Brock were wearing gowns and masks too. She recalled the three of them slipping on green surgical gloves. Benny now squirmed and wriggled in her gloved hands.

Jack delivered the placenta and handed it to Emily. She rushed to the dining room table and lay the baby on a couple of terry cloth towels and cut the cord, then attached a plastic blue clamp on the stump before placing the cord and placenta in a gleaming metal bowl on the other end of the table.

Holding Benny, Emily walked him into the office against the far white wall and weighed him in a nine pounds six ounces on the baby scale. There she stood; a quiet baby pressed on her shoulder after swaddling him in a yellow receiving blanket. He yawned in her ear and stilled. She watched Jack hover over Asia. Brock had crawled on his knees on the floor to be at her side. The room spun in shades of red. Jack prayed out loud, his voice cracking. A distant hum closed in, Emily's throat tightened as the whirling siren hit a high pitch and came to a dead stop outside their door.

Chapter Ten
Gone

Oh death, you steal without mercy. What is your power? Is it that final tick of the clock that man cannot change no matter the vastness of his wealth, the desire to hold onto the fading breath of life, the longing for those loved that are left behind? Cruel destroyer of flesh and blood flee, leave me be! Claim me if there be a true God ~ offer thee me paradise for all eternity. What wilt become of me? Sixteenth century poet ~ Ephraim Algiers

A small grove of pine trees clustered spreading evergreen branches wide like sheltering wings of guardian angels gathered to shield and protect their charge from the eyes and ears of the world. Jack sat alone on the weathered wooden bench under the cover of the forgiving circle of the interwoven needled arms filtering the oncoming autumn light of mid-day. Head buried in his hands, he wept, his body rocked in rhythm with his sobs—heaving, halting, gasping.

Moments passed before the presence of another person sitting beside him, the warmth of another body against his caught his attention. Jack remained huddled, head down and did not look up to see who had also ventured to the secluded corner of the hospital grounds built for the privacy of the grieving seeking to be alone.

The stillness of the air surrounding Jack offered no solace. The usual crisp snap of October was stifled by the heat, the constant companion the drought coupled with that would most likely carry into January or February again. The seasons were confused, out of sync, needful of divine intervention to reset the timepiece that could recycle the four seasons of the year back to the original sequential order.

"You did all you could."

Jack recognized his father's aging voice, felt his arm stretch across his shoulder, and settle as his hand cupped and squeezed tight pulling him closer. But Jack couldn't raise his head and face the man he knew understood the pain of losing another patient, and the deep anguish of helplessness as you feel life slipping away from the one you are trying to save—knowing that you do not have the power to give another hour, minute, or second of breath to the dying.

"You did all you could." Doc repeated.

"Brock is alone now, with a baby." Jack wept. "Alone."

"Yes, but he will learn how to love his son. They will go on." John Walter's voice was gentle. He chose his words with tender care.

"Dad, I tried everything." Jack looked up, pleading for some reasonable answer.

"Sometimes there is no answer."

"I know he has cancer. What will he do?"

"Grieve. Cry. Live. He has choices to make you can't make for him. Remember that."

"How many more will end up like Asia? She was a lovely woman. How can I keep practicing medicine like this?" Jack wiped his shirt sleeve across his face and smeared the dampness. His back straightened.

"Just keep doing your job the best you can. You are a good doctor."

Jack shook his head. His father pulled him to his chest and hugged tight until his son's head rested on his shoulder, leaning in with the weight of the world bearing down. The evergreen branches rustled as a cool breeze allowed flitting rays of light to shine before being overshadowed by clouds.

"What can I say to Brock?" Jack said and pulled away.

"Listen to what he needs to say."

Jack squirmed, shifting to the side of the bench. "He will have questions that I can't answer." Tears flowed freely now. "What if, what if it was my fault?" His voice cracked and a thickness filled his throat.

"Don't take that burden on yourself." Doc Walters reached over and placed a weathered hand back on Jack's shoulder. "At one time or another, all physicians ask themselves this question. We can only do so much."

"I should have considered the possibility of complications."

"How could you have known? Births are unpredictable, especially for first time mothers." A strain rippled through Doc Walters voice. "You weren't her obstetrician or gynecologist. Thank God you were there, or the baby would be dead too."

"At least he still has his son." Jack's tone warbled, grief for his own stillborn son resurfaced, intensifying the anguish of loss all over again.

"You understand the depth of Brock's sorrow more than you realize."

"I still have Emily." Jack turned to face his father.

"He still has Benny."

"And yet, we both have less."

"I suppose you can look at it that way." The old man leaned back against the cold wrought-iron frame where they sat. He folded his bulky hands together, fingers interwoven, and pressed tight. "Brock is not alone. He has a future with a tiny new human being that bears a striking resemblance to his mother and will most certainly share some of her character traits. He can choose to focus on what he does have instead of what he doesn't."

"True, but..."

Old Doc Walters interrupted, "then encourage him in that direction. Offer him hope."

Jack sat silent and still. A strong gust of wind swept between the two men and bristled through the forest behind them. Jack tried to form words into a sentence that his father would understand. But he didn't have any. Not a single word.

"You think about it before you speak with Brock. He's inside asking for you." Slowly the retired physician rose; his bones creaked at the knees and spine as he straightened, but his back remained bowed forward at a slight arch. He shuffled two steps, his movements stiff, halting, and somewhat awkward. He turned and said, "Pray, Jack."

"That is what I came out here to do, but I can't seem to start." He slouched down in the bench and dropped his head in his palms.

"It is when we don't have the words that we pray the best." A glimmer of truth shone in Doc's eyes, a knowing from a deep place within, a place well acquainted with pain and suffering. He waited a few seconds before making deliberate strides toward the emergency room entrance.

Jack watched his father's slow movement—arthritis-ridden and in need of his walking cane for support. The elderly man had struggled to journey to the sanctuary on the outer rim of the medical compound to offer his son advice. How Jack wished he could confidently approach Brock in the same way, with the assurance and guidance needed. He lingered at a safe distance. A storm was brewing, the unpredictable winds becoming more forceful by the minute; cracking and snapping branches, knocking pinecones across the dirt, and whipping pine needles off limbs with an increasing ferocity. Jack watched Doc walk directly into the epicenter. He braced himself against the onslaught rather than avoid it until he finally entered the sliding glass doors and disappeared from view. A red light flashed on and off, off and on.

"Tell Brock that everything will be okay. Time heals all wounds. Lie to him?" Jack muttered out loud and shook a fist at the darkening cloudy sky. "If I had lost Emily, I would have died myself." A heaviness weighed on his chest; a heaving sigh escaped. Rain pelted down, a hard driving rain that stung the back of Jack's bare neck like a hundred piercing needles. He dragged himself off the bench and trudged forward. The air smelled of stale rain and chimney smoke. Sirens roared as an ambulance rolled in and the emergency room team ran out; they huddled under the overhead cover as a loaded gurney was lowered with a thud to the ground. The closer Jack got the more his speed picked up.

Thunder clapped and lightening lit up the dark gray horizon. By the time Jack reached the building he was drenched, his shoes sloshing. Bloody wheel tracks marred the once shiny floor to the entry doorway and down the long hallway.

A tall lean figure hovered outside the emergency doors where the tracks started. Brock was waiting for him.

Part Two
Alone

Chapter Eleven
Left Behind

There was but a single thought on my mind. Was he wondering what if it had been me and not Jackson that died when he was born? We moved forward because we still had each other. The memory of the only child we birthed together had not been enough for me in the beginning. It was Jack who brought me through the heartache of pain and loss. How different would it have been if he had lost me instead? ~ Emily, journal entry the day Asia died.

Brock stood motionless and barely acknowledged Jack's presence when he stood beside him. Ashen-faced with a shadow of stubble that prickled his chin, Brock's glazed, glassy stare with pupils dilated, was fixed on the ground below his feet. His disheveled clothing, wet from the slanting rain seemed to parallel his mental state. He was in shock. Jack knew the doctors had medicated him when they couldn't pry him from Asia's body to send her to the morgue.

"Brock." Jack gently nudged his right shoulder in an attempt to stir a response. He remained in place without flinching.

"Let's go inside and get out of the rain."

"Rain." Brock said in a hollow monotone. A blank expression covered his face devoid of emotion.

"Yes." Jack replied. The automatic sliding-door repeatedly opened and closed behind them. Jack waited for it to open again and ushered Brock inside the building while waving aside a security guard at obviously had been sent to deal with the distraught person. Along the now slippery waxed floors, Jack tried to direct Brock ahead to the surgery waiting room.

Multiple sets of footprints already muddied up the smeared tile. Brock had at some point ventured out on the hospital lawns. Perhaps he'd gone looking for his doctor. Perhaps he'd wandered aimlessly about the grounds just to be out in the air. Jack was pretty sure if he asked him, he'd have no answer.

"Let's sit here." Jack suggested and pulled a padded armchair next to him. To his surprise Brock immediately slumped into the seat, resting his head on the wood back, and closed his eyes. His hands, hanging loose on his legs, trembled. Slight tremors began to rack his upper torso but slowly subsided the longer he sat. Jack slid his chair in front of him and relaxed, sitting in a leaning position toward Brock, and waited.

Brock slipped into a fitful sleep of exhaustion, rapid movements sputtered his eyelids and low moans escaped his dry lips. A rumbling from the young father's stomach alerted Jack he hadn't had anything to eat or drink. Brock needed fluids or he would dehydrate, worsening his present physical condition and that would only accelerate his unstable cognitive thinking.

Jack sat back into the resistant fabric cushion and couldn't help but remember. He kept his line of vision directly on Brock, watching for any change. He knew his present condition meant nothing to him. Life currently held no purpose or meaning without Asia. Part of him died with her. Who could tell him anything otherwise? Jack knew it would be the only truth he believed at the moment and doubted that he gave even a thought to his newborn son. Benny was but a stranger that had, in Brock's mind, taken Asia from this earth. Jack knew Brock had no faith in anything. They had discussed this when they talked about the cancer. Asia was his life. What he needed was to be able to grieve for her. Brock's pain ran deep. A day ago, his biggest concern had been for his wife; if she would have to endure a prolonged slow death process with him while tending to a new baby.

That life was gone now. The cancer remained as did the infant. Part of Jack was jealous of the son Brock continued to ignore, refused to look at, or hold no matter how many nurses or doctors encouraged him to bond. Would Jack have reacted any differently if it had been Emily? The two of them had experienced opposite outcomes from the birth of their sons.

Brock jerked in sharp quick spasms, then seemed to drift even deeper into a combination of drug-induced and sheer fatigue slumber. *Sleep Brock, sleep as long as you can. The world you knew doesn't exist anymore.*

Over the next four hours random words rolled off Brock's tongue and past his half-open mouth. He never moved, never shifted an inch in the chair. But pain filled his face, clouded in pale shades of nothingness. Even in sleep reality raged at him depriving him of peace.

"Asia."

"Are you awake, Brock?" Jack answered.

"Asia," Brock murmured, shaking his head right and left, lifting a hand to fend off the awakening drawing him back to consciousness. A frown imprinted his brow and stayed. He shot forward in a jolt; swollen eyes open, lower jaw gaped wide. With both hands Brock clamped onto the wooden arms of the chair and he squeezed tight until his knuckles whitened. Furtive glances about the room only served to remind him of the truth—he had been left behind.

Chapter Twelve
The Walking Dead

Death is not always quick. Despair, Depression, Desperation ~ these companions sidle along not always making their presence known. Lurking in the shadows, they hang back, remain silent until the moment the door opens for their unannounced arrival. Welcome or not, they enter. Some are shielded from their intrusion, mind, body and soul. Others are helpless to the invasion. ~ Jack's annexed medical notes.

"Asia is gone," Jack answered in a low murmur.

Brock lunged forward to the edge of the chair. Wide and wild-eyed he asked. "Where did she go?"

Jack knew this was coming. Asia was a woman of great faith. Brock leaned heavily on his wife's strengths, but they were not his own. She was a Buddhist when they lived together and got married. A few years later Asia came home one day and told him she wanted to get baptized, a full underwater immersion. Brock said she changed, but she never forced her Buddhist beliefs or her new faith on him.

During his appointment Brock had asked Jack if he died from cancer, what would happen to him. Will he just rot in the earth? It had troubled him, the thought of decay setting in, taking over, entombed with no escape, no air to breathe. Brock thought he might somehow be conscious of his own demise. Jack told him he had watched too many zombie movies.

"Before I have to bury her," Brock hesitated, "what happens to her?"

Jack knew Asia had already been transferred to the county morgue. She would be placed on a cold metal tray and pushed into a wall of compartments. In his delirium Brock had unknowingly signed for an autopsy. Something Jack didn't think he would have agreed to in a right frame of mind, though it was necessary to determine the exact cause of death. Brock simply would not be able to bear the thought of the Y-shaped incision into his delicate wife or any other technique involved. Even a body bag would be difficult for him.

"Asia has been transported to another location while you make the arrangements for her at a local funeral home. Do you need help with that?" Jack asked.

"I don't know what to do or how to do it," Brock mumbled, his large shoes shuffling, searching for stable footing on the slick floor. He locked his knees in place with his over-sized sneakers tucked neatly under the chair, out of the way.

"Did Asia ever say anything to you about what she would want?"

"We talked about it, when we thought I might have cancer." Brock nodded his head. "Asia knew exactly what she wanted. No fuss."

"Did she give any specifics?" Jack pressed gently.

"A plain pine box. Some of her favorite songs. Single roses for old folks." He stopped. "Said she knew where she was going." Brock's dry throat stumbled on his last words. "Is she already there?"

"Do you mean heaven?"

"Is there really a heaven, Doc because I don't see how there can be."

"Why not?"

"Who decides which people are good or bad, and who divvies up the dead? How is it fair for Buddha, God, angels, or anyone else to make all those decisions?" Elbows resting on his knees, the tired young man held his palms open as if releasing these questions into the cosmic universe.

Brock had obviously given this much thought. Probably more about him and the cancer. He was not prepared to lose Asia.

A nurse wheeled a bassinet from the nursery up to the rubber tops of Brock's shoes and parked it in front of him. Visible through the clear plastic crib, a dark head of hair peeked out of a swaddling bundle of pastel blue blankets. The infant slept quietly inside; his face turned aside from Brock. Baby Boy Benton was written across a postcard-size label and slipped into a slot at the front.

"You need to hold your son." The older woman flatly stated. "He's been crying for hours and so far, only the doctor's wife Emily has been able to rock him to sleep." Her hot pink surgical pants and smock were brighter than her not-so-perky attitude.

Brock stared blankly at the metal framework under the mobile baby bed, never raising his eyes high enough to risk actually seeing his son. He did not reply.

"Doctor Conner." The nurse held out a plastic bottle of formula. "He will wake up hungry." Jack took the bottle. The sole of her right shoe squeaked each time her heel rose inches above the floor on her return trek down the white-walled hallway. She left a floating mixed-scent layer of baby powder, disposable lanolin wipes, and soiled burp cloth lingering in mid-air.

Brock and Jack sat in silence. There wasn't any movement from the bassinet.

"Asia wanted to breast-feed. It was important to her for him not to have formula."

"There are natural substances, Leukocytes that fight infections, vitamins, proteins and fats in breast milk that help babies," Jack said. "Asia was making wise choices."

"She researched everything." The hint of a smile curved. In seconds it faded, and Brock's lips blanched.

"Asia had a couple of books with her when you two came by the house." Jack tried to encourage Brock with the few happy memories he mentioned.

The baby stretched and yawned. Jack bent over the plastic rim of the crib until he was face-to-face with Benny who had a ruddy round face with a dent in his chin and fuzzy light brown eyebrows. Dark blue, almost brown almond-shaped eyes opened and blinked in the bright fluorescent lights. Tiny red fists flicked about in the air. Successive squeals escaped the newborn and his forehead spread into four rows of baby fat. A mounting joy echoed in Jack's chest at the sound of the baby's cries. He glanced at Brock.

The new father cast an iron stare at the ground. He crossed his arms over his chest and locked his hands around his upper shirt sleeves.

Benny began to sing, loudly. Jack carefully picked him up and held the squalling babe close, then folded him into his arm. Immediately the infant rooted and suckled Jack's hairy skin. A displeased howl rang throughout the room. Jack laughed and pressed the bottle nipple on the baby's tongue and squeezed lightly, enough to release a stream of the milky formula. The baby responded with a greedy grasp of the rubber nipple cleverly patterned like a mother's nipple. The tiny mouth made slurping, sucking sounds that altered the silence.

"Well he certainly isn't going to starve." Jack was entranced with the determination and force with which the newborn accepted the substitute mixture of water and concentrated formula. "He'll down these two ounces in minutes." The baby grabbed Jack's index finger. Jack's heart did flip-flops. This precious moment was one he had dreamed of with his own son. "Hello, baby Benny."

For an instant, Jack thought he saw Brock's face soften. In fact, he was sure the heartbroken father sneaked a peek at his son. "He has his mother's dimpled cheeks." Benny sucked the bottle dry. Jack held the baby upright on his right shoulder and patted the middle of his back until a loud, long burp burst out with a spewing forth of formula. The doctor grabbed the cloth diaper from the baby's bed and blotted the smelly spit-up off his shirt collar.

"A diaper change will be next in order."

"I have to go." Brock stood and moved from the bassinet.

"Don't worry, dirty diapers aren't so bad."

"I have to get home so I can start working on the funeral arrangements. Asia's mother and step-father are arriving early to-morrow morning at the Reno airport." Brock looked ready to bolt for the exit.

"Wait, what about your son? He's ready to be discharged tomorrow." Jack set the infant on his lap and unwrapped the blan-kets. Perfect legs, feet and toes kicked. A hospital band around his left ankle read, Benton. A powder blue Onesie snuggled close to the baby's torso. Jack placed a matching cap over the downy crown of dark brown hair. The infant fussed at the unexpected dis-turbance with a piercing yelp.

"I'm not ready, Doctor Conner." Brock turned toward the ER doors, then looked back, directly at his son. He took one step forward, then halted and lowered his head. "I know he didn't mean to," Brock struggled for words, "but he killed his mother."

Chapter Thirteen
Going Home

Pain cannot be ignored. It will make known the deep expanse it ravages. Pain killers only mask the problem. Different drugs will induce a slumber that will give the patient relief, until they awaken. Other drugs bring on a fog that convolutes actuality. Some doctors mix cocktails to accomplish both of these effects. My patient needs to experience the painful reality of his unforeseen circumstances, or he may lose everything. ~ Doctor Jack Conner's' medical notations about patient Brock Benton.

Asia's mother went to see Benny at the hospital. She didn't stay long. Brock had refused to honor her request to deal with Asia's death within her mother's Buddhist beliefs and funeral rites. The first day of death had already passed. The next four were important because Buddhists believed the person did not yet know that they are dead. Brock told Sue that Asia left specific instructions for her burial. He was fully aware of the huge blow-up and consequential disowning that had separated mother and daughter since Asia's baptism. Mrs. Quon left to join her husband and board a plane to

Hong Kong for business within hours. She did say they would return the following month to see the baby again.

Emily and Jack had hoped Asia's parents would support their son-in-law and grandson, but Brock was on his own. His family was spread far and wide across five continents. The only reply to his notification of Asia's death came from his youngest and wildest sister Amy who offered to fly in from London to help out. She couldn't arrive until after the memorial service and would only stay a day or two. For now, he would be home alone with Benny. He would be burying his wife as she requested, but he did not share her faith, go to her church, or belong to any religion.

Jack focused on the baby. He went to the hospital the morning of discharge to change diapers and bottle feed Benny. Then he helped Brock prepare for the upcoming cancer testing that was scheduled the day before Asia's memorial.

***

Jack's dad, Doc Walters pitched in at Brock's cabin and helped Emily with the final preparations. They moved the white wicker bassinette into the master bedroom and placed it directly beside the king-size bed.

"If that doesn't bring bonding, I don't know what will." Doc nudged Emily.

"Maybe he'll break down and put the baby in bed with him." She smoothed her hand over the plaid cotton comforter. "There's lots of room for the little guy."

Emily filled the freezer with single meals that had a high protein and complex carb content. "These will keep his strength up," she said after stacking the last foil wrapped container.

72

"He's going to need lots of physical stamina." Doc nodded.

Together they set up a bottle feeding system that Brock could run from a small refrigerator in the bedroom and warm up in a bowl of hot water in one of the bathroom sinks. A similar grouping of bottles packed the top shelf of the kitchen fridge.

"There will be a lot of sleepless nights ahead of the new father." Doc closed the oak kitchen cabinet he had over-stocked with cans of formula.

The two of them left a magic marker magnet board on the front of the fridge door, a green coil dangled with a pen attached. Emily wrote, "Welcome home Daddy and Benny."

"Everything is ready to go." Emily peeked in the nursery one last time. A Tahoe bear theme decorated the little room; forest murals filled the walls encircled by the mountains and lake, with a cloudless sky blue ceiling. A fading memory tugged her heart as she closed the door.

They left after vacuuming and turning on the dishwasher.

Asia's friends from the church brought boxes of disposable diapers, coordinated a laundry procedure of pick-up dirty, and drop-off clean clothes and bedding for the father and son. They arranged to have a man from the church stop by daily, either before or after work, to check in and see how things are going. To listen if Brock wanted to talk, watch TV if he just didn't want to be alone, or share a meal with him.

The rest was up to the reluctant father.

And it was time to bring his son home.

Jack went through the discharge routine with Brock and the nurse, then helped strap Benny in the car seat. Brock still had not touched his son. He hardly looked at him while others held him. The October winds had kicked up that morning and there was a definite chill in the air. Could it be possible an early winter would bring an end to the relentless drought? Hopefully, change was in the air.

Benny wailed in the back seat of the car. Jack reassured Brock this was normal.

"How can something so little make so much noise?" The frightened father gave a fearful look at the screaming minion that now possessed his car.

"The car ride lulls most babies to sleep, almost instantly." Jack said. "Benny just downed a bottle, he's been burped, changed, and bathed. You're off to a good start." He patted Brock's back a couple of times and shut the car door.

Brock stood rigid, tall and gangly. The uncombed red mop of hair on his head was sticking out everywhere in wild clumps and clustered-strands. The indifference he had shown his son thus far had transformed into abject terror. "What if he doesn't stop? What do I do?" His face grew paler by the second; full-fledged panic set in.

"Well, he can't cry forever." Jack laughed and tried to lighten the moment. "He will exhaust himself eventually. Right now, he's taking in a lot of air, so be sure to burp him."

"I don't think I can do this." Brock mumbled, shaking his head.

"It just comes naturally. You can read all the parenting books, watch all the videos in the classes, practice diapering dolls, and it all comes down to, just starting on your own." For the first time Jack believed Brock could take care of his son. It was a good thing no one was going to be there to help since Amy bailed out. The two of them needed to be alone, to bond, and get to know each other for the first time. To be a family, even if it was a family of two instead of three.

Brock swallowed hard. Then he noticed. It was quiet. He opened his car door, and nothing happened. The baby had fallen asleep. The car seat was not facing forward, and he couldn't see his son. Slowly, he crept around the car to the window next to where Benny was belted in. He lowered his tall frame, pressed his face against the glass, and checked on the baby. Jack stood back a few steps while Brock did what all parents do. He made sure his son was okay. Then he instinctively rushed back around to get in the car before Benny woke up.

Brock rolled down his window. "Thanks, Doc, I'm going to take off before he wakes up again. Maybe I can get him in the crib at home and he'll sleep until the next feeding." He waved a quick good-bye as the window went back up, and Brock drove home.

Chapter Fourteen
Round Two

There are other ways to approach any problem. People are stupid. They always come back for more. You just need to find another way to play them. You don't have to be a rocket scientist to figure out most of the population. Now we switch to Plan B and if that doesn't work, we go to Plan C, Plan D. You get the picture.
~ Detert's sage advice to Astrid after the failed revival.

Astrid hated the annoying little man who seemed to have over-taken her life. Everything about him niggled at her in a wrong way. He had zero charisma, was bereft of any measure of compassion. He smoked incessantly and tossed the burning embers of his cig-arette butts out into the dry forest never checking to see if anything caught on fire.

"Detert, I have a few ideas of my own." She ignored the scrawny nuisance.

"Really." He slicked back a flop of hair from across his brow and glared at her with contempt, then quickly changed his tone. "Tell me what you have."

"Well," she hesitated.

"Yes?" He strummed his fingertips across the solid birch tabletop, his nails clicking in a numbered pattern.

Her soft snowy hair fell in wisps on both cheeks as she bowed her head. With a slow rise upward, her eyes leveled with his. "I want to offer assistance to the families losing their homes on the south shore."

"What kind of assistance?" He cleared his throat and hacked that horrible smoker's cough that testified of his three-pack-a-day habit that would most likely be the end of him if some-one didn't come along and speed up that fateful event.

"Financial."

"You can't baby these people." Detert swerved across the room like a weasel. He was clever, quick, and full of guile. He was not Astrid's friend.

"I think I can do whatever I set my mind to."

"How?"

"I can map out a plan. It will take time, that's all."

"If you want to gain their loyalty, you need not spend your own money to do so." He drew his wiry body next to hers as a confident smile pursed his lips.

Astrid stepped back to put physical distance between them. She retired to the settee under the burgundy brocade curtains that cast a rosy hue on her aged cheeks. A cool evening breeze blus-tered through the open windows, blowing the drapes in ripples out into the room. Remaining silent, she hoped he would leave, but he pressed on, petulant as a disobedient child.

"Why waste your resources? Build them up instead."

"We see these things from polar opposites."

"Don't fool yourself into thinking you are any better than me because you implement different tactics." He goaded, smoothing his hand over the fabric arm of the sofa until he stopped short of her fingertips.

"Where is your compassion?"

"Same place you tuck yours."

"I beg to differ."

Detert stood over Astrid, staring down with distain, his dark beady eyes narrowed in and settled on her like a heavy weight. He held her upward gaze before sitting beside her and clamping her hands in a tight hold. "Think this out and you will come to your senses."

The sickening-sweet scent of cheap cologne overpowered Astrid. She gasped for air and then held her breath. The noxious mixture of antiseptic mouthwash coupled with too much cologne and a strong antiperspirant was strike three in her book. Detert always overdid things. What he lacked in finesse he made up for in overkill.

"You think about it." Detert stiffened against the puffed out pillow back cushion of the settee and exhaled a disgruntled grunt. He released his grip, rose in one swift motion, and headed for the front door.

"Meet me at the bank when it first opens in the morning." The old woman spoke in a firm, flat tone. She did not raise her voice, nor did she look his way. The discussion was over.

"You are making a big mistake and it will come back and bite hard."

"We are going to find out then, aren't we?"

Detert slammed the door behind him, jarring the framework of the cabin and the moose antlers above the door casing. A barrage of curse words erupted on the other side of the solid oak wood. He struck a match, lit a cigarette and tossed the matchstick into the night, mumbling all the way to his Lexus.

Astrid rose in time to watch him peel off, spewing gravel and dirt from her driveway as he hit the asphalt in the distance and accelerated well over the twenty-five MPH limit; doing about sixty plus down the road. A heady whiff of Detert's special blend still hung inside her home like an invisible, toxic cloud. She flipped the ceiling fan switch on high speed and opened the door. Her eyes followed his red taillights until they disappeared from view. Astrid stepped out onto the porch and emptied her watering can on top of the ashtray of accumulated matches, cigarette butts, and cigar nubs littering her thimbleberry bush and mums flower bed.

"That man has no class or moral convictions." She muttered under the full orb of the luminous moon that cast a wide path across the lake. The clear blue waters of the day now flowed like black ink from the north to the south shore. Moonlight played a moody symphony on the glassy surface. Who knew what secrets moved in the lower depths? Millions of stars spiked the dark sky. Astrid raised her arms reaching out to them and swayed back and forth as if in a trance, closed her eyes and hummed a familiar melody. The melancholy notes told of lost ones, and the savior that came to find them. The lost and the found. The wounded and the healer. The poor and the provider.

Astrid slept a deep slumber that night. Her decision was final.

Chapter Fifteen
The Needful Things

The potency of prayer hath subdued the strength of fires; it had bridled the rage of lions, hushed anarchy to rest, extinguished wars, appeased the elements, expelled demons, burst the chains of death, expanded the gates of heaven, assuaged diseases, repelled frauds, rescued cities from destruction, stayed the sun in its course, and arrested the progress of the thunderbolt. Quote ~ Saint John Chrysostom (347-407) Greek Ioannes Chrysostomos, archbishop of Constantinople.

Emily, Jack, and Doc made many a trip to help out the young father who was barely making it from one two hour feeding to the next. Brock lived five miles down Lake Shore Boulevard, a quick jaunt when the phones rang and pleads for immediate help came frantically from the distraught voice on the other end.

Though Brock was making some progress. He had learned how to change diapers, clean the umbilical cord area, and mix concentrated formula. Only once did he forget to add the water and fed pure liquid concentrate to a fussy baby that later broke out everywhere in pin dot blemishes. Jack assured Brock it was a natural way for the body to work the rich substance out of the system. Brock switched to powdered formula, just to be sure he didn't repeat the mistake.

Men from Asia's church stopped by for breakfast, lunch, or dinner. Brock welcomed the adult company and conversation. Sometimes he snagged naps, sometimes he asked questions, and sometimes he fell asleep holding Benny after they left. The church ladies had replenished the fridge and freezer with a full month supply of food. A couple of Asia's friends used her recipes and baked foods Brock was used to eating, his favorites from the recipe box on the kitchen counter. It made him miss Asia even more.

The laundry arrangement turned out to be the biggest help of all. *That baby* soiled more clothes and crib sheets than Brock could keep up with.

The memorial seemed to bring a measure of healing. Father and son sat in the front row alone, until Doc Walters, and Jack and Emily scooted beside them on the light pine wooden pew. Mr. and Mrs. Quon were anticipated no-shows. The little stone A-frame church filled up on both sides and extra chairs were brought in to accommodate the overflow of Asia's, *Holy Trinity* family.

The service was not at all what Brock had expected, or at least what he'd seen on TV shows which was all he had to go by. He thought the floor to ceiling, arched stain glass windows were works of art. Each one told a story in the three-divided panes. Six windows lined the side walls of the building, and a massive one filled the wall behind where the preacher stood. Flocks of sheep pastured on rolling lush green hills below brilliant blue skies. Little children gathered around a hippie-looking man Brock assumed to be Asia's Jesus. They sat at his bare feet, clung to his robes, and every child's face shone with a delightful smile or spoke in laughter.

Lisa, the woman in charge of the laundry ladies was the first to stand and share a story about her friend. "Asia taught me what it means to live what I believe. Not to be afraid of what might happen." She ran her hands over a near full-term pregnant mound. "After four miscarriages, I wanted to give up. Tomorrow my daughter will be delivered by caesarian section."

One by one people stood to share scripture verses Asia had prayed for them. Brock listened to stories he knew nothing about; thoughtful things his wife had done, and ways she'd helped out when needed.

"They loved her." Brock whispered in Benny's ear.

Tears trickled a slow journey down Brock's flushed cheeks. He clung to his son and listened, pressing Benny against his chest, rubbing the baby's back through the bundle of blankets he'd wrapped around him. "These people loved your mommy."

Emily grabbed Jack's hands when Brock referred to Asia as Benny's Mommy.

Communion was offered. Brock stayed in his seat and fumbled for a bottle in the diaper bag. Music played that he recognized from home; full symphony instrumental CDs his wife loved and sang along with in her perfect pitch voice. The memorial closed with five teenagers singing "Amazing Grace" acapella. The reference to a wretch, troubled Brock. Asia was not a wretch. But the song was strangely beautiful. Lost and found.

The women's Bible study hosted a full meal downstairs in the old church basement after the private burial at the north shore cemetery. No limos. No preacher. Just Brock and Benny.

"I wasn't sure I wanted to come back." Brock acknowledged to Jack.

"Glad you did." Jack drew Brock closer with a hug.

"These people are different than how I imagined." Brock set the car seat carrier with a dozing baby on the floor next to him. "Asia asked me a couple of times if I wanted to come here with her." He combed his fingers through the red crop of hair he'd had cut short because Benny grabbed fistfuls of the longer locks with a power grip that would make any father proud.

"Why don't you fix yourself a plate of food? That lasagna is layered with veggies and steak." The pastor suggested. He stopped and offered to walk Brock over to the buffet.

"I, shouldn't leave the car seat sitting on the floor." Brock's stomach was growling but the invitation surprised him.

"When you are ready, help yourself." The preacher turned, then said, "The vase of single roses is by the bookshelf. Everyone knows to take one when they leave to give to an elderly person in one of the local rest homes, or to a neighbor that lives alone."

"That was what my wife wanted." Brock's voice trembled on the edge. He had forgotten about the roses. He glanced at the simple clear glass vases brimming with an assortment of vibrant, long stem large roses. Asia loved flowers with a passion. A sudden twinge reminded him that he had neglected her garden since her death.

"Thank you."

"I hope the flowers bring a glimmer of joy into the life of each person to receive one in Asia's memory." The preacher patted Brock's shoulder with a reassuring fatherly-type touch.

Brock actually welcomed the contact. "I think I might get the plate of food now. I am kind of hungry." He glanced at his son.

"Em and I will watch Benny along with the crowd of admirers gathering around him." Jack pointed to the teenage girls sitting on the floor beside the car seat.

"I fed him a bottle at the cemetery. He should be good for about three hours." Brock assessed the moment weighing a walk with the pastor as a major risk of being indoctrinated. "Thanks." He headed off to the buffet.

"My name is Ted." The pastor shook Brock's hand and held on. "I know I'm a stranger to you and I hope I am not overstepping my bounds here."

Great, here it comes. I knew it.

"Some of the women helping out at the house have mentioned that the garden needs tending. Would you like a hand with that? We have a few master gardeners and a few apprentices. Green thumbs and not-so green thumbs."

"Oh." Brock paused.

"You can think about it." Ted Hamilton moved over to the dessert table. "First the chocolate cake, then the casseroles."

Brock laughed; he had been thinking on the same lines as he eyed the dessert table.

Chapter Sixteen
Things that Grow

"Someday the garden will extend beyond the east side of the yard. We can grow enough vegetables to share with our neighbors and have plenty of room left for a butterfly garden. You can build a butterfly house. I'll plant Black-Eyed Susans, Coneflowers, and Zinnias. Maybe some dill and parsley plants by the aspen trees where I placed the flat rocks so the butterflies can bask in the cool mornings. The baby will love a butterfly garden." ~ Asia

Benny yawned a big, perfect O-shaped, full-gum yawn that made Brock place a hand over his mouth to block a bigger yawn he couldn't suppress. The two were stretched across the king-size bed where they'd fallen asleep after coming home from the church. Brock didn't quite make it to the bassinet to lay Benny down for the night.

"Four hours, you slept four whole hours in a row." Brock spoke in a low, muted tone while he stroked the baby's back in a slow, gentle circular motion. "How did you know I needed to catch a longer nap this time?"

"Today was nice. Your mommy would have liked every-thing about her service." Brock said face-to-face, father to son. He explored every tiny facial feature with two long fingers, running over the curve of Benny's ears down to the lobe, then smoothing the pads of his fingertips across the lines creasing his forehead. The lanky copper-crowned father appeared almost giant-like beside the miniature babe bundled in bright yellow and blue receiving blankets.

"You do look like her. Everyone says so." A slight frown crowded Brock's brow. "That was one reason it was hard for me to look at you at first." For a second or two the father's fingers froze in place before they moved to caress a pudgy, tan dimpled cheek. "You have the softest skin." Brock cupped his hand on the dark brown hair that formed a perfect downy cradle cap.

Benny responded with a mew-like snore, a sweet sound that brought a gradual smile to his father's lips.

"What did you think about today? The people reminded me of your mom, the way she was with others." Brock waited a while for an answer. "They can't be that bad if they keep picking up your dirty laundry. That's some powerful stuff." He crinkled his nose.

The baby lips quivered, and his eyelids rippled but didn't open.

A loud silence echoed in the room dividing the words spoken and the words still guarded in Brock's heart. Darkness hovered around the two, the only light cast a warm glow from a lamp on the nightstand next to the baby illuminating an angelic aura on his tiny face. The distinctive radiance caught his father's attention.

***

"Please don't lower her into the ground until after we leave." Distraught and weeping, Brock pleaded with the two funeral home ushers plastered in black suits and gray ties. Their shiny shoes left deep indents in the tilled soil surrounding Asia's gravesite. "I need more time to say good-bye." The young man whimpered, clinging to the wailing infant in his arms.

"We can come back." The older man nudged his partner to leave with him.

Brock collapsed at the trunk of a mighty pine towering above his wife's burial plot. Red-faced Benny screamed, sucking in air and expelling the air, in a relentless cycle. Tears streamed, then rushed mercilessly as the bereaved widower fumbled in the diaper bag until he fished out a lukewarm bottle and jammed it into the demanding baby's mouth.

The trembling newborn latched on with a fierceness that alarmed Brock. "What does it matter?" He wept. "She's gone." He leaned back against the uneven puzzle bark of the tree and pushed his flesh hard against the wood. With robotic motion he pulled his knees up to support the baby. Benny's little legs kicked repeatedly onto Brock's heaving chest.

They sat separate but together.

Sweat beaded on Brock's neck and dribbled down his spine in sticky, hot droplets.

As the baby drained the last remaining pool of formula in the bottle, he began to calm down and released the nipple. Satiated and full, he stared up at his father.

"Feed me, burp me, change me. That is the entire scope of your existence." Brock sat head hanging and shoulders sagging.

Benny cheeks puffed out.

With swift precision Brock kneeled, grabbed a cloth diaper from the bag and turned Benny, his tummy in the palm of his hand. The first burp blurted out. Followed by another, and another laced with projectile formula that spewed into the grass below.

"Asia, I don't know if I can do this without you."

Knees digging into the ground, Brock crawled and struggled to stand, but couldn't. He strapped Benny in the infant seat and reached to touch the casket. "Where are you?"

***

The midnight sky outside leaked through the walls. Brock welcomed the outer darkness, in. He watched his son begin to stir, the blankets conformed to his every movement, the gap in the air between them was widening as the seconds ticked.

The distraught father had the routine down ~ bottle ready to go, diaper ready to change, burp cloth for the usual return after mealtime, but his heart kept coming up empty.

Benny had soaked through his clothes and needed a sleeper change. Brock smoothed his hand over the comforter underneath the baby to be sure it was dry. "Good thing tomorrow is laundry day." After tossing the wet clothes into the basket on the floor, Brock washed his hands, and got the bottle out of Asia's sink. All her make-up and hair accessories now took up space on Brock's side of the double countertop.

"Drink this down and let's see if we can get another four hours sleep."

Usually the baby fussed during diaper changes and objected to the time it took to offer him the warmed up milk. Tonight, Benny gazed intently at his father, his eyes following Brock everywhere in the room. Out of the darkness and into the light. Close-up and far away.

"What?"

Benny took the bottle and continued watching.

"What?"

Nestled in the crook of his father's arm, Benny remained quiet, making mild suckling sounds as he drank his late night snack with a rare relaxed approach. Brock responded in like manner, propped up on pillows pressed to the headboard of the bed. In the stillness of the room the two strangers' breathing patterns synchronized in rhythmic unison. Moonlight filtered through the window where willowy drapes were tied back on brass knobs. A hazy panel of misty moonbeams played on the shadows across the room.

Brock studied his son's face; his almond eyes already turning a muddy brown, dented chin, dimpled cheeks with wide cheekbones, smooth tan skin, and a small nose. Teardrops caught, then released over his freckle sprinkled face. There was Asia. He need look no farther. She had been there all along when his tortured thoughts fought to save her from a cavernous grave that would seal her in an utter abyss of pitch black, buried deep, far from him.

Benny opened his mouth and nudged the bottle away. He lie there in the comfort and warmth of his father's strong arm, gazing a fixed stare upward. Brock eased the baby on his chest to pat his back with gentle firm taps, his massive hand encompassing most of the baby's torso. The infant's head rested on a soothing, beating heart, and burrowed into the soft cotton fabric covering the steady heartbeats. The half-full bottle was tucked into the folds of the bedding when peaceful sleep fell upon tiny fluttering eyelids.

Brock nested his son in the sea of pillows and embraced him, then the exhausted young man stretched out in the rumpled jeans and shirt he'd worn all day. He drew Benny closer and curled around him building a protective shield with his own flesh and bones.

"Your mommy wanted you to have a butterfly garden." He whispered with a kiss.

Ribbons of flowing moonbeams illuminated the empty bassinet next to the bed, and a hushed tranquility settled upon the two sleeping forms as they cocooned into one silhouette.

Chapter Seventeen
Healing

The world is full of walking wounded souls that we pass by everyday unaware of the depth of their struggles. In this hurried, modern culture that becomes less and less personal, and more and more detached, people fall through the cracks on all levels of society. We physicians do our best to help heal the sick, mend their broken bones, diagnose ailments, and treat diseases. But we have limits. I only know of one who created spirit and body, cures by miracles, and in love. It is this Great Physician and Healer who called me to my work, catches those who fall between the cracks, and holds them in the palms of his hands. You will know him by his voice. Listen. Hear. ~ Doctor John Walters journal notes written in the autumn season of 2017.

"Dad, what happened?" Jack helped Doc to the recliner, leaning his cane against the stone hearth within an arms' reach from the chair.

"I'm not sure. I think I tripped over the edge of the area rug, fell, and hit my head on the coffee table." Doc eased himself into the leather seat conformed to fit his body.

"How long were you down?" A tight clenching squeezed in Jack's chest.

"I think," he blinked, scrunched up his forehead, and frowned, "I blacked out." His fingers curved inward from arthritis and he repeatedly stretched them outward, and back in.

"Maybe we should go to the hospital for an EKG and make sure it wasn't another heart attack." The squeezing increased.

"My pacemaker is working fine." Doc patted his chest with a wrinkled hand, bluish-purple veins bulging in a V- shaped pattern of thin lines on the surface.

"You know it's made to kick in if needed. Let me throw together an ice pack for that lump."

"That is probably a good idea." The addled man rubbed the swollen knot on his left temple.

"What's the last thing you remember?"

"I wanted to make myself a bacon, tomato, and lettuce sandwich for lunch."

"Lunch," Jack dropped the ice in the kitchen sink. "It's six pm and dark outside."

"It can't be. I was finishing some journal notations and getting ready for lunch. The sun was shining, and it was twenty degrees hotter than it should be this time of year."

"Dad," Jack stood in the doorway between the two rooms. "That means you were out for five to six hours. You always eat at noon, like clockwork."

"How can that be?" A stunned look clouded over Doc's face. "This growing old stuff isn't for the fainthearted."

"That's it, we're going in for tests." Jack put some ice in a baggie and zipped it shut. "Make sure you have your insurance ID card in your wallet. I'll pack you something to eat on the way. You probably haven't eaten since early this morning." *How could this have happened?*

"No, no I haven't. Not since my oatmeal and coffee at six am. Or did I eat my lunch at noon?" Doc visibly struggled to remember. "Not sure, just oatmeal, I think."

"There isn't any external bleeding from that bump. Let's make sure you aren't bleeding internally." Jack worked to keep a balanced tone to his voice. "Come on, let's get going." He did a quick triage check. Doc's pupils were dilated. A slight pinch of dry skin on his hand indicated dehydration, and his reflexes were slow to respond to touch. *There's more than one thing going on here.* Jack's trained eyes followed every sluggish movement his father made. A rush of adrenalin flowed through Jack's body as he fought off the fear of losing his dad. Reddened rims moistened his eye sockets as he strained to maintain a calm presence in front of his father.

"Sorry, Jack. I know you were going over to check on Brock."

"It's okay, Dad." Jack spoke softly and helped his father out of the recliner. "And actually, we haven't gotten a call for help since the night of the memorial service."

"Well that's good news." Doc held onto his son's arm, grasping his flannel sleeve, and leaned over to get his cane. He hobbled forward about a foot and tried to stand on his own, but immediately began swaying and reached to steady himself leaning into Jack. "It's been a full week. He may have turned a corner in parenthood."

***

"What did the tests determine?' Emily asked when the front door closed. A ripple of wind flitted the two lit tall candles in the middle of the dining room table. She placed the corkscrew down next to the unopened bottle of merlot and two crystal glasses that reflected the red-orange flickering flames in a double halo.

"He's had a couple of minor heart attacks very recently." Jack joined her at the kitchen table. "He's asleep by now. It's midnight." He glanced at his watch. "They kept him overnight for observation."

"Is his pacemaker working?"

"Yes." Jack hesitated, "Em, he seemed, so feeble. So old."

"He is old, Jack. He's eighty-eight now."

"They figure he stumbled on the rug because of the heart palpitations. Falling and hitting his head was a direct result." Jack groped for words that caught in his throat. "You know he's all alone over there. He refuses to move in here, and I could never put him in a home."

"Let me see if I can convince him to move in the guest room. That way he won't have to deal with stairs. It's right next to the bathroom." Emily tried to reassure Jack with an offer to plead on his behalf. "I have my wiles, and maybe I can reach him in a way you can't."

"He understands the tests. His body is tired, Em." Jack's voice cracked. "I guess I always think of him as being there for me. You know, everyone loves Doc. All my life I've shared him

94

with this town, all the way around the lake, and to Reno." Jack slumped in his easy chair and stared at the floor. The wind rattled the windows across from him, the glass panes trembling in the casing as pine branches scratched back and forth, obscuring a clear view. Jack shivered.

"Yeah, I know. Me too."

"He still plugs away, helps out. Like with Brock. I know he misses seeing patients since he retired." Jack settled into the welcoming leather, flattening his palms over the thick arm rests. "I think Dad was more concerned with how I would take the news."

"That's the father and the doctor in him." Emily's chose her words with careful concern.

"He's never fallen before. You and I both know what that means."

"We should have moved him over here a few years ago."

"Well, now is the time. It's not optional anymore." Jack sat forward.

"All we have to do is switch out his furniture for what is already in there. We can do it this weekend. The girls can sleep with their families upstairs whenever they visit." Emily reached out and took Jack's hands in hers and squeezed.

"He'll buck and argue."

"Yes, and then he'll cross the path and make this his home. It's not so far to walk."

"It's not like I didn't know this day was coming. I knew." He cupped her chin and dove into the boundless blue lake in her eyes. The eternal sea where their story is written, their beginning, middle, and end. "Are we ever ready to say good-bye to someone we love?"

"No, we would always choose another time, another place." Emily kissed his forehead.

"Dad said when he was over the morning before Asia's service helping Brock get ready for the day, that he found him in the nursery, talking out loud to Asia. At first Brock was embarrassed, but Dad told him that he used to talk to Annie the same way when she died. He told him some people never live as much as Asia did in her twenty-six years of life. A lot of people die inside first."

"Asia left much of herself behind. She kept a pregnancy journal for the baby. The nursery is decorated with all her collective creative talents. Benny sees her art every time Brock walks him in that room and shows him the murals. Asia painted Tahoe birds on the ceiling over the changing table ~ Canada geese, Black-Capped Mountain Chickadees, Western Tanagers, Robins." Emily sighed. "It is all so vibrant, so beautiful."

"My heart breaks for Brock to have lost Asia so unexpectedly. And Em, he said I could tell you that his cancer is midstage—two on the very edge of three."

"You were right." She sat back against the wooden slates of her chair.

"How I wish I'd been wrong." He has a year or two, maybe more with Benny. That is the medical diagnosis. If he is healed though, he can have a lifetime with his son."

"Maybe that is why he was so resistant to bonding, because he thinks he won't be around for long?" Emily paused and blew out the candles.

"We guys don't come as natural to parenting. I am not being sexist here. Brock is trying to be mommy and daddy. I suggested to be daddy and let the rest happen as it may."

"I hope that comforted him." Emily stood and took Jack by the hand. "Has all this made you think about our baby? I've been thinking a lot about Jackson, missing him."

"How could I not be remembering? I don't ever want to forget."

He rose and followed her up the stairs, her bare feet padding on the wood, each step slow and measured. A drizzle of rainy mist breezed in the open window next to their bed as sheer panels billowed in the cooler midnight air.

"I'm right here, Jack." Emily promised. "I'm not going anywhere." She nuzzled, massaging his neck and shoulders in languid, fluid movement.

Emily pulled her husband in close for a kiss. Jack put up no resistance. He leaned in and pressed her lips to his, lingering, exploring.

"I love you, Em." He whispered in her ear, breathed the words with a longing from so deep within him that breathing was not easy. His heart hurt and pounded at the same time with desire. His mind traveled to places they'd already been, intimate rendezvous' that left him weak in the knees and beyond breathless. Jack wrapped her in his arms, and embraced the love that completed him, the love that pleasured him, sheltered him, where he made his home.

Chapter Eighteen
Four Decades Later

Change comes. It rides in town on a proud Palomino horse and hitches to the post in the center of Main Street. Everyone sees the animal, walks by him and stares, but not everyone accepts his arrival. Many desire his departure. Even if Change leaves town after a season, nothing is as it was before. ~ An old western saying accredited to anonymous.

After moving the last of the furniture from the guest room over to Doc's cabin, Jack waited for his father to settle in and make the transition of living in his son's home. It shouldn't be too hard because it was originally Nana's cabin; the one her husband Harold built for his beloved Hannah in their early years together. The one Emily inherited when Nana passed away, and Em sold her house in Sacramento. The house where she and David had lived since their girls were born, until he left her for his mistress the weekend he was killed in a hit and run accident. The home Jack moved into when he married Emily and sold his bachelor condo. The cabin next door, down the granite stone-lined pathway that Emily and Jack cleared when they were kids.

The same pines grow along the path, but now they tower high into the watery blue sky. Smooth reddish-brown branched Manzanita bushes fill in the spaces between the tree trunks seven feet high or more, their oval leaves blending in with the pine needles. Withered Snow Plant stumps dot the low ground, some bloom as late as July, and will soon spring up again if autumn ever fans her skirt and winter follows dusting the earth with powdery, needed snowfall.

"Dad is puttering in his new room." Jack tip-toed down the hallway in his socks to the silence of the wool rug covering the living room wooden flooring.

"I think he'll be okay, or as Doc says, 'Time will tell'." A sentimental grin spread across Emily's face.

"Saying it and living it are two different things."

"He's such an independent person. There's no way this isn't huge for him. But I already like having him here with us." Em patted the sofa cushion next to her.

"He's all we have left. They're all gone now." Jack rubbed his palms together, resting his elbows on his knees.

"He still has us. I guess now we are the up and coming oldsters."

"Speak for yourself. I'm still middle-aged."

"Barely." Emily nudged Jack's mid-section with a pinch.

"It counts. We Baby Boomers have to stick together." He sucked in his gut.

"Oh, I don't mind claiming to be a Boomer, Jack, but I'm one of the youngest Boomers around these parts." She winked.

"There is a whole new generation here at the lake that I have trouble relating to, Em." Jack got serious in a hurry. "Change is everywhere around us."

"Yeah. The original homeowners that built here have all passed away and left their cabins to their children. A lot sold out in the 1990's." Emily leaned in on Jack's shoulder.

"Then the mansions started rising. Ostentatious, pretentious, and over-priced."

"That's why so many people started losing their homes. Greed, plain old greed." Em snuggled closer.

"The fall out has been overwhelming." Jack sighed.

"Most of the lake isn't even American owned anymore. Tourists fly into Reno, rent a car, stay at a south shore resort, and go house hunting with their real estate agent until they find their dream second, or third house, pay cash, and fly home." Em, somewhat disgruntled by her own statement, sat straight.

"Many of the middle class owners can't make their mortgage payments. The number of abandoned cabins around the lake increase by the day. People stealing away under the cover of night, some leaving their furnishings behind too."

"Doc can sell or rent out. Does he need the income?"

"No," Jack stretched and crossed his arms behind his head. "He paid that place off decades ago. He has no debts. He just drops by in person to pay his utility, phone, and water bills. I think he enjoys chatting with the folks and it gets him out of the house."

"That was a wise generation, they only bought what they could afford. My grandparents never used credit cards either.

Nana left this earth indebted to no one. She lived frugally and had some savings." Em relaxed back against Jack.

"We struggled with my student loans and your bookstore mortgage until you had to sell. 2008 took a toll on the country." Jack shuffled his feet on the carpet. "There has to be hope some-where."

Doc's door opened, his cane tapped, tapped down the hall and across the kitchen cobblestones with divisive care. He stopped at the edge of the flooring and countered his pace with a little speed.

"You good in there now?" Jack asked. Doc looked tired; shoulders sagging, and frame bent forward, but he wore a beaming smile that lit up the entire room.

"Just takes me a little longer these days, that's all. I can still do it myself. Okay to sit in your recliner, son?"

"Sure, dad. I'm zoning out with Em." Jack hugged her and resisted the urge to rise and make sure Doc's cane cleared the rounded edge of the thick rug. He sat and waited, ready to jump to his feet.

Doc lifted his cane on top of the throw rug and adjusted his stride to accommodate the change. He stood in place for a second or two before moving ahead and settling into the comfortable chair. "This feels good." He ran a hand down the soft leather arm before resting his cane against the hearth. "Haven't moved since Annie and I came to Tahoe from Idaho in 1949."

"Just a few years after Nana and Papa." Emily fanned her face with a magazine.

"If the weather was as it should be, we could start a fire and eat supper out here together." Doc wiped his brow with a folded handkerchief from his shirt pocket. "Too warm these days."

"And it's not getting any cooler. The weekly forecast is all in the low 80's." Ugh." Emily rose. "Does anyone want something to drink? Lemonade, iced tea, a soda?"

"Lemonade sounds good." Doc replied and pulled the lever to lock the footrest in place.

"Me too."

"No beer, marguerites, or blended smoothies?" Emily laughed thinking blended, iced anything was the way to cool off. She parted the lace curtains above the kitchen window, looking for the birds chirping in the nearby trees. The three-tone whistles grew sharper and a flutter of wings took flight. A quick flash of movement below the deck caught her attention in time to see a man, short in stature, exceedingly thin in khakis shorts that exposed blinding white, hairy legs, turn and run. In his haste, he dropped what looked like a pair of binoculars.

"Jack, someone was watching the house!" Her head snapped back and forth like a little red ball attached to an elastic string on a paddle board. "Quick, maybe you can catch him!" Emily surveyed the yard again, but the stranger was nowhere to be seen in the thick forest or surrounding neighborhood.

Chapter Nineteen
Destiny

"Alliances form where and when you least expect. Just look at us. Who would have thought we'd find each other in that crowd at the Governors Re-Election Dinner? A sprawling Nevada mountain mansion with all those occupied guest rooms and we bump into each other in the same one. What were the odds? Some things are meant to happen. Call it fate. Call it an accident. Call it destiny." ~ Detert's comment to Astrid upon her return from the latest fund raiser.

Astrid lingered on the beach listening to the waves rippling in and lapping at the shoreline, frothing in peeks and swirls before rolling back out. The edges of her cotton dress hung down the sides of a webbed chaise lounge chair and soaked up wet, gritty sand. Hands dangling to the ground, she raked trails with her fingernails in the soggy silt. Transparent water washed away every trace, then receded, leaving a smooth surface waiting for the continual cycle to repeat.

Ignoring the little man sitting on a tree stump behind her, she listened to the calming rhythm, the repetitive routine, as the afternoon ebbed into evening. Her bare shoulders welcomed the fading warmth of sunlight. She'd cast her straw hat off to the side hours ago. A slight pink tinged her exposed white limbs. She cared not. If only this precise moment could last the rest of her lifetime. Autumn had fooled the lake, the trees, and the weather. Summer delayed.

"Why did you drag your chair so far out?" Detert stood and shouted.

To get as far away from you as I can.

"Astrid. Come in before it gets dark."

Before dusk settles. Before the waters chill and you catch your death from the cold.

"Astrid. We need to talk. Tonight." Detert stomped his feet like a petulant child.

She raised an arm skyward and let it sway from side to side, hoping he would head to the house and wait there for her. But the demanding twerp was relentless. She turned to face him.

"Meet me at the house!" Her feet sank deeper in the sand as she rose and gathered her chair and hat, then slipped into her zories, letting the water wash between her toes to cleanse all coating granules. She draped the beach towel from her chair around her slender figure. The dampened hemline of her garment weighed close to the ground as she trudged the long distance inland. The setting sun dropped like a brilliant fireball throwing flames of red and bronze behind the ring of mountains. She twisted her stance to gaze directly into the sunlight before adjusting her sunglasses to deflect his image descending upon her when she turned.

"Why must you always make this harder?" Detert grumbled, his hand raised shielding the last rays of light though bright streams filtered between his boney fingers.

"I needed a day off."

"There isn't time for that right now. The clock is ticking."

Astrid rushed past him practically running and hurried up the long grassy slope leading to the storage area under her deck. She dumped the chaise next to the stairway and climbed each step with increased speed until she reached the top and bent over, short of breath, gasping for quick gulps of air.

"You should have gone with me."

"I told you to wait." Moisture blurred her vision. She straightened and took deep breaths.

"Emily saw me."

"How could you be so careless?" She fumed, clutching the towel at her neck.

"I wasn't. She just looked out the window at the wrong time."

"It's always something with you." Astrid's heart raced, pounding in her chest and rattling her ribcage making her feel the years that limited her capabilities. She slid open the glass door and headed to the sink to get a glass of water. With care she slipped a bottle from a side pocket of her dress and took a pill that she placed under her tongue. She said nothing to Detert.

"Get over it." He smirked.

She swallowed and tilted her head back, closed her eyes and imagined him gone like a little puff of smoke that trailed after him when he smoked his cigarettes and cigars. A mere rising vapor, dissipating in the air without even a hint of a previous existence. Gone for good.

"I can fix this. Go back for my binoculars. Tell them I was bird watching." His tedious voice droned on as his smoke saturated clothes tainted the air between them with that obnoxious odor that smokers subject non-smokers to. "Yeah, that's it, bird watching. I'll walk right up to their door and ask if they found the binoculars and I'll look all innocent and hopeful."

"Stay away." Astrid warned in a steely tone and opened her eyes.

Detert sat at the dining room table in a rumpled heap, emptying his pockets and stacking one hundred dollar bills in three neat rows of ten each, counting out loud. He pushed the piles toward Astrid like a peace offering. "I collected the accounts in Tahoma earlier. Everyone paid on time. No delinquent penalties this time, stupid conscientious borrowers don't want to pay any interest."

"You're nothing but a sniveling loan shark." The color was slow to return to her cheeks, she flushed with anger that fueled a rush of energy running down her spine.

Detert sniggered and parted his hair back with one long fingernail, revealing his wide forehead and distended ears. "I am the man." He pat a black pistol handle under his belt.

Chapter Twenty
A Limited Friendship

Friendship with the enemy allows for both possible advantages and grave disadvantages. Weighing the cost is either a timely decision or a life or death mistake. History has proven this over the ages. And yet history does tend to repeat itself either in wisdom or folly. Choose wisely. ~ Astrid's journal notes to herself in the belated months of the lingering Indian summer. 2017

Whispering trees overheard their conversation. The heady scent of pine permeated the air Astrid and Detert breathed in and out. Interlocking branches shielded both light and the harsh elements. Darkened clouds gathered above the two wayward figures like opening umbrellas. Bickering bitterly in subdued tones, they soon reached an impasse.

"Just shut up and observe." Detert uttered in disgust, his greasy brown hair flattened under a Raider's ball cap. Fingers twitching, he reached in his shirt pocket for a pack of cigarettes and book of matches.

"Wait." She insisted and pressed a hand against his chest, smashing the near empty pack. The paper wrappers crinkled, and he pulled back a step.

Astrid observed all she needed to know from her hiding place. Her next move would be swift and decisive despite Detert's opinions. She remembered a verse from her youth, one that guided her throughout her years…*Upon the wicked he shall rain snares, fire and brimstone, and a horrible tempest: this shall be the portion of their cup.* She cast a piteous glance upon Detert, certain this was the fate he deserved.

The thick grove of trees in the forest camouflaged their movements as the three trucks pulled away loaded with stolen goods from a neighborhood robbery in the elite Incline Village neighborhood on Lake Shore Boulevard in Nevada. It had been quite the haul; jewelry, art, electronics, furniture, imported wines and champagnes, coin collections, and a library of first edition books. How Detert managed to find out about the heist and secret meeting place where the crooks divvied up the spoils, was beyond his usual capabilities. Or was there more to the little man than there appeared to be?

Nevertheless, he had been right about this theft. He told her the trucks were headed out in different directions to different states. Each truck bore the name of a different national moving company. The pre-planning needed to pull off a robbery on this level indicated the detailed organization of a possible mob connection. During the off season, the daylight burglary had gone unnoticed. All the summer dwellers had long since gone back to their city homes. The few locals that lived on the lake year round resided on neighboring streets. No one would be calling the police. So much for Neighborhood Watch.

"Just saying, they are cutting into our would-be take." Detert sputtered around and spoke inches from Astrid's face. He flicked a match and lit a cigarette, sucking in, then blowing smoke in a long stream past her head, up close and personal.

"We don't rob houses." She reminded him.

"Well, they'll be back and I'm thinking they don't plan on leaving much behind."

"They must have some kind of a major fencing operation. This is the big league, Detert. Be careful what you get involved in. I want no part of this." She turned to walk up the hill toward the main highway, away from him and his smoke.

"Look lady," he stretched to stop her but couldn't quite make contact as she increased her pace, "you need to re-think your plans."

"I have not shared all my plans with you." She snapped back, then accelerated forward.

"Oh, I'm aware of that fact." The thick waffle soul of his hiking boots crushed twigs and cracked a large branch as he kicked a couple of pinecones across the forest floor. He scurried to catch up with her, mumbling repetitive expletives along the way.

Astrid walked to where they had parked the Ford Expedition in someone else's driveway. Out of breath, she struggled to regain composure. She clicked the door open and dropped her keys in her jeans pocket as she stepped up into the vehicle. Rain pelted down the moment she got inside. Detert seemed to be limping as he huffed the final distance, then slid into the passenger seat, slamming the door with an unnecessary thud.

"Temper, temper." She tapped her fingernails on the steering wheel and started the engine. Trying not to smile, she backed out onto the two-lane highway.

He flipped the heater on full blast and shook the raindrops off his hat. Water dripped down his stringy hair and hung in big oily droplets.

"Stop it!" She hated how he rattled her nerves and made her lose control.

"I think we should cut in on this action." He reiterated.

"You would." She drove, eyes on the road ahead of her. "I need to get home and deliver a meal to a young widower. His wife died after giving birth to their son."

"How charitable of you." He sneered; his yellow-stained teeth gritted tight.

"Keep your distance from these criminals. It's too dangerous, too sophisticated and orchestrated." Astrid lowered her agitated tone and spoke in a calm voice. She managed to carry on a civil conversation for the rest of the drive to the cabin.

Detert switched off the heater when the cloudburst finally came to a sudden stop and rolled down his window to let in some fresh air. Astrid did not allow him to smoke in her SUV. He craved another smoke but suppressed the urge, her disapproving glare answering his unasked question. They were around the corner from her place anyway. He would light up first thing they parked.

"I'll be back in a couple of hours." She dropped him off at the front porch. "The ground is damp from the brief rainfall, but it is dry right under the surface. Be careful where you extinguish your cigarettes." She tossed him a house key on a separate key-chain.

"Don't you need to come in and get that meal?" He asked and stepped out.

"It's in the back seat, frozen." She shifted into reverse gear. "Lock up once you go inside."

"Why, you afraid of getting robbed?" He laughed.

***

Astrid combed her hair, freshened her caked-on face powder and rouge then reapplied a brushing of light-red lipstick. She puckered her lips and rubbed them together until a glossy sheen brought new life to the faded shriveled flesh. She gathered the two handle bags from the back seat; one weighted down with a baked Zita casserole with meatballs in a CorningWare dish, a tossed green salad, and a loaf of garlic-buttered sourdough bread. The other bag stuffed with blue tissue paper contained baby boy blanket sleepers for the coming winter and a big brown teddy bear with a green scarf, knit sweater, and ski hat.

The short walk to the front deck was challenging. Careful not to slip on the steps still slick after the rainfall, she took the steps one at a time up to the door. Balancing the bags on her arms with her overloaded shoulder-strap purse, she pressed the door-bell.

No one answered.

She pushed the small round plastic button again.

Within seconds a frazzled young man cracked the door open and peeked out. "I thought you ladies from the church just left the meals on the bench at 4 o'clock?" The droopy-eyed red-head leaned against the wooden oak door.

"Oh dear, I am sorry if I disturbed you. I'm not from the church. But I knew your lovely wife, Asia." She struggled shifting her bags side to side. "I've brought you a meal and a gift for the baby." Astrid tripped on a loose plank and nearly fell when she tried to hand him the bags.

The door opened wide and two arms caught her before she hit the ground. "Come on in."

"Thank you. These are a bit heavy. I hope you haven't already eaten an early dinner." She entered the house following close behind and handed him the bags exposing red imprints on both her arms.

"No, Benny is still asleep. I was napping with him." Brock rubbed his eyelids and accepted her gifts. "This is so thoughtful of you. Did I meet you at the memorial service?"

"I had a cold and didn't want to risk spreading germs to anyone. I'm Astrid."

"Nice to meet you. I'm Brock." He shook her hand. "And thank you for dinner." He turned toward the bedroom when two sharp cries rang out followed by steady wailing.

"Let me heat up the oven for you and pop in the casserole, Brock."

"Oh, thanks." He dashed to the bedroom.

Astrid did that and so much more. She set the table, tossed the salad into a bowl from the cupboard, and foil wrapped the bread, placing it on the oven rack when the meal was near ready to be served. She tucked a one-layer chocolate cake in the fridge but left the wine in her purse.

Down the hall the baby's cries had diminished to whimpers. Brock soon reappeared with a freshly changed Benny attached to bottle of formula he was draining like a hungry bear cub.

Astrid had taken in the disarray of the little cabin. Baby paraphernalia littered every surface: disposable and cloth diapers were crammed into a SF Giants gym bag, a hamper of dirty laundry that emitted an odd odor sat near the front door. Rattles and stuffed animals covered the sofa and love seat. A wind-up swing, car seat, baby bouncer, and portable playpen filled the living room crowding out the grown-up furniture.

"He seems to have taken over your life."

"We're still working out all the kinks." Brock blushed and stumbled on an Audubon squeaky toy that squawked in protest under his shoes as he made his way across the room to his recliner. He plopped down in the chair and held Benny close to his chest, the baby's mouth locked on the bottle nipple like a suction cup.

"You have your hands full." She picked up a stack of furry woodland critters and settled next to the father and son in a small open space of the loveseat. Cradling the soft miniature zoo in her arms, Astrid focused in on the baby.

"He is adorable. Has his mother's eyes, hair, and dimples."

"Everyone says so."

"That's a good thing, isn't it?"

"He reminds me of her, has her sweet nature. Except when he's hungry."

"I imagine that is most of the time." She laughed when the baby slurped and started drawing in air through the nipple.

"He's become an expert belcher." Brock beamed with pride and pat-patted two big burps from Benny within seconds of bracing him on his shoulder. He was quick to catch spit-up on a cloth diaper draped on his shoulder and down his back.

Astrid and Brock chatted while the baby relaxed in his lap. Soon the aroma of basil, rosemary, buttery garlic and a hint of thyme floated through the room.

"Did you say the casserole has meatballs?"

"The timer will go off any minute. I should let the dish set." Astrid rose and completed her task. The Zita now cooled on the kitchen counter and within minutes butter bubbled between slices of the sourdough bread.

Brock placed Benny in the bouncer on the floor next to his dining room chair. "You're welcome to stay for dinner."

"Oh, I couldn't impose." Astrid said and lowered her snowy head.

"Sure, you can. I'd enjoy the company." He grabbed another plate and some silverware.

"Thank you, Brock." She hesitated, "do you think after dinner I can hold little Benny?" She offered the baby a rattle from the table, and a ring of primary-colored keys. He grasped it in a clenched fist after crossing his eyes to focus in on the flash of bright red, blue, and yellow.

"Sure. I'll change him first, so he doesn't christen you. He's a pro at that."

"Let's eat." Brock set the covered dish and bread on the table. "My mom used CorningWare when I was a kid."

"This is my favorite piece; it bakes everything evenly, no hot or cold spots." She smiled and added. "I'll come by sometime next week and pick it up when you've finished the Zita. Let me know if you need anything else. I'm happy to help out in any way I can."

Astrid thought about offering to say a grace before the meal, but Brock was loading up his plate to the point she became concerned he might finish the food tonight. She took one spoonful of the pasta and a single meatball then filled her dish with salad and bread. Comfort food has an intoxicating smell that men are weak to resist and makes it them dopey, like Thanksgiving Day. Astrid was counting on that.

Part Three
Deception

Chapter Twenty-one
Confusion or Clarity?

Sometimes I still struggle with short term memory loss and thought confusion from the car accident. It hits at the most inopportune times when I need clarity. Jack instinctively keys in most of the time. It feels like I lost part of my identity that cold winter day. My life was spared, but what was lost may never be fully restored. In my prayers I ask for healing. ~ Emily's journal.

Emily shuffled around in the kitchen trying to remember what she went in there to do. After opening and closing a couple of drawers and turning off the coffee maker she plopped down in a chair, lowering her head on the table in frustration. *I know it was important.* She interlocked her fingers and cupped her hands around the back of her neck. Once, twice, three times she lowered her forehead on the oak surface. Nothing.

Jack walked up behind her and caressed the palm of his hand in slow circles on her back. "Did you pour me a cup of coffee?" He glanced around the room.

"Was that it?" Emily rose and immediately ran her finger over the plug and secured it in the outlet. She filled a mug to the brim and set the steaming brew in front of her husband.

"Where's your cup? I thought we were going to sit out on the deck and relax for a while." A frown arched across his brow, then a knowing look smoothed it out. "I'll get it."

Emily wandered out to the deck and curled up in the chaise lounge. The sense she'd forgotten something still niggled at her, triggering a moody rush of emotions, deeming herself mentally impaired. *How can I trust my suspicions about Astrid if I can't even remember the reason I entered a room in my own home and what I wanted to do when I got there?* She kicked her shoes off, pulled her knees to her chest and wrapped her arms tight around them.

"You okay?" Jack held her mug out until she unfolded herself. The concentration on her face softened. After a few sips of coffee, Emily relaxed.

"Thanks, one sugar and lots of cream, just the way I like it."

Jack reclined in the seat next to her and waited. The strong Jamaican brew would make her chatty. Caffeine kicks in and inner defenses lower within minutes of the legal stimulate hitting the system. Emily was no exception to the rule. If he were patient, she would say what was troubling her. If he asked, she'd clam up and retreat to small talk. He swallowed a gulp, then slowly sipped another.

"Do you think I'm over the edge with Astrid? I mean, should I back off?"

Jack chose his next words carefully. "She is a mystery. One that appeared out of nowhere."

"You didn't answer my question. Do you think I should back off?" Emily poked her toes through the spaces between the webbing of her chair and ran them in and out, in and out. "Come on, Jack."

He hedged for a minute then answered, "I thought you were a little too quick to speculate when we first met her."

"And now?"

"Now, I think she is an odd old woman."

"Do you not see anything shady or distrustful in her actions?" Emily scowled; her voice tinged with a hint of disappointment. She pressed the hot ceramic cup against her lips as if to seal them.

"There does seem to be more to her than you can see." Jack set his mug on the wobbly metal table next to him and swung his feet around to rest on a rattan ottoman. "She is pretty active for someone her age and she does turn up at places you wouldn't expect to see her."

"Have you run into her lately?"

"Yesterday, at the hospital meeting for local physicians."

"Really."

"I wasn't there long because of dad, but as soon as she saw me, she left."

Emily chugged a few gulps, opened her mouth to speak but closed it instead. *So what. So she was there. Why do you care?* "Was that little dweeb with her?"

"That man everyone calls Detert was nowhere in sight."

A stream of bright sunlight shone through a passing patch of clouds and hit Emily directly in the eyes. She blinked a few times and shaded her face with an open palm. When she glanced back at Jack all she could see were shadowy outlines that warbled with movement as he spoke. She could hear his words clearly, but they didn't make any sense. She smiled and nodded, spilling drops of coffee on her jeans which she brushed dry. Jack was coming back into focus as she sat still and listened, the sun slipped behind increasing cloud cover.

"Em, you okay?"

"Fine. Just listening."

"Well that's a change. I figured you have some theory for Astrid's presence at the monthly meeting of the docs."

Squinting, Emily directed her response to the right side of where Jack sat in full shade under a cluster of Jeffrey pines. "Perhaps I have been too opinionated concerning her."

"Perhaps." Jack stood and moved in toward her.

"Old people are allowed to be eccentric, especially women." She laughed and winked at the empty chair across from her.

The warmth of his cheek against her own, startled her. "Maybe you are due for another eye examination." Jack kissed her upper lip before drawing her in for a lingering kiss that left her breathless. He ran his hand down the length of her shoulder and arm until he clasped her hand in his. "The bright light still bothers you." He sat beside her on the picnic bench.

"Only when it hits in quick flashes." She confessed knowing she hadn't fooled him but wishing she had. The taste of black

121

coffee from his tongue mingled with the remainder of the sweetened creamy residue in her mouth.

"It's been a couple of years, right?"

Emily gazed out toward the lake longingly. *How should she answer? No, her vision has never been fully restored. She simply became a master of disguising flare-ups. Or, yes, this is something new, not to worry, it will pass. Just like all her conclusions about Astrid were probably misguided by her own mental imbalance, snippets of lost memory, and possible paranoia induced by her lessened ability for articulate thinking and processing of what was once cohesive brain activity.* With a lowering of eyelashes, she closed the open windows of her eyes.

***

The car crash happened in the dead of winter on a snowy day when Emily was in a rush to get to the bank early and to make the deposit that might save the bookstore she had then owned. She hadn't seen the truck that slammed her vehicle head-on when she spun on black ice after pulling out of the parking lot. She only had seconds to focus on the bright headlights, brilliant beams of blinding light. A wall of icy snow replaced her windshield and pushed against her forehead and chest, pinning her in the driver seat. She remembered the warmth of something thick trickling over her heavy eyelids and down her face.

Many nights she saw Forrester's face in her dreams, piercing slit eyes, dark and evil, a cigarette dangling from the corner of his twisted mouth, embers burning a red hot glow against a pure white background of hard-packed snow eight feet high. Days of stubble shadowed his cheeks and chin hiding any pink flesh tone.

He gripped the steering wheel, jagged, dirty fingernails curled in a deadlock. He never spoke a word, just stared a hole through her and sped up until impact. She always saw Forrester, not the man who drove the truck that fateful day.

Soft wispy swirls of filtered moonlight surrounded her. The blue lake was smooth as glass, the still waters ahead, just inches from where her SUV had stopped. Her first thoughts were of heaven. Wondering what it would be like. Her limbs seemed weightless and she desired to float above the scene below, fly like a winged angel. A powerful flush ran through her body and a sense of deep inner peace flooded her mind smoothing any fears into snowflakes that lit on solid ground and melted.

She had to try harder now when the dream came to hold onto the perfect peace and tranquil thoughts that now drifted into a foggy mist. The last time Astrid walked out of that mist and spoke to her. Or had she already been talking when she walked out? A tall forest lined both sides of a powdery pathway. Far in the distance Emily watched the sapphire waters of Tahoe blend with the sky. She concentrated on trying to make Astrid disappear. And she did, not even leaving footprints in the snow. The path was inviting. All the pine boughs were dusted with fresh snowfall. A silent earth filled the expanse of the world before her with a quiet grace and beauty. Her heart longed to be a part of it—whether earth or sky, water or creature.

Before she awakened at the same place and part of the dream every time, her ears fine-tuned to music playing and voices singing. Emily did not recognize any of the instruments, but the melody was alive, that much she knew, or felt, or believed.

123

Stringed instruments and a language of song blended with a multitude of voices; some vaguely familiar, all in gentle harmony—a symphony of notes and vibrations lifting effortlessly.

A sudden burst of intense light always ended the dream; radiant, vibrant, translucent rays shone beyond her vision extending universes away in uncharted galaxies. This was a conclusion Emily came to after years of dreaming the reoccurring dream. It was something beyond her. Something greater. Something of a holy presence.

One thing she was certain of, she was never alone. When Astrid had appeared uninvited, Emily did not doubt the Presence would protect her, and she did feel the need for intervention as Astrid walked closer and closer. Emily was aware of the old woman's eyes changing from blue to hazel, and back again. She also seemed to grow younger with each step toward Emily, decades younger. Her clothing had no color and was but a shadow covering.

Though it seemed Astrid beckoned, Emily did not respond. A foreign language she did not understand, it seemed like an ancient tongue from thousands of years past, the elderly Astrid spoke with complete authority and in a demanding tone. Emily noticed Astrid's appearance in her dream was the first time shades of gray and black obscured all vivid colors and the purity of the fresh fallen snow. Did it mean anything, or was she grasping for more than there was?

***

The dazzling light flashed, and Emily sat straight up in bed. A stunned expression on Jack's face was the first thing she saw upon awakening. He pulled her close and held tight.

"You were dreaming again. This time you spoke a word I couldn't quite make out; 'Qudash'. What does that mean?"

Emily buried her head against her husband's warm chest and nestled in. "I don't remember saying that word."

"Was Astrid in the dream again?"

"Yes. This time I was watching for her."

Jack hugged Em and ran his fingers through the tangles in her hair. "Usually this dream brings you comfort and peace." He strained to see her face.

"I was more apprehensive, not wanting her to intrude."

"Did she speak to you?"

Emily gazed up into his penetrating blue-green eyes, flecks of gold and amber encircled black pupils. She wanted to stay lost there where she felt safe, where he held her closer than his arms could ever embrace her, where their lives entwined beyond words and touch. That oneness now offered her sanctuary in the midst of uncertainty and self-doubt that crowded her thoughts. "I feared her coming back." She burrowed close and listened to his heartbeat.

Jack understood. He continued stroking her hair, smoothing it out until it was silky again. His breathing calmed her, steadied her, and soon she relaxed in a drowsy slumber beside him in bed, snug in the curve of his body.

Jack lie awake uttering silent prayers long after Emily fell into a deep, peaceful sleep. The doctor in him recognized the outward physical symptom of confusion and the sensory sensitivity to light from her head trauma. But the husband and lover knew intimately the heart and soul of his wife; her depth of compassion and kindness, and her spiritual gift of discernment. These were all muddled at the present and trying to separate her disrupted cognitive thinking issues from what may very well be valid concerns about this strange woman who keeps intercepting their lives.

"Don't be afraid." Jack whispered in Emily's ear, "You are not alone."

Chapter Twenty-Two
Spiritual Questions

The spiritual realm leaves much unanswered. Faith is required to walk the earth through the unknowns and all that is unseen. Faith. How much of it does a soul need? How is it measured and meted out? Can I ask for more? Will I ever have enough? I searched the big book to find answers and this is what I came up with ~ Lord, increase my faith. ~ Emily's journal entry after the recurring dream changed.

Astrid bumped into Emily at the Safeway right in front of the huge Thanksgiving display of canned pumpkin and jellied cranberry, bags of breadcrumbs, mini marshmallows, and sage seasoning.

"Hello, Emily." The elderly woman stared through her to the point Emily wondered if she knew they had met again in her dream last night. To be more accurate, that Astrid had walked right up to her and spoken that word *Qudash* that Jack told Em she said the time before.

Today Astrid wore a frumpy burgundy and beige pantsuit that looked like a thrift store reject. Last night a black hooded cape that appeared melded with the midnight sky covered almost all of her. Emily glanced at the woman's shoes; brown slip-ons gapping around her bare, spider-vein ankles. Last night she wore nineteenth century button-up boots. Today Astrid looked to be one hundred. Last night she appeared as a young, vibrant woman of mesmerizing beauty. As she had drawn closer, Astrid held up one hand, palm aimed at Emily's forehead. Em was certain it was her. Well, almost certain.

"Good morning." Emily replied and continued pushing her shopping cart past the display where she'd intended to select her purchases, past Astrid and into the next aisle.

"Don't let me get in the way of completing the list of items for your holiday dinner." A knowing smile spread like molasses across Astrid's wrinkled face. She kept her lips pressed together as she pointed to the paper crinkled in Emily's right hand.

"I'm pretty much done with my shopping." Em patted the breast of the fresh turkey; weighing a good twenty-five pounds which took up most of the room on the top of the two level metal cart. She smiled and moved forward, increasing her speed with each step.

"Are you having family visit? That is a rather large bird for just you and Jack." Astrid pulled canned yams, pumpkin, and a bag of brown sugar from the endcap and scurried up to where Emily stood frozen.

"Yes, we are."

"Do you mind if I ask who?"

"Well," Em hedged, "my daughters." She wound a lock of hair around her pinkie.

"Do they have husbands and children?"

What's up with the intensive interrogation?

"I hope you don't think I am prying." Astrid flashed a wounded look that could guilt the pope himself.

Emily took a long deep breath and paused before answering. "Why would you ever ask such a thing?" Score! One for Emily. Zero for meddling aged woman seeking pity.

Astrid's cool, controlled façade experienced a stress fracture. She waited Emily out, crafting the perfect response in the next moments of silence.

"I am alone this year. I was hoping you and Jack would be blessed with lots of family surrounding you." She lifted a package of chicken legs. "This will be my holiday dinner."

Emily stared at the six measly drumsticks. They were scrunched together on a bright yellow Styrofoam tray and bound by clear cling wrap pulled so tight you could see a few stray bristles in the puckered pores of loose wrinkled flesh. All her resolve disintegrated into a tidy pile of ash. Emily backed up her cart and began pulling cans and bags from the endcap that were not yet checked off her list.

You should invite her to join the family for Thanksgiving. No! What are you thinking?

"I asked Brock and baby Benny if I could cook for them at their house but apparently you asked them first." Astrid tossed the chicken in her cart and picked up a can of creamed corn, turning the label like Vanna White offering an ocean cruise after turning the correct letter of the board.

"Yes, Doc invited them. I hear you have been spending considerable time over there babysitting and making meals." A sense of dread filled Emily from the tips of her toes to the hairs on the back of her neck starting to prickle on end.

Do not ask her. Do not ask her.

"What about your little friend? What's his name?" Emily found an out.

"Detert? He's traveling home to be with his brother's family in Arizona. Big gathering, like a reunion." Astrid placed the can of corn next to a can of string beans and shuffled them next to a red box of instant stuffing.

"Oh."

"Have a lovely Thanksgiving, Emily." Astrid moved slowly toward the check-out counter, her shoes dragging on the worn tile without lifting when she schlepped forward.

Say nothing. Keep your mouth closed.

Emily's shoulders sagged and her feet remained planted. Scripture verses ran through her head, one after another. The pastor's Sunday sermon rang in her ears, his sincere face popped in front of her, "we all have enough to share with the less fortunate and lonely."

"You are welcome to join us, if you want." *What?* "There's plenty of food to share." *Who said that?*

"Really? I can bring a pie. I canned thimbleberries this summer for mixed berry pies." Astrid perked up, like an old coffee percolator rescued from a musty basement. Yes, plugged in by Mrs. Olsen herself, donned in a crisp white apron, and carrying a polished silver tray with a variety of pastries and delectable desserts. Who even remembers those old Folgers coffee commercials?

"Sure, you can bring a pie." *I will not be eating anything she prepares. Who knows what ingredients she adds in her mixing bowls?*

Astrid rushed Emily with a gush of gratitude and moved like a spry elf. Emily continued envisioning the worst possible scenario for this now ill-fated celebration.

"I will bring an extra little surprise treat for Benny. One for Brock too." Astrid hurried to purchase her cart load of goods. "I am most grateful for the unexpected invitation." Her voice trailed off behind her; too cheerful and too victorious.

Unexpected? You master of guilt. Your minion will probably deep fry his turkey in one hundred plus degree heat in Arizona. I should have suggested you go with him. There's a solution. But no, I fell for your sad, sob story. Poor Astrid, all alone with nothing but ugly chicken legs, soggy creamed corn and waxy string beans. I've been set-up.

The devil is coming to Thanksgiving dinner at my home and I personally invited her.

Chapter Twenty-Three
Alternatives

Wickedness isn't always overwhelming to the point you recognize the evil descending upon you. Most often it is subtle, insidious, and cleverly disguised like acid rain that brings not relief and restoration, but destruction; utterly depleting all living organisms, one drop at a time. The full wash of damage is complete before anything can be done to withstand the onslaught. ~ Detert's favorite lines from his cherished book ~ *Illusions*.

Lying back against the firm cushions of Astrid's sofa, Detert turned the page of the worn paperback; the bottom right corner of the cover and first dozen pages bent upward and creased in a permanent triangle. His Birkenstock sandals were propped on the far arm, exposing hairy toes and unclipped yellow brittle nails. He rested his head on the pillows Astrid always made him stack on the floor.

There is nothing like a good book. He sipped a hard lemonade chilled to perfection. A moist sweat ring left a widening circle on the glass top of the antique Duncan Phyfe oval table he'd positioned beside his head. The four small brass claw feet had etched a few grooves into the hardwood panels when he moved it. But he needed a sturdy receptacle for his ashtray, pack of smokes, matches, and his next drink.

Astrid would be gone all day buttering up Brock. He actually felt indebted to the needy father for accepting all the hours of help Astrid spent with that spoiled brat of a baby, Benny. She lavished way too much time and money on the greedy mush face. Detert could smoke inside, finish his book, and not worry about being surprised by the boss's early return. Shifting his weight to get comfortable after his mid-day trip outside to dump the full ashtray, he pondered how he would change the cabin when it was his.

These antiques will be the first to go after the old broad finally passes.

Detert flicked his fingernails on the table's Mahogany rim of the precious find she so reveled in, then rubbed his hand across the oily sheen of fresh polish onto the sparkling inset glass. The resulting smear pleased him. Pressing the open spine of the book on his chest, he lit another cigarette and inhaled a long drag. Hot amber tobacco burned sparking flecks of ash in the air. He squashed the empty cigarette pack against the lip where the glass rested on the solid wooden surface, then let the paper fall to the floor, a crinkled mess dropping shreds of tobacco like dirty brown snowflakes.

Detert drew in a few drags and exhaled a stream of smoke to the rising haze above his head. He fixed his gaze on the crystal chandelier as the hand blown glass pendants clinked together each time he blew more smoke upward. "I could do this all day."

I'll ditch all this old garbage and buy a new black leather sectional. Yeah. And a pool table and a bar. He mapped out the room in his mind picturing his poker pals and a few of his other trusted business associates engaged in a high stakes game, with the biggest pile of colored chips in front of him, ashtrays spread throughout the room. The dining room transformed into a fully stocked bar with a sexy blonde bartender who only had eyes for Detert. She mixed, blended, and shook cocktails for his buddies' custom orders. A spread of food covered the kitchen table; bowls of potato chips and salsa, hot and spicy barbecue wings, and a tray packed full of meaty, cheesy, submarine sandwiches filled the center of the table. *And all my buds can bring any babe they want to this house, my castle.*

Astrid thinks I am just some stupid two-bit criminal. But she's wrong. I have big plans.

Detert raised his head to finish off the last swallow from his bottle and set the empty glass on the floor. After ripping open a bag of pretzels, he dumped half of them on the table and licked the salt from his fingertips. Nesting his head against the chintz floral fabric of the top pillow, he opened his book and began munching a handful of pretzels he laid on his chest.

The sun beat through the sliding glass door. Detert wished he'd at least opened it for fresh air on his last trip with the ashtray. Too lazy to get up, he fanned himself with a magazine he grabbed from Astrid's rack below the arm of the sofa. Her coveted English House and Garden magazines were always off limits. The Tahoe region ski mags and New Yorker were approved for leisure reading. Detert batted an English Gardens magazine back and forth with increasing speed trying to gain some relief. He dropped it behind him, missing the rack altogether and listened to it hit the flooring as he resumed reading the next chapters of his book.

Falling asleep was never part of the day's plan.

***

Detert jumped to his feet in a dazed state of upheaval and tried to make out the time on the mantle clock through blurred vision. Pretzels toppled over with the paperback when the five o'clock hour chimed. He scurried to scoop up all remnants of evidence. Jamming his big toe against the carved foot of the sofa, he fell back onto the cushions and vigorously rubbed the throbbing appendage, whining and wincing in pain. He muttered a string of obscenities never allowed in Astrid's presence and hobbled to double check the clock.

Astrid should already be home.

In a mad rush Detert ran and opened the sliding door, the front door and flipped on the overhead fans in the living and dining rooms. He sprayed his trusty bottle of air freshener to neutralize the smoke stench on the sofa, in the air, and all over his clothes. He dumped the cigarette butts and ashes out back in his ordained mini-trash can and hid the Harvey's ashtray under a nearby Manzanita bush. In a flurry, he cleaned up, washed up, and disposed of all evidence of the day's activities including carefully repositioning the claw feet of the Duncan table over the new scratch marks.

He did a quick inventory check, room to room, flushed the downstairs toilet, and snatched up the crumpled pack of cigs from under the sofa. His heart pounded like African drums in his chest, a death sentence for sure. *She'll still know. That witch.*

When Astrid pulled in, Detert watched her from the front porch steps. It was eight o'clock in the evening. She parked and flung open her door not waiting for Detert to open it, noticing he didn't flinch a muscle to come and help her unload.

"How big a turkey did you get?"

Without a word she shoved a couple of reusable grocery bags in his arms and headed up the steps. Her hair was a mess, flying every which way under her straw hat, stray strands flopped over her eyes blocking her vision. Huffing and puffing Astrid took each step slower than the one before. She reached the porch practically dragging her shoes across the wooden planks all the way to the front door.

"Phew." She tried unsuccessfully to blow the hair away from her eyes as she entered the kitchen, stopping where she stood as a long yawn forced her mouth wide open to the point it seemed her jaws locked.

"These don't feel heavy enough for a turkey, not even a twelve pounder." Detert peeked in the bags as he walked inside and set them down on the kitchen table.

"There isn't going to be a turkey this year."

"Why not? That's what you went out to buy, a big fat bird for that new dad and us."

"Thanksgiving Day plans have changed." She took off her hat and sank in the armchair at the head of the table. Sweat beaded at her temples, droplets trickling down to her chin. A glazed stare overtook her.

"What? But it's part of the plan. A big part of the plan." Detert fumed.

"Doc had already asked Brock over to Jack and Emily's for Thanksgiving dinner." She wrinkled her nose and sniffed at the air, her nose twitching like a rabbit.

"Yeah, but you've been over there babysitting and cooking him meals for two months."

"No matter."

"You look tired." Detert realized his mistake and practically dove to retrieve the words.

"Well if you babysat for eight hours today you would too." She laid her head against the pressed high back of the chair and let her arms flop down at each side. Her hat dropped to the tile and rolled over up-side-down.

This was uncharacteristic for Astrid and Detert wasn't sure what to do so he started unloading the grocery bags. "What's this chicken for?"

"That dear Detert, is your Thanksgiving dinner."

"You're joking right?' He shoved the canned goods in the cupboard.

"No, I'm not."

"Six chicken legs?"

Astrid rose and wobbled on her feet. She arched her back and placed a hand to apply pressure at the sacrum. Her face scrunched in pain. She pressed harder. Her face drained of color and her voice garbled, like something was caught in her throat. She stared hard at Detert and frowned.

"Here's what's going to happen. You are going to your brother's home in Arizona for a family reunion for Thanksgiving."

She stretched and yawned. "I…" She yawned again. "I am going to Jack and Emily's."

"But I don't have a brother in Arizona or anywhere else. I'm an only child." He argued. "You know that. And I'm not going to eat canned food and drumsticks." He threw the chicken in the fridge and slammed the door.

Astrid turned and set her icy blue eyes on him. "Oh, yes you will."

"Ah, I'll just go to one of the local restaurants." Detert slumped down in the chair where she'd previously been sitting.

"We can't risk someone seeing you."

"Who if they see me?"

"I care. It will make me look like a liar." A low hiss separated her lips and a forked tongue might as well have slithered out and wrapped around his neck.

"Why don't I just go to Jack and Emily's with you?" The little man knew better than to pursue the point, but he was determined not to be cheated out of the turkey dinner she'd been talking about preparing for weeks.

Detert watched her face redden, her nose flare, and her voice deepen. He half-expected her head to twist in a complete circle and spin around on her protruding neck.

"Because you weren't invited." She squeezed the stair railing with her claw-like wrinkled hand and steadied herself clenching the wood, her blue veins bulging to the surface. As quickly as she become enraged, her voice softened, her eyes calmed, and she appeared to regain control of her emotions.

"We still have time to get you a small turkey to roast." Astrid offered another solution. "I'll even bake you a pie." Her thin smile widened. She turned her back to him, walking up the stairs with just the slightest bounce of newfound energy.

"And Detert."

"Yes."

"Don't you ever smoke in my home again!"

Chapter Twenty-Four

Tears

"Rock-a-bye, don't you cry, Daddy loves his, little baby. Mommy's near, don't you fear, she's watching over her, little baby. Rock-a-bye, wave and say hi, to all the birdies flying in the sky. You and me, one day we'll climb a tree, and reach for the stars and grab the moon. You and me, my little Benny. Shush-a-bye, No more time to weep, let's rock to sleep, slumber deep, my little Benny." ~ Lullaby Brock made up to sing to his son.

Brock pulled the last of the diapers from his gym bag and tried to change Benny in the back seat of the car. "You've got to quit squirming little guy." Benny's legs kicked wildly, and his fists punched the air while he screamed. "You never have been much for changing time—and oh boy, you soaked that one." With one hand Brock slid the dry diaper under his son's soggy bottom, baby wipe in the other hand for a quick clean-up. The disposable was taped, and Benny was dressed in a new sleeper in under a minute.

Brock drew the baby to his chest, grabbed the bag, and backed out of the car. His feet angled toward where he'd tossed the wet diaper, he scooped it up and dumped it in the trash can sitting curbside for the morning pick-up. The motion sensor light blinked until the front door closed behind the two weary travelers.

Benny's howls had subsided to a whimper that barely registered on the adjustable scream scale.

"Pretty much wore you out going to see your grandparents." Brock kissed the bobbing top of Benny's soft brown hair. "I had hoped for more. Sue was obviously smitten with you, but she didn't seem too eager to sidetrack their world travels. Asia was right. They come first."

The gym bag hit the floor. "Let's warm up a bottle and get you to bed." The baby seemed to nod in eager approval. With Benny tucked close, Brock washed his hands, pulled a pre-made bottle from the fridge and placed it on the stove in a pot of water to boil. "No Microwaves. Your mommy said they zap all the nutrients and minerals out of everything." Benny's eyes followed his father's every move.

"How about tonight you sleep in your comfy crib? He looked deep into his son's curious brown eyes. "Yes, you say. Well then Daddy will catch some ZZZZ's tonight." Brock walked Benny to his bedroom crib and pulled back the big bear comforter. The baby instantly began whining before he laid him down.

"Okay, we'll start with the rocker in my room, and then the nursery. Asia worked so hard to make it a haven for you. Try it out, you just might like it."

Back in the kitchen, Brock turned down the heat so the formula wouldn't boil. He lifted the plastic bottle and wiped the water on his shirt, then lightly shook it before squeezing the nipple to test the temperature on his wrist. "Almost there buddy." He bounced Benny on his hip.

Benny's eyes remained glued on his dinner.

Brock opened the fridge and snagged a half-eaten deli sandwich from the previous day. "Looks like I'm fine-dining with you." He tossed the butcher paper and wrapped the remainder in a double fold of paper towels and set it on the counter.

After retesting Benny's supper, Brock turned off the stove and cradled their meals while Benny wiggled to reach his eight ounces of pure delight. In his bedroom, Brock managed to set his salami, ham and cheese sub on the nightstand next to the rocking chair and grabbed a cloth diaper from a stack near the lamp.

He settled into the corduroy cushions and immediately began rocking. Benny fit perfectly in the nook of his arm and merrily latched on the bottle sucking. Brock glanced down at his son. The baby looked more like his mother every day—his almond-shaped eyes were identical to Asia's as were his dimpled cheeks and tiny nose. Even his mouth resembled hers. "I sure hope you are going to like to play basketball like me. Asia loved watching me shoot hoops." A tired bitter-sweet sigh escaped Brock's trembling lips.

"Slow down a bit Benny Bug." Brock took the bottle away and positioned his son for a good burping. Benny obliged with two loud almost immediate, successive belches. "And that my son is how you take after your dad." After checking the cloth diaper for spit-up, Brock resumed the feeding.

The baby petered off to sleep when he got down to about an ounce, and he opened and closed his eyes keeping them trained on his father. He never glanced around the room, never looked at anything but Brock.

In a quiet but steady voice, Brock began singing. The nipple fell to the side from the baby's milky lips. Brock blotted the dribble running from Benny's chin and replaced the burp rag on his shoulder, raising the drowsy baby and pressed him to his heart. Benny's head rested beside his father's neck.

"Rock-a-bye, don't you cry, Daddy loves his little baby. Mommy's near." Brock took a breath and his voice cracked. "Don't you fear, she's watching over her little baby." He started humming the familiar tune fighting off tears. "Rock-a-bye, wave and say hi, to all the birdies flying in the sky." His voice quivered and Benny let out a loud sigh. Brock stroked a comforting circle pattern on the baby's back. The rocker creaked with each forward and backward sway.

"You and me, one day we'll climb a tree, and reach for the stars..." Brock leaned his head against the hard oak, "That's where she is, up in the stars." He whispered in the curl of Benny's ear. "We'll grab the moon. You and me, my little Benny." Straining to hold a level tone Brock paused, his son's heart beat against his, strong and in matching rhythm. Brock longed to see Asia one more time, to hear her loving voice he now believed was no longer captive in the depths of an earthen grave. To see her hold Benny. To hear her say his name out loud. These things he ached for. He held Benny tighter and breathed a promise when the baby let out a small piteous cry, and then another.

"Hush-a-bye, don't you weep." Brock rocked the chair the slightest bit slower and cuddled Benny with a quilt from the foot of the king size bed. He hoped the warmth would sooth his son. "Let's rock to sleep, slumber deep, my little Benny."

He lay the baby beside him in bed and gathered all the bedding over them like a covering of protection, a layer of impenetrable oneness that no one else could separate. Benny burrowed close. "I'm trying so hard Ben Bug to be mommy and daddy for you."

"You have the face of an angel when you sleep." Brock wrapped an arm above the baby's head and nestled closer. "I never believed in angels before like your mommy." Brock hummed so low it was barely audible. The room fell silent other than their breathing.

Brock's red hair touched Benny's brown crown; the father's thinning locks were beginning to fall out in patches from his chemotherapy. He picked up a clump of hair from the sheets and let it fall to the carpet. The shadow of his large hand cradled the baby's little head. Tears stained Brock's fair cheeks and dark circles formed half-eclipse moons under heavy eyelids. "Soon the chemo will be finished, and the radiation treatments will start. I'm already so tired Ben. What are we going to do?" A haggard wave of exhaustion swept through Brock.

"Asia." A yearning moan escaped his lips as he drifted off to fitful sleep.

Chapter Twenty-Five
Undertones

Doc faltered and clutched the shirt covering his heart. A slight squeezing sensation made him gasp for air. Within seconds it passed but left him queasy and shaken. He drifted over to his favorite log and sat on the shore where he'd been walking. The sky dipped into the lake and drank greedily. He watched the already low water level diminish until the dividing line separating the heavens and earth blended lake and sky into a blur of crisp blues and murky undertones of gray. ~ An unexpected and defining moment in a physician's life.

After Doc returned home from his early morning walk on the beach, he recognized Brock's voice on the message machine though it was garbled and undiscernible. He placed a pill under his tongue before packing his black bag to drive over. For a brief moment he stopped wondering if medical necessities could be needed, or if Brock's call was more of a personal nature.

Doc tucked a book under his arm, grabbed the worn leather handles of his bag, and left a detailed note for Jack and Emily— Brock needs help and I'm not sure if it is of a physical or spiritual

145

nature. Will call if I need assistance but am pretty sure I can handle this alone. Just relieved he did not contact Astrid for whatever is troubling him. Love, Dad

After placing the paper in clear view on the fridge under a Ski Tahoe magnet, Doc left without locking the back door behind him.

Brock answered the front door the minute Doc knocked. All it took was one look and Doc knew. Disheveled and half bald, Brock was a mess.

"Thank you for coming so quickly." Brock was careful to close the door with a gentle push. "And thanks for not ringing the doorbell."

"I know you have a sleeping baby living here." Doc grinned and patted Brock on the shoulder at the same time. "They make signs, so people won't disturb your little fella."

"I really need to pick up one of those next time I go into town. Benny tunes into every sound as if he is going to miss out on some new discovery." Brock half-laughed and half-cried.

"You look exhausted." Doc took in the haggard, baggy dark circles that overshadowed the youthful features of the young father. "The cancer and chemo are taking a lot out of you these days?" Doc knew the answer, but he hoped Brock would open up.

"Doc, I don't know if I can do this. I can't seem to catch up even with Asia's church still bringing homemade meals and doing all the laundry." Brock slouched deep into his recliner in the living room. Doc followed him. All the curtains were drawn shut blocking out the bright sunlight warming the outside world.

Benny's toys were strewn on a quilt in the middle of the floor and the TV was broadcasting the afternoon news with no volume.

Brock rose and turned it off. "Just more bad news about the drought. It's depressing enough seeing the blighted images flash across the screen. I don't want to hear more news about the unprecedented damage, and how the lake may never recover."

"It is the worst I've ever experienced." Doc sat across from Brock and set his bag and book next to him on the sofa. "Change comes and goes. That's a fact of life. It won't last forever." He folded his hands in his lap, prepared to listen.

"I won't last either." Brock glanced at the darkened window. "Then my son won't have any parents. He turned to face his friend. "Asia's mother doesn't want him. Benny will interfere with their world travels and spontaneous road trips." A terrible sadness ebbed across his face and washed over him. "But she did offer to watch him here for a weekend every now and then."

"I see." Doc waited. He knew if he gave Brock the time he needed; he would make his way to the point of the phone call.

"My hair is falling out in gobs." Brock swept his fingers through the straggly remnants of his once thick ginger mop. Long strands of hair clumped in his hand when he showed Doc his open palm. He sat there staring at the tangle, then closed his fist. "Asia told me she first noticed me because she loved the color of my hair."

"It will grow back, in time."

"I don't have a lot of time. And—Benny deserves better than what I have to give him."

"Where is that coming from?" Doc scowled. "Benny loves you, Brock."

"I know he does, but he may be better off with a mommy and a daddy."

"He has a daddy, and he had a mommy that loved him very much." Doc hesitated, then pursued the subject deeper. "Has someone suggested this to you?"

Brock stated with reluctant submission, "Astrid mentioned it last time she babysat."

Doc clenched his teeth and forced himself to remain silent.

"She said there are adoption agencies that will search out to find a married couple like me and Asia—a woman of Chinese descent, and a Caucasian father with red hair." Brock tried to perk up at the mention of these facts, but his speech and facial expressions told the truth. He sat forward, his elbows on his knees, hands pressed together, and head hanging low exposing a bald patch on the right side of his head.

"Is this what you want for your son?" Doc reached across the coffee table and placed a hand on top of Brock's. "All that matters is what you want for the two of you."

"I wanted the three of us and that will never be." His voice trembled. "Am I being selfish keeping Benny from a happier, normal life with two parents?"

"No, you are not selfish at all. You make sacrifices for your son every day. I watch you put Benny first. That is what real love is, Brock." Doc grasped both his hands on Brock's and opened his fist, releasing the red locks to fall. "You are doing double-duty, trying to be a mom and a dad. All Benny knows is that he loves you."

Brock wept in halted, broken fragments and laid his head on Doc's hands. "But I can never give him a normal life. Not the life I want him to have."

"Brock. All any person wants is to be loved. The hole in your heart aches because the woman you loved died. I am so sad for you to have lost her. She was precious. Benny only knows you. You are his life, his world. He doesn't care that your hair is falling out."

"I love him, Doc. That is why I think Astrid may be right. He deserves more. She says I can visit him. They set it all up."

With a strain in his voice Doc asked, "But is it what you want? A life without Benny? Going to visit and watch someone else be his dad? Think long and hard about whether you will be able to do that."

"No one else could ever love him the way I do."

"There's your answer." Doc said. "You are fighting this cancer the best you can. So, your son is about to have more hair than you will. Do you really think he will care about that?

Actually, when I called you to come over, I wanted you to shave my head."

"Of course, I will." Doc relaxed and sat back. "You do have scissors and a razor?"

"Doc, what if Benny, what if he doesn't recognize me?"

"Well, he'll do a double take at first. But the minute you speak to him, say his name and lay him on your chest, he'll know it's you." Doc assured Brock. "He knows the sound of your heartbeat and your voice."

"I won't scare him, will I?"

"That buckaroo is a tough cookie. He's been through a lot already. A bald daddy, well, he may actually like it." Doc laughed heartily. "If he doesn't, he'll adjust. Let him touch all he wants. You okay with that?"

Brock stood. "Okay then, buzz away. I bought one of those kits last time I went to Reno. I guess we can turn the kitchen into a temporary barber shop. If we hurry, you can finish before Benny wakes up. We're on grace time now."

"Grace time?" Doc noted, "That's a new phrase for you."

"Yeah, it was one of Asia's favorites. I never understood it before. I have to tell you Doc; this is a big deal for me too. Haven't been bald since I was born. I looked like a Martian with giant ears in all my baby pictures."

"There is no danger of you being a little green man." Doc followed Brock and took his bag. "Just in case I nick you."

"What?" Brock stopped short of the kitchen doorway.

"Just kidding." Doc winked. "Now take me to your leader."

Chapter Twenty-Six
Regrouping

Planning takes time. The irritations that creep up don't change the final outcome. They simply require strategic maneuvering and patient restructuring. Every once in a while there is an unprecedented need for a dramatic altering of course to get back on the original track. A little subtle sub-plotting and no one gets in your way. And if they do, they become collateral damage. ~ Astrid's journal entry on Thanksgiving Eve 2017

The more Doc thought about Astrid trying to influence Brock to give up his son for adoption the more he stewed on his drive home. Certain her intentions were far from honorable, he tried to figure out how twisted her true motives could possibly be. He gripped the steering wheel and tried to calm himself. Anger would not be productive.

Jack's car was there when Doc pulled in the drive. He sat in the car trying to diffuse the rage inside that overwhelmed him. The girls would be arriving within hours. Sarah and Olivia were

151

bringing their families for a happy Thanksgiving Day. He determined to give them just that and deal with Astrid after they all went back home.

He carried his physician's bag inside, tugging his collar up against the crisp air. The scent of pines along the path was strong and heady. He hoped it meant a permanent change in the weather. It was the first day with a nip to it and the brisk breeze accompanying the chill was a welcome indicator of a seasonal progression from summer to fall, then hopefully to winter.

Joining Jack in the living room, Doc dropped his bag in the entryway and headed straight for the comfort of the sofa. Delectable scents of apple and pumpkin pies rippled throughout the house, a sweet spicy mixture of cinnamon, ginger and nutmeg wafted in layer upon layer. The enticing aromas had an immediate calming effect on Doc's addled temperament.

"You forgot your cane, Dad."

"I just can't get used to using that thing. I try to remember Jack, I really do."

"Saw your note. How did it go at Brock and Benny's?"

"It went pretty good." Doc relaxed. "What have you been doing?"

"I've spent the day inhaling and savoring Emily's pre-Thanksgiving Day baking escapades and availed myself for all needed test sampling." Jack patted a full belly, stretched and yawned. He flattened out in his chair feeling spent from a full day of work.

"Where's Em?"

"She's napping before she begins the lesser activity of chopping, mincing, and grating."

"The kids will all be here tonight?

"Yep. We have about two more hours of peace and quiet. Got them all bunking together. It's going to be a party tomorrow. Brock is still coming, right?"

"Oh yeah. He's pretty excited about it."

"What was the phone message about?"

"He wanted me to shave his head." Doc took on a more serious tone.

"How does he look?"

"Bald. Very bald."

"And he's okay with that?"

"He's adjusting. He was more worried about Benny not recognizing him or being afraid of him." Doc weighed the wisdom of saying more but chose to leave it for after the holiday.

***

Olivia and Theo arrived first. Their girls rushed in searching out their Nana and Papa. Both blondies were tall and slender for seven and nine. The little one, Nina, wrapped herself around Jack's legs and held on tight. Emmaline quickly donned an apron and went to help her nana in the kitchen. Olivia was alongside them within minutes. The men congregated in front of the TV to discuss tomorrow's game.

Sarah and Jim came later. The twins, Zeke and Conner were teenagers now at fourteen. Both had deeper voices and bigger feet. Conner had passed up Jim in height at 5'11" and Zeke wasn't far behind. "They make me look like one of the little people." Sarah commented as she munched on carrots from the veggie tray. Her raven hair offset her porcelain complexion as she pulled off a scrunchie and let her silky mane drape just below her shoulders. She rolled her sleeves up and washed before chopping the celery and onions for the bread stuffing. The teens joined the men in the other room but not before snatching a couple of refrigerated appetizers.

The house bustled with laughter, voices overlapping until the evening spread out into the early morning hours and one by one they drifted to their rooms. The last sounds as lights went out was the gurgle of water poured into the coffee maker and the bean grinder on the midnight shift. The house fell quiet. Pies lined up on the kitchen table like a mini-assembly line for the local bakery ~ cherry, apple, pumpkin and pecan. The dining room table was set for the next day in the fine bone china and crystal stemware Emily had inherited from her nana. A cornucopia centerpiece spilled over with a harvest of squash, gourds, and Indian corn. All was ready to welcome Brock and baby Benny, and Astrid the devil's handmaid with her mixed berry pie.

***

Benny and Brock landed on the doorstep precisely on time bearing potted plants of rust and yellow mums. "I know you like to garden, and I didn't want to bring flowers you'll have to throw away." He told Emily.

"Thank you. That is so thoughtful." She placed the plants in the entryway next to a grouping of pumpkins and a three-foot scarecrow in a calico shirt and denim overalls.

Brock removed his ball cap and hooked it on the hat tree. He turned and ran one hand over his shiny white head. He glanced up with a slow shy expression, not sure what to expect.

An awkward silence followed.

"Well, I must say you carry off that popular look quite well." Emily blinked in surprise.

"Doc was kind enough to be my personal barber yesterday. I was worried that Ben here might not recognize me, but he came around after rubbing the crystal ball a few times."

"Brock, come on over and meet the guys." Jack motioned toward the living room. "We hang where the snack spread is laid out."

"Will the baby let us hold him?" Olivia reached out for Benny, but he clung to his dad.

"Maybe after a while. I think for now he's heading to the man cave." When Brock turned a bottle stuck out of his back jeans pocket. Benny's eyes were trained on his next meal.

"I brought some beer, but I wasn't sure if you all drink or not, so I left it out in the truck."

Doc offered Brock a cold beer from the fridge. "We also serve red and white wine with dinner. You've got to try some of Emily's olive cheese balls. Perfect with brown ale."

"I think we may be spared Astrid's presence." Emily spoke just as the doorbell rang twice and the elderly woman let herself in, arms loaded with packages, a bouquet of cut flowers, and a pie edged in burnt crust with dark blue, almost black syrup running through the lattice center.

"Hello all, Happy Thanksgiving." Astrid strode past the girls and made her way directly to the men. "I have presents for Benny and Brock." She handed over two gift bags and gave Jack a six-pack of beer. She was quick to cover up a shocked gasp that slipped out when she noticed Brock's bald head. She wiped misty tears from the corner of an eye as she turned to approach Emily with the rest of her goodies.

"A thimbleberry and mixed fruit pie as I promised." She set it down next to the other pies. "Oh my, you really don't need my pie at all." Her voice drained of any enthusiasm.

"Of course, we do." Emily responded and shuffled it into the middle.

"I tried to order you a floral centerpiece but didn't quite get around to it in time, so I brought these winter flowers. Do you have a vase?"

"Thank you. I have a lovely amber glass vase." Emily gave the flowers to Sarah and was quick to introduce Astrid around before returning to the stove to check on the rolls. "Your timing is perfect, Jack is ready to slice the bird and as soon as the rolls come out, we eat."

Doc entered the kitchen and ushered Astrid to the living room to make the rest of the introductions. "Follow me." He urged her to join him, but she walked on past and began introducing herself to the sons-in-law first, then Conner and Zeke. She picked up Benny and bounced him on her hip and headed into the dining room ahead of everyone. She switched her name place card with Jim's card, so she'd be seated next to Brock and the highchair.

Doc offered grace before the meal and sat at the head of the extended table with Jack seated at the other end.

"How did you ever manage to fit fourteen people at one table?" Astrid inquired.

"We just placed two tables together. Papa intentionally built a large dining room for family gatherings." Emily answered but Astrid wasn't listening. "The highchair was Sarah's." Emily continued as if Astrid had a sincere interest in her question.

"Nana's a terrific cook." Zeke helped himself to stuffing and gravy.

"And baker." Conner passed one of the turkey platters to Astrid.

It took some time for everyone to fill their plates and conversation to get started. But before long Astrid initiated one that was of particular interest to her. "I understand that you adopted Emmaline when you married Olivia." She directed her statement to Theo.

"I sure did. Love my girls." Theo took a minute to give his wife a hug before digging into the buttered yams on his plate.

"And Doc and his wife Annie adopted Jack, well maybe not legally, but they brought you in as part of their family. Right?" Astrid munched on her roll and nothing else.

Jack smiled warily as he noticed Brock's face go blank.

Doc interrupted, "We are a big family. We were even bigger before when Annie, and Hannah and Henry, and Em's parents were still with us. I guess all of us are adopted sons and daughters when you really get down to it."

157

"I read that in the book you left on my sofa, Doc. I wanted to ask you about it later." Brock spoke in a low, muffled tone.

"I'd be pleased to talk with you later tonight if you'd like, Brock."

"Well, I'd like seconds of the stuffing before my brother polishes it off." Conner passed his plate to Astrid and motioned to the near empty bowl. She sat motionless. After a second or two Conner reached over her and grabbed the bowl, dumping the remaining contents in the middle of his plate.

"Don't worry, I have another casserole in the stove warming." Emily rose.

"The gravy boat is empty too." Jack handed it to Olivia. "Can you help your mother?"

"Look at Benny." Doc laughed, "He's got his little mitts in his daddy's dinner."

"Starting him out young. Good for you!" Jim squeezed an arm out and slapped Brock an approving pat on the back. "He won't be settling for that bottle of formula at the table next year."

"Yeah, Ben, he's a foodie like his dad. He watches me eat with rapt attention." Brock pried the slice of turkey from Benny's fist but not without a fight and some fuss.

"Way to go little guy!" Jim and Theo thrust their thumbs up.

"We are your future, Ben. One day you'll be in the man cave with us." Zeke spoke and Conner agreed.

Brock offered Benny a teething biscuit as a substitute which he eagerly accepted.

"You still going to eat that turkey?" Nina asked Brock.

"Sure am." Brock doused it with fresh gravy and cut it up."

"Yuck." The girls chimed.

"Men, go figure." Olivia scrunched her face in displeasure.

"As long as I get a drumstick, I'm good." Doc offered the other one to Astrid, but she declined and grit her teeth, grinding them back and forth.

Benny dribbled milk on his tray until a puddle formed and he smacked his hands in the center of the pool, splashing some on Astrid's face and silk blouse, and on his dad's jeans. Brock mopped up the spill and blotted his pants, but Astrid excused herself to the restroom to clean up.

"I'm so sorry." Brock tried to use his napkin to help her.

"It's okay." She stood. "I'll go dab some water to clean up." A forced smile pressed her paper thin lips and a crease etched across her forehead. Her eyes bore down on Doc.

"Thank you for understanding." He stepped aside to let her out. "Did you notice Benny is wearing the Baby's First Thanksgiving bib you gave him?"

"Yes, I did." Astrid replied rather terse though the smile remained plastered on her face.

After a prolonged absence, Astrid returned to the table that had been cleared and set for dessert and coffee. She requested tea if it wasn't a problem. Emily went into the kitchen to brew a pot. The girls went with her leaving the old woman alone with the men except for Brock and Benny.

"Did Brock go home?" She asked with concern.

"No, no." Doc said. "He's laying the baby to sleep in my room. Ben just tuckered out all of a sudden."

"Oh, I see." I am kind of tired myself. She yawned and said she thought she should probably head for home before she was too tired to drive. "I drank a little too much wine."

"I can drive you home." Doc stood.

"Oh, my goodness, no you youngsters carry on and enjoy."

"Well at the very least I can walk you to your car."

Astrid bid everyone a good-night and followed Doc out the front door to her car.

She hesitated before clicking the lock open. "You do know I can still change his mind."

"I think he has made his decision." Doc opened the door for her. "Good night, Astrid."

"This isn't over just yet." She pinned her hazel eyes on Doc. "It's what is best for both of them."

"I think for some unknown reason it is what is best for you."

With an abrupt swiftness Astrid pressed her hands on Doc's heart and mumbled words he did not understand. In an instant, pressure built up in his chest that brought back the squeezing sensation that had seized him earlier the day before. He gasped for air and tried to speak.

"Be careful old man. Heed my warning. Your health is at risk." She removed her hands and there was a sudden draining of all pressure and energy as he struggled to catch his breath. Staggering, he leaned onto her car.

"Are you," he strained to regain composure, "are you threatening me?"

"I am merely suggesting you not exert yourself in such a way that you experience anxiety or unnecessary stress. Bad for the pacemaker." She patted his heart again and an electric shock shot through him that jolted him to his knees.

Astrid uttered an unknown word, then walked to the other side of her car, got in and drove away.

Doc raised a hand in the air and his eyes rolled back as he collapsed to the gravel.

Chapter Twenty-Seven

A Twist in the Story

They say your life passes before you in slow motion, not a quick flash. For me it simply went blank. ~ Doc

"Has anyone seen Dad?" Jack called out to no one in particular, just a general inquiry when the first eager diners started filing to the table for coffee and dessert.

"He walked Astrid out to her car. They are probably still out there talking. Do you want me to go get him?" Emily asked.

"No, honey. You finish up here. I'll go." Jack words trailed behind him. He shut the front door and glanced at the driveway, scratching the side of his head. "Well, that's strange." He strode down the porch steps. His boot heels hit the loose gravel and hard pan dirt, stirring a dusty cloud of the parched soil. Within seconds of passing the old claw foot bathtub planter, Jack spotted Doc sprawled on the ground.

"Dad, Dad!" He rushed beside him, skidding on his knees. An immediate check for blood, bruising and lumps came up empty. He was careful not to raise his father's head and risk possible spinal cord injury. "Dad, Dad!" Jack cried out loud, cupping

Doc's cheeks and forehead. When he reached for his hands, a pill bottle rolled out against his leg. Jack twisted off the cap, took a pill and placed it under Doc's tongue.

"Oh God. Help." Jack watched the shallow rise and fall of the chest and ran his palm over the pacemaker. He began to administer CPR when Doc's eyelids weakly open and closed.

"Dad! Can you hear me?"

Doc nodded and moaned. "Ohhh…" One eye open, pupil fixed and dilated. A spasm shook his torso and the other eye floated lazily before freezing in place.

"Can you move?" Jack pulled back from his crouched position, giving his father space and air.

"Son?" Doc's legs bent up at the knees and he drug his Dockers until the soles flattened on the pebbly surface. "I think I can get up now."

"I think you are going for a ride to the ER." Jack took his hand in his and pressed it firmly.

"Ouch." Doc recoiled. "Hurts."

"Do you think you had another heart attack?"

"Not sure." He relaxed against the bulk of Jack's body trying to push himself up.

"Whoa." Jack intervened holding his arms out to embrace his father. "We don't know if you've had a heart attack, or a stroke."

Doc wiggled the fingers and thumbs on both his hands. "I am moving my toes in my shoes too." Carefully he sat upright, his actions were slow and defined. "I think it's just another episode. The Nitroglycerine is doing the job it's supposed to do."

"We're going to the hospital."

"Let's not ruin Thanksgiving for everyone. That is just what she wants."

"Who? Are you talking about Astrid?"

"Yes." Doc shuffled for a more comfortable position, aligning his lower limbs with the rest of him.

"You mean she left you like this? On the ground?" Jack's voice teetered on the verge of complete outrage, and his nostrils flared with increased rapid breathing.

"She flat out threatened me and placed her hands on my chest. Next thing I knew, I was going down." Doc shook his head in disbelief. A shudder swept through him as he repeated the incident. "It was, as if she had some kind of power over me. And you know I do not believe in that."

"You mean a supernatural power? Or something like the power of suggestion?"

"I don't know for sure. She said she'll still convince Brock to put Benny up for adoption and told me to back off or my pacemaker may not work."

"What? This is all crazy talk." Jack took Doc's pulse. "You're stabilizing. Let's take it slow."

"The mask is off. You know she tried to use our family at dinner tonight as examples for the good cause of adoption. And we are, but not in the way she intends. There's something sinister lurking below the surface." Doc winced.

"You think Emily's been right all along?"

"Help me to stand." Doc let Jack brace him up by straddling the ground below him, his arms under Doc's armpits, pulling him toward him.

"Slow, Dad." Jack strained to keep his boots from sliding.

"Your slacks are torn and bloody. We need to clean up your pants first thing we get inside. And yes, I think Emily saw through Astrid before the rest of us. Brock is blind to her motives."

Struggling to bear the brunt of their weight without slipping on the moving gravel under foot, Jack anchored his left leg in place against the planter and used his right one to bolster Doc's gradual rise to stand. When nearly there, Doc stumbled backward, but Jack tightened his grip and hauled him forward until he regained balance. Perspiration dripped down his neck to his collar.

"Let's keep this incident between us for now." Doc smoothed his hair back and brushed off his clothes. "She wants drama. I'll not give it to her."

"Okay, Dad. But tomorrow we make a trip to the local Doc-in-a-Box before the weekend. You might need x-rays." Jack locked one arm under his fathers, and they made their way up the porch steps ever so slow.

"Agreed. I know Emily has a Hannah Mae coconut cream pie hidden in the fridge. Let's focus on that." He stretched to make the final step falling inches short.

Jack caught him and they landed together just as Conner opened the door. "See, I told you everything was alright." He hollered over his shoulder. "Papa, you're going to get it for ripping those jeans. Is that blood?"

"Never mind, Conner. We are seriously ready for pie and a strong cup of black coffee." Jack urged Doc ahead of him so he could disappear and change his clothes before Emily noticed. Once he got his father comfortably seated, Jack left to wash the road rash and put on another pair of jeans. He was back at the table before Emily finished the whipped cream in her mixer and rang the traditional bell call for dessert.

Brock arrived at the table bleary-eyed. "So sorry. I nodded off with Ben."

"Tomorrow morning, Dad. It's a date." Jack leaned in and whispered. The noisy din in the room rose in tempo over his adamant declaration. "And we'll discuss this recent issue more in depth." Jack glanced at Brock, gaunt and pale, hungry for so much more than turkey and pie. The last thing he needed was Astrid messing with his head.

Emily set the pies in a line down the center of the table with Astrid's Thimbleberry and mixed fruit directly in front of Doc. He and Jack exchanged a skeptical look.

"Em, let's put aside Astrid's pie for a time when she can be here to enjoy it with all of us." He lifted the dish up to her. "Why don't you bring out that coconut custard you have tucked away in the back of the fridge, bottom shelf, behind the veggies?"

"You think she'll be coming back?" Emily took the sticky stoneware pie plate that hadn't been cut into just yet.

"Pretty sure. I'd be happy to serve her a slice then.

Chapter Twenty-Eight
Letting her Hair Down

I vented on the first unsuspecting available living breathing body. I killed a cat. That darn thing ran out on the highway in front of me on the way home. What was I supposed to do? Swerve to miss it? I think not. So maybe it was in the other lane and I crossed over to nail the tabby fur ball. I feel so much better now. ~ Astrid's journal entry Thanksgiving evening.

"Detert! Don't get in my way." Astrid stormed in fuming and flung her purse on the floor. She headed to the alcohol cabinet. "I need a real drink, not a half-empty glass of wine."

"So how was dinner with the folks?" He sneered.

She took the bottle of Glen Livet from the shelf and poured herself a full glass and belted down a couple of gulps that burned.

"Want some turkey? I'm just about to cut up the bird. Did you even stay long enough to eat?" Detert stood over his fourteen pound bird like a proud peacock. He strutted over and offered her a plate. "I did pre-taste the stuffing mix you bought."

"Didn't you set the table?" Astrid was almost indignant. She drank almost half the alcohol in her glass.

"Not just for me. I wasn't expecting you back this soon." He picked at the perfectly browned, brined skin over a breast and yanked off a leg.

"Sit down and I'll carve. We'll need napkins." Astrid washed her hands, letting the water run while she soaped up and rubbed them together. She drew a knife from the butcher block and started slicing at an angle. When she noticed he hadn't cut the string and emptied the cavity of extra stuffing, she made one swift upward cut, opening the bird.

"Detert! You left the gizzard, heart, and liver inside the bag. You baked everything you're supposed to remove when you wash out the cavity to prepare the turkey."

"What bag? Where?" He asked befuddled. "I pre-heated the oven, brined the bird, and covered it with foil until I removed it to brown. And I basted every half hour." He beamed.

"You idiot! You'll give us food poisoning." She threw the knife in the sink.

"I read the wrapper and it came with a meat thermometer that pops out at just the right time. Get off my case. I didn't screw this one up. You did." He cowered when she lunged at him.

"I can't eat any of this." She countered in a howling screech.

"You ate over at the Conner home." He looked over the drumstick before biting into the meatiest section. "Tastes good to me."

"No, I didn't. I munched on a couple of rolls because I knew I had a turkey dinner to come home to." She tried to calm herself. "Brock always worries that I don't eat enough."

He let loose with a belly laugh. "You eat like…"

"Watch yourself." She interrupted.

"You were supposed to break him down tonight with all the family talk, so he'd go home with his baby alone and depressed. Then we were moving in with the adoption papers after he realized he could never give his son what a mother and father can." Detert munched down to the bone. His lips smacked slick with grease. "It's a good plan."

"I'm running out of time."

"And I wasn't there to flub it up." A pleased Detert helped himself to heaping servings of the creamed corn and green beans still simmering on the burners. He scooped some instant mashed potatoes out of a pot onto his plate and smothered them with slabs of margarine.

"Gloating can be hazardous to your health," Astrid warned him, glaring until that nervous twitch in her right eyelid hitched with a vengeance.

"I'll be nice tonight, boss lady." He raised a toast to her glass, his lips curved like a crescent moon. "Bye-bye baby, good-bye." The low light setting on the chandelier above them cast a hovering shadow over him.

Astrid clinked her lead crystal glass to his tumbler. "To patience, power and persistence." She watched him eat, gobbling the food before his taste buds had time to discern what flavors nipped at his tongue as he washed down the mixture of canned and prepackaged sodium and nitrates. Then, he started shoveling it in all over again. "Doc is in our way." She took a slow sip of whiskey. "He can still mess this up." She paused, swishing the amber liquid in a circular motion. "Can you take care of him or do I need to?" Her wispy white hair fell across her brow like a lacy curtain you can only partially see through between the variegated patterns.

"The old man?" Detert swallowed a mouthful. "He's no problem, bad ticker."

"He is a delicate matter."

"Did you bring some of that pie home?"

"Concentrate."

"Come on Astrid. You left it there."

"That was specially baked for the Conner family. Brock doesn't like berry pies." She mused perking up, her autumn leaf silk scarf now vibrant against the blush of her rejuvenating cheeks. "I kept waiting for a compliment about my scarf tonight and no one said a word."

"Well ain't you pretty." Detert gushed with a wide grin.

"Thank you, Detert. Thank you kind sir." She stood and waltzed around the table with graceful, precise pacing, her scarf flowing as if a breeze had entered the room and caught it by surprise. "Come on, join me." She held her arms out, hands and fingers fanned in perfect pose.

Detert wiped his hands clean with a couple of napkins, then bowed before he pressed his palms to hers, and timed when to step in. Astrid loved to dance. It brought out the best in her and he was for anything that accomplished that goal. She took the lead of course. He deferred and followed her mastery of movement. With a quick dip, she whisked up a remote from the end table, and flipped on lovely waltz music that filled the air and space between them. Her scarf trailed behind as if in obedient compliance and flawless rhythm.

Astrid turned up the volume. Detert was a perfect partner if she closed her eyes. She turned her gaze inward and the man she saw was decades younger, dashing, darkly handsome, and hopelessly in love with her. He led, she followed, emerging breathless as he danced her across an elegant ballroom of gilded gold archways, polished marble floors, and a dozen crystal chandeliers with prisms twinkling like a million stars lighting a midnight sky.

Towering over her by at least a foot, he compensated with shorter strides and enfolded her intimately close to his chest. The cerulean brilliance of his blue eyes was the only light in the room that caught and carried her attention. They moved in an encapsulated momentum, a timeless hourglass trickling grains of sand glistening granule by granule, century by century.

His caress stimulated sensations she yearned for and brought to memory a life once fulfilled of dreams though now long forgotten.

Trying to hold onto the illusion longer, Astrid captured it to carry in her skirt pocket throughout the days and nights to come. The mere essence of youth revived her, restored her waning passions, and filled a craving she could no longer ignore.

The gentleman's touch was light upon her skin. Her memory was fading, vague, and once she opened her eyes, he would become invisible. She squeezed her eyelids tight and held him there, though faintly so. The music played out and the magic of the moment passed despite her efforts. It was Detert that she beheld when the room stood still. A bewildered stare offset on his face, his lips parted seeking speech, but he uttered not a word.

Astrid stepped back from his arms and surveyed the room, searching. *Why did you leave me?* The quiet inside the house was left undisturbed by the wind brushing against the windowpanes on the north side; the intensity of force increasing.

She wandered past a shaken Detert and opened the sliding door to welcome the full impact of the storm with anticipation. A howling gust blew through and past her aged body, yet she stood unfaltering against the blast, then walked directly out into it, her clothing willowing in layers of sheer organza and chiffon.

Detert followed her and forced himself to slam the door shut. The glass seemed to ripple like agitated waves when it closed, and an acrid smell entered the room, burning the inside of his nostrils. He drew the drapes to block out what he did not understand nor desired to see or meet. Fumbling for a pack of cigarettes, he lit one with a trembling hand, the filter dipping from his quivering lower lip.

As quickly as the wind had whipped up, it stilled to an unearthly calm. A silhouette of two figures embracing each other appeared in shadowy form through the opaque drapes. Then simply, disappeared.

Chapter Twenty-Nine
The Value of One life

In a physician's life there are things we understand and things that no matter how hard we try to figure the science of it or the logical nature, there is no explanation, no rational grounding or medical evidence for the outcome. Divine intervention, whether it be a complete healing for the good, or a supernatural attack to the harm in illness or mental impairment, to be contemplated. In our Western culture this is far less accepted than on the other side of the globe. I have seen much in my lifetime that leans to both sides of this equation. I believe prayer to be a powerful weapon in this spiritual battle. Now nearing the end of my days here on the earth, I am seeing the increase toward evil. Whatever the outcome that weighs the balance of my individual life - to God be the Glory. ~ Doc's journal entry notated with a sealed letter for his son, Jack.

Jack took Doc for x-rays early the next morning at the packed clinic overflowing with holiday revelers and other afflicted patients. Nothing was broken from his fall. Blood labs did not show any enzymes indicating a recent heart attack, but Doc's heartrate was slow, so an EKG was performed, and he was released with an appointment for a pacemaker check the following week. They returned home in time for the big breakfast as the Conner clan assembled at the dining room table for turkey and spinach omelets, mashed potato rehash, and thick slice hickory bacon. A side of pumpkin pie was available for the ambitious.

"You promised to be on good behavior, Dad."

"Yes, I did, and I intend to honor my word." Doc assured Jack. "I look forward to this breakfast every year. I so appreciate that Emily carries on my Annie's traditions with the omelet and rehash. I know the bacon is for you." Doc inclined and whispered, "We'll talk after the youngsters all head for home."

Clear skies and unseasonably warm Tahoe weather prevailed ushering in the day with lively conversations and talk of the annual family hike after departure; meeting up at General Creek and ending at Lily Pond in D. L. Bliss State Park. This year Emily and Jack declined but sent the younger generation on their way with full backpacks and canteens.

"You sure you don't want to join the kiddos?" Doc questioned Jack as they got into his truck. "You drive. I'll sightsee."

"I'm sure, Dad. Em needs to rest up and I thought you and I could go on a little memory lane drive around the lake." Jack hedged before saying, "I'd like to talk out this Astrid situation while we're out if you don't mind.

"I think that's a good idea. Can we end up at Brock's on the return route?"

Jack noticed Doc's normal pleasant demeanor seemed to be weighed down by an unrelenting burden. He watched a cloud of concern erase the joviality of the past few days. He knew the look well; saw it on his father's face when they were in practice together and he had to give a patient bad news. "You're worried about Brock." Jack belted up and pulled out onto the highway in the direction of Tahoe City.

"I think he has fallen under Astrid's spell of deceit. And for some reason she's determined to talk him into giving up Benny for adoption."

"How will that benefit her?"

"I don't rightly know, but it's clear she has an undisclosed reason."

"Did your seatbelt click?"

"I'm good." Doc gave his belt a tug. "I prayed about this whole situation last night."

"Did you get any answers?"

"We need to stick close to Brock. He's about to crack and Astrid knows it."

"But he seemed fine yesterday, Dad." Jack kept his eyes on the road ahead. "He exercised an air of confidence with Benny I hadn't yet seen."

"She has been systematically breaking him down under the guise of helping out. Brock's every other sentence is prefaced with, 'Astrid said, or Astrid thinks'. She's been brainwashing him, and he doesn't have a clue." Doc rung his hands together and shook his head. Beyond the passenger window Doc watched the evergreens breeze by. Tahoe pines crowded the shoulder of the roadside.

"Why is he listening to her?" Jack shot a nervous glance sideways.

"I suspect she's been sending the church people home, therefore occupying most of his time by filling in as cook, babysitter, and general do-gooder. His main sole influence."

Jack passed Fanny Bridge after the Y and headed down the west shore toward the south shore. There was a noticeable lack of holiday tourists out, no bottleneck as they cruised through Tahoe City, a grove of golden aspens fluttering in a gentle breeze as if waving good-bye.

"What can we do?" Jack asked.

"Counter her influence. Be his biggest encouragers. Offer him hope in the middle of his struggles. Simply love him."

"That's what you did for me, Dad." Unexpected emotion overcame Jack. He sputtered a word or two, then halted to regain his speech. "You just loved me."

Doc smiled. Aged lines creased his saggy eyelids and leathery forehead. Jack believed Doc possessed a humble wisdom beyond his eighty years.

"Brock needs love too, Jack. His physical body is weak from disease and the chemical treatments meant to save his life are draining him from thinking clearly."

"What can I do to help?"

"He needs you, someone who has experienced depth of loss."

"I still have Em."

"Yes, but you know the pain of losing a child." Doc's voice wavered. "He will soon know that sorrow too if he keeps listening to Astrid."

"He trusts you, Dad."

"He respects you too, son. Trust yourself through this." Doc motioned toward picnic tables at the water's edge on the opposite side of the highway. "Can we pull over and talk for a while?" He caught his breath, winded, but drew in a couple of deep chest breaths.

"You okay?" Jack parked on a patch of dried grass and wilting weeds. "We can walk across lakeside. Sure you can make it?"

"Oh yeah. My generation are a bunch of tough old birds."

The two men waited until there was a break in the traffic and walked over where the shimmering sapphire waters beckoned. Doc gazed at the still glassy surface. A peacefulness filled him with a kind of incomparable unity and intimacy that sustained. His stride had slowed, and Jack fell in step behind him when the gritty beach hindered the surety of Doc's footing. Jack shored him up when he stumbled on larger stones interspersed with the tiny pebbles. Doc bypassed the bench and proceeded directly to the pristine waterline where the waves rippled in a successive, orderly pattern.

"After all these years, I still stand in awe at the majesty of this bit of heaven on earth."

"It is an inspiring beauty." Jack cast his glance upon the swell rolling in that was sure to soak their shoes. Neither man moved back. Doc wrapped an arm around Jack's waist and held firm, his shrinking frame visibly frail. In the silence between them, the water's constant ebb and flow seemed to bridge the past decades of their lifetimes. Jack's strong muscular arm draped over Doc's shoulder, resting on his old weathered tan jacket.

"You are all I ever wanted in a son, Jack. Flesh of my flesh, bone of my bone, blood of my blood." Tears pooled in the crevices of Doc's eyes and traveled to his chin. He looked directly into Jack's misty eyes. "I prayed for you from my youth, when my brothers and I were wild Scottish lads on the coast of Maine. Always in trouble of some sort whether we found the trouble, or it sought us." Doc turned his head toward the south shore of the lake and his smile faded. "When they both died in the war. I was lost, angry, bitter, and more alone than I ever had been in my life." The water lapped thirsty licks at the edges of his pant legs. "Then Annie found me and loved me in a way I had never known before. In time, I changed. I kept on praying for you, and truly began to believe you would come one day." A rogue wind wedged Doc's jacket collar upright and stiff in a vigorous current.

Salty tears nipped at the tip of Jack's tongue as he bit down trying to hold back a rush of emotion. Doc had never told him any of this before.

"Isabella came to us for, but a short time and our hearts were broken beyond what I thought we could bear in losing her. And I loved her, Jack. Annie and I did." Doc drew in a deep breath before he could go on. "You had already come to us by then. I knew the first moment that I saw you standing on our doorstep, that it was you that I had prayed for. Your cheeks were whipped ruddy by the fierce wind, your eyes were downcast to the boards below your feet, and snow was caked on your winter coat and rubber boots. Annie and I took you into our hearts."

"You saved me." Jack spoke softly.

"We loved you." Doc replied. The glint of his tears reflecting the shimmer of the lake.

"When Isabella died, I was still going between my parent's home and yours. As a teen I thought somehow I was responsible at the time because Isabella might take your hearts away from me. A foolish thing I later realized." Jack choked up, no longer ashamed to tell his father.

Doc turned to face Jack. "I never knew." He took Jack's hands and interwove their fingers, his wrinkled and bony, and Jack's strong and calloused. "You are our firstborn. We became consumed with grief for a season after losing our daughter, but the love for our son grew. Annie loved you so." A sudden hush fell upon Doc, his words and emotions tumbling together.

Jack was struck with a deeper understanding of why his father had such empathy for Brock. "It's been hard on you these years since their deaths." Even in the years when Jack and Emily were at odds, they still had each other, though they wasted too many years bickering.

"My blessings far outweigh my sorrows." Doc bent over and untied his laces. "Let's shed these wet shoes and walk in the lake for a spell." The two men tossed shoes and socks under the picnic bench, rolled up their dripping pant legs under their knees, and walked quite a ways in the shallow, cold water. The sandy bottom sank under their feet, silt rising from the imprints they left behind until the next wave washed in. Sunlight warmed them as long as they stayed in motion, quelling the initial numbing sensation. They continued out, sloshing steps forward toward the buoys, goosebumps prickling their shins.

"We haven't done this since I was a boy." Jack slowed his pace.

"I guess when you live on the water you can take for granted that it's always there. We used to swim and boat often. But this is nice, son." Doc leaned against Jack.

"Quiet out here, no cell phone, no technology."

"Man and nature. Imagine how simple life used to be." Doc scanned the continuous stretch of blue, water cresting at his kneecaps. Glancing back to the shoreline, he observed the great distance they had come. "Such a different perspective from this vantage point."

"You can almost forget your troubles." Jack stood a towering figure next to his father, rippling waves splashing at mid-calf. His legs still a summer bronze clashed next to Doc's stick white limbs now completely immersed under the crystal clear mantle of the watery surface.

"Almost." Doc repeated. An intermittent breeze whistled by, an echo bouncing off the lake's shallow sounding.

Jack knew they should turn around and head back. A myriad of mundane and critical responsibilities awaited both of them. But he was caught up in this perfect place and time that he longed to last and seal forever in his memories. The encircling mountains and mighty evergreens sheltering the great spill of the lake to the depths of the crater holding it as if in a celestial bowl.

"And what shall we do, Jack? We physicians that mend the broken bodies and heal the terrible diseases that ravage mankind." Doc held steady as a stronger undertow swept against them, and they swayed in rhythm with the increasing advance, the water heavier.

"Return to the work destined to us." Jack answered knowing it to be the plain truth, their calling, their commitment.

"Wisely said, Jackson Luke." Doc nodded in agreement as the men stood below the canopy of blue billowing sky that mirrored the now calm lake while they breathed in the magnificence encompassing them.

Chapter Thirty
Counting the Cost

Death steals and kills, but it does so in more ways than just the act of dying. Many spend decades not living, merely existing never experiencing the scope of what life offers. Choices are made along the way, either thought out decisions, or reckless, directionless indecision. A drifting in the living world, feet never touching the ground as if already in the spiritual realm. The waste of a human life while still walking the earth is a sorrow to the Creator for his beloved ones. ~ Doc's journal entry simply dated—today.

Doc knew Astrid would not leave things be for long. He visited Brock daily. She called and Doc always answered the phone. The strain in her voice mounted each day. It wouldn't be long.

"The chemo treatment is almost done." Brock managed a hopeful smile. He lie on the floor with Benny, a calico quilt spread under them with dozens of toys everywhere. "I'm going to start calling you Bouncing Benny the Boy Wonder." He tugged the string attached to a wooden dog that clicked as the wheels turned under his elongated body and sideswiping, tail wagging with a clickety-clack, clickety-clack.

Benny giggled, saucer brown eyes widening the closer the toy drew near him. Each time Brock pulled it back, Benny's little legs kicked in the air at Olympic swimmer speed and his arms reached, hands grasping. "He's so easy to please, Doc."

Doc finished loading plates that clanked together in the dishwasher and came out to join them. "He is pretty self-entertaining. Not that you aren't doing a bang-up job. He loves the interaction." He sat on the end of the sofa beside the *2Bs,* he'd dubbed the father and son duo.

"He is a people person, for sure." Brock's smile warmed the pallor of his exhausted face.

"Do you believe that we are created for relationships?" Doc asked.

"You know before I would have said no, but since Ben came along I think differently."

"Why is that?"

"Well, I'd always thought of us a three, with Asia." He raised his head and laughed when Benny's eyes crossed in concentration as the dog waggled close enough for him to touch. "She would have been such a wonderful mother." He let the plastic string go. Benny pounced on the opportunity to make contact, and with one fell swoop he was teething on his conquest.

"You are a pretty good father."

"I'm getting the hang of it." Brock grinned at his slobbering son and grabbed a burp rag at the same time. He wiped Benny's mouth and the soggy toy, then tucked the cloth in his back jeans pocket. "Jean pockets have a new functional capacity to me these days as built-in bottle, burp rag, and pacifier holders. As re-lationships go, it's him and me now."

"That's good to hear." Doc swallowed. "I lost the woman I loved too, Brock."

"I've heard many wonderful things about your Annie."

"It was sudden, like your Asia. No warning, no time for goodbyes. Just, gone."

"It's hard that way. I understand you lost a baby too, a daughter." Brock focused on Benny, rolling over on his back, his gums locked tight on the dogs wagging tail.

"We had time to say farewell to our Isabella. A week. But it's never enough is it Brock?"

"No."

"Jack and Emily lost their stillborn son. Sorrow speaks a quiet language of few words. Most communicate through tears during sleepless nights and days that blend without rising suns but hold the darkness under moonless night skies."

"You do know." Brock longed for that something more Doc had. He couldn't see it. He couldn't touch it, but he knew it was there.

"I still have my son. And our family."

"Your adopted son."

"We never legally adopted Jack. His parents refused. But Annie and I raised him, loved him. He is my son. His parents emo-tionally left him when he was seven. They didn't physically exit until he was thirteen, and they never came back."

"You'd never know. You two are much alike. Especially as physicians. I know losing Asia was devastating to Jack." Brock hesitated. "I think he blamed himself. I think maybe I blamed him for a while too. It was the easiest thing to do. Blame someone, anyone." His head lowered and he fumbled with the floppy ears of a stuffed grey elephant.

"It's human nature." Doc spoke in a hushed voice. "With Isabella, I wondered if I missed something during the pregnancy, something a doctor should have noticed."

"How did you forgive yourself for not protecting her?" Brock lifted his eyes to meet Doc's, struggling to hold the gaze.

"I could not forgive myself." Doc admitted. "But there was the offer of grace, a grace that set me free of guilt, free of accusations that I was to blame. And there I left my heavy burden."

"This is in that book you left me. I've been reading it. Astrid misplaced it a couple of times, but I went searching and found it in the oddest place."

"Where was that?"

"Buried under the laundry the church ladies pick up. Don't know why I looked there."

"Do you understand what you're reading?" Doc sounded serious.

"I do. It's strange. Like it's being revealed to me. Does that sound crazy?"

"Not to me." Doc spoke in a gentle tone. "Have you been praying, Brock?"

"I don't know if it's exactly what you call praying. I mean I'd see Asia on her knees, and I don't do that. Don't even use words. I kind of speak in my heart and Doc this may sound like I've really lost it, but someone answers me." Brock whispered.

Doc leaned down and ran his hand across Brock's shoulder. "Makes perfect sense to me."

"At night when I can't sleep and Benny finally nods off, I read and cry, then I read more, sometimes most of the night. Time is seamless. You know?"

"Yes, I do."

"Astrid would show up in the morning and babysit Ben, so I'd fall back asleep with the book in bed with me." Brock pointed to a drowsy Benny curled up with a stuffed oversized brown bear. "That was the first thing we bought for him after we found out it was a boy."

Doc leaned forward, "Are you comfortable talking with Jack?"

"Yeah. He has good insight about life. You know, basic stuff and the hard stuff too. He still helps me with the cancer and the insurance mess." The overhead light reflected a blaring glimmer off Brock's bald head as he lie flat on his back and covered sleeping Benny with a receiving blanket. He bent his elbows and interlocked his fingers, hands under his head and stared at the white ceiling. "Jack is like a younger you, Doc."

"I'll take that as a compliment."

"I think you were meant to be Jack's dad, the one that raised him. I'm just guessing, but I don't think he is much like his biological father." Brock continued staring at the white space.

"No, he isn't." Doc asked. "Do you think Benny will be like you, and Asia?"

"He already reminds me of his mom. He has her wonder and delight, her curiosity and gentle spirit." Brock spoke thoughtfully as though he had given this a great deal of consideration.

"And how is he like you?"

"Well, to be honest he has my appetite, the energy I used to have," Brock turned and shot Doc a wishful glance. "He's a determined little guy, he doesn't give up easy. And he has a lot of love in his heart."

"You do too, Brock. Benny responds to that love."

"I do love him, but I miss my wife. Before I blamed Jack, I blamed Ben." He came and she left. It wasn't a fair deal." Brock's face darkened. The gleam in his wide open eyes misted.

"Not a lot here on earth is fair. People lie, cheat, steal and kill. It can get ugly. The boy that rammed the boat carrying Annie is still in jail. All his friends turned on him to get lighter sentences, and they did. They were all drunk. One almost died from alcohol poisoning. The little girl who was out on the lake with Annie survived the accident. But my Annie never came home. Not a fair deal." Doc's words came out slow. Aching. Honest.

"How did you face your life without her?"

"Jack and I faced it together. I believed in God. Jack didn't then. He was angry. He tried to fill the void in many ways for years. It was deeply personal for both of us."

"There is no hatred in your voice, Doc."

"I had a choice to make, either I lived the faith I believed, or I didn't. That is where grace comes in. I was completely broken. There was nothing I could do on my own." Doc paused for a moment. "My faith was not enough to help Jack. Ask him about his journey." Doc gave Brock a reassuring arm squeeze. "Sounds like you have embarked on one of your own."

"I never understood the change in Asia except it brought out a new loveliness in her. I saw something deeper, something she didn't have before that drew me in." Brock stopped short. "But as you say, it was her journey."

"And now, today, where are you? If you don't mind me asking."

Brock sat and crossed his legs in front of him. He stretched his arms into a wide open wingspan, palms and fingers fanned upward, and an earnest look of discovery lit his face. "For the first time in my life I believe in something more than what I can see and touch. Someone greater than me, than mankind. I think maybe there is a God and he has been listening to me. A comforting force envelopes me. Fear leaves, and a peace remains."

"I know that same peace, Brock."

"Asia's pastor stops by on Sundays after Astrid leaves. He brings dinner and we talk. Well, he mostly listens. He never tries to trick me into going to the church. No pressure. He just makes time for me and Ben." Brock tucked the blanket tight around his son.

"Do you want me to turn down the air conditioner?" Doc rose.

"Yeah, do you mind?"

"Not at all."

"Astrid still thinks I should give Ben up for adoption. He'd be better off with two loving parents. I know I come up short for the little guy without his mommy here. With the cancer."

Doc started to reply but remained silent. He returned to his seat and faced Brock.

"I go back and forth. Weigh the positives and negatives." Brock gestured as if weighing the balances of a scale about even. "The biggest negative is him not being in my life anymore. Just having visitation rights." He wove his hands in his lap, one thumb repeatedly rubbing in a circular motion on his palm. "One thing I know for certain."

"What's that?"

He explored Doc's eyes. "If I'd died, Asia would never give her son up for adoption. Never." His back straightened and he arched his shoulders until a crick in his neck popped.

"Brock, is Astrid a mother? Has she had children of her own?" A quizzical look flashed across Doc's face as the question popped into his head.

"I have no idea. I just assumed."

"Has she ever mentioned any children? Mothers always brag about their kids, you know. Their kiddos are the best at this and smart about that." Doc relaxed back into the sofa. "Has she shown you any pictures? That can be endless. Take it from me, those still came out even when I was looking right at their little ones in person in my office."

Brock's thumb froze. "How can she make suggestions to me if she has no experience of her own?" A look of betrayal and utter disbelief washed over him.

"You might want to ask her. She's dropping by sometime tomorrow. I took that message on the phone this morning and posted it on the fridge." Doc stood to head home.

"Thanks for coming today." Brock pushed himself off the floor. It proved to be a more laborious task than he'd anticipated as he lurched to one side, then the other before rising to meet Doc at the door. "I appreciate the company, and the listening ear." His shoulders bowed down to Doc's level and he embraced the old physician.

Benny stirred and cried out as if awakening from a bad dream.

"Go while you can." Brock teased as he rushed over to lift his squalling son.

Doc complied, sympathetically watching Brock bounce Benny on his shoulder as he closed the door behind him.

"Going home? The day is just getting started."

Startled, Doc turned and bumped face to face into Astrid.

"Don't worry. I plan to pick up right where you left off." She reached for the door handle.

"How long have you been standing out here?" Doc asked.

"Long enough." Lips pursed in a beguiling smirk, she leaned in toward him expecting Doc to pull back in fear. "He's all mine now."

Doc stood firm. "There is nothing you can do to me unless God choses to allow it. The Lord be the judge between you and me."

Astrid withdrew in an astonished stupor that immobilized her. The air of confidence in which she had spoken, vanished. An impenetrable unseen force shielded the old man. She knew the power from which it emanated, the only power she truly feared, that she hated with all her being.

Chapter Thirty-One
Doctor John Ailbert Walters

Night falls, a voice calls. My soul longs to draw nearer. All earthly ties, that once seemed wise, slip away, slip away. Aches and pains, aging strains, remain contained in my human body. Lighter still, surrendered will. My spirit soars unhindered. Brilliant, bright, this second sight. Love beyond imagination. Born again. Freed of sin. Eternity unfolding. ~ Olde English poem

And at that time shall Michael stand up, the great prince which standeth for the children of thy people: and there shall be a time of trouble, such as never was since there was a nation even to that same time: and at that time thy people shall be delivered, every one that shall be written in the book. And many of them that sleep in the dust of the earth shall awake, some to everlasting life, some to shame and everlasting contempt. And they that be wise shall shine as the brightness of the firmament; and they that turn many to righteousness as the stars forever & ever. Daniel 12:1-3

***

191

Doc puttered around the house before sitting down with Jack and Emily for an evening chat in the living room. A cool breeze traipsed in through the open bay windows that held a full view of the sun setting on the lake. Amber rays rested upon golden layers of light blanketing below the jagged mountain ridges. A hazy shade of purple cast an outward luminous glow surrounding the giant, fiery orb that would soon disappear from sight.

"Pretty amazing tonight, huh Dad." Jack cast his eyes in the same direction where his father's seemed fixed.

"How does one even try to describe such beauty?" Doc responded.

"I leave that to poets and literary novelists." Jack pulled Emily closer. She nestled under his shoulder in a custom fit nook where she relaxed and stretched her legs on the sofa cushion.

A quiet settled in the room. A momentary reverence. Light and shadows played on the still waters reflecting the last remnants of the day as though an artist's watercolors splashed across the horizon. Eventually dusk established the coming of the night. Dots of electricity turned on throughout the lakeside and shone streaming pathways from the water's edge out across the now darkened glassy sea.

"Takes your breath away every time." Jack broke the silence.

"Did we lose our Emily?" Doc asked.

"Yeah." Jack ran his hand through the length of her hair. "She put in a long day with Benny here while Brock went for chemo."

"Trying to keep him from Astrid's influence?" Doc arched a snow white eyebrow.

"That's the plan. She offered to keep him overnight incase Brock spent another night throwing up, but he picked up the little guy and headed home."

Doc rose and turned on a lamp. "He's becoming a better father every day. If only he could see the truth of it."

"Em said he was reluctant to leave Benny. The little guy put up quite a fuss when Brock left." Jack whispered. "It took her the better part of an hour to calm him down. He kept watching the front door."

"Good to hear." Doc relaxed back in the recliner and lifted the footrest up.

"You've got some serious edema in that left ankle, Dad." Jack pointed to a swollen puffball of flesh that overlapped Doc's scuffed corduroy slippers.

"We old folk endure our share of uncomfortable ailments." Doc turned his ankle sideways and examined the distended skin." He frowned. "Definitely some fluid retention."

"That's new for you. Yesterday your ankles were boney." Jack shifted to rise.

"Stay with Em. Let her sleep." Doc urged in a calming tone. "I'm sitting here with my leg elevated above my heart. What more can I do?"

Jack hesitated, then deferred and eased himself under the warmth of Emily's contour. "You know, I don't think of you as old folk. More like the guardian sentinel of the lake and the people."

"Somehow I don't think Astrid would agree with you on that one."

"No, but she'd be wrong. She fears your reputation with the locals. Something you've earned over decades of caring for them."

"She fears no man, Jack. Remember that. She will lash out at all others who get in her way. That includes you, me, and Emily." Doc cautioned.

"I was pretty hard on Em about Astrid at first." Jack got serious. "I think maybe pride got in the way because I helped her at the castle. I thought she was a harmless old woman."

"That is what she wanted all of us to think. I wonder if that initial meeting was accidental. It set the tone, you helping an old lady in distress at Vikingsholm." Doc stopped and took a few deep breaths, his chest wheezing. "Emily was wise to trust her spiritual discernment. She only began to doubt herself because of her head trauma. You two need to trust each other's gifting." A hacking cough caught Doc off guard. "You—balance one another." He coughed.

"You okay?" Jack asked. "Wow, Dad. Do you think she set us up, even then?"

"We've been played from the beginning, son." Doc took sips from a glass of water on the coffee table between them until he regained his speech, but his voice remained horse.

"Maybe she's an imposter. Not the young woman she professes to be from the early days at Vikingsholm. Emily did some checking. There really was an Astrid who stayed with Lora Knight during the summers, and she was from back east." Jack stated.

"With today's modern technology, you should be able to keep digging. Astrid gained a lot of her initial acceptance here using that persona. If she's a liar, everything's a lie."

"The research went cold. The young lady did go to England, but the trail stops there."

"Ask Em to pick up where she left off." Doc suggested. "The truth is out there. If Brock can see her for who she really is, he may find the strength to pull away completely."

Jack agreed and leaned back. "There's supposed to be a thunderstorm rolling in tonight from the south shore. Maybe some hail too."

"I can smell rain in the air." Doc inhaled the increasing wind blowing in through the open windows as the curtains flapped like a flock of birds taking flight. "Perhaps we should close things up for the evening?"

"The weather changes so rapidly here." Jack slipped out from under Emily without disturbing her, and latched the windows shut. Then he drew the curtain cord until heavy pleated drapes met in the center over the bench seat pillows, rimming the 'Welcome to the Lake' over-sized one with the words spelled out in dark pine branches.

"That glorious sunset hinted of a brooding rainstorm. Such beauty before the fury." Doc pulled one of Annie's quilts from the rack beside him and spread it out from his chin to his feet.

"Usually I see it coming. But even the weather is confused these days." Jack nudged Emily to head upstairs to bed. She stirred and peered through blinking eyes trying to focus. "You staying out here for a while longer, Dad?" He asked.

"Yeah." The lamplight flickered on and off in successive flashes. "We may lose electricity."

"Sorry guys." Em muttered in a drowsy fog. "Cute baby." She stood and leaned on Jack's arm. "Lots of energy." She stumbled past the coffee table. "Need sleep." She followed Jack to the stairs. He stood beside her, step by step as she staggered to the top.

"See you two in the morning." Doc called out.

Lightening cracked across the sky, streaking bright tails of light through the woven fabric of the curtains. Loud claps of thunder followed in bellowing booms. Doc sat listening. He read a few passages in his book following each line with his finger under the dimming light. His lips moved in an unbroken cadence, sometimes his words were audible, sometimes only the sound of his shallow breaths filled the room. He'd close his eyes and utter words interspersed with tears and groaning. Then he'd read where he'd left off before. Rain pounded hard, then hail against the other side of the glass window as if demanding entry to the solace of the little room. Hours passed without any change from within and from without.

***

But thou, O Daniel, shut up the words, and seal the book, even to the time of the end: many shall run to and fro, and knowledge shall be increased. Then I Daniel looked, and, behold, there stood other two, the one on this side of the bank of the river, and the other on that side of the bank of the river, and one said to the man clothed in linen, which was upon the waters of the river, How long shall it be to the end of these wonders? And I heard the man clothed in linen, which was upon the waters of the river, when he held up his right hand and his left hand unto heaven, and sware by him that liveth forever that it shall be for a time, times, and a half, and when he shall have accomplished to scatter the power of the holy people, all these things shall be finished. And I heard but I understood not: then said I, O my Lord, what shall be the end of all these things? And he said, go thy way, Daniel: for the words are closed up and sealed until the end of time. Daniel 12:4-7

***

Jack sat up in bed. The room was a cold pitch black. Rain pelted on the roof shingles and windowpanes with a steady, unrelenting rhythm. Emily slumbered deeply beside him without rousing He stared into the surrounding space, his eyes adjusting to the smallest fusion of light. Wide awake and not certain why, he rubbed his eyelids and lie down to try to go back to sleep. The absence of ticking from the alarm clock caused him to look and note the face was dark, no numbers were visible. *The power must be off.* He sat again and picked up the clock/radio. The cord was still plugged into the wall. Bringing it in closer, he struggled to read the hour when time had stopped; twelve thirty-three.

A clap of thunder shook the house, almost as if it had hit. *That was close.*

Replacing the timepiece, Jack grabbed his robe and slipped into his moccasins. He turned and kissed Emily on her forehead. He watched her for a second then brushed a few wisps of hair behind her ear. A knowing smile crested his lips and brought a warm flush to his cheeks.

Jack tied the belt snug around his waist and shuffled across the floor with caution. When he got to the doorway, he expected more light but there wasn't any. With one hand on the railing, he took the steps one by one. The soft sole of his worn leather slippers padding in a quiet unbroken repetition against the wood.

The downstairs rooms were dark also. He wandered to the living room where they'd left Doc, but his chair was empty. It was much colder on the foundation level of the house. All heat had risen to the second story. The clock on the fireplace mantle had stopped at the same precise hour and minute. *Power will probably be out all day while they work on the storm damage. No tourists to appease.*

Jack walked to the kitchen and dug out a flashlight from the junk drawer. The chill from the cobblestones penetrated through to his feet, sending a shiver up his spine. A small brightness shone through Doc's open bedroom door. Jack turned in surprise. As he drew near, a flame burned orange and red, a white wax candlestick melted halfway down in an old brass thumb-handle holder. Doc was sound asleep, his face illuminated by the sole source of light in the home.

Jack realized Doc had wisely taken one of the all-night, dripless candles Emily had purchased for power outages. With a closer look, he noticed Doc slept on top of the bedding with only Annie's quilt covering him. He walked into the room looking for another blanket to add on top. The tiny flame dissipated the near blinding darkness. Jack didn't need to switch on the flashlight in his hand. He took an extra comforter from a stack of linens on an old hope chest in the corner of the bedroom. It smelled freshly laundered, like spring flowers. One of Emily's lavender sachets was probably tucked somewhere in the pile.

Something caught Jack's eye. It appeared a book and pen had fallen to the floor on the opposite side of the bed, the side where Doc usually slept. Jack stooped to pick it up. He immediately recognized the handwriting. It was Doc's journal. An envelope was tucked inside pages dated a week ago. Jack read the words ~ *to my son, Jackson Luke Conner Walters.*

Clasping the book and envelope in hand, Jack stood still. The rain peppered against the wood siding, and the wind whistled and blew outside, but not a sound emitted from the small space around him. Jack strained his ears to hear Doc snoring, and his eyes settled on Doc's back to watch for the rise and fall of his breathing.

But the room remained silent and Doc lie still.

Oh God. Oh God, Oh God, no...

The flashlight fell and bounced on the oval braided rug onto the floor with a crash. Jack circled back to the front of the mattress, stumbling, grabbing the first and second posters of the foot board. His heart leapt in his chest and thudded, skipping beats. The candle flickered, revealing up close the peaceful expression radiating Doc's features. Jack knelt beside him and reached for a hand to take his pulse. But he knew. The hand was unnaturally cold. Jack pulled it to his chest and wrapped himself around his father, burying his head into the quilt.

Dad, Dad. Why did you have to leave me now?

The journal tumbled to the floor. The pen fell.

Jack clung tight. But it wasn't tight enough. A terrible force rose from a deep place he'd never known before. A place of anguish. A place of pain. A howling from his own spirit. A sorrow that shamed the outside winds that knew nothing of grief. Knew nothing of love of a son for his father.

Part Four
Loss

Chapter Thirty-Two
Grief Interrupting Life

"One of the most difficult times in a physician's life is seeing patients after the death of their loved one. We doctors work our entire lives to bring healing to the human body. The broken-hearted come looking for more than what is in an old physician bag or anything that modern medicine has to offer. Death leaves a gaping hole behind. I think perhaps the comparison a famous author makes in one of his books, that loss leaves a person like an amputee, is closest to the truth. Those people will never be the same again. How can we who patch, stitch, and mend dare to think we can tell even one person their grief is not intense? There is one who heals the soul. That is the grace of it all." ~ An excerpt Jack read from Doc's journal referring to author C.S. Lewis' words in ~ A Grief Observed.

"The service is tomorrow, Brock. Please come." Emily pleaded on the phone. "It will mean so much to Jack, and me." She waited and listened to weeping on the other end of the line.

"I can't. I don't understand," he gulped. "How a loving God could take Doc too."

"It was Doc's time. He was prepared to go home."

"Well, I wasn't prepared for him to go!" Brock threw his cell across the room and Benny started to wail.

Emily stood listening to carnage until she couldn't bear it anymore and hit, end call. Her own heart was breaking. Jack was more wounded than she'd ever seen him. More than when Annie and Nana had passed away. More than when Jackson was born dead. Death permeated their lives these days. The town was in a state of shock. She couldn't handle it when people said something, and she couldn't handle it when they didn't. There was no going back, ever.

Doc left this world peacefully in his sleep. A heart attack in old age. A natural way to go. But the aftermath was all but natural. Jack and Brock took it the hardest. Emily wasn't far behind. The only one around glorying in the loss was Astrid. She was obviously delighted.

Emily paced her steps up the stairs to the bedroom with a determined focus. Jack needed her more than ever before. He'd been there for her with Nana. And he was hurting then too. She opened the door. The curtains were still closed. It was noon. Jack lie motionless, a blank gaze fixed across his face. But she knew he'd been sobbing again. She'd heard the muffled sobs in a pillow an hour ago when she'd first come up to check on him.

Emily crawled into the bed behind him and enclosed herself around his body. He surprised her when he pulled her closer and took her hands in to his.

"I was hoping you would come."

"Davidson called and took your patients for another week."

"He's a good man."

"Will that be long enough?"

"Probably not. But I'm going to try."

"Okay."

Jack turned to his other side, then faced her. "I'll never be ready."

"I know." Emily thought he looked as though he'd aged a decade the past week. She knew he hadn't eaten yet today, the tray of food she'd brought up in the morning remained untouched. Her fingers caressed the outer ridges of his handsome face where several days of stubble grew unattended. He wore the same jeans and shirt he had on three days ago. The Jack of their youth seemed to have vanished and been replaced by someone so broken, so crushed and vulnerable in a way never foreseeable. She ached for him. She hadn't hurt this bad since Jackson left before he arrived. Jack had longed for him with such joy, his son. Losing his father had left only part of the person she had known for all but five years of her life. Doc was, irreplaceable. But that is not what Doc would say, if he were here.

"What are you thinking?"

"How Doc is irreplaceable."

Jack smiled. "You know that he would refute that statement."

"A smile Jackson Luke. How lovely to see you smile again." Emily kissed one eyelid and then the other. Her fingers lightly touched the softness of his lips.

"Dad would say to see Christ within him. I saw Him there. And he would say, 'then, you will see the one who will never leave you.'"

"Harder to do now?"

"Yes. So much harder." Jack pressed in closer to Emily. "I was praying you'd come upstairs and just hold me. And you did." He sighed. "Tomorrow I have to face the outside world. Not so sure I'm ready." A tremor warbled his wavering voice.

"I called Brock. He's angry."

"Of course. He's lost so much. He needed Dad too."

"The chaplain called from the hospital and said they are preparing for a large crowd at Commons Beach."

"Thank you for taking and making all the calls this week for me. You are the only one I want to talk to." Jack struggled to keep his eyes open and wrapped one leg over and one leg under Emily. Their faces touched; the warmth of her breath was comforting. His eyes spoke the language of sorrow, the unspeakable language without words. His lips parted to speak. His mouth opened and tried to think of what to say. Tears gathered and pooled in the corner creases of his eyes, but before long they flowed. He laid his head on her heart and listened to it beating.

"I left the downstairs unlocked for the kids with a note on the fridge for them to pick their rooms and get settled. That we're down for the night and we'd see them in the morning."

"Okay."

Emily held him for hours in their private place apart from all others. They slept and when they awakened, they talked and then slept again. She understood the impossibility of reality when loss takes over your life. And she was grateful they still had each other. Jack's birth parents were nowhere to be found. Emily had tried. His mother's last known phone number in Paris was no good. His father had divorced again, and the new ex had no idea where he'd moved to and didn't care. She just complained about the lack of money.

Emily had turned off their phones and left a new message on the home machine that answered all possible questions about the memorial. Tahoe World, the Reno Gazette, and all the local TV stations had sent out press releases. It was covered.

Her mind traveled to all the side roads she could have forgotten. She closed her eyes and let it go. Tomorrow would come. There was no way to stop it. And it would end as surely as it would start. The physician needed healing now. A distracted mind would be of no help, or comfort.

Jack's breathing pattern regulated in his sleep. She rubbed the circular strokes on his back to calm him the way he always did for her. The slow repetition was soothing. *Sleep, Jack. Tomorrow Doc will rest beside his beloved Annie and Isabella. But they are all already His. For those of us left behind, the difficult journey continues forward without them.*

Chapter Thirty-Three
The Language of the Lake

The mourning came, and they came, and they continued to come. I thought I would not want to see or talk to them. How wrong I was. They brought healing words, loving stories, and cried with us. My father cared for and loved so many. I had no true idea the impact a life lived for others has. To me he was mine. To them he was theirs. To him he was His. ~ Jack's journal entry the night of Doc's memorial service at Tahoe City, Commons Beach. December 8 of 2017

By the time they arrived in their cars, the beach was already packed. Jack drove past the people lined up on North Lake Boulevard downtown. With wide-eyed wonder he watched the babies in strollers and in back packs, the elementary school children, teenagers, adults, elderly with canes and walkers, and shop owners he recognized. He turned the left turn blinker on at the old fire station and drove down into the Commons Beach parking lot. Local policemen directing vehicle and foot traffic waved for Jack to pass everyone. The front three parking spaces had been marked off and saved for their cars.

The entire beach where the lake normally rolled up, was now a bare pebbly stretch of barren sand. The grassy park, and the wood chip play gym area, was full of people who'd brought their own folding chairs, blankets, rafts, kayaks, and canoes. The Conner clan parked and sat in their cars and stared, mouths agape. Finally, Olivia opened the passenger door of their rental silver Toyota 4Runner. Sarah's twin sons poured out of their red Expedition next. Emily and Jack sat in Doc's old 1975 tan Ford truck George Fernley's Auto Repair had fixed for today.

A simple makeshift stage stood where the bands play during the free summer concert months. Local pastors from all different denominations sat in metal folding chairs in three long rows. A small podium stood beside an old square card table Jack recognized from Annie's board game nights. On the table sat Doc's worn black physician's bag, his stethoscope, and his faded brown felt hat. His Tahoe wood cane leaned against the right side of an aluminum leg.

Several of Doc's fellow retired physician friends came to escort the family to the chairs reserved on the left of the podium. A sound system was manned by the local news stations.

Jack noticed the absence of flowers. That had been Doc's one request and almost everyone had honored it. The simple setting would have pleased his father. There were two tall woven Indian baskets filled with letters and cards off the far side of the stage. Doc's best friend, Fred Matthews; a mild-mannered man with short gray-haired stepped up to the podium. Fred knew Doc from the early days of his practice from the 1940's in Tahoe City.

He now pastored a small church on the northwest shore where Doc had attended.

Fred looked to Jack for approval before speaking. Jack nodded. Then Fred adjusted his horn-rimmed eyeglasses and opened with a prayer from the book of Nehemiah, noting the rebuilding of the walls of Jerusalem was one of Doc's favorite stories.

"All of us are here today to say our personal goodbyes to Doc John Walters. I cannot think of a better place to meet than out here, lakeside." Fred stopped and choked up; a catch in the back of his throat held captive his intended words. He turned his face toward the center of the lake. "Please excuse me." He continued. "I see that many of you are also struggling to fight back tears. I say, today we let them freely flow. We may be suffering a terrible drought with a grave lack of water in this majestic lake, but today, may the sharing of our loss and love of Doc Walters, fill this basin."

"Doc lived a life for others. As did his Annie. They helped many of us and never told a single soul. It has been said before that the broken and bleeding came to Doc John Walters. He had a healing touch. If he stood here now, he would tell you all that he did was born out of divine grace and mercy, not of nor from him. He never once sought to bring attention to himself. Rather, quite the opposite." Fred cleared his throat, paused, and placed both hands on the sides of the podium leaning in more for support than for preaching momentum.

"I will not speak for long. What I have to say cannot possibly express the depth of what is in my heart; the respect I have for a man that so influenced me to change the way I was living my life. Not because he judged me, but by the example he quietly lived, day by day. Our troubled world is in such need of more men and women like him."

"If you were blessed to be one of Doc Walters patients please raise your hand." Fred raised his hand first, followed by a whooshing of air as hands went up throughout the crowd of several hundred. "We have all lost much." Fred's voice waffled as he lowered his hand.

Jack gazed out into the sea of people and began to weep. Consumed with his own grief, he'd forgotten the truth of who his father was. A servant. One who prayed for the gift of humility and knew the cost of the answer to that prayer.

"If you believe that Doc prayed for you, please raise your hand." Fred rose his hand first again. A mighty rush moved among the people as they not only raised their hands, but many stood. There in the drought ridden lake, wave after wave of living water washed onto the shore as they continued to rise. Parents held their children with arms reaching to the sky. Three and four generations of families stood side by side, bearing each other up.

"I tell you; those prayers are deathless and live on." Overwhelmed with emotion, Fred reached out to the people, then he sat down beside Jack.

A song came over the sound system. Jack recognized Doc's favorite song from an older children's CD he played it at the office all the time. A single voice sang out that was soon joined by many others, mostly children. He glanced at Emily. "Perfect choice." It was not at all a traditional funeral service hymn. But it was his father's heart. One voice after another joined in from the crowd; the ones Doc used to call the baby buggy brigade. They all knew the song by heart. The sweetness of those innocent voices lifted Jack's heart.

Three other people spoke as briefly as Fred. Jack had hand-written a short eulogy and he was expected to speak at the end to bring the memorial to a close. He saw many of his own patients in the crowd, but the one face he searched for, he could not find. Brock.

A hush fell over the people when Jack stood to speak. The distance to the podium might as well have been a marathon run. *What can I possibly say to add to what these men and women have said?* He reached into his father's corduroy sport coat pocket and pulled the piece of paper he then placed on the flat wooden surface of the podium. Looking down at his brown loafers, he wondered if he'd been disrespectful not to wear his black suit, white shirt and a silk tie. All of a sudden the brown coat and taupe pleated slacks seemed too casual. He tugged on the tail of his cotton earth tone shirt and straightened his paisley print tie. Doc had given it to him when he'd graduated from medical school. Jack looked out to the waiting crowd. Most of them were dressed like him.

He tapped the mic and drew in a deep breath. "My family and I are so grateful to all of you for coming here today." His speech faltered and his knees weakened as though they would collapse beneath him. He clasped his trembling hands together in the middle of the podium, on top of his prepared paper. Jack hung his head.

"This is a struggle for me." He managed. "To talk about my dad without weeping. I brought something I wrote, but I'd much rather just talk with you." His slouched shoulders straightened. "All of you that live here know Doc and Annie *adopted* me when I showed up on their doorstep when I was seven. They simply loved me just as I was." Jack's pressed his sweaty palms together. He arched his back and looked directly at individual faces in the gathering.

"My father loved unconditionally. He practiced medicine with a wisdom beyond his own human capabilities. And he lived a life of integrity never concerned about financial gain. All his patients know this to be true."

"There were years I was not exactly a model son. In fact, I was quite the opposite. Dad never gave up on me, even when I did." Jack held his head high and smiled. "I think quite frankly, he adopted all of us in his own way. I have met very few men like my father. You honor him today by being here as his engrafted brood." Jack turned to Emily and their family.

"Dad recently told me how he grew up on the shores of Maine with his two older brothers and he claimed they were wild ones. I don't know..." Jack leaned to one side.

The crowd laughed.

"His brothers were both killed in the war and it left him bitter, and angry, and lost. Then he said God sent Annie to him and she taught him how to love again. He told me he was never the same. I think he was trying to show me there is always hope for redemption."

Jack's voice cracked. "Please do not grieve the loss of my father, and I say that, admitting to you, that this is exactly what I did all last week." Jack moved away from the podium and walked to the edge of the platform with the microphone in his hand. "Remember instead the joy he found in living his life even after Annie and Isabella left ahead of him. He knew sorrow intimately. But he also knew where his strength came from. He didn't try to go it on his own."

"These are not the words I wrote to read to you today. But it is the truth, which is one thing Dad taught me is most important. Thank you." Jack walked back and left the mic on the stand, then sat beside Emily. She wove her fingers through his hand and held tight, their arms dangling in the space between their two chairs. Emily's dress ruffled in folds, flowing in a breeze cooling the crowd from an unseasonable eighty-four degree sun.

Jack stood to sing the closing song, 'In Christ Alone'. Sophia Williams Turner walked up to the microphone. She was thirty now, all grown up with a husband and two children of her own. The oldest, eight years old, the same age Sophia was the day of the boating accident when Annie died. The lyrics comforted Jack. He'd heard his dad sing the song when shut in his office, buried under stacks of patient's folders. Doc's baritone voice, deep and in perfect pitch, carried through their shared wall. He hit the higher notes with a smooth transition. Sometimes his throat would catch, and Jack knew he'd gotten emotional. Doc never did anything in his life halfway. He put his all into whatever it be. And Doc loved music.

The crowd sang along. It appeared most knew the melody, though the words were posted on a big screen for all to read. People joined hands. Some held them high in the air. Others wept openly, barely making it through the verses. Jack caught a glimpse of Brock with Benny on his hip, standing on the stairway midway between the beach play area and the highway above. A young girl about age ten with blonde pigtails, in a yellow dress stood beside them, grasping both of her hands around Brock. Benny was imitating the people, reaching his pudgy fingers up to the sky. He came. Brock came for Doc. Jack closed his eyes and sang the end of the song.

Chapter Thirty-Four
Convincing Lies

Fools, they're all fools believing in things they can't see and trusting in people that can't offer them anything profitable, or of any worth. They've wearied me with their incompetence. It's time to purge. ~ Astrid's journal entry after Doc's memorial service.

"Astrid, I keep telling you I went to do the job, but the ambulance was already there. The coroner was there too. The old man was already dead. To be honest," Detert stuttered, "I thought maybe you'd done him in from here." He stared past her, afraid to look directly into her angry eyes.

"You should have gotten there earlier that day and taken care of things." Astrid screeched like a trilling bird of prey. Her hair was wild, unkempt, and that was unusual for her.

"There was a storm, hail and buckets of pouring rain. And he wasn't alone either." The small man cowered before her, then stepped back as she raised a hand to strike him.

"They think I can't figure out why the service ended with that blasted song! *'No power from hell, no scheme of man!'* " She fumed and ranted making no sense for an entire hour. Detert retired to the back room where he sometimes spent the night. Usually he went out back on the deck to sneak smokes, but he hadn't gone there since the night all that supernatural weirdness personified into something or someone he did not want to know more about.

Even the closed door didn't block her shrieks. Detert flipped on the TV and channel surfed with the remote until Jeopardy appeared on the screen. After a couple of pots and pans banged on the stovetop, he turned the volume up to the highest level. *Dead is dead. What is wrong with her? He's out of the way just like she wanted.* He flung himself in the secondhand recliner she'd purchased for his room and sunk into the vinyl. Cheap. Her chair is leather.

One thing he knew he could count on was that she'd cook up a feast. Astrid dealt with frustration in one of two ways; she either cleaned or cooked. Tonight, she's chosen cooking and baking. No fast food or Chinese take out for him today. Since the pots were already on the stove, she'd made her choice. Sometimes he worried about what she put in those maniacal meals. She didn't always eat from all the different dishes. So, he only ate what she ate. Just to be safe.

The music would come on soon. The same CD she played over and over again every time she lost it; a compilation of songs where she sought refuge or revenge. All depended on her current motives and expectations. Detert was pretty sure this was for revenge. He'd know when the first song blared throughout the house. Classical piano for refuge, rap for revenge. Detert was hoping for rap, no danger of that mysterious apparition reappearing when the rappers reigned.

Double Jeopardy came on after a lengthy string of commercials and so did the rap music. The walls vibrated; the bass was off the charts. *Sure hope no one's dumb enough to get in her way tonight.* Detert could only make out her words or phrases intermittently, usually cursing this and that. She was in a foul mood alright. She replayed the first song an unprecedented four times in a row.

Astrid poured herself a martini, extra gin, more than slightly shaken. She knew Detert was hiding out. *The coward.* With Doc's hero funeral, she'd have to work extra hard to break Brock, and keep him from turning to Jack for advice now. So tomorrow she'd deliver Brock's favorite cheeseburger casserole with an added tasteless ingredient to impede clear thinking. She'd have the falsified adoption documents, and the photographs of the Asian-American couple she'd hired in Reno as Asia and Brock look-a-likes.

Astrid sipped the cocktail, put her feet on the ottoman and stretched across the fullness of the oversized chair which smelled vaguely of cigarette smoke. Her brow knit instantly into four wrinkly lines that etched deeper than she was willing to acknowledge. *Who cares, he'll be gone soon too.* She wiggled her painted toes admiring her recent pedicure. The audacity of that girl putting on a pair of Latex gloves before she'd touch Astrid's feet and legs. What an insult. The salon was definitely luxurious, and they served perfectly chilled champagne in flutes while the chair mas-sager vibrated easing her tight muscles. The owner compensated Astrid by not charging anything after trying to quiet the ensuing tirade she masterfully unleashed in the packed salon.

The fiery red polish matched her thoughts. Astrid flicked her fingernails testing the strength. She'd wanted the French tips filed to a one inch point, but instead went with her regular tips. She'd cooled down enough to be nicer to Detert when he crept out of his cavern to find the special dish; chicken chili verde with huge dollops of sour cream. Oh, he would watch to make certain she not only took a helping, but actually ate it. And she would. It was baked in a divided dish. She'd serve him from one side and her portion from the other, leaving the center untouched, then load him up on the rice, beans with tortillas he so relished sopping up all the juices. She grabbed the remote and turned the music down low.

Astrid sat straight up. *Maybe the mixed berry pie did its work after all. Maybe it wasn't natural causes.* She swallowed the last of the martini and smacked her wet, gin tainted lips. Oh well, maybe not. No time to get caught up in the disappointing way things ended up. She should have Benny by tomorrow night, and he'd be out of the country by two nights after that, headed to a confirmed location from which he'll never return. Ever.

***

The knock on the door was steady. Brock finally rose to answer leaving Benny crying in his crib. The morning chemo has been harsh, and a splitting headache unrelentingly pounded until he thought his brain might burst. The immediate flash of sunlight made him squint and hold a palm out in front of his face to fend off the onslaught.

"Hello, Brock." I brought an early dinner. Astrid stepped over the threshold before he could shut the door. "Oh, I hear little Benny. Not happy at all." She left the hot dish on the stove and headed for the bedroom.

"He's in the nursery."

"The nursery?"

"Yeah, trying to get a schedule started." Brock closed the door with an extra shove. Shadows moved across the walls following Astrid, but he didn't notice.

"Are you expecting anyone else tonight?" She called out loud enough to disturb the baby.

"No. It was a rough chemo treatment."

"I'm so sorry. Good thing I brought dinner. You look like you need nourishment." She disappeared down the hall and brought squalling Benny as close to Brock's ears as she could get. "Here, you hold him while I make us a plate."

"I don't know, Astrid. I think I might upchuck if I try to eat anything." Ben squirmed and squiggled in Brock's weary arms, then went rigid without warning. His son's face scrunched a deep crimson yet not a whimper came from his wide open mouth. Within seconds Benny spewed forth such an alarming ruckus that Brock held Benny away from him.

The left corner of Astrid's lips curled as she suppressed a devious smile. She set their filled plates on the table, then took the baby from Brock. "Let me try to rock him so you can eat. I'll join you as soon as he calms down for me."

"Well, okay. I know I need to get some protein in me so I can function. So tired." He flopped in the armchair at the head of the table and stared at the food.

"Maybe I should give him half a bottle?" Astrid headed for the fridge.

"He should wait another hour or so. I think he's crying because I put him in the crib. He's not thrilled about sleeping in a different room without me." Brock poked his fork at the cheesy elbow macaroni and fished out several large chunks of meat.

Astrid grabbed a full bottle. "I'll pour half in a glass, so he doesn't drink too much." She unscrewed the top and turned her back to Brock. "I know you prefer I warm the bottle on the stovetop instead of in the microwave." She ran water in a pan and turned on the electric burner. "You really should switch to gas. It's so much better."

"That takes money."

"Are you running low on funds?"

"I'm still not working full time, just part time hours around his schedule and mine." Brock took a few bites, then a couple more.

"Not your usual appetite." Astrid seemed concerned.

"Yeah, I know." Brock pushed the plate away. He sat against the back of his oak chair and stared out into the open room.

"What is it Brock?" The rocker creaked with each sway. Astrid tilted the bottle at a high angle so the baby would not get any air. Benny gazed at her with a quizzical expression.

"I miss Doc." Brock swiped a tear, and then another. "I wasn't going to his service. Too soon for me after Asia. But—."

Astrid interrupted. "We all have to learn to go on without him." Her teeth clenched. "He would want that." She forced a hint of a smile to appease Brock's searching eyes.

"He was so wise. Did you see all the people at the beach?"

"Yes, I did. Many loved him." She turned her head to the side hoping to hide the strain as the veins in her neck pulsed in a wild rush.

"Did you?" Brock turned and locked eyes before she could glance away again. "Love Doc?"

Astrid answered in a misty voice, "I did. It was hard not to get a chance to say good-bye." Wells of water oozed from her hazel eyes. She was at a loss for words to back-up her declaration.

Brock anchored his hold. "Astrid, do you have children?" He pushed the plate to the middle of the table.

"What?"

"Do you have children?"

"Well, I." She paused, briefly. "I, I did Brock. A baby boy." She drew Benny closer and hugged him to her chest. Her eyes wandered about the room, darting. Then she relaxed. "I wasn't married so I never talk about it. Back then, it was not at all acceptable and unwed mothers were shunned. It was during WWII. I fell madly in love. He never came home so I gave our son up for adoption." She kissed the baby's forehead. Then added. "When he was about Benny's age."

Stunned to silence, Brock watched her face. It seemed to soften. A sadness settled upon her features, her lips trembled, and her eyelids closed tight. The pace of her rocking slowed to a near stop. Her head lowered and bowed down over Benny's face. Her

221

chest heaved a great sigh moving the baby as she breathed in and out. Brock sat transfixed, his head resting in his hands, elbows on the table in front of him.

"Sorry, I have kept these emotions buried for decades." She croaked out and took one of Benny's little fists into her wrinkled palm and cradled it. "Since I never married, people assume I never had a child of my own."

Brock was fighting off a desire to doze off that he felt was inappropriate at the moment. He struggled to concentrate and continue the discussion, but he was losing focus.

"Giving a baby up for adoption is a selfless and loving thing to do, Brock." Astrid rose and walked over to the table. Benny had quieted down and cooed peacefully close to drifting off to sleep. "What will you do if the cancer gets worse and you don't have time to seek out the parents you want for Benny?"

"I don't know. A bit fuzzy right now." Brock's head slipped through his hands down on the tabletop. He yawned, stretching his long arms toward his son.

"I brought the photograph of the couple I showed you before. They actually resemble both you and Asia. Remember, you commented on that likeness last time we talked?" She grabbed the shoulder strap of her purse and set the bag on the chair between them. "I have the paperwork too. You looked at that before too and almost signed but then you told me you wanted more time to think about it." Astrid took note of Brock's glassy eyes and sluggish movements.

"What?" He asked. "Give me Ben—Benny."

"Just sign here, on the bottom of the last page." She lifted a red folder out of her leather bag and shuffled through several documents before placing papers directly in front of Brock. "I know you feel you just can't give Benny everything he needs. Real love means making hard decisions that are the best for the baby. If anyone understands that, it's me." She pat his shoulder.

Brock tried to take Benny, but he was just out of reach. "I'm trying to be a good dad."

"Yes, yes you are." Astrid listened to the slurred words and knew this was her moment. "You love your son like I loved mine. Two dead parents won't help this little boy."

"I hate cancer." Brock strove to move closer. "Hate cancer."

"It would have been nice if Asia's mother would have helped when you asked her, or any one of your sisters, but with no family to adopt, what else can you do?"

"I don't know." Brock looked right into Astrid's eyes. "I tried." He bemoaned barely holding his head up.

"Here's the pen, Brock. Just sign here." She pointed to the long line at the bottom of the page. "Remember this says you will have visitation rights on weekends and holidays. They will send you pictures." Astrid shifted Benny on her hip away from the table, out of Brock's view.

With a final of surge of determination, Brock tried to stand, but slid back into the chair without rising. Whimpering, his speech jumbled, making no sense.

Astrid took Benny to the nursery where she'd seen the car seat and diaper bag. When she came back out, Brock was sniffling, his head laying one side facing sideways, on the oak table. She sat and wrapped her arms around him. "Your son knows you love him, and he'll always be there for you to check in on. All you have to do is call first. That's all."

"That's all?" He drew himself up and held the papers up to read."

"Yes, yes Brock." She placed the pen in his right hand. After he put the papers back down. She pointed to where his signature was needed.

Brock's eyes glassed over and closed to the faint click of a door shutting.

Chapter Thirty-Five
And Then There Was One

Innocence fades too fast. The wonderment of a babe's awe is never recaptured later in life. The gift of a child is precious and undeserved when bestowed on parents. There are no instructions how to assemble a lifetime of growing and learning for little ones. Just the willingness to try, make mistakes, and try again. Somewhere in the midst of it all, the magic happens. ~ A page in Doc's journal Jack read the morning after the memorial.

Jack turned through the pages with great care. He read each word, each sentence, and each paragraph with intense interest. The journal offered deeper insights to his father's life. Doc had recorded his thoughts after unexpected emergencies and mundane events in his patient's lives. The passages were conversations with another, who answered.

Sunlight flooded the back deck where he sat under the shade of his favorite pine tree. The ponderosa branches stretched out in evergreen splendor offering both shelter and respite from the well-intended but overwhelming outpouring of condolences. Jack was grateful for the kindnesses people expressed in a myriad of ways, but he longed for quiet solace. The deepest part of his father's soul was inked in those journal pages and he immersed himself in between the lines.

Beginning of summer of 2017 ~ "The days are hotter than any I've lived through on the lake before, even in past droughts. It's difficult to keep cool. So many elderly are suffering heat stress and heat stroke. Tourists don't give themselves time to acclimate to the thin mountain air. Jack will be a busy man throughout the season. I miss doctoring, especially my regular patients, but I'm not as sharp as I used to be. Never thought I'd be admitting that. The process of aging takes a toll on the human body and mind. I'd say the spirit too if I didn't know my best friend so well. My flesh is tired. I remember once asking my Annie what she saw in this tired old bag of bones. I was in my late thirties, but it was my first of many more to come; endless days of this practice. Had I known the depth of this commitment would I have still pushed onward?"

"I know what you mean, Dad." Jack used his thumb as a book marker and closed the cover. Running his other hand over the worn texture, his fingers smoothed out the curled-under corners where the sewn seam of the leather had separated and split open, exposing frayed threads that continued unraveling. Jack pulled the lose threads between two fingers until they flattened out. "It's hard to follow in your footsteps." He held the book pondering whether to read on or take a break. He'd risen before the sunrise. Emily was still asleep. Perhaps he should awaken her. Or at least make a pot of coffee. The freshly ground bean aroma would drift upstairs and enticingly arouse her heightened sense of smell. Maybe she needed the sleep more.

He reopened the page and read the next entry.

"The frailty as compared to the resilience of man is a constant challenge. We docs have quite the charge to encourage to recovery while taking care with our words. Young Sophia Williams came to me for years with survivor guilt after the boating accident. My grief was still fresh. I struggled at first. How do you answer an eight-year-old why one lived and the other died? Her questions came from a deep place of hurt in her heart. I did not have the answers. So, I listened. She shared the things I had wondered about—how Annie spent her last hours doing what she loved best. Sophia has no idea what healing she brought me. All through the eyes and mouth of a child. She told me about the fun they reveled in before the collision; the laughter, their silly conversations about third grade fashions, and the weeny and marshmallow roast Annie had invited her to that night. The last thing Sophia heard was Annie praying out loud for her. A prayer I believe was answered and saved her life. What happened was destined to be. My Annie did not ask for her own life, but for the life of another. When Sophia came to me after the birth of her first child and told me the guilt had been lifted, that she'd found the peace that had eluded her; I held her and cried. Sorrow is not forever, truly joy does come."

Jack fumbled to turn the page. Doc had inserted a snapshot of Sophia and Annie that Emily had taken that morning so long ago. Annie's gray streaked chestnut hair flowed in the breeze under a red bandana. White-rimmed sunglasses covered her eyes and she stood on the boat in her blue denim capris with a sleeveless crisply ironed, tucked-in white blouse. She leaned in, her tan arms wrapped around little Sophie who stood in front of her decked out in a matching shorts and shirt khaki set, tied in a knot mid-waist. Swimsuit straps slipped off their shoulders; Sophia's were spaghetti thin and Annie's a much wider band. Both wore zories that matched their clothes. Sophia struck a model's pose, turned sideways, head tilted back at an angle. Her honey sun-bleached ponytails and bangs blew in the wind. She anchored one hand on a hip and the other in the air fanned out toward the camera. Annie mimicked her little shipmate in a similar stance. Or was it visa-versa?

Jack laughed. Then he remembered how much Emily had insisted tagging along that day. She'd worn her one-piece Speedo under her clothes. But Annie had insisted Em accompany Doc on the drive to Reno to deliver the handmade quilts to Washoe Med Hospital for the unwed mothers and babies in the maternity ward. Emily had given in begrudgingly and pouted the rest of the day. Later telling Jack she'd even packed an extra meal for herself in the picnic basket.

The vintage square snapshot showed more than they'd all realized back then. Doc had kept it close at hand. The last image of Annie—bright, beautiful, and always playful.

Leaving the journal open on the table beside him, Jack wandered into the kitchen to grind the coffee beans and fill the pot. He selected a new organic brew Emily had purchased her last trip to Truckee from Wild Cherries Coffee House. It was 9 am and he'd been up, without any caffeine since 5. It was already hot inside and outside, and the humidity was increasing.

After pouring enough filtered water for six cups, Jack climbed the stairs two at a time and almost got to the top when the doorbell rang, and an insistent knocking began and didn't stop.

"Not now." He peered out a slit of the closed curtain to see who was on the front steps. The person was too close to the door to be visible. "Who would stop by this soon?" He tweaked his head to try to get a better look. Before he overlapped the center folds, he glanced one more time. Brock stood back from the door and looked straight up. A hollow look of terror filled his eyes.

Jack raced down the steps and across the room calling out, "Coming, just a minute!" Panting, he flung the door open. Brock crumbled to his knees breathing in jolting spasms. Papers were scattered on the deck. "What is it?" Jack scanned the porch for Benny's car seat, then glanced to the truck. It was empty.

"He's gone. He's gone." Brock's monotone voice tapered off, and he doubled over grabbing the pages up one by one. "I signed the adoption papers."

His head hung low, his eyes cast lower, and he struggled to say more.

"When?" Jack stepped out to the porch. Acid churned his stomach.

"Last night, or maybe early this morning." Brock pressed the paperwork to his chest.

"You're not sure?"

"Astrid came to the house last night. Benny was gone when I woke up this morning." Brock pushed himself off the porch decking and leaned onto the door jam.

"You didn't go to a lawyer's office or an adoption agency?" Jack tried to control the tone of his questioning while he led Brock inside to the sofa.

"No, she came to me. Alone. The car seat and diaper bag are gone. Some clothes from his dresser too, and a big box of diapers from the closet."

"Anything else?" Jack reached out for the papers.

"All the pre-made bottles of formula from the fridge. Enough for a couple of days and nights." Brock pleaded. "Where can they be?" He was pale, his skin pasty, and his eyes bloodshot, lids swollen. "It's all legal. There's nothing I can do." Brock moaned in pain.

"There are lawyers. You can get him back."

Brock's body shook. Jack worried that he might seize and knew he had to calm him. "Is this your signature?"

"It looks like my scrawl."

"Do you remember signing?" Jack tried to get a straight answer from him.

"She showed me where to sign and handed me the pen, pointing to the last line on the paper."

"Do remember signing?" Jack persisted.

Brock pulled his head up from his hands. "No." He considered the question, trying to concentrate. "No, I don't."

"May I call a lawyer friend of mine to check out these documents? He lives in town and can be here within minutes." Jack urged, "Brock, can I make that call?"

"I don't have any money to pay him for legal fees."

"He won't charge for this. I'm certain." Jack drew close, Brock's acrid breath soured in his face. "Are you still throwing up from the chemo?" Jack didn't wait for an answer. "If we get right on this, we may be able to get Benny back, but we have to move immediately."

"We can get him back?" Desperation glazed over Brock's face. "Please, call him. I got sick early this morning. I think the casserole Astrid brought disagreed with me."

Emily stood at the foot of the stairway, half-dazed from all she'd heard. She moved closer to Jack. "What can I do?"

"Don't leave Brock alone. Get him into the kitchen for a cup of coffee. Sit with him. Do you understand, Em?" Jack whispered and went into his office to make the call.

"I am so sorry." She knelt beside Brock and took his hand. "Come with me."

"You must think I am a terrible father." He avoided eye contact and rose letting go of Emily's hand. "Benny must be so frightened. He won't understand why I'm not there."

"Benny knows you love him."

"Then how could I let him go?" Brock moved robotically and pulled out a chair but didn't sit. He stood waiting.

"It doesn't sound to me like you signed those papers. That is something you would remember." Emily pulled three mugs from the cupboard, the ceramic cups clinking together hooked in a finger and thumb hold.

"Grab a fourth, Em. Steve is on his way over. Can you sit with me, Brock?" Jack grabbed a chair. "Steve did not recognize the name of the adoption agency on your papers and he works on legitimate adoptions."

Brock dropped into a chair. "These papers might be falsified. Why would Astrid go to all that trouble?"

"I don't believe she had honorable intentions. Has she introduced you to the couple adopting your son?" Jack was careful with his questions, not to be accusatory.

"No. She brought a picture of them with a family medical history. I requested that, wanted to be certain there wasn't any cancer. All that paperwork is in my truck." Brock sat forward in the chair, his lanky legs spread apart, and his elbows braced on his jean clad thighs, head buried in his palms. "Emily, may I have water instead of the coffee?"

"Sure. Are you nauseous?"

Brock looked stricken. He rose and dashed to the bathroom and hit the floor with a thud. Strenuous retching continued until it sounded like dry heaves. He fell against the open door and laid out on the floor, his bright orange shoes sticking out in the hallway. Jack went over to help him stand and clean up. "Here's a towel. Your skin is clammy." What did you eat last night?"

"Astrid brought my favorite cheeseburger casserole, but I only ate a little. I just didn't have an appetite." He turned the faucet on and splashed cool water across his face.

"Do you mind if I have the lab at the hospital test what's left?"

"Why? Do you think she put something in it?

"Yes, I do." Jack eased himself out of the little mosaic tile bathroom to give Brock room to move. "Were you drowsy, not thinking clear? Memory lapses?" Jack figured it had to be some form of poison, but he didn't want Brock to worry what the old woman would do with Benny. He figured she had a rock solid plan in motion and the clock was ticking. About twelve hours had already passed, the next twenty-four are critical.

"Yeah, all those things."

"Do you know where Astrid lives?"

"Somewhere near Tahoe City. I've never been there."

Jack looked to Emily. "Did you ever find out where she lived when you were asking about her at the bank?"

"No, only found out her name then, and her P.O. Box number 84."

"None of us knows where she lives?" Jack asked in amazement.

Emily sputtered. "We always run into her somewhere in town, or she comes to our homes. This is all beginning to make more sense."

"It is?" Brock exploded. "Because I don't get any of it!'

"Let's get that picture from your truck." Jack headed for the door with Brock on his heels. They hurried back with the medical file too. "This all looks official." He flipped through each page. "But there isn't a doctor's signature on the records. These should be copies, not originals. All medical records are digital now, so copies have to be requested."

"This couple looks so much like you and Asia." Emily scrutinized the 8 by10 glossy. "What are their names?" She turned to the backside, but it was blank. "She looks familiar."

"I thought so too." Jack agreed.

Brock took the photograph from Emily and stared hard at the happy young couple. He wanted their life, their health, their new son. "You're right! She's in the advertisement on the side of the bus that transports tourists on the south shore casino hops." He gasped. "She's an actress, not a stay-at-home mom!"

Chapter Thirty-Six

Fire

The magician's trick didn't seem real. It's all sleight of hand. He knew that much after years as the understudy. You don't look where he wants you to look. The key is to keep your eyes on the action being performed. ~ Excerpt from Detert's favorite book, *Illusions*.

Detert stewed for hours. Astrid was late, she was always late. If he set his watch an hour ahead, she'd arrive on time. This was their big pay-off—a million to split for the fake adoption. No more piddling stuff—they were high stakes now. He had everything ready to go to the airport tonight. All important papers were bound together in a leather folder he'd stashed in his suitcase.

Who pays that kind of money for a squalling kid? Detert was almost jealous, the sick guy's baby had inflated value. Better to make a profit from him than to complain. But he wondered; hadn't the new parents thought out the possibility that the kid might get cancer too?

Boss lady had already moved her precious antiques and some personal effects to storage in Reno. The house would finally be his. No one knew where they were anyway. She'd purchased the property and cabin under an assumed name several years ago. And they'd both been careful not to be noticed by even the closet neighbors. Well, maybe his smoking had been an issue a couple of times, but contact had been minimal. Astrid was strict about that. She was flipping strict about everything and he was tired of all the restrictions. She had new digs and he liked the idea of them running operations from separate residences.

Detert checked his watch, then headed to the kitchen to nuke a plate of leftovers. He'd slept so deep last night he didn't even dream, and kind of woke up with a headache. A six pack will do that to ya. He stuck his head in the fridge to nosey around. Astrid divided their food, left side all hers, right side his. And her champagne was looking darn good. She'd popped it open last night.

"I'll just polish off the last half of the bottle." Detert pulled it out and struggled to pop the cork, it took some effort. He'd shaken it up a bit more than he had intended, and the bubbly gushed like a geyser spraying and wasting the expensive import. He cursed and placed his thumb over the opening and pressed trying to save what was left of the contents.

"And I'm drinking out of the bottle, Astrid. Did you hear me? No?" Detert tipped the dripping green bottle and read the label. "Man, I'd never spend a hundred bucks on this." He guzzled down most of the French sparkling wine, walked to the recliner, sat and pumped the handle until the footrest snapped into place. He rested comfortably and chugged another big gulp. And another. The last slurp emptied the bottle.

***

Detert smelled smoke and wondered if he'd forgotten to put out his cigarette. He tried to get up, but his legs wouldn't move. The harder he tried, the more leaden his calves and thighs became. A constriction in his throat tightened and he tried to gasp for air, but his mouth remained shut. Smoke visibly rose around him in vaporous clouds. He heard a baby cry, and the slamming of a door. This was not a good dream. He tried to awaken himself or at least change the direction the dream was going.

"I knew you'd go for my champagne." Astrid appeared over Detert's face. "You are so predictable." She wore a paper mask, but it was her voice. A huge white bottle weighed her arm and shoulder forward. His eyes were wide open, and he couldn't close his lids. The sound of liquid pouring surrounded him. No matter how he strained to move his neck to see what it was, he remained immobile in the recliner.

"These are yours. I gathered them from all your hiding places in the house."

Detert could make out the red and white defining brand of his cigarettes. The smoke choked him as she stuffed the pack of crinkly paper in his shirt pocket and pulled a cigarette, carefully placing it between his left fingers. Eyeballs dry and burning, he tried to blink but nothing happened.

"You wanted the house. It's yours." She sneered and knelt beside him. "It's a rental. And I got two million for the baby. All mine since you won't be using your half." She placed a used glass ashtray directly below his arm. The smoke was thick, the room white.

Tears rolled down his cheeks.

"Too late." She wiped his tears. Astrid pulled the mask up and coughed, burying her face in a wet towel. A lighter clicked, and a blue flame flickered. She lit a cigarette and took a long draw, then showed him the leather case she now held in her hand. "They'll think it was your idea, the illegal adoption. They'll think you burned the house down when you fell asleep in the chair smoking. They'll find the paper trail that will lead them to *your* extortion, a bank account with a little too much money." Astrid blew smoke in his face and took another drag. "They won't look so hard for me with so many answers pointing to you."

Astrid recovered her mouth and nose with the mask and stood back far enough to quickly exit the front door. She turned and tossed the lit cigarette behind her on the rug. She didn't wait for it to ignite.

The door closed again. Smoke billowed in plumes and pillars to the twenty foot ceiling, enclosing him in a world of white haze. Crackling, snapping sounds preceded a big whoosh and orange flames rising across the room burning bigger and brighter. Detert couldn't breathe and struggled to suck in air. It was his worst nightmare.

Chapter Thirty-Seven
Hope

Open your eyes, open your heart. Faith moves mountains, love's where you start. Don't look at obstacles, focus on Him. The battle before you, is the victory within. ~ Brock's new favorite song lyrics.

Brock tried to process all the information the lawyer had given him. The adoption papers were fake. All the promises Astrid had made to him about the non-existent couple and how they would keep in touch, were a stinking pack of lies. She just wanted him to think he'd signed legitimate documents to give her time to snatch Benny and run. But where? And why did she want him if it wasn't a legal adoption? For an illegal adoption?

Jack and Emily helped Brock call every authority in the county. Brock filed a missing child report and the sheriff and police issued an Amber Alert, and then began searching for the illusive Astrid and her partner Detert. By mid-day, drained physically and mentally, Brock headed to his home with Jack to search for any possible clues.

"I have no idea what I am looking for." Brock tossed his backpack on the sofa.

Jack handed his friend a checklist Emily had quickly drawn up for them after talking with Derrick Thomas from the Placer Sheriff's Department. "Anything that might have her fingerprints; a glass, coffee cup, a pen, anything of Benny's that she might have touched. The sheriff will be here in a few minutes. Don't touch it. Just make note of what and where."

Brock flipped one of the sofa cushions and threw it on the floor. "She always wore rubber gloves when she did the dishes. There can't possibly be any prints." He slipped to the floor in a heap of despair; arms and legs trembling, hands shaking, sweating. "I let her take my son."

"No, you didn't." Jack knelt beside him. "She tricked you, she tricked all of us. Everyone makes mistakes. She got cocky, Brock. That's when people mess up. Come on, keep looking."

With hollow eyes Brock glanced up. His shoulders sagged. "What hope is there of finding him now? We have no idea where to begin looking for her."

"One thing I know for sure. There is always hope." Jack helped Brock get to his feet. "You said she brought you a casserole and left it. Try the kitchen first but remember not to touch a thing until Derrick and the team of specialists arrive."

"I don't know where to start." Brock picked up a magazine and tossed it down again.

"Think. Astrid had to go in Benny's nursery yesterday to get clothes, diapers, things you said were missing. Think about what isn't here."

A loud knock on the open front door interrupted their conversation as several uniformed men and one petite woman asked to enter. "Jack, this is the team assembled to the case." A sheriff shook Jack's hand then turned to address Brock. "Sir, are you Brock Benton?"

"Yes." Brock stood between them and offered his hand. He read the name on the man's shirt. "Sheriff Thomas, thank you for coming to help me. Please come in." He moved aside.

"Call me Derrick. Have you had time to go over the list I gave Emily yet?" He gave Brock's a firm handshake, then started to take notes on his cell phone as he stepped in.

"We just started." Jack answered and motioned to the officer to take it easy on Brock.

"Em went to Vikingsholm to make inquiries. Phoned ahead so she could take the road in. The staff still works during the off season to maintain the grounds. That seemed to be this woman's main hub other than wherever she lived with this Detert. I have officers on the way."

Brock replaced the cushion then sat on the edge of it, his long legs pressing against the coffee table, his bald head noticeably following the people now roaming through his home. He watched the team open cases full of materials and get right to work.

"What were Astrid's habits?" Derrick sat across from Brock. "What did she touch?"

"She cooked and she cleaned. She was always cleaning." Brock rung his hands.

Jack shot Derrick a knowing look as he sat beside Brock. This was all too familiar. They both knew how critical time became with each passing hour.

"Did she use your utensils and pots and pans, or did she bring her own?" Derrick asked.

"Astrid usually brought her own then took it all home a few days later after I finished what was left in the fridge."

"So, she touched the refrigerator and stove, and the microwave?" Derrick turned and pointed the crew toward those appliances.

Two young men clad in dark blue jumpsuits with shield patches on their upper shirt sleeves headed over. They set their black leather boxes on the kitchen table and unbuckled the tops. Compartmental trays unfolded out in triple layers with a full center storage area. The team grabbed thin yellow Latex gloves and didn't touch a thing until the snug fitting material covered their fingers and palms. Both politely acknowledged Brock with a nod of the head, then went straight to work. The men carefully laid out zipper lock bags in a variety of sizes across the table; setting up a central area of operation. Another officer with salt and pepper hair headed for the baby's nursery to set up a similar station with his kit.

"You know it's strange, now that you mention it, she never used the microwave." Brock spoke in a surprised tone. "She even prepared the leftovers in small container to be warmed up at 350 degrees. You know that pattern all grandmothers have; that white dish with the blue flower."

"CorningWare?" Derrick asked. "Did she leave any here in the cupboards?"

"She took everything home. She did use my aluminum foil to cover the casseroles in the oven." Brock's words barely left his lips before the team started opening drawers. "Left of the sink, second drawer down." He pointed, then watched in amazement as they dusted for prints.

"Did she have a favorite show on the TV? Listen to the radio? Use any of your electronics?"

"I took naps when she watched Benny and never heard anything electronic before I went to sleep or when I woke up." Brock paused. "The house was always quiet, and the meals were set with placemats and dinnerware on the dining room table. Pretty formal, like when you're expecting company."

"What did she eat and drink?" Derrick pressed for answers.

"She picked at her food. I used to worry because she never ate much. She took tiny portions." Brock stopped. "What am I doing? This woman was nice to me." His body sank in the sofa as if weighted down by some invisible anchor. A heavy sensation compressed against his chest and he tried to grasp the scope of what these questions meant. "This, this is all craziness. How can someone who helped me so many times turn out to be such a bad person?" Brock grabbed his bald head with both hands and squeezed tight.

"These criminals act swiftly. This has all the appearances of being premeditated, painstakingly orchestrated, and executed." Derrick stated, a clear urgency peaked in his voice. "These next hours are critical for us to get your son back."

"What do you mean—hours?" Agitated, Brock stuttered trying to get his words out.

"What did she drink?" Derrick asked again.

"Wine, she drank wine with her meals. Once in a while, champagne."

"Your wine?"

"I drink beer." Brock stared at a brown spot on the carpet next to his shoes. He wondered if he'd spilled coffee. The matted fibers compressed below the raised pile of the carpet.

"She brought the wine with her?"

"Yes."

"Did she ever leave any?"

"No, no, she always took it home." Brock stopped short. His tired eyes widened into full twin moons. The hand tremors he'd been trying to suppress increased in intensity.

"What?" Derrick moved in closer, close enough to smell the vomit on Brock's breath.

"She left a bottle once that I put in the cabinet under the hutch. In case." Brock rose and walked into the dining room. "She wanted to have it with the next meal." His tall frame bent below the beveled glass doors of Asia's antique walnut sideboard. He pulled the loop handle hanging from a bronze dragon's head on the burled door. And there it was, a green glass bottle of merlot with a burgundy stained cork sticking out. Brock stepped back. "My prints are on it."

"So are hers." The sheriff put on a pair of gloves and grabbed a large zipper lock bag.

Chapter Thirty-Eight
Selma

Familiarity can be deceptive. The obvious can be hidden in plain view. It takes concentrated effort to think outside your own assumptions and preconceived notions. Past experience can come in handy. In fact, it can illuminate the present. ~ Emily's journal entry the night she helped look for Benny.

Emily pulled up and met Rachel in the driveway. Vikingsholm was closed for the winter though they could have left it open due to the warm weather from the drought. Not sure what she might be able to find at the castle, but hoping for anything, Emily followed the docent inside.

"Other than occasionally taking the Tahoe Gal or Queen paddle boat cruises, I can't think of anything unusual about Astrid. She is always here on the grounds." Rachel's voice echoed in the empty entryway. "She'd keep to herself. Packed her own lunch in an old knapsack and always had water bottles with her."

"No water bottle the day Jack and I found her on the trail suffering heat exhaustion."

"Really." Rachel strung the word out. "That old woman is sprier that most hikers we get half her age. Seriously Em, she can't be as old as she says."

"Everyone around here believes she's the young woman who used to visit Lora Knight back in the 1930's. She has to be as old as she says to be that person." Emily scanned the rooms as she spoke, but nothing caught her attention.

"There's a docent that has worked here for thirty-seven years and was a regular visitor with her parents for fourteen summers. Helen Henry Smith's the real deal. They lived in Santa Barbara near Mrs. Knight's winter home. There are many photographs of her here as a child." Rachel stopped in front of Selma. "I've never seen a single picture of this Astrid."

"Maybe they didn't visit the same month?" Emily wondered.

"Maybe she was never here. You'd think Helen would know about her. She knows the Vikingsholm history inside-out. Tea was at four o'clock in the afternoon. Morning rides on Mrs. Knight's largest boat the Valkyrie, a magnificent mahogany cabin cruiser that was well known on the lake in its heyday." Rachel stood opposite Selma and checked the time against her watch.

"Is she keeping correct time since Jack's friend fixed her?"

"Yes, she keeps perfect time again. Thanks." Rachel sighed. "Look, I don't mean to be snippy with you, but I am fond of Helen and this Astrid is no Helen Smith."

"I find it interesting that they have the same last name."

"Smith is Helen's married name. Her maiden name was Henry. Daughter of Mr. and Mrs. Benjamin H. Henry. All were well-known visitors in the old days."

"Is there anything you can think of that might help us find a home address for Astrid?"

"When she is here, she picnics on the beach, walks the grounds, and hikes. She keeps to herself, but I will admit she acts as if she had a right to be here more than the rest of us." Irritation hemmed Rachel's words. "You remember Helen. You and Jack came many times for her special once a month luncheon tours."

"That's how we learned Lora called it, 'Veekingsholm', and in one of the Scandinavian languages it means—bay with an island. Helen knows all the neat personal info. Astrid didn't know any intimate details about Lora." Emily stared at Selma. "There must be something."

"I wish I could help more. You are free to walk through the rooms and see if you notice something." Rachel scratched her head. "Maybe in the woods?"

"Two elderly women named Smith and I *know* only one of them is honorable. If only Selma could talk." Emily patted Selma's shoulder. "What would you tell us old girl?"

"Em, I completely forgot." Rachel burst out.

"What?" Emily watched the minute hand tick a notch over on Selma's clock face.

"Wait here a second." Rachel rushed off toward the office, her rubber sole shoes silent on the tile floors.

Emily went over to the piano, sat on the bench and ran her fingers over the ivory keys. She played Bach's Toccata and Fugue in D Minor filling the home with music that lightened her heart for the moment. All this took her back to her own kidnapping. Terror had finally ceased to resurface when Jonathan Forrester came to mind. She whispered a prayer for Benny.

Rachel returned. "Here, I don't know what this means." She handed Emily a yellow folded piece of thin, brittle paper. "Jack's friend found this when he fixed Selma."

Emily opened the paper and strained to read the faded ink. "It looks like it was written with an old fashioned fountain pen, in impeccable penmanship." Emily held it to the light filtering in from the beveled glass window beside them.

"I've read it several times and it makes no sense to me at all, but I couldn't throw it away. It seems to be genuine; I'd guess about sixty to seventy years old, and important enough for some-one to hide it under Selma's shoes." Rachel watched Emily's face scrunch in a curious expression while she tried to understand the few words penned in three straight lines.

"What could this possibly mean?" Emily brought the paper closer. She fumbled in her shoulder bag for a pair of reading glasses, and finally drew them out. The plastic rims hit the bridge of her nose as she slid them on while still reading the piece of faded parchment stationery. The words were clearly written but they seemed to convey only part of a message or statement.

No time ~ good-bye
Return my forest
Across the pond

"It almost seems like some kind of a code, a personal letter. Why was it left with Selma?"

"You know as much as I do. Take it with you. Maybe it will help. Bring it back if it doesn't. It's just stuffed in a desk drawer here and I'm the only one who knows it exists." Rachel stared at the strange note again. "Beautiful handwriting. Nobody writes like that anymore."

"It's definitely from another era. Selma must hold a special significance. Hasn't she ever been painted, you know, spruced up?"

"That would have been before my time. If she was. Maybe the painter just put this right back where he found it thinking it was supposed to be there. I can look into that."

"You sure it's ok for me to take it with me?"

"It's not something Helen ever mentioned. I honestly don't think she knew about it." Rachel added. "And she would have, trust me. That lady knows everything about this place."

Emily refolded the paper with great care and searched her purse for a safe place to tuck it away. She slipped it into her business card holder after removing all the other cards and clicked it shut.

"Across the pond is a reference to England. I get that. 'No time' seems it would be about Selma herself. Time—clock. But I can't come up with anything for 'Return my forest'. Maybe Jack can figure it out."

"Hope it helps in some way to find that baby, though I don't know how it can." Rachel lowered her voice. "If it was one of my children. I'd be going crazy right about now." She walked Emily to the heavy wooden doors where they'd entered the castle.

"The father is in shock." Emily hugged her purse close pressing her arm snug against it. She adjusted the shoulder strap to keep the heavy handbag from sliding off. "Still no home address for Astrid is bad news. The bank had a P. O. box number and said her account was closed two days ago. She used cash every time I saw her in a place of business. No other checking account and no credit cards. It makes her harder to trace without a paper trail."

"Sounds like she knew what she was doing. She seemed odd to me, but harmless."

"Thanks, Rach. This may end up being helpful." Emily waited while the docent locked the doors behind them. "Where are you off to now?"

"Home. Kevin left the kids with his mom. He got called out on a fire in Homewood. A rental cabin burned to the ground before it was phoned in. Kind of an isolated area with a private beach area. They have requested the arson investigators."

"Who would burn down a cabin in this drought? They could catch the entire forest on fire." Emily shook her head in disgust.

"Well, that's not all." Rachel leaned in closer. "There's a body burned beyond recognition. They found evidence of cigarettes and a fried Jack Daniels label on a bottle that burst from the heat. The nearest neighbor said that a tenant used to smoke out back by the deck despite her rants. They've notified the owner that his cabin is toast. The firefighters were able to contain it before it spread into the forest and to any of the surrounding structures."

Chapter Thirty-Nine
In the Ashes

It is not that which we see that holds our attention, but that which is unseen. That which we must search out to behold if only for a brief moment. ~ One of Nana's old wise sayings.

Emily met up with Jack and Brock back at the Conner home. The investigative team was still taking samples at Brock's and he had a difficult time with them riffling through Benny's nursery. He'd answered every question, but it made little difference. Other than the wine bottle, he was certain all the fingerprints would be his. When they disturbed Asia's art studio, a place he considered off limits to all except himself, he'd lost it.

"I made tuna and egg salad sandwiches. We still need to nourish our bodies for strength." Emily offered one to Brock which he reluctantly accepted. She set the full plate in the center of the table with a bowl of fresh fruit, a pitcher of water, and glasses. Warm sunlight streamed off the three tall empty glasses reflecting brilliant rays of light on a wall across from the kitchen window.

"What's the news from the castle?" Jack sat between Emily and Brock at the table. The drain of the past two days made him ravenous and he immediately devoured a sandwich and reached for another.

"Not much. No address. Just a strange note that was found adhered under Selma's shoes when Toby fixed the clock for them. Rachel had stuffed it in a desk drawer. She let me bring it hoping we might be able to decipher the meaning of the words and that would help in some way." Emily dug deep into her purse and retrieved the hopeful clue.

Jack unfolded the scrap of paper and read it without speaking.

"What does it say?" Brock asked.

"No Time ~ good-bye. Return my forest. Across the pond." Jack read the three lines with slow, intentional pauses after each period. "There is distinct punctuation after all three phrases. These aren't exactly sentences, but three separate thoughts." He mouthed the words again in a stronger tone of voice. "You know, like someone was in a hurry but wanted to say something of specific importance. To Selma?"

"I'm no expert," Brock interjected, "it sounds personal. A promise of sorts."

Jack pressed his lips together and nodded his head, then he opened his mouth wide. "You know. I think Brock is right. It's as if the writer knew the reader would understand. But why tape it under Selma's shoe? She can't talk."

"But what if there *was* a real Astrid back then. Maybe a teen about the age our Helen Henry Smith." Excitement flashed across Emily's face. "It's a farewell—a promise, to return some-day. Maybe she never made it back. There's an intimacy binding the phrases together."

"With a wooden clock?" Jack was trying to understand.

"With a friend." Emily stood, her chair scraping the tile floor as she hurried toward her desk and nearby computer. She turned back and faced the men, "I believe there was a real Astrid. A young woman nothing like her imposter. If I can find out who she was it may lead us to this fraud. And we now have a sample of the real Astrid's handwriting."

***

Brock woke up from a short nap on the Conner's sofa when the phone rang. Jack picked up and listened then grabbed a pad of paper and started writing furiously. Emily was still typing on the computer. Flashes popped up on the screen, she'd minimize a window and go to another, and another. Brock stared at his wrist-watch, barely an hour had passed.

"Let's go." Jack hung up the landline wall phone in its cra-dle. "There's been a fire in Homewood, suspected arson. Remote area. One dead male. The rental contract was signed by a woman who used an alias, an old woman." Jack pulled keys from his jeans pocket and brushed a thick cluster of dark hair peppered with sil-ver from his forehead. "It's someplace to start."

"Rachel mentioned that fire." Em called out. "Her hus-band's working it."

"Come on, Brock. You might be able to help. Just stay out of the way on the sidelines."

"What can I do?"

"You may recognize something. No one else spent as much time with her as you."

"It's all burned up."

Brock's voice drifted off. His ashen face bore the strain cancer was physically taking. His movements were slow as he rose to walk toward them. He stooped forward as if to straighten his stance was painful. The bones in his legs cracked and popped, and a low wince emitted from his pursed lips. Jack waited. Brock was not showing any signs of improvement. In fact, he seemed to be spiraling in the opposite direction as depression had set in over the past two days.

***

Brock sat motionless on the other side of the bench seat of Doc's truck. It had been a quiet ride so far and Jack wondered if it was wise to continue to let his passenger mope. The vehicle hit a pothole and the two men's heads jolted at near whiplash force before the ride smoothed out on newly paved asphalt.

"Sorry, I find it comforting to drive Dad's old Ford instead of my Jeep."

"I totally get it." Brock answered. "I wander in Asia's studio and hold her paintbrushes, run the bristles across my face. Sometimes I even sit in the chair in front of her easel and look out at what she used to see from the window over her workspace." He hesitated before speaking again and strummed his fingertips on the dashboard. "It's almost like she's still there. The palettes smeared with her mixtures of color. I open tubes and inhale, not like sniffing glue, just for that familiar smell I so took for granted. I envision her in there with the blank canvases. And I try to picture what she would have painted next."

An unnatural heat stifled inside the truck. The men rolled down their windows, cranking the metal handles in circles until a warm breeze blew in cooling the stagnant air. "This trusty old Ford has a certain smell too. Like Dad." Jack said. "It's okay for us to miss them."

"I think about Asia every minute of every day. I keep waiting for the ache to lessen. But it doesn't." Brock ran his hands over the baldness of his scalp. "I look like a different man than the one she married. The one she loved." His voice carried out the window on a gust of wind.

"Asia knew what the cancer meant. She told Em it killed her father." Jack shifted gears.

"She loved her father. Her step-father is a hard man. Not a warm person."

"Is he hard for you too?"

"I think her mom would step up to the plate as a grandma if he wasn't so distant and superficial. There's depth hidden in that woman. Like mother, like daughter."

"Maybe she'll come around for Benny's sake."

"They leave Reno tomorrow night for yet another vacation somewhere. When I told them told them that Benny's gone; Frank didn't show any emotion. They'll be gone for a couple of months. So, what's the point?" Brock slumped lower in the seat.

Jack rounded the Y in Tahoe City and turned left toward Homewood.

"Not a lot of traffic."

"Yeah, the off season works for me."

They lapsed into a pensive silence. Both preoccupied with their own thoughts. Jack was concerned the fire might be too much for Brock—seeing what destruction Astrid was capable of. Road construction was in full gear; laying pipes for winter drainage had been going on for a couple of years—ironic since there'd been little snowfall for snowmelt. The flagman waved them on, they were the last car in the line to go through before he held up the red stop sign.

"Asia would have painted Benny next." Brock stated with clear conviction. "Do humans look down from heaven like angels after they die? Do they have a spirit form instead of the body they leave behind?"

"I think she would have painted Benny too. If he'd sit still long enough. Maybe when he was sleeping." Jack drew in a deep breath before answering Brock's other question. "It's not like you see on TV shows and read in most books. No one knows for sure what heaven is going to be like. You're right, the body stays behind. Without the soul, it is an empty shell once the breath of life leaves."

"But what Asia believed, in an eternal soul, is true?" Brock trained his eyes on Jack.

"Yes."

"That's all I need to know. She lives."

***

The location of the burn was pretty remote, a long winding dirt road off Highway 28. They passed three new and expensive cabins before arriving at the charred site. You'd never guess a cabin used to be in that same spot. The truck had kicked up big dust clouds in the dirt, so Jack parked quite a distance away. They walked a good quarter of a mile to get to the yellow tape section where the police and investigators were sifting through the ashes.

Derrick called them over to the far side. A middle-age woman dressed in a lime green outdated polyester pantsuit and what looked to be shiny white vinyl ankle boots with black block heels stood next to him. The closer they got, the more she stood out like the J-ello molded salad that you bypass at the buffet table. Brock was certain her slightly askew platinum blonde hair and full bangs had to be a wig.

"Mrs. Quinton, this is Doctor Jack Conner and Mr. Brock Benton." Sheriff Thomas introduced them. The men shook her hand and she smiled; her lips slickered a thick glossy red.

"Just call me Flo. It's short for Florence." Her eyelashes batted like heavyweight boxers.

"Mrs. Quinton, can you please repeat what you told me about the recent tenants here for these gentlemen?"

"Well, it's like I said. The weasel of a guy, the short, thin man that was always with her, I had to yell across the way to him all the time because he would smoke out by the deck. He'd toss the butts in that coffee can over there." She pointed to a twisted piece of metal sitting on a large green trash bag. "If the SUV was gone and she'd left him alone, he'd smoked inside and never once came out until she returned. I just knew something like this was going to happen. He drank a lot of beer too. You can see the cans over there in the recycle container. Well, the plastic is kind of

melted over and molded. But the cans are in there just the same."
She bent down and cocked her head in a perplexed way fixated on
the blob of black that didn't resemble a recycle bin at all.

Brock watched her in a state of disbelief. Was she for real?
He moved closer to Jack.

"And the woman?" The sheriff encouraged her to continue
as he shot Jack a direct glance.

"She was a different story. I only saw her a few times other
than when she'd get in and out of the vehicle. They both came and
went a lot. But I never saw anyone else come here. No visitors.
The old woman stayed inside. One night not too long ago, strange
lights lit up the back deck and I saw two figures dancing. They
almost looked like ghosts. But that man was taller than the
woman." Her whole body shuddered before she finished talking.
"Loud music played every now and then. That same strange light
sometimes came from one of the upstairs bedrooms. It was bright
and supernatural in nature." Her tone lowered and she looked
nervously over her shoulder as if she'd said something she
shouldn't have.

"Thank you, Flo." Derrick tried to get the woman to look
at him. "Did you ever hear their names?"

"Oh, I heard her shriek his names many times. She yelled
at him often. She called him Deeddirt."

"Are you sure you heard correctly?'

"Deeddirt." She placed one hand on a hip and shot the
other hip out to the moon. "You have to ask yourself what kind of
a misguided mother would give a baby a name like that."

Derrick motioned Brock over to the outer line of the yellow tape that snaked around the entire foundation of the cabin and left Jack to fend for himself with Flo.

"This is all we have been able to pull from what used to be the kitchen cupboards. Can you look over to the right where I placed a few things for you to check? You'll notice I placed some items on the top of the table where we're still sorting and sifting through the ashes. Use these gloves but don't touch a thing. I'm just going for recognition here." Derrick said.

Brock immediately spied the familiar blue flower from where he stood, then another, and another. Some were just broken pieces, all were charred, but one was whole. He stepped back instead of forward. Those were Astrid's. She had been here and burned this place to the ground.

Chapter Forty
Fear

Horror is but a mere word, what it describes; the torture of mind and body, also impacts the soul. ~ Dr. Jack Conner quoting his father's journal.

The ride back to the Conner cabin was filled with anything but conversation. Jack sensed Brock's need to process the implications of the fire. Astrid was capable of anything. She had Benny and no one knew her true intentions. What did she plan to do next?

"We are doing our best to find him."

"I know. But will it be enough?" Brock continued staring out the passenger window.

Jack cleared his throat. "When Em and Olivia were taken back in 2008, Livie was six months pregnant. Forrester kidnapped her on a last minute whim. Em was his main target. I know these are different situations, but I've lived through similar fears that you're now fighting."

"Where is this loving, all powerful god my wife so believed in?" Brock's voice rose with bitter venom. "Benny's an innocent baby."

Jack clutched the steering wheel, his eyes trained on the road ahead. "I believe in what I cannot see, or hear, or touch. That is how I fought my way through the last time."

"You talk like it is some kind of a battle in a war." Brock raged, his arms up in the air.

"Because it is, all-out-war." Jack knew he was taking a risk, and a big one. That Brock might completely pull away from everyone that believed in the power of an unseen God. "You are up against pure evil; do you believe that?"

"I think that old woman I trusted, let into my home, let hold and rock my son to sleep, is the devil incarnate." Brock's body stiffened and his words snarled out sounding less than human.

A big rig sped past them in the opposite lane followed by a string of construction trucks that rattled the asphalt under Doc's old truck. They had to be going twenty miles over the speed limit. The roar drowned out Brock's angry outburst but did not lighten his stone-faced glare.

"Try to focus on what we can do." Jack slowed to a complete stop after a flagman held up one hand and waved a stop sign side to side. He stepped in front of the mounting line of traffic. A long snaking lane of oncoming vehicles slowed down until they were bumper to bumper. The forest on both sides of the highway was hemmed in by construction products and giant pipes stored along the shoulder of the road. Drivers were frustrated and short-tempered, honking horns and yelling profanities through open car windows at the Transit workers.

"You have every right to be angry. At Astrid, at God. But what purpose will that serve?" Jack turned to engage Brock.

"I don't really care right now."

"You need to care. It can make a big difference. Any small thing you remember, something that you might not even consider significant, can help recover your son."

"It's my fault if they can't find him." Brock's demeanor altered with that admission.

"This is not your fault." Jack shook Brock's shoulder. "She's been drugging you for weeks, months. Trying to cloud your thinking while she gained your trust. You are just as much a victim of her trickery. But, you can fight back for both of you."

"How?" Sobs jerked Brock's torso, the harder he tried to suppress them, the more he trembled. "That wicked witch burned that pitiful little man to death. What will she do to my Benny?"

"Concentrate on what we can do to help catch her. Right now, she is protecting your son to accomplish whatever she wants him for. She will not hurt him."

"What is there other than an illegal adoption? I'll never find him without the adoptive parents allowing contact conditions." Brock beat on the dashboard like a drum. "I don't believe like you. I have no faith like Asia did. And look where her faith got her—dead."

His voice droned off like a dying motor. The cycle of fear had set in and begun its overwhelming, destructive work. Brock had already given up. He reached for the door handle.

"Where will you go?" Jack asked without trying to stop him.

Brock flung the heavy metal door out into the brush of trees along the roadside and turned to get out. "Anywhere but here, he lunged, one shoe out, and unbuckled his seatbelt.

"I'll drop you off at your home. You can deal with the sheriff instead of me."

Brock froze, one leg in the car and one leg out, his tall body scrunched to the passenger side of the vehicle. He wanted to run for the hills and keep running. But Benny's face kept flashing in his mind—his silly grin when a bottle got within range and his chubby arms and hands reaching for it, his sleeping cherub face next to him on the bed, and the curious look when Brock cried, like Benny knew he was sad, like he cared.

"I have tried to think of anything that can help. I've got nothing."

Horns honked. The cars were beginning to move by inches.

"Derrick is the sheriff that got shot protecting Emily. He helped bring her home to me. I do know how you feel. Let us help you." Jack's arm stretched across the top of the bench seat.

Brock's head flopped downward and he squeezed the bench seat under his hands. With pleading eyes, he glanced up. With a measured shove, he pulled his leg in and drew the door close until he gave it a sharp tug and shut it behind him.

Jack waited while Brock buckled up, then began moving with the molasses flow of traffic. After a few minutes they were up to the posted speed limit of thirty-five. "I know the black hole widening inside you right now. It seems bottomless, but I tell you. It is not the end."

"How can you believe? A second time?"

"Because I have seen victory. Even from the pit of hell. There is more, Brock. That much I know for certain. The muck and mire of the middle is not the end of it all. Neither is a burned up building."

Brock wanted to trust Jack, to believe like he did. But he didn't. First he lost Asia. Then he lost himself. Now he'd lost Benny. He listened to the low rumble of Doc's truck that had out-lived him. Sturdy heavy metal sat on thick tread tires spinning circles over a new road that was full of cracks and potholes on one side, yet smoothly paved on the other. Freshly painted double yellow lines separated the two lane highway. A giant roller vehicle was headed their way to go over the particles one more time, to flatten, condense, press until the road was usable for all. Brock thought about throwing himself under it. Then he thought about the guy driving it and how he would feel about squashing the life out of a person he didn't even know. How unfair that would be to do to someone? It wasn't any different that Astrid burning her ex-partner to death. He probably didn't have a say in that decision either. He wondered if these similar thoughts had run through Jack's mind back in 2008.

"I got desperate." Jack answered as if he'd read Brock's thoughts. "I had let down two people that I loved."

Shame outlined Brock's face, flushed his skin a crimson heat. Jack didn't have to take his eyes off the road to see it. He knew. "You have just made it over a major hurdle. The war is still raging, but you have come through the first battle. She did not defeat you. She defeated Detert."

Jack gauged with great care what he would say next. "Do you believe in demons?"

"You mean the devil?"

"I mean demons, plural."

Brock squirmed and tried to find a comfortable position on the worn seat. He'd been thinking witch, but not about the devil until the fire. Then he saw the covered burnt corpse in what used to be a recliner, all melted into one horrific heap of smoldering ash. Astrid had changed from an attentive, harmless elderly babysitter, cook, and house cleaner into a what?

"If you believe in good and a heaven for Asia, there has to be an opposite dwelling place where evil lives and prevails. God has angels and the devil has his own evil minions; a fallen third of former celestial beings. I would not lie to you." Jack spoke with an air of authority.

"It all seems impossible."

"You need to know the enemy you are up against. This is a spiritual battle."

"How can we fight demons?"

"With spiritual weapons." Jack could hear the intensity of interest in Brock's voice.

"But Astrid is human, like you and me."

"That's right, but we choose to either follow God and truth into battle, or to follow demons and lies. Astrid has chosen the losing side. I believe that with all that I am."

"I don't know, Jack. I just want my son." Brock backed himself next to the door.

"There are already warriors praying for your son; at Asia's church, at Emily and my church, Pastor Fred's church where Doc used to go. Doc prayed protection for your son before he died. Just because Astrid took Benny, does not mean those prayers are not answered. Remember what Fred said at dad's service? 'Every prayer he prayed is deathless. The prayers live on.' It does not mean an absence of battles. It means we are not alone in the midst of them."

"This is just a lot to take in." Brock moved closer to Jack and stated, "But I do believe I have just seen the result of evil. And I did not recognize it at first because it had the outer appearance of good. I saw what I wanted to see because I needed help."

"Deception is usually very subtle. Astrid played all of us."

Jack's cell rang. Brock picked it up off the seat and glanced at the caller's name. "It's Emily."

"Can you answer it for me?"

"Emily, Jack's driving. It's Brock." He listened until she hung up. "Hurry home. Emily found news about the real Astrid online and some woman at Vikingsholm found books in the library she signed. Derrick put out an APB and got a hit in Carson City. Someone saw her, with a baby."

Chapter Forty-One
Found

Books tell much about a person. The story within the pages opens wide the readers imagination and leads them to new worlds and adventures. How dull the world would be without the words recorded and thoughts unleashed. ~ Inscription in a book published in 1913 and donated to Lora Knight's library at Vikingsholm by Astrid Annalisa Hughes in 1939.

Emily was almost giddy when they walked in the door. She ran and hugged Jack first, and Brock second. She gushed forth with such exuberance that neither of the men could make out a word she was saying. Waving computer print-outs in their faces like newspaper headlines fresh off the printing press. Her desk was a wild mass of scattered papers, yet she foraged through the pile, and pulled more pages and a file folder filled with still more paper.

"I found her! There was a real Astrid!"

"Was? Past tense?" Jack asked glancing at Brock who did not share Emily's celebratory attitude. He sat sullen at the kitchen table.

She plopped the file in front of Brock. "Good news. This imposter tried to pattern herself after a very real and wonderful person. They had to have met at some point and talked about their lives. I am working on that now and I think I'm right there."

"Where?" Brock leafed through the pages.

"England. Astrid was last known to follow her father, William Hughes, to England before America formally declared war in WWII. He was an officer, a pilot that flew with the RAF in the Battle of Britain. Well, one of the unofficial listed as others, with the registered eleven American pilots that flew before we sent troops over."

"Rachel did some checking after I left Vikingsholm and found a people on the south shore that knew the Hughes family that used to visit Lora Knight. The grandmother remembers Astrid well. They knew each other. Astrid read to her and many other children when the Hughes visited from Michigan. Nine years total. One year, 1939 to be exact, the father got a telegram and left in haste the next morning. The mother and daughter followed the next day. And Jack, she read to the children in a forest clearing. *Return my forest.* I get it now. It was a promise to return to Vikingsholm one day. But she never did."

"Slow down, Em. How does this help find Benny?" Jack took the pages she handed him to look through.

"Astrid was real. The imposter met her in England. I am this close to finding her true identity. That's how." Emily flung her arms up in the air. "Why did I drop all this before? I thought I was losing my mind even though I was so suspicious of her. I figured it was my head trauma. You know, my memory loss, confusion, headaches. But I was right from the start." She collapsed in the chair next to Brock.

"This is pretty amazing stuff. She left to volunteer at the hospitals in London and the surrounding villages. The Hughes family had relatives all over England in London, Cornwall, Norwich. No wonder they went." Jack said.

"What about the mother?" Brock asked.

"She remarried in the 1950's and moved to Maryland after neither her husband nor her daughter ever returned. He was killed on a mission over London, his plane exploded in the sky, no remains were found. Astrid filled in wherever needed in hospitals. After a major blitzkrieg over London, she's never mentioned again. No death recorded, no body."

"How convenient for Astrid Smith. She just stepped right into Astrid Hughes' life and added a supposed married name that's practically untraceable." Jack huffed.

"The Hughes family were close personal friends with the Stoddards in Cornwall. This lady on the south shore says she has letters postmarked London from a flat the Stoddard family rented to Astrid. She lived there and helped the British nurses in overflow makeshift triage-type locations when the bombing was really bad."

"Doc suggested I ask Astrid is she had any children because she was so interested in Benny. She told me she'd given up a baby boy for adoption because she'd never married. What a liar! Do you think the woman who took my son was one of the Stoddards?" Brock spoke up.

"I do. And I'm working on a first name. There's a young woman mentioned in these letters, but she is a decade younger than Astrid who was in her twenties.'

"That makes sense. All of us felt the imposter had to be younger. A decade seems about right." Jack nodded.

"Well, if it's her, her real name is Mildred Ethel Stoddard. Astrid referred to her as Mildy in a few of the letters. They shared the flat for a short time before the other young woman went back home. Nursing was not her interest after all. She studied herbs and flowers."

Jack and Brock looked at each other at the same time. "It sure fits. Her use of poisons to hinder thinking capabilities." Jack responded.

"The letters are ours if we need them. The woman would like them back later. Rachel recognized the handwriting from the note left with Selma. She's actually seen these letters before but, who knew? That's when she remembered books that had been donated to Lora Knight's library in appreciation for the invitations to stay at Vikingsholm."

"Is there anything in the imposter's handwriting?" Brock scratched his head.

Jack and Emily shrugged. "None of us ever thought to get her car license number. We never grasped the entirety of her ill intentions." Jack admitted.

"What about this APB in Carson City, Em?" Brock pressed.

"Derrick is going to call your cell after he follows up on it. He couldn't get through to you when you were at Homewood. So, he called me. A text message should pop up on your phone any-time now with more information."

"This Mildred, she's a piece of work. One letter says she black marketed ration cards for profit and stole drugs from the family business. Pretty despicable to pirate medications from wounded soldiers during a war." Emily read from her notes.

"Mildred has to be our Astrid Smith." Jack voiced a new confidence and hope.

Brock grew quiet listening instead of joining the excitement. He closed the file and handed it back to Emily. "What could she possibly have planned for a baby? If she isn't adopting Benny out, do you think she might black market him?"

Chapter Forty-Two

Time

The ticking of clocks, the opening of locks, oh keepers of time, will it all unwind? Who frames the lives of men, says how and when? Who rules supreme, this unseen immortal Being? If thou art God, and saved not thine own son, I pray thee, why hast thou shown thy favor to me? ~ Old hymn Brock found at Asia's church while searching for the book.

Brock's words left all in the room stunned. The tick-tock of the clock on the mantle counted seconds of time like a heavy breath exhaled. It hung in the air dressed in all the implications of thoughts that had not yet been voiced. But, there it was.

"Don't tell me you haven't wondered too." Brock stuttered.

"I didn't want to worry you." Emily admitted.

"There's a big difference between a mixed-race couple in Reno legally adopting my son in an open adoption with visitation rights, and child trafficking." Brock blurted out and stood, his chair falling backward to the floor. "Be honest, Jack, this might have been her intention from the start."

"You could very well be right."

"This Mildred." He spit out her name. "She sold ration cards and drugs during World War II." Brock raised and crossed his arms over his head, cupping his scalp. "She'll sell Benny to anyone, to whoever bids the highest." He bowed forward, doubled over, head bobbing. "Oh God, oh God."

"Whatever she's planned, she'll be taking care of him until you get him back." Jack stood, a hand on Brock's back. "To her Benny is an asset, and she will protect him at all cost."

"Bartering for human flesh is evil!" Brock's arms rocketed up like a ship launching into space.

"If we think like her, we can anticipate her next moves. That is how we closed in on Forrester. That and a lot of prayers." Jack stayed beside Brock, waiting. "It's spiritual warfare."

"I will take any help I can get. This Mildred scares me. She's been doing this a long time. We're up against a pro."

"Okay then, let's brainstorm." Jack pulled back a chair for Emily. "Do you mind if Emily and I pray first?"

"No." Brock sat in the chair at the head of the table. He watched Jack and Emily take each other's hands. They wove their fingers together and closed their eyes. Jack started talking first in a soft, low tone. Emily nodded her head as if in agreement and would add words every now and then. It wasn't anything showy or spectacular like those TV evangelists he'd seen at revivals his mom dragged him and his sisters to for a couple of years. Big circus tents packed full of shouting half-crazed zealots of all shapes and sizes that scared him. This was intimate, like they became one person with another unseen spiritual being Brock couldn't see or hear. He felt a presence, a peaceful sheltering cover of safety. Basically, all they were asking for was, help. Protection for Benny. Brock had come upon Asia like this a few times, but she was on her knees at their bedside. She'd known this same presence, and she'd trusted whoever it was right up to her last breath. There hadn't been any fear on her face.

"Alright, Brock. What do you think she'll do next?" Jack opened his eyes.

"She'll try to leave town."

"I think you're right," Jack agreed. "Where to?"

"As far away as she can get." Brock braced his forehead with a hand, elbow on the table. "A drop off point—pick up point."

"Do you think she'll try to flee the country? Maybe head back to England?"

"She has no reason to stay here and risk getting caught." Emily added.

"Derrick has posters with an artist's depiction of her at all the bus stations, airports, and taxi hubs. She won't try to drive cross-country with a four-month-old in a car seat. Too confining for her."

"An old lady with a baby is pretty noticeable. They'll stick out." Brock decided.

"Astrid will make sure they aren't conspicuous, hang out in big crowds, near casinos?"

"Carson City isn't big. Did you check your text messages?"

Brock checked his cell. "It just says—they were here yesterday. Caught on a hidden camera in a grocery store. No license plate, no vehicle, no hotel."

"It's a starting place. She didn't fly directly out. Why?"

"Maybe she has loose ends to tie up?" Brock laughed. "Benny will slow her down for sure. She wasn't what I'd call baby smart, but she thought she was."

"My guess would be she is not maternal by nature." Emily added.

"Good point. Slowed down by her lack of experience of being alone full time with an infant that cries when you want him to be quiet, needs regular diaper changes, and bottle fed on demand." Jack agreed.

"Not this Astrid or Mildred's lifelong MO. This will work against her at every turn." Brock seemed to believe his words with more conviction.

"I texted all the imposter info I could to Derrick. He knows the Stoddard family name and locations in England, and Astrid's real name." Emily offered more assurance.

Brock glanced at his watch. "It's four p.m. Time for Benny's dinner. Astrid and I butted heads over this. She'd try to stretch it out. She had this thing about supper at 5 pm. Table set all formal and everyone eating together."

"And there you go, Brock. One of her quirks that is sure to throw this escapade off kilter. Benny's sure to demand his supper on time. Babies have built-in alarm clocks." Emily said.

***

The hotel room was stuffy and smelled of the last two runny diapers. A bellhop came to the door again to carry off the soiled clothes and disposable diapers in another triple layers of garbage bag. The old woman held the trash out and offered no tip for the young man's efforts. "Grandma, maybe you need to get the parents to take the next shift." He laughed and exited from the persistent cry of a howling infant he could still hear after she slammed the door.

"Benjamin, I said enough. It's not time for supper yet." She cradled a box of hair dye in one hand as she clenched a fist. "I have just enough time to let this process and shower it off before we eat. You lay there and play with your teddy bear and toys." She opened the bathroom door without looking back and flipped on a fan that started to whirl. The baby cried even louder.

The chubby infant sucked his thumb instead of the pacifier that had been in his mouth. Saucer brown eyes held pooled tears of displeasure while gripping a blanket imprinted with rows of basketballs on one side and a soft flannel plaid on the other. A fat brown fuzzy bear lie next to the baby's side. With concentrated effort the little one strained until his head rested on the soft belly fabric of the stuffed animal. A wide-mouth yawn ended the twenty minute long tirade with a few whimpers until tired eyelids closed and sleep brought needed rest. The baby was but a diminutive figure in the center of a massive king size bed.

A car seat and overstuffed diaper bag sat near the hotel door next to a black leather valise containing a pile of one hundred dollar bills tucked in a side pocket with maps of Europe—Italy, France and Spain, poking out. Two online plane tickets were folded in half with the money. A plastic major brand store bag and cardboard box took up space in the forefront of the cluster with two pieces of carry-on size Samsonite luggage, and a set of keys dangling from the locks.

The open double doors of an oversized whitewashed armoire exposed a flat screen TV with a Blue Ray disc playing, the volume blaring. Closed caption wording ran across the bottom of the set ~ *Un bicchiere di vino rosso, per favore* ~ *A glass of red wine, please.* Rolling hillsides of vineyards laden with grapes bursting to be picked filled the 42 inch screen with a new vineyard photograph accompanying every new Italian phrase ~ *ripeti dopo di me* ~ repeat after me.

Several items overflowed a woven trash basket in a far corner of the room; a navy blue sleeper, white t-shirts, and tiny basketball baby sneakers topped off the pile. All the custom drapes were drawn. No light illuminated the room except a thin stream filtering in from a large window above where the baby slept. It cast a pathway glow angled up to the sky outside. A half-luminous, half-shadowy mask divided Benny's face.

***

Derrick dug through the garbage in the bathroom at a gas station where footage showed an old woman with an infant on her hip entering the restroom. The proprietor had called in when he saw her sketch on the evening news. Even with the ball cap bill lowered over her forehead, he'd recognized Astrid. A taxi waited at the pump until she returned.

Other than a couple of disposable diapers and wipes, nothing unusual caught the sheriff's attention until he stepped back outside and closed the door near slivers of broken glass. Flecks of gold metal glinting in the late afternoon sunlight reflected off the clear shards on the ground. He slipped on a Latex glove from his pocket, stooped over and picked up what appeared to be a broken charm like the ones his wife collected for her bracelet. Sure enough, the loop was severed but the charm remained intact. It was an odd shape not familiar to him; a dragons head and body with a triple-forked tail of flaming fire. It was expensive gold with possible diamond chips for the eyes.

He pulled a small plastic baggie from the same pocket, took a picture, and sealed the item inside. After a careful check for anything else, he got in his patrol car, recorded a message on his cell, then texted an update to Brock—found a charm that may have at least a partial print.

The information from the husband and wife that owned the Carson Station was far more valuable. They could ID Astrid and Benny. She'd panicked and asked for their help when the baby hyperventilated after she'd waited too long to give him his bottle. "That old woman knows nothing about babies." The proud grandmother of eight complained. "Poor little fellow. He just wanted dinner and she kept telling him it wasn't time yet. Babies don't stick to schedules when you're on the road." She'd huffed as her husband nodded in agreement. *Good thing.* Derrick thought, or she'd have slipped out of here and we'd never known. When they saw her on the news, they called in immediately. "Didn't like that one much." Old Russ had grumbled and snapped his suspenders on his chest. "She's a mean cuss."

Derrick figured Astrid intended to sell the baby and ordered alerts at the airports. She'd make her move soon. There were flights out tomorrow to states where she could connect to the east coast and head overseas. He'd zeroed in on the Reno airport. But he did not expect an obvious departure and thought she might cause a distraction to divert attention elsewhere. Jack was certain this woman was capable of anything. This had an all too familiar feel to it.

Derrick pulled over, stopped the car, and called his wife.

"Hello?"

"Hi, Honey. Do you have a free minute?"

"I can take a break. What's up?"

"I'm going to send you a cell pic of a charm I just found. If you recognize it or know what it signifies, can you get right back to me?"

"Sure."

Derrick sent it off and got ready to pull out when his cell beeped.

"Helen."

"Where did you get this Derrick? I don't wear demonic charms." His wife sounded upset.

"This is from the case I'm working."

"Babe, this is a demon charm, symbolic for the devil himself. That three flame tail is counter to the Father, Son, and Holy Ghost. This demon is supposed to devour the Trinity."

Part Five
Hope

Chapter Forty-Three
Family

Asia's profile was immensely pregnant. Benny was full term and only days from being born, three days to be exact. Brock towered beside her and they both cupped hands around their son. He lowered his skyscraper physique before she took the selfie, so that his head was just above hers. It was their only family portrait. ~ Framed picture Brock fell asleep holding.

Brock's head was about to burst from the facts and unwanted knowledge about the real person who had kidnapped his son. He'd begged off sleeping in one of the Conner's guest rooms and headed home for the comfort of his own bed. Once there he immediately regretted his decision.

Everything reminded him of Asia and Benny. He wandered into the nursery to try to find something that smelled like his son and rifled through the laundry hamper until he found hooded jammies that made Benny look like a bear cub. Inhaling deeply, he absorbed the mixture of baby bath lotions and his son's scent he'd grown to love. Ben's personal signature. The soft terry cloth ears folded between his fingers and thumb. *Remember to suck*

281

your thumb for comfort little bear. The mental image of Ben with Astrid or Mildred or whoever she was, incited a deep brooding anger that began to fester.

Brock walked over to the rocking chair, grabbed the crib quilt the church ladies had given Asia at her baby shower, wrapped himself inside it, and rocked. He turned on the windowsill iPod and listened to the music Emily had recorded for him from the CD after Doc's memorial. He clicked over until the song he wanted, *Out of the Mouths of Children*, played. Each song played through. The voices of the children spoke to his soul, to the hurting place he bared to no one. He held onto Ben's sleepers in his lap.

The creak of the antique wood swayed with the rhythm of his movement. Asia's forest murals surrounded him with all the woodland animals she so loved at the lake. Brock continued rocking, taking a closer look around the room. He noticed for the first time the innocence she'd painted on each face. A wide-eyed bear family of four struck him most. Only the papa bear had a reddish hint to his fur. The mama bear was not much bigger than the two cubs, one cub had a pink bow tucked close to an ear. A sudden awareness sunk in—she'd wanted more children.

Brock heaved in sorrow and folded in half. His cries echoed in the empty room. The music had stopped. His size 15 shoes didn't match the habitat of the fantasy forest on the walls or child-sized furniture in the room. He seemed a giant visitor from a neighboring kingdom that didn't fit in this magical world with raccoons playing saxophones, and pine tree houses he was too big to climb. In one corner there was a strange creature he'd not noticed before. At the top of the mountain range behind Lake Tahoe. What was that? He rose and walked over to get a better look. It was actually two creatures laying with their front legs overlapping. A lion and a lamb.

Asia had painted two worlds. He examined the few clouds in the blue sky. The formations were spirits with wings, just outlines, but he was certain of what he now saw. Some held musical instruments, some were open-mouthed in song, and all were facing the same sun. In the center of the round ball of fire a cross stood weightless and rays of light streamed out from that central point to the entire room. He ran his hand along all four walls then stretched to touch the ceiling. There were wisps of yellow sunlight blended with faint hues of orange and red. His fingers followed the thin lines out the window ledges and on the doorframe to the hallway.

Asia told another story on the mountaintops and in the varying shades of blue in the lake. When Brock got to the middle of the water the word *Holy* was present in the sapphire swirls and teal strokes. He spun in a circle, eyes comprehending the revelation of layer upon layer of paint. How had he missed it all before? The imagery was crystal clear. The creatures were worshipping the sun, raising arms, singing, and dancing in celebration. Granite boulders were engraved with the words—love, hope, peace, and joy, but to a blind eye, there was nothing but stone.

Brock collapsed on the carpet and bent over, hands covering his face. The rise and fall of his body releasing pent up anger and frustration. He was physically spent. How she'd longed to share all this with him. She'd painted the language of love for her son—a living picture that traveled in timelessness to another haven where he hoped she now lived. Eternity. Did it begin here on earth? Asia had painted it all reflecting back to the cross in the center of the sun. And in that center, tiny letters spelled out, the way, the truth, the life, across the horizontal beam.

Brock turned to see what the Benny bear was doing. The little cub stood on his hind legs, his front paws reaching up to the sky, his eyes directly on the sun. He stood on his own with huge brown knowing eyes. He was a strong little bear.

As he left the room, Brock picked up a picture framed in smooth pine from Benny's dresser that stood by the door. He gazed at the 8" by 10" photograph and remembered the day it was taken.

It had been one of those bad-from-start-to-finish days you'd like to forget. Had he known then is was to be one of his last days with his wife, Brock would have behaved differently. Asia wanted a picture of them with the baby before he was born. His hours had been cut in half that day at work with no warning. He came home early, in shock, not in the mood for a photoshoot. On the way home his ATM card had been denied at the grocery store when he stopped for a twelve pack of beer and a frozen pizza. At least the pizza went through after the clerk took the beer off. The red reserve gas light lit up on the dashboard as he pulled into the driveway. Tourists had parked in his assigned slot, so he had to back out, and park along the shoulder of the highway. When he grabbed the mail, it was all overdue bills which they had no money to pay.

A perky Asia greeted him at the door all dressed up and ready for a photo shoot. She was persistent and he'd snapped at her. He wanted a couple of beers to take off the edge. She baked the pizza and found a tall can of beer in the back of the fridge for him. He popped the tab and guzzled it down. At least is was cold.

Asia had just finished painting the nursery and wanted to show him. She was excited to take pictures in there as a kind of christening. Brock hid her Nikon camera; just a friendly game of hide-and-seek. He thought it was hysterical. Asia did not. She offered to massage his shoulders when he sat in his recliner. They talked about the possibility of cancer. He shared little with her not wanting her to know how scared he was. Terrified.

Finally, Brock begrudgingly followed her into the nursery and was quite amazed when he saw the murals. He told her so too. When he moved in for a kiss, she was ready with her cell phone. He playfully obliged. He still needed some down time before he had to show up for split shifts the next two days at work. The following day he had a cancer screening appointment with Dr. Conner. He smiled at the picture. She glowed. So full of life that he'd watch drain from her as she gave birth to Benny. The last light he remembered in her eyes was when she first saw the baby and reached out to touch him.

Benny was the desire of her heart. At first Brock had been jealous that she looked to her son, and not to him before she left. Things changed so fast. All their preparations from classes for a natural delivery, disappeared. By the time he realized they were in trouble, it was too late.

Brock curled up in the quilt on top of the comforter and set the picture across from him on the other side of the mattress. His eyelids grew heavy. But his mind was clearer. This was a battle like Jack said. Now he knew where to go for the help he needed.

Chapter Forty-Four
Looking Through the Hourglass

Are the instants, periods, and decades of time encapsulated or they overlapping around us? Can we actually feel time move in and through us? If every second is calculated, is it possible to stop the clock to change the order of events? ~ Questions Brock peppered at Asia's pastor.

The lightness of Asia's laughter floated in the air like a refrain of musical notes that echoed in Brock's dreams. They were dancing in the kitchen and she told him she was pregnant. His long red hair draped across her shoulders like a protective cloak. Strength rippled through his veins and a surge of energy pulsated through his limbs. She was beautiful, the curve and angle of her face enraptured his thoughts as he lifted her in his arms. He tried to hold onto her image, capture the measure of the moment framed in his memory. But it slipped away. For the first time he didn't feel the burden that usually remained.

He called out for Benny.

There was no answer.

A heavy sleep came, he succumbed, surrendering to the much needed rest.

***

Officer Thomas sat at his desk surfing the web checking out the latest information Emily had forwarded to him. This breakthrough in the case offered hope as minutes ticked into hours. Time was on Astrid or Mildred's side, not theirs. But his gut instinct told him that was about to change.

Derrick reread the letters the woman on the south shore had handed over for the investigation. He regarded them as actual historical records—documentation of proof from another era that connected two women with polar opposite personalities. The Stoddard family seemed to have been honorably rooted through the parent's hard work in building up the chemist business, but their three children appeared to have systematically torn it all down to the ground.

The oldest daughter, Mildred was a proven scam artist that mentored her younger sister Agatha as her personal protégée. Their brother Leonard, previously involved in petty local crimes, had escalated to the heightened level of activity that the sisters pursued internationally. All three had ventured across the pond to America in recent years. No arrests thus far, but their names and fingerprints were popping up across the states during and after several unsolved criminal investigations. One hit after another came up after entering the set of prints from the wine bottle Brock had provided.

Derrick suspected Mildred had begun dabbling in an international ring of infant trafficking for wealthy clients with no concern for the validity of legal adoptions. But where was Benny headed? To what continent? In a recent case, the couple had flown in on their private jet to pick up the baby. If that was the situation here, the chances of finding Benny just decreased by half. He tried to focus on other possibilities. The Stoddard siblings had a pattern. Had this imposter Astrid stepped outside those perimeters to take Benny when the opportunity presented itself after his mother's death? If so, there was a better chance of her making a mistake.

A cell phone on the officer's desk vibrated across the hard oak surface. "Hello?"

"Derrick Thomas?" A croaky voice inquired. "This is Brock Benton. I need some answers."

"Okay. What do you want to know?"

A silent pause was followed by a hesitant plea. "Do you think my son is still alive?"

"Yes, I do."

"I want to help find him. Like Jack said, I know this Astrid better than anyone, and I remembered something."

"What?" Derrick picked up a pen and notepad off a stack of papers.

"She was fascinated with a photograph in Benny's nursery, a picture of my wife and I three days before our son was born. Last night I was looking at it and noticed the back had been pried open. It looks like the picture was removed and later replaced. Do you think she would have a reason to show the picture?"

"Please don't touch anything. I'll be right there to pick it up. We'll put the pic on the afternoon and evening news." The officer rose and grabbed his gun. "On my way." He shoved the cell in his shirt pocket after calling the lab technicians to meet him at Brock's address. *She blew it. I knew she'd screw up.* He headed out, his right leg hitching from a slight limp as he ran to his car.

***

"Everything's sorted. I've booked the Villa Le Scale in Capri overlooking the Amalfi Coast. It has seven bedrooms. They'll meet us there. Lenny's flying them in from Hong Kong." A hint of a British accent filtered through the cell as a woman continued speaking. "Give you a bell tonight. Don't be late."

"Sod off."

"Act Toff, nothing dodgy." Astrid clicked off and checked her hair in the lobby mirror. A bit too brunette for her taste but it was temporary. A day spa treatment awaited her in the next forty-eight hours. She was ready to be pampered, every pore in her body screamed for more than the maintenance she'd been enduring. A reservation for complete head to toe indulgent make-over was in the computer just awaiting her scheduled arrival.

With precise timing Astrid maneuvered the elevator ride up to the fifth floor room. Careful not to be too chatty, she politely acknowledged the uniformed operator and the young couple standing beside her. Nothing to draw unwanted attention. She exited to room 523 at the end of a wide hallway, her pump heels pressing into the high pile of the maroon floral print carpeting. Her card key signaled a green light to beep, and she opened the door, but left it ajar.

Inside the infant slept in the middle of a king-size bed bordered with pillows surrounding the peaceful form curled up in a footed sleeper. A sweet smell saturated the room like fresh bloomed lilacs. Astrid called for room service and ordered. "A fresh fruit salad with proper condiments for scones, and a bottle of chilled champagne, please. No thank you, just scones, no complimentary breads, pastries or desserts."

After slipping out of her shoes and reclining in a plush eggshell upholstered chaise, Astrid glanced over at the baby. She checked her watch, adjusting the diamond-studded band until the clock face was centered on her wrist.

A pleasant thought crossed Astrid's mind. Something she hadn't dare to consider before. This had been easy enough. Higher stakes, higher profit margin. Perhaps they should break in the east coast next time. Would her siblings object to hastening the mothers' exits from this world for the prime-priced orders? Asia's untimely departure could be the springboard of a new career. A low rap at the door interrupted her planning. "Please, do come in. I left the door open."

A cart pushed by a slender dark-haired, clean-cut young man rolled in almost silent over the thick rug. He parked the two-tiered silver butler right up to the side of the lounge chair. "Shall I open the champagne for you, Ma'am?"

Her leisurely grin disappeared, a deep scowl creased her forehead, and her thin lips pressed tight, so tight the steward stepped aside to wait for instruction.

"Do not, call me, Ma'am." She forced a faux smile. "Just leave the cart." She shooed him off with a wave of her hand and without a tip. "Close the door behind you. Only old women are called, she drew out the word in a mocking tone—Ma'am." She flung her silky chestnut hair over a shoulder. "The nerve of that chap."

Leaning forward she pulled the dome lid off the tray to inspect her brunch. A delectable array of berries and melons filled a crystal dish in an eye-pleasing artful array. A matching divided bowl with clotted cream and a lovely lemon curd rested beside a plate of scones.

"Home." She mused and unfolded the cloth napkin before replacing the cover and taking a fluted Waterford glass to raise. "Cheers, my multi-million dollar baby." I have a few surprises for you. Yes, I do." She popped the cork off the champagne bottle with little effort.

The baby stirred on the comforter and turned to the side. A little pink satin bow was Velcro-stripped on her brown hair. Her wide brown eyes opened and blinked. Deep dimples in her cheeks puckered as she rose her head and looked around the room.

"Cheers, my little Beatrice. Awake from your kip? Ready to join the party?" Astrid rose to get a baby bottle from the mini refrigerator and set it to warm up in the bathroom sink under a steady stream of hot water from the faucet. "My drink is more festive than yours but there is an age requirement and for once, older is more desirable." She poured herself a glass brimming with ice cold champagne, tilted her head back, and downed the bubbly before coming up for air. Her iridescent taffeta dress clung to her boney hips and hung mid-calf length. A row of tiny pearl buttons ran up to the scoop neckline trimmed with an over-stated collar.

Loose flesh jiggled on her upper arms where the tapered sleeves pinched at a single dart line. She tugged at the gold buckle on the thin waist belt sewn in matching fabric.

"There now, your drink should be just about the right temperature." Astrid set her empty crystal flute on the edge of the black granite counter, turned off the water, and fanned through the steam with her hand. The double mirrors fogged over. She tugged a towel off a rack and wrapped the plastic bottle in the thick white cotton. After turning her wrist upward, she squirted formula from the nipple on her bare wrinkly skin. "Not too hot, and not too cold. Perfect." With a sense of bravado, she walked the liquid lunch over to the baby. Big brown eyes fixed in on the nipple sticking out the top of the towel. The baby reached out to Astrid to be picked up, but she simply rolled the baby on her side against one of the fat pillow shams and propped the bottle in her open mouth. She braced another pillow closer to support the bottle, so it wouldn't roll away.

"I would hold you, but then I couldn't enjoy my drink." After retrieving her glass, Astrid filled it and sat across from the bed, watching the baby. "Slow down a bit, you'll get a tummy ache guzzling it so fast. We have to finish packing. Our extended check out time is in just two hours. You drain that special drink, so you'll sleep on the plane. Auntie gave you a little something extra to help you relax. No stress on this cross-country flight. Then we have a big— she stretched her arms apart—wide ocean to cross in a Lear Jet being sent just for us. Cheers, little princess." Astrid held her glass high and forward before taking a few sips, then swallowed the rest. "Maybe you have the right idea after all." She winked.

A loud belch sounded out, then another as the empty bottle fell to the side of the outer pillow. "Absobloodylootely! Better to burp so you don't get sick, then I'll have to change your nappy and you wouldn't want to soil auntie's pretty frock."

The baby lie quiet on the bed gazing around the room focusing where light brightened areas near open windows, and sheers billowed in a calming breeze like the fluttering wings of an angelic visitor. The see-through panels flowed inward until the hem of the curtain landed on the mattress. The delighted infant raised arms and legs in motion, emitting a succession of pleased coos directed at the open space above the bed.

Astrid eyed the scene with suspicion, moving in to take a closer look. A stronger wind blew in the nearer she drew to the baby. The sheers settled back, still against the window as the blustery circulation of air seemed to encircle the large bed. With an increased enthusiasm the baby girl stretched her pudgy fingers toward the ceiling in what appeared to be an effort to touch some invisible delight.

In a huff Astrid turned and slammed the windows shut one after the other to eliminate the disturbance, then stood in the center of the room waiting. The breeze was subdued. With renewed confidence she returned bedside to address the gleeful infant. A flurry of sweet lilac rippled in the air. She glanced at her watch. "Beatrice, time for a nappy change." A small stack of diapers sat on the nightstand next to a container of disposable wipes. She grabbed both.

"Let's get this done the first time." The baby didn't pay any attention, her mesmerized eyes stayed on whatever wondrous spectacle hovered above. Ignoring the implication, Astrid unsnapped the sleeper and changed the diaper without any trouble. She sat the baby up bent forward over one of the pillows and patted her back until another loud burp spewed projectile contents from most of the bottle, splattering her dress bodice.

"Little Blighter!" Astrid exploded, jerking backward while trying to wipe off the smelly spit-up. The baby teetered precariously in the sitting position with no back support, then Astrid lunged forward, her hand raised.

A swirl of motion stirred the air around them and the baby gently lay back on the bed, not a hair on her head blown out of place, as if cradled in caring arms. Astrid stared, then slowly lowered her arm. Each time she attempted to move, she couldn't. The air stirred again like a ceiling fan on high speed. Astrid cursed so hard she rattled her false teeth.

In an instant the wind disappeared. The room fell silent. All was as it had been before.

"Tell *me* what to do." Astrid shook both fists defiantly at the empty space surrounding her, more determined than before to complete her task.

The babe slept on her tummy sucking her thumb.

Cell phone out, Astrid made an immediate call. "We have a problem. I'll take care of it. Request to have a pram waiting in Capri. Meet me at the assigned rendezvous on time, not early, not late."

"You   sure   you   don't   need   my   help   now?"

"Don't be a tosser! Just do what I say." She abruptly hit the red, end call button.

Astrid gave the baby a nervous glance. "Fine, you sleep while I clean up and change my frock. The milk will sour before I can have this dry cleaned. It's rubbish." She stared hard while walking past the bed to the bathroom and grabbed her carry-on clothing bag. After flipping on the lights and turning the shower on full blast, Astrid grumbled the entire time she shed the soiled dress and threw it in the garbage. "You want to battle for control. I'm up for that. Just watch me."

Chapter Forty-Five
Prayer

Some decisions take more time than others. Weighing the possible negative consequences as opposed to the positives can sway the end result. Brock made a big decision, one that will change his life forever. The cost could be devastating; the outcome, yet to be seen. ~ The inner thoughts of a young father.

Sheriff Thomas came and went in a matter of minutes. Brock watched the team go to work and stayed out of the way hoping the sooner they left, the sooner the photograph would make the Tahoe news, Reno too, maybe farther. More exposure meant better results especially with the baby pictures of Benny that went out on the air within hours of discovering him missing.

Brock hung onto the officer's words of encouragement, "I believe this will help break the case." while he waited for Jack and Emily's arrival.

He grabbed a basketball from the nursery and dribbled down the hallway and into the kitchen. Asia used to ask him to keep the ball outside, but she understood it calmed him. Still, if he got too close to the stove when she was cooking, she'd fan her spatula through the air like a warning flag. He stopped and grinned at the memory of her standing on the step stool he'd custom made for all four foot eleven inches of her. Asia, trying to look formidable in a child's orange poke-a-dot apron that went to her ankles. He'd clock in several warnings before exiting out the front door where the basketball hoop was mounted on a tire with cement.

"I should have been a better husband." Brock spoke out loud and stared down at the solid slab of the wooden stool and shoved it out of the way beside the oven. A collection of Benny's toys were now piled high on top of it. "It's as if your presence is leaving our home." The basketball dropped and rolled across the room. Brock collapsed in the closest oak wingback chair. The hard surface offered no comfort or relief. Everything was hard right now—decisions, facing mistakes, and trying to remember things that might be as important as the photograph.

"You home?" Jack called out as he knocked on and opened the door. Emily stood beside him.

"Yeah, come in."

"Shooting hoops?" Jack scooped up the ball and passed it to Brock who jumped up and caught it mid-air.

"I like the scuff of it on the floor and the curve of it in my hands." Brock rolled the ball between his hands and spun it around, then tucked it under his arm.

"What's up?" Emily got right to the point. "Need help with anything?"

"Yeah, I need some advice."

"Okay, what about?"

"Prayer."

Jack and Emily looked at each other then sat next to Brock's empty chair. "What do you want to know?"

"I need to know if I am doing it right." Brock sat with the ball on his lap, hands folded on top. "I need to be sure that God hears me, so he'll protect Benny from anything that Astrid has planned, or if she screws up and puts him in more danger."

"All you have to do is talk to God. He'll listen." Jack assured him.

"But Benny can't. Babies can't pray. He doesn't know how to. Only Asia knew, and well, sometimes the people she prayed for, it didn't go so well for them."

"How do you mean?" Emily asked, her eyebrows quizzically arched.

"I noticed things got worse sometimes. People got sicker." Brock shifted position, leaning in toward the table. "Or, they died, and that wasn't what I heard her asking for." He looked to Jack, catching a direct line of vision he locked onto. "Did God hear her wrong?"

"No, he heard her heart, not just her mouth." Jack rested his elbows on his knees and linked his fingers together, squeezing his knuckles.

"Then what went wrong? If anything goes wrong, I will lose Benny forever."

"Do you ever remember hearing Asia say, 'your will be done.'?"

"She always said that. Why would her God not heal the people? Are some things too hard for him? Are there just times when he can't help?" Brock let the ball fall to the floor, and it bounced it a couple of times before ending up in the laundry room.

"Prayer is direct contact with God. His answers aren't always what we want, and we don't always understand."

"This may surprise you, but I have been talking with him for a couple of months. Maybe more at him. I just talk out loud like he is listening. Astrid caught me a couple of times and I felt an urgency to be quiet. I didn't want her to hear me. Was that some kind of an answer?"

"It was, Brock." Emily pressed in closer, her voice low but firm.

"I prayed to be a good father to Ben and not give him up for adoption. But," he hesitated, "I blew that." His tone changed, and his shoulders sagged.

"You were drugged. You didn't actually sign those fake adoption papers. She stole your son." Jack reached over and said in a strong, steady voice, "you are a good father."

"I have been praying for Benny's protection, something I heard Asia call, divine intervention. I take that to mean that God will step in to keep Ben from harm."

"And many people here are praying that same prayer with you." Jack told him.

"If God hears my heart, then he knows exactly what I mean. No drugs, no private jets out of this state, no devil woman Astrid or Mildred or whoever she may be, that burned Detert, can hurt my son." Brock's voice cracked; his hands trembled.

"Do you believe that God can do these things?" Jack asked.

"Yes." Brock strained harder to not lose control. "Because he will not leave Asia in a grave. He'll take her spirit to be with him."

"I agree with you." Jack spoke with a reassuring confidence. "Keep trusting him, no matter how bad things look. He works in the spiritual realm that we cannot see."

"Do you agree, Emily?" Brock surprised her.

"Yes." Emily faced Brock head on.

"Even though you and your daughter were abducted too, and you can remember all the fear?" Brock persisted. "At least Benny is too young to remember any of this."

"We were never alone with Forrester." Emily relaxed. "That still comforts me to this day."

"Then Benny isn't alone either." Brock sat back in his chair. "When I told Asia's mother about the adoption and kidnapping, she was off the charts mad at me. I was shocked by her reaction; she was so detached before. She started to cry, and that woman never shows any emotion." Brock shook his head. "I get a sense more is going on with her that I don't understand."

"Keep praying and listening." Jack stated. "I've seen mountains tumble in this place before."

"I never believed in much of anything before Asia, except basketball." Brock's eyes widened like clearing skies. "For the first time in my life I *know* things don't happen by accident. There is supreme presence that cares about me and Benny. And it is more powerful than Astrid and all the evil she draws upon."

Chapter Forty-Six
Increased Media Coverage

Darkness is frightening only if you don't know the light that breaks through in even the minutest measure. Tiny spheres of light burn to brighten the deepest abyss, the blackest sky, and hopelessness that overshadows the helpless. ~ Words Jack shared from the last pages of Doc's journal that encouraged Brock.

Local news stations: Channel 9 News, 2 News KTVN - CBS, KRXI Fox 11, KOLO 8 TV-ABC, KRNV 4 TV - NBC and others including online streaming stations all offered sympathy to the widower in the photograph with his beautiful pregnant wife as the search continued for their four month-old baby boy, Benny. A more recent picture was flashed onscreen of a bald cancer stricken Brock at Thanksgiving holding his son. An artist sketch of the elderly woman suspected of the kidnapping was broadcasted with her known aliases, Astrid Smith and Mildred Stoddard.

A detailed description of Benjamin Benton was televised: Brown hair, almond brown eyes, of Asian and Caucasian descent, about fifteen pounds with dimpled cheeks and a clef dent in his chin. He was reported to be a chubby, happy baby boy.

Random people were interviewed on the streets of downtown Tahoe City and Reno with interesting opinions and suggestions.

"What do you think about this terrible news?" A young street news reporter thrust her mic in front of a local grandmother in a grocery store parking lot.

"I am shocked to hear that a woman in her eighties or nineties could do such a thing. It is simply unthinkable." Reno grandmother Vera Meyers stated with contempt. "I hope they find her in time before any harm comes to that sweet baby boy." She teared up and waved the cameraman to stop filming. "It's just so sad." She walked away covering her face with a handkerchief.

"And you sir, what is your opinion?" The reporter spun on his heels to catch a middle-age man in a brown business suit, probably an executive from downtown Reno.

"Hey, I'm in a hurry to get home and need to pick up a few groceries first. I haven't watched the news in the past couple of days. Been too busy at work. But any kidnapping is awful. Hope they get the kid back." He smoothed out the wrinkles on his slacks and walked off.

A young mother with three children that looked to be under the age of five, one attached to her hip, was interviewed in Tahoe City. "I'm a tourist up here with my family for vacation, but I feel for the widower father. This is tragic. And after losing his wife in childbirth. Hope they catch the old lady and put her in jail for a long time, well at least until she dies." Her towheaded little girls clung tight to her floral sundress, burying their faces into the fabric.

"May I ask how old your baby is?" The reported pressed for more of a reaction.

"She's six months old." The mother stroked the baby's hair. She placed a pacifier that hung from a ribbon around the baby's neck, back in her mouth when she started to fuss.

The camera zoomed in on the sisters holding hands as the mother reached down to link hands with the one closest to her. The four walking up to the store together was the final footage shot with a close-up of the baby lifting her head to look straight into the camera with big blue curious eyes.

"This is Dancia Stevens reporting the local news for The Tahoe-Reno region with the latest information about the Tahoe Benton Baby kidnapping and alleged arsonist and murderer. Please report any suspicious behavior or sightings of the suspect, an eighty or ninety year old woman, white mid-back length hair, five foot three inches, about one hundred twenty pounds, with blue eyes but known to wear hazel contacts. Call information into this number on the screen"

Brock watched the news and shut it off without saying a word to either Jack or Emily.

"The Facebook and Twitter feeds are full of suggestions and condemnations, with hundreds of comments and even more likes." Emily scowled.

"We could do without the sensationalism that the media perpetuates." Jack interjected. "But if that couple at the gas station in Caron City saw it on the news, someone else might too."

Staring at the little television Asia kept in the far corner of the kitchen counter, Brock remained silent. She had mostly used the CD player included in the unit to fill the kitchen with music. But at times like now it was convenient to watch her little twelve inch screen from the kitchen table.

"I keep asking myself, what would Asia do if she was still here?" Brock rose and shuffled through the stack of CD's sitting beside the TV. He read titles and the names of groups, most of which he wasn't familiar with. "Clocks by Coldplay, this one I know."

"She would be doing what you are doing." Jack said and plugged in the coffee maker. "Any one up for a cup?"

Both Brock and Emily nodded.

"She would have put Benny on the church prayer chain, and on every prayer chain in the Tahoe region." Emily said. "That's already done."

"You did that?" Brock asked.

"We both did. And on some missionary chains in Africa, China, Russia, the Middle East, pretty much around the world." Emily answered. "Go straight to the front lines of the battlefield when waging all-out war." She gave Brock a sheet of folder paper from her jeans pocket.

"Wow." Brock read the email printout prayer request that went out to all seven continents.

"What else do you think she would have done that we haven't" Jack asked. "Short of jumping an old woman to get her son back."

"Oh, Astrid would have met her match with Asia." A smile broke through and that crinkled the corners of Brock's mouth.

"My wife may have been petite in stature, especially compared to me, but she sure could get a point across when she wanted."

"This is the hardest part. The waiting. Your mind can play tricks on you if you let it." Jack pulled mugs from the cupboard, looping all three handles on his forefinger and thumb, careful not to clink them together. "I remember."

"I have to let it go." Brock pulled the sugar bowl across the table. "I worry that Astrid will leave him alone wherever they are so she can run errands without being seen with him. That she's forcing him to wait to eat on her ridiculous timetable and not changing his diaper often enough." He glanced off to the side. "She hated changing diapers. She'd wait until he cried." Brock stopped. "It's just that he gets a rash really easy."

The landline phone rang, and Brock rushed to pick it up.

"Brock Benton?"

"Yes."

"I saw the picture of your baby on the news tonight."

"Who is this?"

"Looked your number up in the phone book. I think I can help you. I'm a physic."

"I don't need a physic." Brock held the phone out in disbelief.

"Don't hang up, it could mean the difference between life and death for your son!"

"Call Sheriff Thomas." Brock stammered before speaking again. "Or the 800 number if you have anything to report."

"I saw him in a dream, he's underwater…"

Brock hung up while the man was still talking.

"Turn down the ringer on your home phone. Derrick, and the investigative team call your cell." Jack walked over to a shaken Brock. "Ok if I shut it down for the night?" He poured a cup of coffee and handed the mug over after flipping the volume switch off. Then he filled the other two cups and grabbed some milk from the fridge for Emily.

"He saw Benny underwater."

"I heard him, in a dream. We all have dreams. That doesn't mean it's real." Jack sat at the table and urged Brock to return.

"Did you get calls like this?"

"I got calls like that at home and work, and Emily got calls from Forrester at the bookstore. Hard is hard. It gets intense as the clock keeps ticking. That is the nature of this beast." Jack opened the sugar bowl for Brock when he sat down, coffee dripping off the side of the mug, onto the table.

Emily sopped it up with a napkin, then poured milk in hers. "The threat is very real. You have to look beyond, or it will swallow you whole." She grasped Brock's arm. "Ask yourself why this man did not call the hotline or go the direct route to the police or sheriff?"

"Because they might think he's a nutcase?" Brock dropped two sugar cubes in his coffee and used the spoon from the bowl to stir.

"He wanted to get to you while you're vulnerable. But you handled it, Brock." Emily ran her hand over his sleeve.

"Then, why am I so shook up?"

Jack said, "I can offer you my take."

"Okay."

"Some people truly think they are helping, some feed off circumstances like this, and others, well, they are looking to make financial gain off the suffering, or as Emily said, the vulnerable." Jack sipped from his mug. "Hot."

Brock rubbed his palms together like washing his hands. "I've had dreams about Benny. He's sucking his thumb. He's looking all around him. I'd like to think he's looking for me. One time," he drew in a long breath, "he was alone, and a rush of wind swept over him. He liked it."

"You never saw him underwater?" Jack pursued.

"No."

"Can you shake it off?" Jack asked.

"Yeah. I need to stay focused."

Brock's cell vibrated on the table. He was quick to answer. "Hello?"

"This is Officer Derrick Thomas. I have a new update for you, Brock."

"Is it good news?" Brock ran a hand over his head and put the phone on speaker.

"Yes, I do believe it is. We have held this back from all the media. Are Jack and Emily still there with you? Tell no one except them. Do you understand?" Derrick was firm. "We have a better chance of catching her if this does not get out. The team is here going over everything."

"Yes. They're still here and my phone is on speaker."

We got a call from the Montblue Resort on the south shore of Lake Tahoe. They had a guest check into one of the expensive suites alone, an older lady that fits Astrid's description."

"There wasn't a baby with her?" Brock sounded desperate, his voice weakened, and he braced himself for the worst.

"Not at check-in, but she had a baby with her at check-out and one of the bell hops saw an infant in the room with her during her stay." Derrick continued. "There's more."

"Okay." Brock squeezed his eyes shut.

"The maid had to clean up a huge mess in the bathroom."

"A mess?" A dry clog hitched in the middle of Brock's throat.

"Brunette hair dye. The woman checked in a white-haired old lady and checked out looking twenty years younger as a brunette dressed in two-piece designer suit and shoes. The admitting desk clerk observed her departure through a two-way mirror. She could not see him." Derrick breathed in deep before exhaling. "And the baby."

"Yes, and the baby, the baby?" Brock grew impatient and stood, his free hand pressed against the ceiling. His feet spread like he was ready to shoot a free throw from across the court.

"The baby was dressed in a frilly lavender dress and she had a pink bow in her hair."

"What? Are you sure?" A look of horror washed over Brock's face. His big shoes stumbled over the legs of his chair as he tried to move from the table, and he almost fell to the floor when all the oxygen seemed to evaporate from the air in the room.

A stunned gasp escaped Emily's lips before she covered her mouth.

Derrick reiterated his words with clear distinction. "In a dress and pink hair bow. Can you hear me, Brock? She's going to try to pass Benny off as a girl."

Chapter Forty-Seven

The Countdown

Bait and switch is a trick as old as time. Whether the criminal is a lone amateur, an intermediate studying under a mentor, or a time-tested professional, they practice this over and over. It has to be flawlessly perfected, and it usually is how a scam is plotted out like the outline for a novel. The edits, rewrites, and additional drafts all are necessary to finish the book. ~ *How-To Basics for the Determined Thief*—a book anyone can check out from the library or order online.

Loading the baby in the rental car took a lot more energy and expertise than expected. This time Astrid had to actually properly secure the car seat before she was allowed to leave the covered loading zone in front of the hotel. An observant bell hop noticed the seat was not belted in, so the young father of twins offered to help taking up all the extra time needed to catch her flight.

"Bless you. I couldn't have done it without your help." She tipped him twenty and waved like the Queen Mother greeting her royal subjects.

"I couldn't care less if you fly to the moon you Little Blighter." She grit her teeth in a pasted smile, checking her rearview mirror until the man was out of sight. "How the bloody hell am I going to get you out of that contraption? It was just for looks and it cost more quid than it's worth."

The baby gurgled with glee from the back seat. "Don't you be laughing at me. You've made a shamble of things. Now we're behind shed-yul."

Astrid made a call on her cell. "On time, but spare timetable is spent. Be ready." After adjusting her electric leather seat forward, she tapped the Beamer dashboard. "I can afford one of these now." Five blocks down the road she pulled over into a strip mall parking lot and tossed an orange plastic bag with a brown wig hanging half out of it into the trash. She parked under a shady cluster of pines at the far end of the lot, used voice control to turn off the engine and waited, glancing at her watch every few seconds. A passenger door opened and closed—a wave of heat seeped in and hung like a stifling sauna. "Bloody time." The air conditioner blasted on when she voice commanded the car to start before pulling out into oncoming traffic. Horns blared and brakes screeched. She stared ahead, never looking back.

Benny babbled happily from the back seat, arms stretched out and legs kicking, his white Mary Janes with dainty lace bows in constant motion.

"What's the bugger so cheery 'bout?" Her passenger asked.

"Got a kip in." Astrid made a sharp right onto Mt. Rose. "Nice dye job, sis."

"Yours isn't too bad either. The couple deposited a million into the Barclays account this morning. The rest is direct deposited upon delivery. And there's this lovely all-expense paid fortnight in Italy. Maybe we should ask for more?"

"Let's go with the plan. No deviations. No problems. Have you contacted Lenny yet?" Astrid voiced for cruise control and let her foot off the accelerator.

"No. Not yet. He flies them in tonight."

"We do this my way. You were supposed to make contact. Make sure nothing went wrong." An icy hand palmed the back of her sister's neck, and gripped tight. A low hissing spewed from the driver's seat increased in intensity. Cars sped by a good ten miles over the speed limit as the incline up the highway increased. The car automatically shifted into gear with a slight jolt from the transmission. Another car blew past. Astrid shot glaring disapproval.

"Okay, okay. Don't get your knickers in a twist."

"Cruise control off." Astrid's right foot hit the gas pedal. She exceeded the 65 miles per hour speed limit and hit seventy-five.

"Slow down, you'll draw attention."

"Don't be daft, you old bird." The cruise control went back on without the voice control activation.

Sunlight disappeared behind cloud cover that moved in and settled overhead. There was minimal traffic coming from the opposite direction, an occasional big rig whizzed by, but otherwise, they were pretty much alone on the highway now. Conversation in the car hit a lull except for the banter bubbling from the back seat.

"Didn't you dose the baby?"

"He threw it up. I have another bottle ready for an hour before we board the plane." Astrid squeezed the steering wheel with both hands. "I've handled everything so far."

"Don't get snippy with me. You are always too chuffed for your own good and it's put us in a bad spot more than once before." An air of authority accompanied the delivery of the comment with a saucy tone of irritation.

"Who thought to take advantage of this opportunity when it popped up?" Fingers drummed on top of the wheel. "This was my idea. Best not forget that fact."

"Whine, whine, whine." Sis heaved a sigh, then the radio blipped on and channels changed until stopping on a country and western station. Dolly Parton was belting out, the beginning of the song, "Jolene".

"Turn it off, now!" Astrid demanded and slapped at her sister.

"You know Dolly wrote this when she first married Carl Dean in the early 70's and a flirty redhead at his local bank branch came onto him." Sis leaned in and whispered in the curve of Astrid's ear, "It always comes back to him. After all this time."

"Because he should have been mine!" Thunder reverberated and lightning bolted across the front seat of the vehicle. The deafening roar was not of this earth.

"I just thought he was a looker. All your wiles and seduction never swayed him from the only one he loved." Sis sneered with pleasure, taking time to scrutinize the anguished, aged face across from her. "And you employed every power from hell." She continued her rant, knowing better than to do so. "I'm not the one he chose over you."

"Radio off!" A primitive scream pitched through the vehicle, rattling every glass window. The baby sniffled, lower lip quivering in a wavering pout, that progressed to full blown wailing.

"We need the baby to be calm, you old tosser."

"I hate being old." Astrid quieted as quickly as she'd become enraged.

"Well, I'll agree with you on that." Sis lowered her sunglasses to the bridge of her nose and glanced in the rearview mirror. "Shush, shush, little baby. The scary lady is going to behave herself now like a good auntie."

"What is that sweet fragrance? Are you wearing some kind of a time-release perfume? It seems to be getting stronger."

"Lilacs. You smell it too?" Astrid grew more annoyed.

Benny whimpered, tears rolling down his chubby cheeks. The subsiding turbulence appeased his mood and a calming force stilled the atmosphere. Blinking, then rubbing his eyes he dozed off, his head resting on the soft side padding of a neck pillow built into the car seat.

"You must learn to control your temper and keep your voice down. Let the baby sleep or we'll be dealing with a cranky, crying, attention drawing nuisance." Sis stretched. "Nothing to spoil the fortune waiting for us."

"No spoilers then."

"As long as Lenny comes through at his end and delivers the package, we Stoddards will have our fortnight, vineyards, Tuscany's best, and spa days until we tire of being mollycoddled."

"I left a trail of false clues that should lead them away from us. They'll be looking at the private airport." She jingled the gold charm bracelet on her wrist and checked the diamond studded watch one more time. "On shed-yul."

Chapter Forty-Eight
Taking Flight

A child changes you for life. Before the person born of your flesh arrives, you wonder if you will be a good parent, a parent that will love no matter what. I have dreamed of you since I first found out I was pregnant. When you move within me, I cradle you in my hands and speak to you as if you understand every word. You know the sound of my voice and responds to my moods. By the time you are born into the world, you will recognize me. I know this to be true. ~ Asia's cell video message to Benny.

"Shouldn't we let my son-in-law know we are leaving the country? What if the authorities wish to contact us about Benjamin?" Sue Quon questioned her husband and straightened the waistband of her skirt until the hemline hung even below her knees.

"They have our cell numbers. Our tickets and reservations are non-refundable. We've been planning this trip for two years." Frank slipped their online tickets in his sports coat pocket and loaded the rest of the luggage in their SUV without looking at his wife.

317

Sue stood waiting for him to open the door for her as usual. She glanced in the side mirror to see if her make-up needed a touch up. Pulling a lipstick from her purse, she applied a new layer, pressing her lips until she acquired the deep berry shade sheen she desired. Resting on her high heels, she tap-tapped the tip of her shoes until Frank circled to her side of the car and opened the door.

"If something happens to the baby, we'll be on another continent." She persisted.

"Brock can deal with anything that comes up." Frank took her hand and helped her to step up into the car. He stole a quick look at this Rolex while she situated herself comfortably in the leather seat. "We have to hurry. You know I like to arrive at the airport with a couple of hours to spare."

"Yes, I know." Sue set her Coach handbag to the left side of the passenger floor.

"You made all the arrangements; cancelled the maid service, the cook and the paper?"

"Yes, yes." She leaned her purse against the middle divider before swinging her shoes, one-at-a-time, on the beige carpet and positioned herself back in the seat.

"But you retained the gardener?" Frank held the door open, his eyes scanning the garage for anything they may have forgotten.

"It's taken care of." Sue turned to face him just as the door closed. A gnawing in the pit of her stomach had pursued all day. She'd tried to broach the subject of what was troubling her with Frank twice, but he dismissed her each time with a wave of his hand, then he'd delve back into the novel he was reading. She'd texted Brock but he hadn't replied other than to forward more pictures of Benny as she had previously requested. The shock of seeing the photograph of Asia on the news had crumbled all her feigned defenses. But her husband would have none of it. They were sticking to the pre-planned schedule.

Frank hopped in the driver's seat and checked his perfect teeth in the rearview mirror before voice starting his new 2017 Lexus LX. He loved his new hand-polished custom lady. He inhaled a whiff of air, "Still has that brand new car smell."

The creaking garage door opened while the couple sat in silence. Frank backed out and the door closed behind them. "I've got to get that blasted door oiled. The noise drives me crazy." He ran one hand through his thick white hair along the side part so he wouldn't mess where he'd spritzed a light cover of hairspray.

Sue stared at her shoes. The cranberry color seemed too much at the moment. She thought she should have gone with a more subdued, neutral shade, maybe a taupe. Her size 5 feet fit snug in these heels and the open middle was stylish enough. She would have skipped the nylons, but Frank believed women should dress up, not down. The balls of her feet were already sweating.

Sue wanted to stay behind this time. The trip to Greece and the Mediterranean cruise no longer captured her interest, they'd gone twice before. Brock's last visit left her desiring a more active part in Benny's life. He so resembled Asia as a baby, it was quite remarkable. Benjamin had taken to her too, most babies cried when she held them, and she couldn't wait to hand them back. Benny had been different from the first time he smiled and reached his chubby arms out to her. He cozied in, a perfect fit. She'd noticed Frank's disapproving stare and his comments later. "Don't even think about a baby visiting in this house. It's not child proof and Brock might start to take advantage, ask for free babysitting."

"Moping is not attractive." Frank slipped in a CD and turned up the volume.

"I can exercise my prerogative to change my mind." Sue spoke over the classical music.

"You'll forget about this development once we're sunning on the Grecian coast." He shot her that charming smile, one corner of his mouth cocked at just the right angle delivered with a flirtatious wink. "Martinis poolside, after dinner dancing, moonlight strolls on the promenade deck." His famous double wink followed, as expected.

"All the cruises are the same." She stated.

"You never even reconciled with your daughter." He huffed and rolled his eyes.

"I am," she struggled to continue, "quite aware of my mistake." She turned to him with a pleading expression, every feature of her face outlined with regret, and her eyes reflected pain from a deep, hidden well. "Benjamin is of my ancestors."

"Where is this coming from?" The twinkle left Frank's eyes and his mouth formed a thin, level line. "This is guilt talking. You went on cruises after all of Asia's phone messages, and you had fun. I recall laughter and midnight lovemaking."

"I cannot change the past."

"Would you if you could?" Ridicule sliced his words and still he did not look at her.

The cruelty that hinged his mocking attitude stirred an anger buried beneath a transparent veneer he'd spent decades sanding the varnish off, layer by layer. Her hollow heart lost all desire to share more of the suffering that left her raw, exposed. It took but seconds for her to dry her own tears with a tissue from the console between them.

He glowered when she missed discarding the make-up smudged Kleenex in the accessible trash bag clipped to the inner passenger door compartment.

"You did that on purpose."

Sue drew her handbag up to her lap, slipped her cell from the side pocket and viewed the pictures of Benny that Brock had texted to her. The pointed sole of her right shoe crushed the tissue into the carpet until they arrived at terminal B at the Reno Airport, and she tossed it in the bag. A dark blotch of lipstick marred the floor. Frank came around to help her step down and she swung her legs around, one at a time, careful not to reveal the new stain on his precious plush carpet. His divorced friend Alan was taking a taxi to pick up the Lexus tonight after work and park it in their garage while he house sat for them. She imagined one of Alan's lady friends would do worse damage to both the house and the car. Frank could deal with it when they returned, and he sported his winter tan and he'd had his fill of flavored Mediterranean martinis.

***

Officer Derrick Thomas decided to cover both bases and sent some of his men to the private Calvada Meadows Airport in Pahrump on NV 74, which he believed Astrid wanted him to think she was flying out of. She'd left enough clues, addresses and directions on the hotel stationary, maps with that section torn out. There was a good six hour drive between Reno International and Pahrump.

 He figured she was vain enough to fly out of Reno, Tahoe International, right under their noses, banking on whatever clever disguises she'd manufactured. The box of brunette hair dye was a diversion too. Though she'd disposed of all indicators a baby girl would be accompanying her. He was certain there were more surprises coming. With all of the Tahoe/Nevada region searching an elderly woman and a baby boy, Astrid thought she had them all by a nose ring.

After researching the other two private airports at Gerlach and Round Mountain, which were only three to four hours away, Derrick figured cagey Miss Stoddard would connect with an east coast flight from Reno and head for anywhere in Europe except England. A privet jet was somewhere in those connecting flight plans, but he was ninety-nine percent certain, not out here on the west coast.

Still he alerted all the commercial and private airports and asked for ID checks for the next forty-eight hours. She'd have fake identification and passports, so would the baby and any other traveling companions. Though nothing suspicious jumped out at him from the RNO manifests and passenger list, he took the Reno Airport and headed for East Plumb Lane.

He was still breaking in a new partner and all the bumps that come with inexperience and bravado. Derrick had learned a few things from Forrester, like staying a step ahead, not behind.

"Craig, let's go over it one more time." Derrick was about to exit I80 into Reno.

"Yes, sir."

"Go."

"First—ignore all media reports. I am not looking for a helpless little old lady, white-haired or brunette. Notice anyone with a baby girl, a teenage mother or father. Astrid/Mildred can pay anyone to travel with her. The baby may be drugged. There are no impossibilities, sir."

"You are a good ex-marine, son." Traffic snaked to a slow crawl. Derrick wove through.

"Sir, yes, sir!"

They both laughed. "Okay, that breaks the tension, but we are dealing with a life and death scenario. Be aware. Be alert. Nothing will be as it seems."

"Do you think Benny is still alive?" The young rookie looked at his partner for hope.

"Yes, I do. And I believe we can safely put him back in his father's arms by tonight. Tomorrow morning at the latest." Derrick nodded, his shoulders and back straight.

"I would like to help do that, sir." Craig swallowed the last of his Starbucks double espresso. "My brother has a six month old son. This hit me hard.

"I know what you mean, the younger of my two sons is nine months old." Derrick held his breath, then let it go. "I can't imagine what Brock is going through."

"Yeah." Craig hung his head.

"I learned a few things from Forrester, the one that shot me." He turned to his partner. "We have to think like them, react like them, walk in their shoes, inhale through their nostrils."

"How?"

"Everything you value, every moral you believe in, every instinct you usually act on—will be contrary to their nature. Watch for what appears to be routine. You will start to smell a stink. Trust your gut."

"This is going down in a large public crowd. Innocent civilians."

That's why I think Astrid picked Washoe County. Bigger crowds mean more insurance for her to get away if things unravel. And mark my words, she will flee with the baby. She will not leave him behind. I expect at least one perpetrator to be armed." Derrick urged. "Use your weapon. The imposter will shoot to kill."

"Vest on."

"Rookie, any questions?" Derrick turned onto East Plumb Lane. The airport was crammed. "Start watching the cars driving by."

Derrick squinted in the mid-afternoon sun after removing his shades. The flight he suspected Astrid might board was taking off in two hours. Time was back on Astrid's side.

Chapter Forty-Nine
Seconds Away

The mental state of patients affects their physical wellbeing. Healing is hindered by fear, anxiety, even unforgiveness. Sanity is a borderline; any person can cross over given the right circumstances. I've seen patients beat impossible odds, life and death situations. There is no expiration date stamped on an individual. Medical science has boundaries, faith has none as eternity starts here on earth. ~ 1973 Doc John Walter's journal entry days after his infant daughter Isabella died at one week of age. With an additional notation inked in the day Jack and Emily's son was stillborn. 2001 ~ I rejoice, I weep, I praise for my grandson.

Jack finished rereading his father's journal while Brock catnapped on the sofa. All three cell phones sat in the middle of the coffee table anticipating word from the detectives. Derrick had called an hour ago to let them know he was arriving at the Reno Airport. Emily kept busy in Brock's kitchen making a vegetable casserole.

Jack longed for his father's wisdom, and the sound of his reassuring voice. Doc's presence made the hard things in life easier. What would he do if he were here? There was no guarantee for Benny's safe return, but there was hope. The statistics for abductions were staggering. So many never returned safely home and others remained missing as the families try to go on with their splintered lives. There was tragedy mixed in with recovery too, especially for the older victims who could remember their captivity despite efforts to forget. For them, time rewound, unwound, and rewound again.

Closing the leather book, Jack's heart beat in sync with the grandfather clock on the wall behind him. The massive timepiece reminded him of old Selma at Vikingsholm. Both sentinels filtered intervals of time, the fabric of the air they inhaled and exhaled, while waiting. The ticking of the second's hand reverberated in Jack's ears. He turned to look into the face of the old English Grandfather. The antique had measured the hours of the day for over one hundred and fifty years. Today the hands of time were unyielding, moving forward.

The five o'clock hour gonged, startling Brock awake. Evening had come, afternoon had passed. The final sixth chime struck. Jack, Emily and Brock stopped where they were, suspended in apprehension for news that had yet to be delivered.

"I don't know how much more of this I can take." Brock buried his head in the throw pillows. His long body heaved muffled sobs, his bare feet hanging over the opposite side arm of the couch, rising and falling with his torso.

Emily walked over but Jack shook his head and mouthed the words— "Let him be." Tears welled in her eyes. She knew the other ugly side of this. Sitting beside Jack on the loveseat, she rested on his chest and looked up to his reddened, glistening eyes.

The hour had come.

***

Astrid had moved with ease through the airport, no one gave her a second look. Pleased, she relaxed and sat on a blue cushioned chair linked to a row of chairs in a silver metal framework. She held the current issue of The New Yorker, licking her forefinger and flipping through pages, enjoying the satirical cartoons and political articles. A half-eaten bag of salted mixed nuts sat on her lap and she balanced a paper cup of coffee on her knee before setting it on a built-in table.

"Long wait tonight." She mentioned to the mop-headed teenage boy seated beside her. A set of lemon yellow earbuds were plugged in snug, and the string cords dangled from his neck. He remained bent forward eyes trained on a cell phone in his hands, both thumbs in rapid movement playing a game that flashed bright reds, oranges, and blues across his mini screen. He never looked up but repeatedly jerked, shaking her seat, uttering curses.

A quick glance down the lines and rows of chairs revealed similar activity on a variety of electronic devices, e-readers, laptops, and cell phones of all sizes. Most heads were downcast, most ears were plugged, and the conversations were minimal among strangers and those who appeared to be traveling together. *How lovely, a detached world so reduces the threat of discovery.* Astrid resumed reading the magazine and shoe shuffled her carry-on bag under the chair. All other luggage had been checked upon her arrival. She was traveling light.

***

Derrick and his partner met in terminal "C" at gate 147. They had walked the length of the passenger areas and came up empty. Chattering travelers rambled past them, drinking bottles of water and soda as they lugged backpacks, pushed empty strollers, and managed multiple pieces of beat-up or matching designer luggage.

"Unless our imposter is under that burka over there, I don't see her or her sister." Craig whispered. His black shiny shoes squeaked on the indoor-outdoor carpet near the gate. "Breaking in a new pair. Bad timing. Got a blister." Three female flight attendants hurried by in their crisp, ironed navy skirts, white blouses and short jackets with wings pinned on the collars. One gave the rookie a nod and lingering smile and cocked her head back to take a second look.

"Maybe it's all a trick and their brother Leonard is the one boarding this flight and the sisters have already flown out?" Derrick offered the suggestion with obvious disappointment. He closely monitored males and females of all races, married couples, and grandparents, aged hippies with dreadlocks, moccasins, and tie-dye shirts.

"Just a few babies and the only girl is black." He mentioned to the rookie. "She looks more like a six to nine month old." The crowd had settled in a line wrapping around the boarding desk and filled up all the chairs at the gate. Teens sat on the carpet eating microwaved fast food under the huge windows along the runway, their bags under their legs or stowed behind their backs as pillows.

"I'm still looking for the normal, the everyday, like you said." Craig strained to keep a couple of teachers wearing "Teachers learn faster" t-shirts and jeans in his line of vision.

A family of five passed the officers and all three of the children waved to them. The mother scuttled her children closer to her while trying to keep up with her husband.

Derrick's cell rang. He glanced at the number before picking up. "Yes. Really. What's your call? Okay, I'll get right back to you." Pizza fumes wafted from a brick oven in the nearby food court.

"Great. An anonymous tip was phoned in. A sighting of an old woman with a baby boy in Gerlach at the Black Rock City Airport. Three hours from here. The next flight to leave from there is charted to lift off in four hours."

"A diversion?"

"Most likely. She's timed it so we'll miss this flight out if I go for it. Probably called it in herself." Derrick shifted his weight to his left hip and leaned against the column where they stood.

An overhead speaker broadcasted: "Flight 147 departing to Atlanta, Georgia is delayed another half hour due to fog. Please check in at the ticket counter for either A or B seating."

Derrick's phone rang again. "Yes. I figured as much. Ask the local police for back-up."

"Round Mountain?"

"You got it. Someone wants us out of here. She'll be watching. Maybe we're close and don't know it yet." Derrick looked over his shoulder and called Gerlach back suggesting they also request more local back-up. "The departure flight I'm watching to Atlanta is delayed due to a strange fog that's rolled in."

"I could be wrong." He hung up and started walking the aisle. "Check the men's bathrooms again." Where is she hiding that baby? His eyes darted at every passing person, he looked them up and down in seconds, then moved onto the next group. "I'll have the matron recheck the ladies rooms." He brushed up against two men in business suits; one charcoal gray, crisply pressed, the man about thirty-five, 160 pounds, green eyes and over-whitened perfect teeth. The older man of about forty-five in the blue suit wore a lopsided necktie, 190 pounds, muscular, gray eyes, coffee breath. They each carried briefcases.

"She's probably drugged Benny into a deep sleep. We won't hear him cry." Derrick leaned in and whispered. "Meet me back at the column in ten if you get nothing. And watch for the undercover Federal agents. Don't get in their way." With that the two went in opposite directions.

The matron rifled through the garbage looking for diapers while a woman changed her baby at the fold-out table in the restroom. "All stalls are clear, just teenagers and businesswomen rolling carry-on and overhead stow-away luggage." She reported back discreetly then blended into the crowd.

Derrick's heart pounded hard in his chest and sweat beaded at his temples. If he was wrong, Brock was going to lose his son. He looked at soft-sided luggage as it wheeled by. A sleeping baby would fit in there. Cut unseen air holes at the top by the handle. It could work. He started glancing around at the vast number of them being wheeled back and forth on either side of him. *Was he going crazy?*

The noisy din grew louder. Flight announcements echoed, departures, delays, lay overs. He stepped over a spilled cup of Starbucks. His nostrils kicked into overdrive when the stronger scent of lilacs floated by, diminishing the aroma of the heady ground coffee beans. He caught sight of parents with a baby girl and picked up his pace until he stood beside them. Suspiciously he eyed the infant who looked too young, barely a month old, maybe. The parents were too young also, teens barely high school age. When the mother proceeded to change the baby on her lap and it was obvious the child was a girl, Derrick moved on.

"This is Leslie with American Airlines. We will prepare to board Flight 147 for Atlanta, Georgia at Gate "C" in the next fifteen minutes. Please check your tickets. Make sure all carry-ons are the correct size. Passengers with babies and first class will board first, as will frequent flyers. Section "A" will board second with Section "B" to follow. All passengers are allowed *one* legal-size carry-on that will fit in the overhead compartments and one stow-away bag for under your seat."

Craig waited for Derrick at the pillar. Neither had seen a single questionable suspect.

"Maybe they've split up until boarding? Less conspicuous that way." Derrick spoke under his breath to his partner.

"So, we should be looking for—one adult with a baby. And a single adult. Male, female?" The rookie made a slow start to the kiosk across from the gate and watched for people walking up. The mid-section had somewhat emptied after the flight at Gate "D" departed to Pittsburg, Pennsylvania. That left Gate "B" and Gate "A" a little farther down. Both waiting areas were as packed as Gate "C", but most people were seated and hunkered down for another hour or two to wait. Two restaurants were sparsely filled, except for the packed bars.

***

Sue Quon stood at the head of the line ready to board first class. Frank was still at the bar downing his pre-flight martinis. He always carried a flask with him for a nip or two or three. She held her handbag close, turning her back to all the other passengers beginning to file behind. Her heels dug into the carpet and she bent to stroke a muscle she'd pulled when she tripped over a pacifier.

Frank stumbled next to Sue. "Sorry folks, not cutting." He said and fanned his hands out and laughed. "This here is the wife." Frank moved in for a kiss and missed. "Aw, come on, honey. Don't be that way."

"You're drunk and making a scene." Sue brushed by him and stepped forward.

"Just tipsy. And you usually like that." He winked.

"Behave or they'll knock you off the flight." Sue turned and whispered in his ear.

"Not with all the money I spend on this airline." Frank's hair stuck straight up on the right side of his part. He kept trying to smooth and flatten the lacquered silver-white unruly shock, but he made it worse with every side-swipe of his hand. He smooched the back of Sue's neck with a slobbery kiss, his lips lingering a bit too long.

"Five more minutes to first board. Anyone with children go to the front of the line."

The desk attendant motioned to an older blonde woman from the mid-section. She waved for her and the baby asleep in her arms to go to the front of the line.

"It's okay. We're fine here." The woman called out.

The attendant persisted and reached for the speaker, but the woman complied.

"I hope you don't mind us taking your first place position." She wheeled a brown piece of luggage that hit a snag in the looped carpet fibers.

"Frank, help her." As she spoke, Sue noticed a sheriff move closer, within earshot.

With a quick jerk, Frank popped the plastic casing across the bottom of the suitcase free from the frayed carpeting, then he rolled his own luggage next to his legs.

"What a cute bonnet." Sue commented.

"Thank you."

"I used to dress my daughter in pretty clothes like that." Sue sighed and took note of the attentive sheriff motioning for another officer to join him.

The baby began to stir, her fingers opening one by one from a balled fist.

"She's wearing a matching outfit." The woman faced the sheriffs and bounced the baby on her hip a couple of times. She slipped the bonnet off revealing blonde sweaty hair almost the same color as hers. "I love shopping for my granddaughter. The latest fashions are adorable."

Sue forced a faded smile. "The bright colors are so cheerful with that skin tone."

"Yes. Wake up now, sweetie. Time to board." She spoke right into the baby's ear as her hand slid below the blanket the little one was wrapped in. With a sudden jolt, the baby stiffened. One eye popped open and she stifled a wide yawn.

"What unusual green eyes." Sue complimented.

"She inherited them from me. It's a dominate gene in the family."

***

Derrick pulled back and walked down the line. Craig continued farther to Gate "A" and shook his head when he stopped. Derrick met him half-way. "I think I was wrong even though my gut tells me they're here."

"We can still fly over to Gerlach and make it. We'll make Pahrump too, if we leave now." Craig watched his partner's answer.

"Yeah, I guess we should head over. There's a small plane waiting, just in case." Derrick grabbed his cell phone to place the call. He took a last look at the arrival and departure board posted above him. A stroller sped past back toward Gate "C" with two women in a full sprint.

"Wait!' Derrick called out and rushed to catch them. A baby sat covered with receiving blankets, only a cherub face appeared with wide brown eyes and thick, curly brown hair. "How old is your baby?" he questioned.

"Seven months." The two women stalled. "We're going to miss our flight. This is the wrong end of the airport." Both were dressed in sneakers and workout clothes, the taller of the two had multiple piercings on her face and a tattoo sleeve down her beefy left arm. A closer look at the baby was disappointing. She was not Asian skin-toned, but pale as his partner's winter white legs. The women were more girls than grown-ups, most likely in their late teens.

"You can take that shuttle over there." Craig put two fingers in his mouth and whistled. The shrill ring drew attention from everywhere which was not what they wanted. The sheriffs headed for the airport entrance.

"Boarding Flight 147 is temporarily delayed due to increased fog. Please stay in line for a few more minutes and bear with us."

Sue watched the baby struggle to awaken. Her dimpled cheeks were pudgy, and her lips puckered as if ready to deliver a kiss. "Such a beautiful chubby face." A stab of sorrow pierced Sue's heart as she offered the compliment. "My Asia was tiny, not even five pounds when she was born. She had dimples too. I gave her a big name for the continent of our ancestors." Sue leaned forward, closer to the baby's face.

"The father is Asian then?" Sue couldn't help but notice the grandmother's fair complexion.

"Our family is a blend of many nationalities." The woman bounced the child a few times, her hand covering the baby's face from view. She looked beyond Sue and then turned to glance where the officers had gone.

"I think I may move over to the chairs and sit for a while, until they are ready to board."

Sue glared directly in the eyes of the fellow passenger. "You speak with a slight English accent. Cornish? I lived there in the early 1970's for a few years." She took the baby's hand in hers. "Hello little one." A deep clef in the baby's chin caught her interest.

"My legs are tired. I need to rest." The woman shifted a sharp turn away and the baby's hand fell across her face, throwing an unintentional right hook.

"Oh, I'm so sorry." A flustered Sue tried to assist her. "Here, something fell off." She bent down and scanned the carpet but saw nothing.

"Really, not to worry." The woman motioned toward another person sitting two rows from her. A man rose to come to her aid. "I have help."

Sue was still bent down, running her hand along the carpet surface, not sure what she was looking for, when she didn't find it. She stood back up.

The baby rubbed a hand over her right eye and started quivering. Both eyes opened and closed again in a flash. One brown eye, then one green eye.

Sue gasped out loud and drew back, bumping into a disinterested but annoyed Frank.

"Watch it Suisun." He drabbled while scoping out a couple of teen girls walking with a group past them.

She stood without flexing a muscle. Then bowed forward to scour the floor again. And there it was. Sue licked a fingertip and pressed hard on the carpet. When she rose, a green soft contact lens was suction-cupped to the rounded flesh of her index finger. She screamed out loud and held her find high up in the air as the woman moved away in long, fast strides.

"Benjamin! Benjamin Benton! Benjamin!"

***

Derrick heard shrieks and swiveled around without hesitation. "Craig, call for back-up." She'll use the full airport to her advantage. Think fast, move faster. Past gates "A" and "B" he huffed preparing to pull his weapon.

Sue stepped out of her shoes and dropped the contact into one of them. She swung her handbag in the direction of the man and woman fleeing, aiming for their feet, but she missed by inches.

"Talk about me making a scene." Frank stood in place, pointing down to the empty space next to him. "Get back here, Sue!" He apologized for his wife's strange behavior to all the curious onlookers in line and sitting, walking and standing nearby. They'd all responded to her scream of alarm.

"Benjamin Benton is that kidnapped baby boy from Tahoe." A guy called out.

"The woman has a baby girl, not a boy." Another voice yelled.

A rumble of voices grew louder. Mothers gathered their children. People stepped out of line, abandoning their place for first boarding. Several men began walking toward the couple leaving the area, picking up the pace as they did.

"Her baby has blonde hair, not brown."

"Really?" A teenage girl with purple spiked hair tipped in cobalt blue struck a pose highlighting her dyed hair and told the boy next to her. "I'm a natural blonde. Duh!"

"Stop where you are, Mildred Stoddard." Derrick ran trying to catch their sprint that sprung into a dead run. "Everyone down on the ground. Don't panic. Get down." He'd drawn his weapon and people dropped or got as far away as they could while he waved an arm spanning the entire passenger waiting lounge.

Three large round international clocks hung in a row like observing overseers on the wall above. Time zones across the world ticked, second by second.

A man watching the scene from the opposite side of the aisle tossed his backpack at the fleeing couple's feet as he walked past them, then pitched himself to the carpet at the Gate A waiting area. The older gentleman tumbled over it and went down. The woman kept running, the baby jostled up and down, head pressed into her shoulder. She never looked back.

Craig reached the fallen suspect and tackled him as he was rising. "Stop! Stay on the floor!" He knelt beside the suspect and pulled his arms behind his back and cuffed him.

A female voice yelped, followed by painful moans. "Get your hands off me you bloody bugger!" The prisoner kicked hard with thick-soled black ankle boots.

"Not Leonard Stoddard I take it." Under the flat top salt and pepper hair, a frail elderly person cringed in anguish. A gray and silver mustache had ripped halfway off the person's upper lip, leaving a raw strip of red flesh.

The sheriff straddled the woman. Wrinkly, veiny skin and stick legs appeared under her trousers. "You must be the oldest sister."

"Tosser!" She screeched, spittle spewing from cracked lips.

Back-up arrived. Another officer helped the sheriff get the suspect to her feet. An undercover agent read the Miranda Rights and took over, leading the disgruntled woman to an interrogation room in a secluded area of airport security.

Derrick had boxed the other suspect in a corner near the up and down escalators. His main concern was for the baby who was squalling, wide awake and frightened. He figured he had the younger sister; Agatha and she was a piece of work. She'd use Benny for leverage.

"Let me go and I'll give you the baby." She droned over the baby's increasing cries.

"I can't do that." Derrick replied. "Be smart. Give him to me." Craig had joined Derrick with two other undercover agents. Derrick kept his gun aimed at her head. He could have taken the shot right then; it was a clear shot. Even with four guns aiming at her, she couldn't be swayed.

"I'll throw him over." She threatened, swinging their sand-wiched bodies toward the edge.

"Then we'll all shoot you. It's over if you hurt him. He's all you've got." Derrick saw a sharpshooter taking aim from the next wing of the boarding gate area. "They'll take their shot any second." He nodded to the right, so she'd know what was coming.

"Put Benny on the floor and back from the escalator. If you have a weapon. Put it down too. Hands up and behind your head." Derrick watched her scan the area. The only way out was with a hostage, or on her own.

She did not hesitate. "Ok. I'm putting the baby on the floor." She squatted.

"Push him toward me." Derrick's used one hand, fingers cupped, pulling inward in a repeated motion while holding his gun with the other. "Slow and easy, no fast movements."

Cowering behind Benny the entire time, holding his face in front of hers so there was not a clean shot, she maneuvered her stance, shoved Benny in front of her, then she dove for the down escalator, on her belly with hands stretched forward.

Chapter Fifty
The Cost

If we do not choose what is honorable, what is most times the hard thing that will involve personal sacrifice, then we set out on a road that, in time, will lead to discovering we have become less than what we could have been. What then is the real cost of our soul? Because the body will fail every one of us. We can hasten that end, or we can risk a journey that will end in victory though those without honor will never see the value. Thank you for your wise counsel and friendship that helped me to embark on my journey across the pond. I have found true victory in serving these soldiers. Each day their bravery teaches me new lessons, and I am blessed to help bring healing to their wounded bodies. In this country where all now fight for their freedom, I also found love. I hope one day for you to meet my James when I return to the Emerald Bay forest and your Vikingsholm that you so graciously shared from your heart. My life was enriched by the decade spent on those azure shores and my memories travel there to visit you many a dark night when the air raid sirens continually blast, and the bombs fall without mercy. My dearest friend, know I now understand your joy that grew out of loss and sorrow. Respectfully and lovingly yours,

Astrid. ~ Last letter written by Astrid Amelia Hughes in the early autumn of 1940 during the Battle of Britain, sent to Lora Josephine Knight at Vikingsholm, Lake Tahoe, California.

She's going to get away. Derrick went straight for Benny and left the Stoddard imposter to the other officers and agents. The baby was crying when he scooped him up. Derrick scooted over to the seating behind a wall sheltering the child from any possible retribution should the woman venture back up the other escalator. He shielded Benny with his body

A gun went off and a ricocheting bullet pinged on metal and hit plaster before it stopped. The crowd remained flat on the floor and a new wave of fear swept though. People, luggage and electronics remained scattered amid muffled cries for help. From the bottom of the escalator came the sound of a scuffle and loud voices called out before a lone shot rang followed by silence.

Benny clung to Derrick, his pudgy hands clasping the officer's uniform shirt as he rubbed his face repeatedly on his shoulder. Arms tight around the baby, he listened for the call.

"All clear."

Two undercover agents stepped off the up escalator and the sharpshooter emerged from his hiding place near the opposite one. They whispered before turning and told Derrick, "Direct hit." Derrick pulled his cell and sent one text message—Have your son, safe, unharmed.

One by one passengers stood and gathered their belongings. A low murmur of shock and disbelief filled conversations between strangers trying to figure out what they'd just experienced. Who saw what and was it the baby on the news. Were they really safe or was she coming back? Who was the man they'd cuffed and taken into custody? Opinions varied.

A gloved agent came to get the baby. When Derrick was able to pry Benny from his shirt and check him over, he realized a green contact was rolled half-off an eyeball. The female F.B.I. team member was careful to remove and bag it, then slip it in her portable kit. Two huge doe brown eyes blinked and embraced Derrick's gaze. Teardrops stained and trickled down Benny's cheeks. Derrick had to resist the instinct to dry them away. "You're going home to Daddy, little fella. Real soon." A rush of emotion overcame him when Benny rested his head against his chest, muscles relaxing, grip releasing, heartbeat slowing.

"You okay?" She asked and reached for the baby.

"Yeah. I've got one at home a little older." Derrick's words caught in his throat.

Sue Quon rushed to their side from the crowd being restrained. "Please, I'm his grandmother." Words tumbled from her mouth. "She dyed his hair blonde, gave him fake green eyes, and dressed him like a girl." Her voice halted. "Still, he looks like his mother."

"You can come with me. I'm sorry you can't touch him until he goes to the hospital."

"Hospital?"

"For an exam, tests, but he looks healthy, he'll be fine." The agent let Sue walk with her to wait until ambulance attendants came for Benny. They passed Frank, but Sue kept going.

Derrick retraced his steps and ended up under the clocks at Gate "C". He glanced up. The middle clock had stopped exactly at the six o'clock hour. He took a closer look, he noticed fine cracks had created a spider web effect encompassing the glass covering. "It's here, the bullet hit in the center."

"She got off one stray shot." The sharpshooter stood next to Derrick. "I had to take my shot then. She would have kept shooting."

***

Brock arrived at hospital with Jack and Emily. He kept looking over everyone's heads, using his height to get a glimpse of Benny. He'd brought a change of clothes because Derrick mentioned to come prepared for a few surprises. The backpack diaper bag was fully loaded with all of his son's favorites—toys, pacifier, blanket, teddy bear, and his Tahoe bear sleepers. It was late, ten o'clock when he was told he could pick up Benny and take him home. They were going to keep him overnight, but all tests showed he was in good health with only a trace of ground up sleeping pills Astrid put in his formula.

The nurse at the pediatrics desk called Brock over. "I recognize you from the News broadcasts, but I still need to see ID."

Brock whipped out his wallet and produced his driver's license.

"Follow me." She stepped out. "Room 214. He's waiting for you. Such a happy baby."

Her white soft leather shoes squeaked until the freshly waxed linoleum. Brock wished she'd walk faster; she took two steps for every one of his. Jack and Emily stayed a distance behind; he tucked his wife under his arm and held close.

Counting the numbers on the doors, Brock shot looks right and left trying to discern if there was an odd and even pattern. He moved physically toward the right wall. Benny was just a few doors away, alive and as well as he could be after a couple of days alone with the Astrid or Mildred imposter. She was dead now and no longer a threat to any of them. He'd thank the S.W.A.T. sharpshooter first chance he got.

"Room 214." The nurse opened the door wide enough for Brock to see a gleaming metal crib that resembled a cage for animals more than a bed for babies. His heart lurched.

Derrick sat head slouched, chin tipped on his Giants baseball t-shirt, next to the enclosed crib. A paper Starbucks cup butted next to his cross trainer shoes on the floor.

"He wouldn't leave even after he went off duty." She whispered. "Changed his clothes after rocking the baby to sleep. I suggested he get some rest."

Brock eyes fell on the cherub face before him, he drew closer and knelt within inches of the crib. He reached in between the slats and cupped his oversized hand around Benny's blonde head. "Hello Ben Bug. Daddy's here."

The baby stirred, his eyelids struggling to open. One clenched fist opened wide, fingers stretching. A thumb pressed to his lower lip lifted, and a long yawn exposed pink gums and what looked to be a tooth breaking through on the top.

Tears streamed down Brock's cheeks as he ran his pinkie finger back and forth over the ridges of the white enamel. "You got your first tooth."

Benny opened one muddy brown eye, then the other. His legs started to kick in place and his arms shot rapidly into the air, pudgy hands reaching, stretching toward Brock.

The nurse lifted open the opposite side of the crib. "You can take your son out and hold him." Her blue eyes washed aside a lone teardrop as she nudged Derrick awake.

Benny turned his head, watching Brock's every movement. Legs still kicking, arms increasing in speed, he let loose an excited string of baby bird-like chirps until Brock reached in and lifted him out. He drew Benny to his chest and kissed the top of his head, holding him close. Brock's chest heaved a deep sigh that rocked his entire body. He bowed his head and mouthed several words.

Sue stood quiet in the doorway, beside Jack and Emily.

"Wait Mrs. Quon, please." Derrick rose as Sue turned to leave. "Brock, She's the reason we were able to stop the Stoddard women. Sue recognized Benny despite the purple dress, and blonde hair disguise."

"What?" Brock caught his mother-in-law's downcast glance.

"We were leaving, heading to one of the well-planned diversions." Derrick walked over to Sue and looped an arm in hers. "She called out— 'Benjamin Benton' in a voice that echoed through the noisy airport. Everyone heard her."

Speechless, Brock took in the enormity of the sheriff's words. Derrick deposited Sue at Brock's hip. She reminded him of Asia, the largeness of such an underestimated petite person.

Brock rubbed his palm over Benny's fair hair. "We'll have to do something about this won't we?" He leaned down and held out Benny to his weepy-eyed grandmother. Sue didn't move. Benny hiccupped.

"May I hold him?" Benny wiggled into her waiting arms. He squirmed and got comfortable, head to head, eye to eye, and offered her his thumb.

"I will never be able to thank you enough." Brock leaned forward, cupped Derrick's hands between his and shook vigorously without letting go.

"You got a strong grip there, Brock." Derrick grinned before releasing.

"And, Sue."

"Yes, Brock?" She gazed up into her son-in-law's misted eyes.

"The door is open. All you have to do is walk in."

Weeks Later

The Tahoe skies were clear and blue, the temperature was a cooler forty-five degrees at mid-afternoon. The first snowfall was predicted for the next evening. After seven years of drought, there was hope for a full winter—rain and snow to cleanse the thirsty earth and nourish the dry trees and plants.

Derrick inhaled crisp air through his open car window. A blustery wind whipped the waves along the shoreline to frothy peaks causing them to roll in with increasing velocity. It was a welcome change, a needed change. He parked at the base of the road at Vikingsholm, not far from the castle picnic grounds. He and his family were the last to arrive.

"Good of you to join us Sheriff Thomas." Jack laid out another blanket on the last of the grassy area by sandy shores where picnickers have gathered since the first summer in 1930.

"Quiet here today?" Derrick ushered his son nearer to the water with his pile of beach toys, then returned to join his wife.

"Not for long." Helen Thomas sat their nine month old next to Benny. "He looks so much better with that chestnut brown hair. She tussled the top of his head." Benny focused in on the dangling gold charms jingling from the bracelet loose around her wrist.

"I dyed it back to his natural color. Blonde is not his shade." Sue fussed, trying to brush long strands away from Benny's face but he belly scooted closer to the other baby, taking the quilt with him.

Brock sat under the shade of a wide canvas umbrella. "No sun during chemo and radiation treatments. Any new developments?" He asked, a Giants ball cap covered his bald head and dark sunglasses protected his eyes. He flipped off the hat for a second, proud to show off sprouting red stubble.

"Oh yeah, Mildred is singing and no one in any department can shut her up. Everything is Agatha and Leonard's fault so who knows if we'll ever uncover the whole truth." Craig spoke up across the blanketed patchwork of quilts and beach towels where he sat with his fiancée leaning against him, her raven bob cresting his shoulders.

"I still can't believe it was the youngest sister impersonating Astrid all along." Emily rose from lying flat on her belly to sit with Rachel next to a stack of books and letters they were turning over to Derrick for the completion of the investigation. She squinted in the sunlight streaming in through the nearby white fir and Lodgepole pines.

"She was the mastermind of the three. Old Mildy begs to differ, but baby sister told both her siblings what to do, when, where, and how." Derrick nodded at his rookie partner.

"And they have Leonard in custody in Italy?" Brock watched Benny strain to gain an inch nearer his new object of curiosity. He pulled his hand back and let his son try harder. Toby crawled over and perched himself within kicking distance of Benny's busy feet.

"He's behind bars, waiting for extradition papers to be approved. But the couple fled." Derrick answered as Craig gave a thumbs up.

"That's too bad. They may have led authorities to other wealthy couples buying babies for the highest bid. Child Trafficking is a worldwide epidemic." A sadness resounded in Brock's voice. "I've been researching situations like mine. Fewer and fewer children are returned to their parents. Look how fast Agatha found a buyer in Hong Kong for Benny."

"She was a shrewd one." Jack sat cross-legged in the middle of the group. "She saw an opportunity arise when Asia died and moved in like wildfire. She had to be the mastermind. She was the only one here, at Tahoe."

"We do know that Leonard was living in Spain and Mildy was living in Arizona. We've been able to trace their recent activities from credit card charges under their alias names. And they had a number of them, passports too. Leonard is quite the forger." Derrick added. "They each had certain roles. And apparently bickering ran rampant. Agatha was willing to leave her sister behind to save her own skin at the airport. The F.B.I. is still looking for money Agatha stashed elsewhere. At least it's not where Mildy told us to look." Derrick settled back. "I think big sis is getting the picture that there may have been a parting of ways in their immediate future."

"You mean like Detert?" Brock pulled physically back drawing his long legs to his chest.

"I don't think that was the first time she killed someone. Sorry, Brock. I know a lot of this is still fresh." Derrick tried to soften the delivery of this information. "She was originally here for other purposes, bleeding the locals of their savings, bilking the elderly of their mortgages. She went for the religious first and kept going. She'd amassed several million already when she tried her hand at something new, at least according to Mildred."

"She got greedy." Jack nodded.

"What about all that ghostly-demon stuff that the neighbor saw?" Brock asked.

"We're almost certain Agatha dabbled in the black arts, for decades according to Mildy who called that part of her sister's life, sinister. We've uncovered evidence to corroborate those claims at the house in Arizona. The Homewood neighbor Florence saw strange figures, lights, too, remember? We think our imposter burned anything similar she used here in that cabin fire."

"Was Agatha demon-possessed like her sister claimed?" Brock asked.

"There wasn't any indication of such when she was shot." Derrick's forehead puckered. "But Mildred insists her sister would talk to a James as if he were right in front of her."

"There was so much more evil involved than I imagined." Emily's arms looped under her legs, she rocked back and forth, her toes exposed at tips of her sandals. "I never trusted her, yet I let myself be manipulated."

"Who didn't, Em?" Jack reminded her. "I thought she was a harmless, eccentric elderly lady at first. That needed help. You discerned more from the beginning."

The babies played in content, mutual interest while the Thomas's oldest son sifted sand, building a castle with a turret like the stone fortress. One question remained unasked and unanswered. The presence of the real missing Astrid was strong.

Brock broached the question. "Why did she impersonate Astrid Hughes?"

"I think I can answer that one." Rachel pulled the letter she was to hand over and gave it to Derrick. They'd all read it and it offered insight but not definitive answers. "This Astrid built a trust relationship with the locals. She was loved. Agatha used that to her advantage, like the foundation under the castle." She pointed toward to massive time tested architecture, a decade shy of a century. It still stood stone upon stone, layer upon layer, fortified, mortared, and steadfast.

Derrick hesitated, "Mildy shed light about what happened in England to Astrid."

"You don't sound like this is something we'll want to hear." Rachel hedged.

"Tell us anyway." Brock said. "Tell us everything."

"Astrid did follow her father to England and served the RAF troops. She never knew he had been killed when the Luftwaffe had descended on the airfields and radar stations in the months earlier. Mildred was sent to tell her and bring her back with them. Her little sister Aggie insisted on going. Leonard drove them to the outskirts of London. They walked the rest of the way until they located Astrid at a makeshift hospital where an overflow of patients were sent with lesser injuries near an entrance to an Underground station where many people sought shelter from the blitz. Astrid used her own money to buy medical supplies from the Stoddard Chemist to donate for the wounded. Mildred was supposed to deliver those supplies, but she arrived empty handed."

"Mildred hated her. She was also in love with the young soldier that loved Astrid; the James we read about in the letter to Lora Knight. He was mending from a leg broken suffered in a parachute jump. Though barely thirteen, Agatha was quite infatuated with him. Upon their arrival the sisters immediately found out Astrid was engaged to marry James. Mildred insisted Agatha took the news worse than she did."

"Fires burned everywhere throughout London and one was encroaching on the building. The sirens began wailing and the planes and the bombs returned. Astrid refused to leave the wounded like James that could not walk, run, or even crawl away. The Stoddard siblings headed for the Underground station, leaving Astrid covering James's body with her own. From the stairs, Mildred heard a boom and turned to see the blinding flash and white light, pin lights. Then the fire spread, more planes flew over and dropped more bombs. Fires were still burning the next morning when they emerged. There was nothing left of the building but rubble. All the bodies were burned, most beyond recognition. There was not a single survivor in that small building." Derrick finished with a sigh, his last words scarcely above a whisper.

A breeze filtered through the pines behind them at the forest's edge, rustling, stirring the air surrounding the small group. Water rolled in washing the beach, then receded leaving innumerable glistening grains of sand radiant in the sunlight.

"I believe this much to be true. Mildred could barely get it out. She wept on and off while retelling me this story."

Jack spoke into the silence that settled among them, "Courage like Astrid and her father's was repeated over and over during the Battle of Britain. Many sacrificed that others may live."

"My heart longed for a happier end for her life, but I knew deep inside there was a reason she never returned." Rachel mumbled.

"I think though the real Astrid's life was cut short, it was a life well-lived." Emily stated. "Like Asia." She rested close to Jack.

Sue hid behind a fan she drew from her purse. "I do not deserve to be here with you today. I abandoned my daughter, stopped speaking to her." Sniffling, she flushed the fan open revealing a painted scene from the orient. "Asia kept trying, kept loving me."

Brock wrapped a skinny arm around Sue enveloping her. "I was just a basketball jock shooting hoops that Asia loved. I had no real purpose in my life before her. She kept trying with both of us."

"Benjamin is plump, but he is a vision of his mother." Sue's dewy eyes ridged above the lace edging and she held the silk pleated, bamboo framed fan steady. "Perhaps he will open his heart to me, let me be grandmother."

"You're welcome to stay with us for as long as you wish." Brock gave his mother-in-law an option to consider. "Asia would be pleased you are living in her art studio."

The fan lowered to Sue's chin. "My daughter left parts of herself mixed on the pallet of her watercolors. Rooting plants fill her glass jars and flowerpots bloom on the windowsill. I am discovering a part of Asia I never bothered to know before." She hesitated. "Much has happened with Benny's abduction I do not understand though."

"I know, like the fog that rolled in before the plane was about to take off, you and Agatha unknowingly ending upstanding together at the airport." Brock paused. "The evil plot one woman played out, befriending us, drugging us, stealing what mattered most."

Derrick added. "I think from what Mildy has been spilling, we were all spared far worse. She claims both she and Lenny were terrified of the younger sister's demonic activities, said Agatha was possessed by deceiving spirits, plural. She does not believe her sister is dead or can die no matter how many times I assure her Agatha's body was in the morgue and has been buried." A shiver vibrated up his spinal column settling at the base of his neck as he physically tried to shake it off. "She has some dementia, keeps repeating phrases over, has her time frames mixed a bit, but when she refers to Aggie, she watches over her shoulder in utter terror."

"Doc told me he covered Ben and me in prayer." Brock interjected. "I asked God for help. My son was protected while Agatha was alone with him. I don't know how, but he was."

"Some of the good and evil on this earth we'll never understand while still living here." Emily said.

Sandcastles

Derrick left the group and went to check on his son Cody's progress. A mote surrounded the sandcastle, filled with buckets of water he'd hauled up from the lake. He'd built higher up on the beach from incoming waves that could wash away his work. Using his new castle kit, Cody had molded the lower fortress walls with tall towers at all four corners. A turret rounded off the main entrance where he used plastic blocks for a bridge.

"Good job, Cody." Derrick sat in the wet sand by all the discarded beach toys and kicked off his sandals.

"Thanks, Dad. I wasn't sure I could do it by myself."

"I can help, if you want."

Cody kept patting the damp walls to pack it tight, careful not to press too hard, or the solid barriers would crumble. He learned that when the first one went down. Rebuilding had taken time, more time than building the first wall. In the center of the castle interior, plastic green army men stood in a circle facing out, watching, and waiting.

"What are you going to do next?" Derrick positioned himself next to his son who wedged himself near the far end of the castle.

"I'm waiting for the enemies to come."

"How will you stop them?"

"The mote will hold them until they climb the back walls and shoot arrows at the rear guards." Cody whispered. "It's called an ambush."

"Then I will call the battle charge and my soldiers will fight, on all sides. Watch." He stood and sounded an imaginary trumpet high into the sky. "Brave warriors, it's time to fight." He led a charge around the castle grounds, leaving footprints in the sand as he marched in an orderly straight line. Cody called his imaginary men to a second charge and gave a victory cry to encourage them as arrows fell from above. He grabbed a shield, using the biggest plastic shovel to cover his chest, a bucket on his head for a helmet.

Derrick was struck by the wisdom of his six-year-old.

The forest trees, the deeply rooted guardians on the castle grounds, forged an impenetrable hedge of protection around the beach warriors. Unseen angelic beings spread a winged covering spanning earth and sky, to the heavens above.

Chapter Fifty-One
Time Capsule
1940

"I promise to return. You keep safe my grove in the forest and the story time meadow. I leave tomorrow with mother, but I will be joining father as soon I can purchase my ocean passage. Do not forget our time together here. Remember me." ~ Day of departure, early summer of 1940. Astrid's farewell to Selma after she hid her note under her boot, affixed as a keepsake, a memento for a time in the future.

Astrid entreated Mrs. Knight for permission to gather the children for one last story time before she boarded the steamer that evening. Her persistence was met with but one request.

"May I join you, as a listener with the children?" Lora suggested. "Let's say good-bye on the beach. I know you read in the meadow, but I'll have the cooks prepare a hamper lunch for a picnic."

"For all the children that come?" Astrid inquired. "May they swim afterward?"

"Yes, for all of them. Invite any child who wishes to hear you read." Lora leaned back on her chaise lounge and relaxed.

Wisps of her gray hair blew awry in a gentle breeze as she adjusted her spectacles on the bridge of her nose. "The drivers can transport any in need of a ride. Go now, I'll inform the kitchen staff."

"Thank you, Mrs. Knight." Astrid hurried to request a chaperoned drive down the highway to share her invitation. Her mother remained sequestered in her room, but she slipped a note under her door before leaving on her mission.

By noon the beach was transformed—folding wooden chairs leaned up against pine trees, towels and quilts were stacked until needed, canopies for shaded areas, and wicker hampers were filled with fried chicken, potato salad and a variety of fresh fruits. Lemonade and iced tea jars waited on a square table covered with one of Mrs. Knight's hand-embroidered tablecloths.

Lora Knight sat within earshot of the reading circle; small umbrella attached to the arm of her chair. An empty chaise beside her was set-up for Mrs. Hughes, her favorite shawl hooked across the wood back of the lounger. Rose remained at the castle supervising the servants packing for the evening departure and eventual long train ride home.

Astrid read fairy tales and adventures, some of the children brought their own books. She read those too. Boys and girls bunched under a linen canopy staved into the sand on poles and weighted down with sandbags at all four corners. Azure waters reflected the blue sky above. Crystal clear pockets of teal sparkled near the shallow shoreline under the afternoon sun.

The children were giddy, still they listened intently knowing this was their last day until next year with their friend from another lake in a state called Maine. Astrid had shown them on a globe how far she traveled to come to Vikingsholm every summer.

"Is that the farthest you will ever go?" Young Elsa asked, attaching herself to Astrid's swim dress as the other children ran to the hampers for lunch.

"No, I am leaving soon to cross the Atlantic Ocean to Great Britain."

"Why?" The little girl scrunched her face in the sunlight while gazing up.

"To help the country my family lived in before coming to America." Astrid gave her a hug and motioned her to join the others with Mrs. Knight."

"It is dangerous?"

"Any change has risk. Such as when you try something new you've never done before."

"Or try to read a new book or ride a bigger bicycle?" Ash blonde curls cascaded over the eight-year-old's sunburnt shoulders. Her big gray eyes shone like double moons over the lake.

"I will find out when I arrive." Astrid walked her in the direction of the castle picnic grounds, along the edge of the sandy beach, their toes coated in the gritty granules.

"But you will come back next summer?" The child stopped.

"I promise to try my best to visit again." Astrid patted the girl's back.

Satisfied, Elsa ran toward the grand meal already spread out and being served. Astrid lingered on the shoreline, dipping her feet in the cold water lapping at her ankles and legs. Waves rolled in sloshing up to her knees, propelling a deep chill through to her bones.

A sudden movement jolted her. Elsa wrapped her arms around Astrid's waist and held on tight, burying her head into pleats of black fabric. "I will wait for you." She ran off, flapping her arms in the wind like the Golden Eagles circling Fanette Island in the bay.

Astrid turned her head, her thick chestnut French braid down the middle of her back caught in a brisk gust. She waved until the child disappeared into the crowd clustered under the canopy. A pleased smile lit her features as she faced the mouth of the bay. She wondered what lay ahead for her after leaving these azure shores for the whitehead coast of Cornwall, England. The final leg of her journey would be to London where they were in great need of volunteer nurses. The number of wounded soldiers was increasing daily as the bombardment continued without ceasing.

"Astrid, come join us!"

It was her mother's voice that beckoned. She ran to the grassy area that bordered the beach to hug her. Drawing back, she noticed swollen, reddened eyes and puffy blotches that bagged just beneath. The rim of her nose rubbed raw. She clutched a handkerchief tight.

"Oh, Mother. Don't fret. All will be fine." Astrid strained to reassure her mother's fears.

"My dearest daughter." Rose caught her breath and held it before speaking. "This war will reach around the world." A deep hoarseness scratched the back of her throat. She remained silent.

"Papa is a brave man." Astrid clasped her fingers in a binding grip with her mother's. "And he is never alone." She gazed upward.

"There are many brave men who go to war." *And few come home the same. They are forever altered.* Rose looked to Lora who stood stoic, her stance that of one who had been in battles before and survived. "Thank you for your kindness, Lora."

"Yes, how can we ever thank you enough?" Astrid agreed.

"Ladies, let us walk while the children have their picnic."

The three locked arms at the waist and strode the shoreline barefoot, their steps imprinted in the sand beyond the wash of water rolling in and out. Lora grasped her skirt at knee length, the warmth of the sun against her legs. Her trusty straw hat tilted to one side, her laughter a welcome refrain harmonizing with the litany of voices carrying across the sands of time.

Astrid steadied herself between the two women she loved. She adapted to the slower pace of her companions and joined in their conversation.

The castle towered overhead, overlapping pine branches sheltering the worn pathway to the hidden forest grove beyond the south wall. The vanilla scent of bark was heady in the alpine breeze. A foaming spray of chilly water surprised the women, tingling their senses, and baptizing them in a mist of what was yet to come.

Discussion Questions

For Book Clubs

1) Of the many characters throughout this story, who is easiest to relate to and why? Were you drawn to people in both time frames—past and present?

2) The historical background about non-fiction character Lora Josephine Knight is a mix of fact and fiction. She was an amazing woman ahead of her time. Do you feel that she reached from the past and added depth to the contemporary story?

3) This is the last book in the trilogy. Jack and Emily have come a long way in their journey from the first book, ~ *The Language of the Lake*. Do you feel they grew to become all they could be through the twists and turns their lives took?

4) Themes of love and death, truth and deception, and good and evil weave along the azure shores of the majestic beauty of Lake Tahoe. When in the story did you first discern the darkness trying to quench the light?

5) This fictional account of 2017 takes the reader into a seven year drought that ravages Tahoe's lake and forests. It parallels the lives of several characters, but mostly Brock, the grieving widower racked with cancer who

struggles to become a daddy to his infant son. Did you feel Brock's struggle was real, like a drought?

6) Though Asia dies in the beginning of the book, she lives on throughout the pages, in the heart of her husband, in her art, through her loving spirit, and her unshakable faith. How did her death bring a deeper meaning to the unfolding storyline?

7) Emily suspects that Astrid is not who she claimed to be, and yet she doubts her inclination to distrust her. Do you do that sometimes and later regret it?

8) Doc is the same solid rock in this final book that he was in the other two stories. Do you feel his death made a difference as much as his life did? In what ways? Do you know someone like him?

9) Asia's church helps Brock by bringing meals, cleaning, offering free babysitting, and the pastor visits but never forces religion on him. The story never mentions any specific denomination. Do you feel that would matter?

10) Jack moves his medical practice into the spare room at home. The country is going through financial hardship and medical insurance has become more of a detriment than a help for the average person. Is Jack still able to effectively attend to his patients?

11) Emily works with Jack. They are more of a team. Do you think living and working together is a good idea?

12) Detert dies a terrible death by Astrid's hand right when he thinks he's about to profit and be free of her meddling

influence. Was his death too harsh or did it fit their relationship?

13) Did you think Brock made the wrong choice deciding to give up his son for adoption?

14) Baby Benny is the innocent that an evil woman zooms in on and plots to steal through deception. There is an intentional focus on human trafficking. Did you think Brock would get his son back? The odds of that are sadly low in this worldwide epidemic.

15) Both Jack and Doc's lifelong, and Brock and Benny's brand new, father and son relationships are key to this story, as are Emily and Jack, and Brock and Asia's husband and wife relationships. What differences and similarities did you notice?

16) The Vikingsholm, Emerald Bay chapters that bookend this story with Lora Knight, and the Hughes family ~ Rose, William, and Astrid, show the importance of family. Though these stories span eighty-six years in the same locations, do they tell similar or vastly different stories in the choices that people make?

17) When you learned what happened to the real Astrid, did you feel her life ended in vain at such a young age?

18) Time is seamless in this story. WWII and spiritual warfare are parallels that both have casualties. Have you ever fought battles as a soldier on either side?

19) The grandmother Sue Quon had been estranged from her daughter Asia for a season. That fractured relationship is

somewhat restored when Brock opens the door to Sue after he gets Benny back. Do you believe forgiveness can heal broken lives?

20) Is faith real? The supernatural realm in the story shows another belief, in the powers of demonic darkness. Both move the story to what conclusion?

Author Notes

I have long admired Lora Josephine Knight who built Vikingsholm castle at Emerald Bay, Lake Tahoe in California, which was completed in 1929. Her history is rich, and she truly was a woman ahead of her time. I wove this work of fiction to include her, bookending the story's beginning and end, to encapsulate the contemporary year of 2017.

Laura (Lora) Josephine Small Moore Knight's legacy is still alive at the Vikingsholm hidden castle and Fanette Island, now a part of the Harvey West Unit of the Emerald Bay State Park. You can hike the mile down and tour the Scandinavian architecture late May – late September. The paddle wheelers, Tahoe Gal and the Tahoe Queen, offer cruises from the north and south shores to that magical sanctuary tucked away on the edge of the forest.

Lora enjoyed her mountain retreat for fifteen summers until her death at 82 in 1945. She was one of the major contributors to Charles Lindbergh's trans-Atlantic flight. Lora was also a generous philanthropist who donated money to provide educational opportunities for young people, and other groups. She opened her Tahoe home to many people, though the Hughes family in *Upon These Azure Shores* are all fictional characters.

I relied on years of research and the three years from 1978-1981 that I lived in East Anglia, England, to bring fictional American pilot William Hughes' character to life. He is patterned after the eleven pilots that volunteered and flew with the

RAF in the Battle of Britain before the U. S. entered WWII. My hope is that the bravery of those RAF and American pilots is not forgotten as time moves forward.

Thus, ends the Tahoe Trilogy ~ Emily and Jack's years from 1995 – 2017, Nana, Doc and Annie, Derrick, Hannah and Jonathan Forrester, Brock, Asia, baby Benny, and all the other characters who shared their lives in one of the most breathtaking locations on the earth.

Thank you for being a part of the love, loss, forgiveness, and hope these characters faced in their everyday lives. I pray these stories made a difference after you read the books. Hopefully, the characters spoke to your heart in intimate and true voices. That is my prayer for you.

In this final book, I wrote about human trafficking which is a growing national and global crime against humanity. I have listed national information to report abductions and call for help. Baby Benny, my fictional character, is found and returned to his father. Sadly, that is not the usual outcome in most cases. But, there is always hope, and there is always prayer.

I would love to hear from you and your book clubs too. If you have any questions or insights that you would like to share, you can snail mail me at: P.O. Box 1209, Ione, California, 95640-9771 or message me at my website: kathyboydfellure.com

Information Share
Quotes and Scriptures:
Page 68 ~ Quote Saint John Chrysostom (347-407) Ioannes Chrysostomos Archbishop of Constantinople

Pages 93-94 ~ KJV Bible Psalms 11:6

Page 116 ~ KJV Bible Luke 17:5

Page 108 (Hebrew # 6942 qudash 'kaw-dash' prim root/to be, (*canusat, make, pronounce or observe as*) clean, (ceremonially or morally):- appoint, bid, consecrate, dedicate, defile, hallow, (be, keep) holy, (-er, place) keep, prepare, proclaim, purify, sanctify (-led, one, self). x wholly.

Page 166 ~ KJV Bible Daniel 12:1-3
Pages 170-171 ~ KJV Bible Daniel 12:4-7
Page 175 ~ Based on author C. S. Lewis' quote in *A Grief Observed*.

Suggested Reading:

Vikingsholm Tahoe's Hidden Castle by Helen Henry Smith ©1973
No Easy Road by Dick Eastman ©1971
The Battle of Britain: Five Months That Changed History May-October 1940 by James Holland ©2010

Music Mentioned:

Amazing Grace by John Newton
In Christ Alone (My Hope is Found) by Keith Getty & Stuart Townend
Clocks by Coldplay
Go to the Ant cd (Out of the Mouths of Children) by Judy Rogers

National Human Trafficking Hotline:

SMS 233733 (Text "HELP" or "INFO")
Languages ~ English, Spanish and 200 more languages.
National Human Trafficking Hotline 24/7 ~ 1(888) 373-7888
Website: humantraffickinghotline.org

On the Water's Edge Tahoe Trilogy:

Book 1 ~ The Language of the Lake ©2018
Book 2 ~ Lake Cottage Book Haven ©2019
Book 3 ~ Upon These Azure Shores ©2020

Acknowledgements

It is with gratitude that I thank my beta readers; especially Lydia Cameron, and Cheryl Parker who took to heart my manuscript while in the midst of battling cancer, and my amazing editor Daniele Johnson Araujo, who brought to light needed repairs to my manuscript while protecting the voice of my novel. Many thanks to the former Amador Fiction Writers Critique Group; Carolyn Bakken, Judy Pierce, Gini Grossenbacher, Carrie McAlister, Sarah Garner, Jess Moore, and Pam Dunn; and to the Mokelumne Hill Writer Workshop; Antoinette May Herndon, Genevieve Beltran, Sally Henry, Lucy Sanna, Sally Kaplan, Kevin Arnold, and the late Sandy Towle, for their tireless suggestions on endless manuscripts. Thank you to Sacramento Branch of the Historical Novel Society; fellow historical researchers for sharing many encouraging book discussions at Ettore's meetings while drinking copious amounts of coffee and tea.

It is with gratefulness beyond measure I acknowledge late Wing Commander George Raymond Candy, RAF (retired), OBE, and his wife Mary, for their friendship and welcome to their home ~ The Old Rectory in Great Birchum, Kings Lynn, Norfolk, England for the three years I lived there. Ray flew in excess of 30 missions from 1944 – 1945. He served with 279 Squadron stationed at RAF Thornaby and with 1661 HCU stationed at RAF Swinderly, flying both Stirlings and Lancasters. After WWII Ray was in charge of engineering for the UK Victor and Vulcan bomber squadrons at RAF Marham. His stories of the soldier's courage changed me. Mary embraced me into her creative artist world and encouraged me to someday write novels.

I am grateful for the encouragement and support of my dear friend Lynn Cordone, a Lake Tahoe kindred soul from our youth and throughout our adult years. She believed in my early poetry and essays that later bloomed into novels.

To my Tahoe tribe: Lori Hargan at Historic Camp Richardson, Aaron and Lisa Nelson at The Potlatch in Incline Village, Nevada, Jessica Hester at Geared for Games in Tahoe City & Mind Play at Squaw Valley, Deborah Hanna at Gatekeepers Museum North Lake Tahoe Historical Society, Barb Van Maren at Pine Cone Gifts in Kings Beach formally ~ Lauren's Garden by the Lake at Tahoe Vista, Deborah Fish Lane formally at The Bookshelf Bookstores in Tahoe City and Truckee, retired Park Ranger Karin Nicholson at the Sand Harbor Gift Shop, Maggie Nook at Zephyr Cove Resort Gift Store, and to Heidi Doyle, the Executive Director of Sierra State Parks Foundation, who read this manuscript to be sure I held true to the memory of Lora Josephine Knight. I am thankful for all of you.

My wonderful Tahoe Trilogy book cover designer ~ Kim Van Meter, amazingly talented sketch illustrator, Donna Plant, and budding typographer ~ Aaron Cameron, all contributed their best efforts to make *Upon These Azure Shores* a book worth reading.

And to my family for putting up with my zany hours, all-nighters, Tahoe road trips, cabin workshops combined with family getaways, and relished endless research and photo shoots, I thank you Joe, Jenny, Matt, and of course, the Fellure stand-up comedian dogs ~ Jake, Thor and Maxie, our shelter rescues who truly rescue us over and over, again and again. And in memory of Missy, my Girl Friday.

To every intercessor who has prayed me through this trilogy ~ how you have blessed me.

To God be the Glory.

© Hidden Hills Photography

About the Author
Kathy Boyd Fellure, a lifelong history buff,
is a native of Sacramento, California.
She is the author of the ~ On the Water's Edge Tahoe Trilogy:
The Language of the Lake, Lake Cottage Book Haven, and
Upon These Azure Shores.
Kathy is also the author of four illustrated children's
fiction storybooks:
The Blake Sister's Lake Tahoe Adventure Stories:
When the Birdies Came to Tea
Mr. Snowman Ate Our Picnic Lunch
Nana's Tin of Buttons
Bear Cub Adventure
A new novel series ~ Across the Pond ~ releases is 2021;
The Wrong Ocean, followed by, *Harper House,* in 2022.
Kathy lived in England for three years, and currently abides
in the Sierra Nevada, Amador County Foothills of California
with her family.
Kathy is also a photographer, swimmer, and hula hoopster.
www.kathyboydfellure.com

Made in the USA
Columbia, SC
13 August 2020